Summer Moon

Summer Moon

Jill Marie Landis

BALLANTINE BOOKS • NEW YORK

A Ballantine Book
Published by The Ballantine Publishing Group

Copyright © 2001 by Jill Marie Landis

All rights reserved under International and Pan-American Copyright
Conventions. Published in the United States by The Ballantine Publishing
Group, a division of Random House, Inc., New York, and simultaneously in
Canada by Random House of Canada Limited, Toronto.

Ballantine is a registered trademark and the Ballantine
colophon is a trademark of Random House, Inc.

ISBN 0-345-44039-0

Manufactured in the United States of America

To Loved Ones and Friends:
Bill Olson
Jill Nelson
Roberta Davis
Betty Beadon
Florence Gibson
Hannah Glover
Helen Kemerer
Wish you were here.

Pluck from the memory a rooted sorrow,
Raze out the written troubles of the brain,
And with some sweet oblivious antidote
Cleanse the stuff'd bosom of that perilous stuff
Which weighs upon the heart. . . .

—Shakespeare, *Macbeth*

Prologue

"Turn your face to the wall, Katie, and stop that coughin'."

With her chest and throat burning, racked with chills that shook her thin frame, nine-year-old Katie Whittington huddled in her narrow bed.

"Katie, I mean it. Stop it now."

Only half-awake, at first she thought she had dreamed her mother's voice, so familiar, tinged with a hard-edged, soulless quality that held no love. But then she heard it again, clearly and for real, and the sound burrowed into sleep-fogged corners of her mind, waking her completely.

There were the other sounds, too. Throaty moans, whimpers, sharp, keening cries. A man's harsh, ragged breathing. The whining protest of coiled bedsprings from across the cramped, cluttered room.

Katie rubbed her eyes and tried to hold back the hollow, jarring cough, but it erupted anyway. She covered her mouth with both hands and listened to the coupling noises, kept her back to the room and hoped that Mama wouldn't yell at her again.

She lay there pretending to sleep through the noise,

painting pretty pictures in her head, dreaming of another life, another world for her and Mama—the kind of world she had only glimpsed from afar, the kind she could barely imagine.

In her lovely dream world, she and Mama wore pretty dresses, *clean* dresses, with starched lace and ruffles, and there were pretty hats to match. The weather was always warm and sunny, and whenever they walked down the street, no one stepped aside or turned away. No one pointed at them or whispered as they strolled along in their pastel finery.

Mama had tried to teach her to ignore the stares and whispers of the townsfolk, but the rudeness still cut Katie to her soul, and it always would.

She hugged the torn wool blanket and coughed again, then wiped the palm of her hand on the dirty sheet that was little more than a rag.

The linens in her dream home would be soft and clean. There would be a fancy yellow cover on her bed, too, just like one she had seen through the window of a big white house up on Poplar Street. She would have lace curtains, fancy as snowflakes that would never melt, hanging at every window. The sun would stream through them, casting strands of precious yellow gold around her very own room—a room bigger than the shack she lived in now. There would be pretty china plates piled high with more food than any one person could ever eat all by herself.

The roof would never leak. The windows would glisten, and there would not be even one single crack in them. Wind would never sneak through holes in the windows or walls.

She shivered, her teeth chattering. Without warning, she started coughing again, but this time it went on and on until she lay on her side gasping for air like a dying fish.

"Katie!"

"Jeezus, can't you shut that kid up?"

Katie rolled herself into a tight ball, hugging the thin blanket around her shoulders. Her hands were stiff with cold, her feet nearly numb even though she had climbed into bed in her heavy shoes and socks.

She tried to picture her pretty dream house and all the lovely dresses again, and the plates piled high with hot food.

When the images would not come, she looked up at the frosted windowpane above her head. Between the ripped curtain and halo of frost crystals, she could see a sliver of moon and one lone star shining in the night sky.

She closed her eyes and wished upon that star. She wished all her dreams would come true. Then she opened her eyes, thankful that the moon was not full tonight.

On moonless nights it was easier for her to disappear inside herself and shut out the sound of Mama and the men. On moonless nights she was less tempted to watch.

But on nights when the moon hung full and heavy in the starless sky, she would silently turn away from the wall, stare through the milk-white light, and watch the shapes writhing on the bed. She would peer over the edge of her blanket and watch as Mama entertained the men who came scratching at the door.

She must have fallen asleep, for the next thing she knew, Mama's hand was on her shoulder, shaking her awake. The room smelled of burning whale oil. The single lamp on the crate beside Mama's bed cast a weak halo in the corner.

"Katie, get up and put your coat on."

Mama stripped off the blanket and tossed Katie the ugly green wool coat that some little girl across town had outgrown. They had found it in the bottom of the Christmas charity box that the "self-righteous do-gooders" (as

Mama liked to call them) had left sitting on the front stoop last year.

Suffering through another fit of coughing, wiping rusty phlegm on the sheet, Katie sleepily protested. "It's still the middle of the night, Mama."

"Get up. We have to go."

"Where? Where do we have to go in the dark? It's cold out," Katie whined.

Mama didn't answer.

Katie pulled herself up, climbed off the bed. Mama held Katie's coat as she shoved the girl's arms into sleeves that did not cover her wrists. Katie looked around for her faded red scarf, but Mama grabbed her arm before she could find it.

"Come on."

"Where are we going?" Mama would not look at her, and Katie began to worry and wonder why she was acting so strangely. "I'm sorry I keep coughing, Mama. I can't help it."

"You almost lost me a night's wage."

Before she could promise not to cough again, Katie doubled over with another spasm.

Her mother pulled a tattered cotton hankie out of the bodice of her torn gown and handed it to her. Then she grabbed her by the wrist, dragged her across the room, and opened the door. Katie ducked her head to avoid the blustery wind that sailed in off the sea and tried to keep up as her mother tugged her down one cold, deserted street after another.

Katie knew most of the lanes near the wharf by heart. They had trodden them since she could walk, she and Mama. They lived from hand to mouth on the money that the sailors and fishermen paid Mama when she took them to her bed. When times were very hard, they lived on do-gooder charity.

As they passed beneath a street lamp Katie glanced up at the familiar lines and angles of her mama's thin face. Her mama was looking straight ahead with her jaw set.

They were climbing now, up the hill, away from the wharf and the ramshackle houses that lined the narrow byways and shops close to the water. Katie fought for breath as they ascended. The houses up here were larger, prettier, and surrounded by trees, part of a forest that had once grown all the way down to the sea.

Well into unfamiliar territory now, Mama turned another corner. Barely able to do more than shuffle behind her mother, Katie lifted her head and saw a tall bell tower and the steeple of a brick church. Her eyes tearing from cold, she struggled to read the sign on the front of the building.

Saint—Per-pe-tua's—Church.

Mama was fairly dragging her now, walking faster, more determined.

"Ma-ma?" Katie had to gasp for air. She wiped her eyes with the kerchief.

"It's somethin' I have to do, Katie-girl. Somethin' I should have done long ago."

Mama's huge brown eyes were watering from the cold, too. A fat tear slipped down her bony cheek.

The freezing night air, heavy and damp off the sea, burned Katie's lungs. She had never set foot inside a church before. In awe, she stared at a ghostly white statue of a sad-faced young woman in a niche above the door. Something about the statue made her whisper.

"Are . . . we going . . . in there?"

The building looked old and sturdy. It was probably warm as toast inside. If she could just sit down and catch her breath, maybe close her eyes for a bit—

Mama tugged on her arm when Katie kept staring at the

statue. Katie sighed when they hurried past the church and the small graveyard beside it.

Except for the sound of their hollow footsteps, the neighborhood around them was silent. Not a single lamp was lit inside any of the big houses lining the street.

Suddenly Mama stopped to open a small iron gate in a low fence bordering the yard of another brick building, one almost as big as the church. The gate clanged shut behind them, ominously loud, with a sound that shattered the silence.

The cobblestone walk that led up to the front of the brick building was patched here and there with dirty snow left from the last snowfall. Dead leaves trapped since fall peeked through. Katie lifted her head.

Mama had already started up the six wide steps to the front porch. Katie's legs gave out after the first three. She knelt on the stair, doubled over, coughing. Mama stood over her.

"I can't lift you, Katie."

"I know, Mama," she whispered. She struggled to her knees and with Mama pulling on her arm, made it to the porch. "Can I just sit here a minute?"

Mama started beating on the heavy wood door with her fist.

Above the door hung a small gold-lettered sign. There was another statue, too. Smaller, but it was the same sad lady who stared down at her with her empty, marble eyes.

"Saint Per-petua's Home for Or-phan Girls."

Orphan girls.

Katie slowly read the words again, faster this time, and frowned. They didn't know any orphan girls.

"Mama?"

Her mother pounded on the door again, then whirled

around and knelt down beside her. She grabbed Katie by the shoulders, leaned so close their noses almost touched.

Mama was whispering frantically now, her raspy voice ragged and hushed. She talked fast, as if her mind were running a race with her tongue.

"This is for the best, Katie. Someday when you realize that, I hope to God you'll forgive me. I should have done this when you were born so's you wouldn't remember. I've been selfish, Katie-girl, trying to keep you with me, but it ain't workin' out, see?"

Panic squeezed Katie's heart and lungs. She couldn't breathe anymore. "Mama—" She let go of the kerchief and desperately grabbed hold of Mama's coat sleeves.

"I gotta do it. Don't you see, Katie? What kind of a life are you going to have, growin' up with me in that shack? Followin' me around? It's bad for both of us, you *and* me."

"You're scaring me," Katie wailed.

Mama's eyes narrowed and her bottom lip trembled uncontrollably—that frightened Katie more than anything. "I'm leavin' you here with the nuns where you'll have a warm bed and plenty to eat."

Katie stared in horror at the big door and the gold-lettered sign. Inside, someone had lit a lamp. Yellow light bled through plain white curtains. Her heart began to pound in her ears.

Mama's fingers tore at hers as she tried to push her away.

"Let go, Katie!" Mama shoved her away. "Don't make this worse for me than it already is."

Having freed herself, Mama stood up; she stepped back as Katie tried to grab hold of the uneven hem of her coat. Mama dragged the cuff of her sleeve across her eyes and then wiped her nose.

Katie jerked around at the chill whine of the front door's

hinges. An elderly woman wearing eyeglasses and clothed entirely in black stuck her head out, blinking against the icy chill.

"Yes? Who's there?" The woman had a gentle voice, but Katie was still frightened.

Katie expected her mother to answer, but when she turned around, Mama was already down the cobblestone walk, hurrying through the little iron gate.

"Mama!" Katie strangled on the sound, choked on a cough. She struggled to her knees, grabbed the column of the porch rail beside her, clawed her way to her feet.

The iron gate clanged with a lonely, hollow, terrible finality. "Don't leave me here, Mama! I'll be good." Her scream echoed through the empty streets. She was gasping between sobs, fighting the dizziness that clouded her vision.

"Come—b-b-ack!"

As she wilted toward the cold wooden porch floor where Mama's torn white hankie lay, Katie felt the old woman's arms close around her, heard the clack of wooden beads and a hushed prayer whispered beside her ear.

"I won't cough, Mama," Katie sobbed, staring at the empty walk through a blur of tears. "I . . . promise. I'll . . . be good."

1

Kate awakened, heart pounding, blood racing. She did not
move until her pulse settled back into a slow, steady rhythm;
then she drew back the sheet and slowly slipped out of bed.
Moonlight spilled across her pillow.

She had long ago given up trying to sleep when the moon
was full. Nights bathed in moonlight held too many memories of the life she had lived with her mother.

It was fall again. Maine nights had grown desperately
cold already. Kate shivered as she walked through a puddle
of milk-white light to the only window in her sparsely fur-
nished attic room. A utilitarian piece of unbleached muslin
hung limp before the pane, as unadorned as everything else
in this world of routine and orderliness where she had spent
the better part of her life.

I stayed too long.

Kate drew aside the curtain and stared back at the man in
the moon, unable to think of anything except what Mother
Superior had told her after dinner when she had called her

into the office: "I received word today that the archdiocese is closing the school at the end of the month, Katherine. We sisters are being sent to a new church school in Minnesota. The girls will be relocated, but I'm afraid that you will have to find other employment. I'm so sorry, Katherine. I wish it could be otherwise, but there is nothing I can do."

Eleven years before, desperately in need of another teacher, the good Sisters of Saint Perpetua had asked her to stay on after graduation. She was given room and board and a small stipend in exchange for teaching history and elocution to girls of all ages.

At eighteen, rather than face the streets of Applesby, she had accepted the offer without hesitation, knowing that someday she would have to go out into the world again.

She promised herself that one day she would resurrect her old dreams, that she would have that pretty little home of her own and a family to hold dear.

As time slipped away and spinsterhood crept upon her, she devoted eleven years to Saint Perpetua's orphan girls and all the joys and challenges of dealing with them. She had made a home here, one that was safe and warm and familiar. The nuns and the orphans had become her family.

She had a certificate of education. She could read and write in Latin. She was a teacher, a scholar.

A spinster with no living relation.

The thought of having to leave after so long filled her heart with dread.

She had a little money put by, surely enough on which to survive until she found other employment. She would have to find another place to live—no easy task in a hamlet where her mother had been the town whore.

She had nowhere to go, nowhere to turn, and no one to turn to—not even her mother. On Kate's eleventh birthday, Mother Superior had told her that the old shack near the wharf had burned down, that her mama had died, trapped inside.

Even in death, Mama had been infamous.

Kate could not go to her mother and tell her that she had forgiven her abandonment, or that she had cried herself to sleep for months, missing her mama more than she would have missed her heart if it had been taken from her.

Now she looked out the window at the round face of the man in the moon.

"Where will I go? What will I do?"

The moon man smiled back.

Or perhaps he was laughing at her. She could not tell.

At the end of October, when the butcher made his final call to the nuns for an accounting, he found Kate standing outside the kitchen door with a hand-me-down satchel in hand. When he asked where she was going and she said that she did not really know, he took pity on her and told her she was welcome to rent the empty room above his shop. He was middle-aged and married, a portly man with fingers thick as the sausages he stuffed, and almost entirely bald.

With no alternative in mind, Kate accepted. She rode the butcher's cart back to the shop, a sturdy whitewashed building near the center of town that was frequented all day long by housewives and maids.

The room was adequate and clean, a refuge where Kate spent the better part of the morning scouring up the courage to go out and find employment.

That afternoon, the butcher's wife knocked timidly on the door and told her that she would have to leave on the morrow.

"Not that we don't want you here, you see. It's just that, well, some folks still remember your ma, and folks tend to gossip. We can't afford to have our business ruined, you understand. It's nothing against *you*, of course."

That was how Kate learned that Applesby had not forgotten Meg Whittington—that like Mama's, her name was still as tarnished as an old copper pot.

She packed her somber dresses and scant personal belongings again. The next day she held her head high, kept her tears inside, and moved on.

She rented a room in an old, gray weather-beaten shack by the wharf. It belonged to a sickly old woman in need of coin more than she cared about Kate's name or her mother's reputation. The stoop sagged and the corners of the front door had been scratched raw and splintered by the old woman's flea-bitten dog.

It reminded Kate so much of the places she had lived with her mother that once inside the small musty room, she sat down on the lumpy mattress and burst into tears.

To escape the dreary place, she pulled herself together, put on her hat, and picked up her crocheted reticule—a misshapen, handmade gift from one of her girls. She slipped the drawstrings over her wrist and walked away from the wharf, up Main Street and toward the remnants of the tall evergreen forest that once grew down to the sea.

She could not help but notice that some of the older folks stared as she passed by. Slowly the shame she felt as a child began to attach itself to her again.

She drew herself up tall and straight and walked on. The stares of passersby confirmed what her mirror had always revealed—she was the image of her mother. She had grown up looking into a reflection of her mother's eyes, wide-set and dark brown. She thought her lips too full, her mouth far too toothy, like her mama's, so she never smiled too wide. Her arms and legs were long, her waist thin, her breasts embarrassingly full. Thankfully, the few serviceable dresses she owned were unadorned and drab and so overly modest that they did not call attention to her figure at all.

She never thought she'd experience that old shame again, but the sting was uncomfortably familiar, even after all these years.

She stopped by the printer's and purchased a copy of the *Applesby Sentinel;* then she strolled over to the small park in the middle of the town square. She chose an empty bench beneath a maple covered with dried leaves that refused to fall. The paper snapped as she folded it back on itself, the corners luffed in the same breeze that set the maple leaves whispering. She began to scan the advertisements.

Since the school term had already begun, she doubted she would find a teaching position, but someone in a nearby town was surely in need of a nanny.

Quickly glancing past advertisements for real estate, gents' clothes, and Aladdin stoves, she found one ad seeking a maid for a boarding house in a village just up the coast. There was another for a seamstress, but she had no talent for sewing.

A lumbermill needed a cook, but cooking was out of the question, too, unless the men were of strong constitutions. Whenever she was on kitchen duty, the nuns always offered up extra prayers.

Suddenly a small, boxed advertisement set off with fancy block type one-third of the way down the page caught her eye.

```
RANCHER SEEKING WIFE
   SEND A PHOTOGRAPH
 WITH AN INTRODUCTORY
         LETTER
    TO: REED BENTON
LONE STAR RANCH, TEXAS
```

Kate slowly lowered the page to her lap and stared down at the words.

Rancher seeking wife.

Wife.

Her long-buried dream shimmered like a mirage until the letters on the page blurred.

All those secret wishes, all those hopes tucked away in the bottom of her heart, dreams that had faded over the years she devoted to the students of Saint Perpetua's.

What if?

What if she were to leave Maine forever?

What if she were to reach out for her dream?

She ran her finger over the bold type, closed her eyes, and turned her face toward the fragile fall sunlight. Just the word *Texas* conjured all kinds of images. Wild, wide open spaces. Cattle and cowboys. Indians. A handful of knowledge that she had gleaned through reading various periodicals and accounts over the years.

A place to start over. A place to settle down where no one recognized her. Perhaps even a place to start a family.

When a dying leaf drifted down from the maple and touched her cheek, she opened her eyes. The breeze whipped across the square, picked up a few fallen leaves, and sent them scuttling in a whirlwind dance. Kate lifted the lumpy reticule and slid the crochet along the drawstrings. Her savings lay at the bottom of the bag, a wad of carefully folded bills and a few coins.

Surely there was enough to spare for a photograph.

Surely there was enough to gamble a bit of it on a dream.

2

Spring was bleeding into another long, hot summer of raiding and retaliation, another round of blood and death on the prairie.

Hidden in a gully a half mile from a Comanche summer encampment, gut-tight, mounted, and ready to charge, Reed Benton and a company of twenty-three men watched Capt. Jonah Taylor ride down the line of troops, giving last-minute instructions as dawn stained the morning sky.

Sandy-haired and wiry, a born leader, Jonah Taylor was not only Company J Ranger captain, but Reed's best friend.

Reed gave Jonah a nod of encouragement when the man passed by. There were no formalities among the Rangers, no uniforms, no military law or precedent. The men were divided into military units and officered, but all else was loosely run. Unlettered farm boys fought beside educated men like himself. Usually outmanned, they made up for their lack of numbers with daring.

All along the line, horses as well as men shifted, anxious, all fully aware of what they were about to face. Reed wished he didn't know, wished himself anywhere else—which he knew damn well was no way to go into battle.

Back when other men were leaving Texas to fight the last few battles for the Confederacy, he had joined the Rangers to patrol the frontier. He had thought to protect the settlers living there, knew he would be chasing down renegade Comanche, but he had never anticipated rounding up women and children.

Ever since the war ended, the new government sent sporadic help from Washington, but never enough. Texans had suffered nearly thirty years of Comanche attacks, broken treaties, theft, mutilation, and death. They were all sick of it, and rightly so.

Nearly everyone in the state had lost kin or acquaintances to the hostile clans through death or capture. Most Tejanos were of a mind that only the extermination of the plains tribes would ever settle the score and bring peace to the frontier.

"You men know what to do." Jonah kept his voice low as he swung his gaze up and down the line. They were comrades in war, friends, at times pranksters, rarely family men. Rangers were known far and wide for their aggressiveness, and because of that, they rarely suffered casualties. "Three women were taken a week ago, along with two girls, eleven and twelve years old. If they're alive, they'll most likely be hidden in the lodges. Don't set any fires unless you've rousted everyone out. If we're lucky, they're here, in this camp. There don't look to be very many warriors around, just some outlying guards."

Reed drew his rifle out of its scabbard, touched one of the two pistols he wore at his waist, and then reached up and shoved his hat on tighter. He had done this countless times—ridden into hostile camps, rousted out women, children, and toothless old folk that the warriors left behind while they were out stealing horses, burning cabins, and taking captives.

He wished to God the Comanche would simply turn over the captives and go back to the reservation without a fight, but he might just as well have wished horses could fly. It was the way of the Comanche to raid and take cattle, horses, and captives and not only from white settlers, but from other tribes.

Jonah gave a whistle and as one, the Ranger Company swarmed up and out of the gully. Like a dark stain spreading across the prairie, the company raced toward the small encampment, intent on finding the captive women and evening the score.

Comanche sentries shouted and fired warning shots, alerting the inhabitants of what amounted to a clan with thirty tepees staked on the plain. Reed and the others answered back with their own fire, riding straight into the midst of the camp, firing in the air to cause as much confusion as possible so that the captives, if they were able, could break free and show themselves.

Gunfire erupted all around as Reed rode between the decorated buffalo hide lodges, instinctively aware of which Comanche were running frantically to save themselves and which others were armed and ready to defend the camp. All the while, he, like the other Rangers, was on the lookout for captives—a flash of blond or red hair, pale or sunburned skin, blue eyes, cries for help in English.

Some whites had been captive for so long they were indistinguishable from Comanche. Others had been with a clan for so long that they would run from the Rangers, clutching their half-Comanche children to their breasts.

Cookfires were scattered by charging horses. Lodges burned. The acrid smell of scorched hides hung heavy on the air. There was little real resistance from the inhabitants except for the handful of braves, but women and even children would fight to defend the camp.

Reed caught sight of a pack of youngsters, boys between eight and twelve, running swift and free as coyotes across the open plain. Despite the confusion around him, his heart involuntarily constricted. He was compelled to watch. Then suddenly, one of the Rangers behind him called out a warning and Reed whirled around in time to fire at an old man charging him with a long lance.

He had come a heartbeat away from being skewered in the back.

He had no time to react before he thought he heard a woman's cry for help in pure English, so he spun his horse around in the direction of the sound, and before he could respond, a bullet slammed into his shoulder and sent him reeling backwards. Grabbing for his saddle horn, he hung on and pulled himself upright. Then a second shot grazed his temple, and he went down.

"You're a lucky man, Benton."

Doc Harper shook his head as he wound a bit of remaining bandage into a ball and stowed it back into the worn and sagging satchel that served as medicine bag. "Doc" was no more a doctor than any of the other Rangers, but he had a way with sick horses and wounded men and could keep them patched up until they could get some real care.

"Funny, but I don't feel lucky right now. My head hurts like hell." Truth be told, Reed found it hard to focus, but he figured that was to be expected after the bullet put a new part in his hair just above his ear.

"That shoulder's bound to trouble you, too. Best you get yourself somewhere you can have it sewn up. The bullet passed clean through, so don't let anybody go digging for it again. I already did that, and it ain't to be found."

Reed sat up and looked around. They were a few yards from the encampment where the Rangers had set up a holding area for the Comanche they had rounded up. The dead were laid out a few yards away. Jonah was striding toward him, his expression tight enough to cut deep grooves around his mouth.

"I'm not done for yet," Reed told him, hoping that saying it out loud would make it so. He tried to focus and forced himself to keep his head up, but it throbbed like a war drum with every beat of his heart. He expected Jonah to make light of the situation, to make a joke to cheer him, but the man didn't even crack a smile.

Reed's stomach knotted. "What's wrong? Who died?"

"We didn't lose a single man. You were our worst casualty. Killed seven of their warriors, three women." Jonah looked out across the plain. "No children. We recovered two of the captive women and both girls. The third woman died on the way here. The others saw it. They're all in pretty bad shape."

Jonah didn't have to elaborate on what had happened to the captives between the time they were taken and the arrival at the camp. There wasn't a grown Texan alive who didn't know the fate of female captives.

"Sounds like . . ." Reed tried to clear his mind of the pain and fought for words. "Sounds like it went well. Why the long face?"

"We found a boy you should see. He's about the right age. And I'll be a damn polecat if he doesn't have your eyes."

The pounding in Reed's head was instantly drowned out by the beating of his heart.

Doc reminded Reed that he was there by handing over his patient's shirt. Jonah gave Reed a hand up and kept a hold on Reed's arm until the ground stopped spinning and the man could stand on his own.

"Can you walk?"

"Yeah." Reed nodded, shrugging into his tattered, blood-soaked shirt. He could walk. He just didn't know if he wanted to follow Jonah. As they started toward where the Comanche were being held, he hoped with every step that Jonah was dead wrong.

The prisoners had been separated by sex, bound hand and foot, and tied side by side. Older children were huddled in their own area, trying to appear fierce and sullen, failing miserably, their fear so palpable that Reed could smell it. None of them realized yet that they were not facing death or torture, the fate of anyone captured by the Comanche, but that a contingent of men would escort them to the reservation at Fort Sill up in Oklahoma.

Jonah led Reed over to a boy who looked to be about eight years old. He sat alone, separated from the others, but like the others, the boy had been hobbled to keep him from running.

Reed stood over the child, his breath coming rapid and shallow; he felt suddenly light-headed from more than his wounds. He put his hand over the makeshift bandage on his shoulder, felt warm moisture seeping through. He stepped close to the boy, so close the toes of his boots were nearly touching the child's knees, but the boy didn't look up.

Jonah bent down and cupped the boy's chin, forced him to raise his head and look up.

Reed's breath left him in a whoosh. Despite the child's tear-streaked, grubby face framed by dark, shoulder-length hair, one glance into those Benton eyes was all it took for Reed to know what Jonah and the other men standing nearby already suspected.

After five long years, Daniel Benton had been found.

Not *his* Daniel, Reed reminded himself. The child clothed

in a reservation-issue long-tailed red shirt and a hide loin-cloth sat hunched over with downcast eyes. His expression was as grim as the rest of the captured Comanche. He was not the innocent toddler Reed had lost, but what captivity had made of him.

Staring at Daniel brought everything back to Reed: all the old painful memories of his marriage to Becky, the day Daniel was born at Lone Star, his pride upon hearing that he had a son. He recalled the plans he had made for their future, his vow to be a better father than his own had been. Reed had promised his infant son that he would listen to him, try to understand, and above all let the boy follow his heart.

The filthy, half-naked child sitting in the dirt at his feet was the same little boy he had carried on his shoulders, taken everywhere with him, tucked in at night.

He had joined the Rangers driven by the need to rescue Daniel, but over time that incessant, driving need had ebbed until he believed this day would never come to pass.

So much had happened the night that Daniel was taken that Reed had a hard time trying to make sense of his feelings. The man he had been before would have wept for joy. He would have knelt and embraced his son.

Now not only pain, confusion, and uncertainty tempered his reaction, but so did the knowledge that the years Daniel spent among the Comanche had done irreparable harm. Reed didn't know what in the hell to do or to say. His wounds did nothing but befuddle his dazed mind even more.

"Daniel?" The word caught in his throat and threatened to choke him. Could the boy understand anything? Did he remember his name?

Daniel refused to look up. In the midst of the company of men, aware of little but the throbbing pain in his head and shoulder, of all the grim-faced Rangers watching him, Reed reached down, impatiently jerked the rope off the boy's feet and hauled Daniel up by the arm.

Daniel immediately howled in pain and crumpled, dangling from Reed's hand. Jonah hurriedly stepped up to them.

"He's hurt, Reed." Jonah lowered his voice for Reed's ears alone.

Reed closed his eyes and pinched the bridge of his nose, trying to clear his head. Then he looked down at the boy's bare legs. One of his ankles was swelling above his beaded moccasin.

An infant's piercing, mournful wail cut the hot, dry air. Close by, fires smoldered as tepees and hides continued to burn. Smoke tainted the wide, clear blue sky.

"Take him home, Reed. Go back to Lone Star. See the boy settled in and give your shoulder a chance to heal." Jonah appeared uneasy, as if there was more he wanted to say, but he held his peace.

Glancing around, Reed ignored the stares of his comrades. He spoke to the boy again but was ignored, so he wrapped one arm around Daniel's waist and scooped him up. Holding him against his side beneath his good arm, Reed walked passed the gathering of Rangers. He found his horse, tossed Daniel up in front of the saddle, somehow managed to keep hold of the boy and the reins and mounted up.

As soon as he hit the saddle, he suffered an intense wave of dizziness. Chilled and light-headed, he ached to lie down. The last thing he wanted to face in this condition was the long ride back to the ranch. Nor did he look forward to seeing his father again—but nothing short of death was going to stop him from taking Daniel back to Lone Star.

3

LONE STAR RANCH, TEXAS.

Alone at the crossroads where the Butterfield Line inter-
sected the road to the Lone Star ranch house, Kate tightened her grip on the handle of her dilapidated carpetbag
and turned away from the dust that swirled in the wake of
the stagecoach as it rumbled away.

Dear Katherine,
   I cannot wait for you to see Benton House. It is a tribute to the South (where my mother was born), as well as
to the West. Like Texas, it is a combination of both. Two
stories, with wide verandas around both floors, the house
is made of wood and brick, both elements brought here
at great expense.
   Some may wonder why my father chose to build in
such an isolated area away from the working head-
quarters of the ranch, away from stock pens and bunk-
houses. The truth is, Katherine, he always said that even
though cattle made him a rich man, he did not want to
smell them, so Benton House sits alone on a rise, except
for a corral for horses, a horse barn, and a small place out
back for the head wrangler. We are framed by endless

miles of golden prairie that sweep out in every direction
for as far as the eye can see.

In one of his letters, Reed Benton had described his
house in great detail, and yet as Kate stood on Texas soil seeing it for the first time, she was still overwhelmed.

Benton House was nowhere as monstrous as the old
brick orphanage, but was certainly a far grander place than
she had ever set foot in, more spectacular than anything
she ever could have imagined. She anticipated how lovely the
house must be inside, then reminded herself that she had
not come because of its grandeur, but because of what
she hoped to find inside—love, family, and a place to call
her own.

Canopied overhead, the bluebonnet sky went on and on
forever. Her only reference was Applesby, confined to narrow streets lined with shops and stores, steep hills, wooded
lanes, and narrow rutted roads. There was no tangy scent of
salt on the air. No damp sea breeze. She found this raw,
open land staggering, even violent, in its emptiness.

Out here, there was nowhere to hide.

She looked down at her wrinkled, beige traveling gown,
adjusted her short, matching jacket, and tried to salvage her
tired attire by shaking the dust off the hem of her gown.
The outfit was hopelessly worn, but it was the best of the lot
she owned. She set aside a scrap of lingering doubt that she
was not good enough for Reed Benton and tried to assure
herself that she deserved a chance at a new life.

She was not about to put on any airs or play him false by
pretending to be something she was not. She could not live
with herself if she did. She had been honest to a fault in her
very first letter.

She had given all the details of her past, spared nothing as she told the truth about her mother, of how she had been raised at the orphanage and her years of teaching. His prompt response had brought tears to her eyes.

> I care nothing for your life before now, Katherine. I, too, will be truthful. I am a widower. I have lost a son. I desire a wife, not a saint. My paternal grandmother was from the Northeast, which is why I placed advertisements in papers so far away. I am hoping to find a good, honest woman who values family, loyalty, and honesty above all—a woman who will stand by her husband no matter where he goes or what challenges he may face, the way my own grandmother always did. I can already tell by your letter that you are both honest and sincere. And surely brave to have written in the first place.

So that there would be no surprises before they met, she had spent a precious portion of her savings having a photograph made to send to him. Reed had returned a small portrait of himself in a later letter. Kate had kept it near and memorized every detail.

The prairie wind whipped a lock of her hair out of the tightly wound knot at her nape. She reached up, drew it away from her lashes, and struggled one-handed to tuck it into the prim coil as she started up the dusty lane.

Kate shifted the weight of the heavy satchel, wishing there had been an opportunity to freshen up before she met this stranger, her husband-by-proxy that she knew only through correspondence.

She soon reached the columned veranda that fronted the imposing house and realized her heart was not racing from the walk up the drive but from excitement and more than a bit of trepidation.

Her future waited on the other side of the massive front

door. Gathered lace curtains obscured the view through the long sidelight windows that flanked the heavy door—curtains with patterns as pretty as snowflakes. Smiling at the long-forgotten memory, she raised her hand and knocked, softly at first and then, when there was no immediate response, with more purpose.

There was no warning, no sound of footsteps or movement until the door suddenly opened, and Kate found herself face-to-face with a stately woman dressed in black silk. Tall, on the slender side, her coal-black hair was shot through with a few dramatic strands of silver and pulled severely away from her face in a style that emphasized her high cheekbones and the hollow-eyed sadness reflected in her stunning dark eyes.

Sofia.

Sofia is both housekeeper and cook. She is from Santa Fe and has been employed at Lone Star for over fifteen years.

He had failed to mention how incredibly striking, how very regal she was for a woman in her early fifties.

"I'm—" Kate started to introduce herself, but before she could finish, the housekeeper reached out, grabbed both her hands with a familiarity Kate was not used to, and held them tight. Shaking her head, the woman began crying without a sound; then she let go of Kate's hands to wipe her eyes.

"You are Señora Whittington Benton. *Lo siento.* I am sorry. So sorry." The woman whispered the words over and over, met Kate's eyes, and then quickly looked away.

Despite the warm dry air, Kate shivered, not knowing what to make of the forlorn, apologetic welcome.

Finally, the woman in black seemed to realize they could not stand there forever.

"Come in, señora. Come in." She picked up Kate's carpetbag and led her into a spacious, airy entry hall between two larger, open doorways. "I am Sofia Mendoza, Señor Benton's housekeeper. We . . . were not certain when to expect you."

"Reed mentioned you in his letters," Kate said, glancing down at her old carpetbag now sitting just inside the door. It looked lumpy and threadbare and out of place, the most worn and faded thing in such a grand entry. She struggled to hide her embarrassment as she looked at Sofia again.

Still shaken by Sofia's emotional greeting, Kate tried to pull herself together and hide her nervousness by weaving her fingers together. She pressed her hands tight against her waist.

"There was no way to let him know exactly when I would arrive. Is Reed here?" She glanced over at the staircase across the foyer.

"No." Sofia appeared to be fighting for words, her throat working to swallow, her eyes bright with tears.

Sinking into sharp-edged disappointment, Kate made a feeble attempt to smile.

"Will he be back soon?"

Sofia closed her eyes, as if speech was too painful.

Uncomfortable, Kate looked away. Her gaze drifted over the room beyond the foyer: a parlor with fine furnishings upholstered in rich, shining brocade fabrics and warm wood surfaces gleaming with polish; a bookcase filled with gilded, leather-bound volumes; long windows; a massive fireplace of river rock. The room had an air of disuse about it, as if perfected and then abandoned. Each piece appeared to have been carefully chosen for both comfort and style and then ignored.

Suddenly, her breath caught. There, in a bay window at the far end of the room, a wooden coffin rested on two sawhorses. When her knees nearly buckled, she reached for a circular hall table in the center of the foyer for support and then miraculously, somehow found her legs. She rushed into the sitting room.

"Wait, señora!"

Without responding, Kate ran across the endless parlor until she reached the coffin.

In death, Reed Benton appeared to be far older than he had led her to believe, but he was still as handsome as in the photograph.

His hair was thick, dark brown, with silver at the temples. His jaw line was still firm, but his cheeks were hollow and his neck thin. He had been a man of stature, well over six feet, with shoulders so wide he cramped his final resting place.

Before she knew she had even moved, Kate touched his neatly combed and oiled hair, gently ran her fingers over it just above his brow, careful not to touch his skin. She remained surprisingly calm in the face of death's cold finality until she realized she felt nothing simply because she was numb.

In his letters Reed had told of his father's emigration to Texas from Georgia nearly thirty-five years ago. How Reed had married young, buried his first wife, and lost a son to the Indian wars. Kate knew the milestones of his life, but now she would forever be deprived of learning the little things, things a wife should know about a husband—how he liked his coffee, what he liked to read, his favorite foods, what made him smile.

No single word of love, no mention of it had passed between them in their letters, and yet she had fallen in love with him, or at the very least, the *idea* of him, and of sharing his life.

His letters had been insistent, full of a quiet desperation as well as a determination of purpose that matched her own. After months of sincere, heartfelt correspondence full of both intelligence and tenderness, she had agreed to marry him by proxy before she traveled to Texas.

Dear Katherine,
    I want this done so that you will already be irrevocably mine when you come to me.

Had he known he was dying?

The floorboards creaked behind her. Kate turned around. Sofia rushed into the room.

"Señora, we must talk. Please . . ."

At the same time, a man outside shouted something unintelligible.

"Our wrangler," Sofia said by way of quick explanation. She was becoming increasingly agitated. "People will be arriving for the burial soon."

Kate jumped when the front door banged opened. Sofia hurried back to the entry hall. Uncertain of her place in the scheme of things now, Kate waited beside the coffin and listened to Sofia's brief exchange with a man, heard the housekeeper's lilting, slightly accented words.

"Last night . . . sent word . . . no time."

Heavy footfalls rang out. Boot heels and spurs struck high polished wood. A man reeled into the parlor, his footsteps uneven and heavy—as if he was forcing himself to walk.

He was only a few strides into the parlor when Kate grabbed hold of the edge of the coffin for support.

Across the room, just inside the double-width doorway, stood a younger version of the late Reed Benton. He was as tall or taller than the corpse beside her, wide shouldered, with the same dark hair and features. He wore dark pants, a buckskin jacket, and two pistols at his waist. A growth of stubble covered the lower half of his face.

Above it, his haunted, bright blue eyes were glassy, almost feverish. His full mouth was set in a harsh, firm line. He stared right past her, and she saw plainly in his eyes that if he felt anything for the man in the coffin, it was certainly not sorrow at his passing.

Relief washed over Kate and the numbness began to fade as she stared at this man, so vibrant and alive, with such an undeniably commanding presence. He was the living likeness of the picture she had held against her heart all those cold and lonely nights in Maine. He was the man who had opened his heart to her in such touching, heartfelt letters.

I was named for my father, Reed Benton Senior.

He had always written of Reed Senior in the past tense and so she had assumed that his father had already passed on.

Her head swam with giddiness as the shock of the last few moments began to fade. She held out her hand and started to speak when he stepped farther into the room. Briefly he glanced at her, then looked through her, as if she were nothing more than a caller come to pay her respects.

Her hand went to her hair, then to her skirt. Of course, she was travel-weary, tired, dusty, and disheveled—and still shaken by what she had mistakenly assumed. But surely he must recognize her from her photograph. He had been expecting her to arrive any day now.

He started forward, then staggered as if his feet had suddenly grown too heavy to lift. His hand went out as he reached for the back of the settee. Then, without warning, he toppled like a fallen oak and hit the floor face-first.

"Señor Reed!" Sofia cried. Both she and Kate ran toward him at the same time.

The housekeeper helped Kate roll him onto his back. Blood poured from his nose. His upper lip immediately started to swell. Feverish heat radiated from him. The buckskin jacket he wore fell open to reveal a bloodstained, ragged tear in the shoulder of his shirt.

"Ay, Dios!" Sofia cried upon seeing the bloody shirtfront. "He has been shot!"

"He has a raging fever," Kate added, all the time thinking, ... *but he is alive.* She eased the jacket back off his shoulder, carefully opened the shirt near the jagged hole to reveal a bandage soaked in blood.

"I will get someone to carry him upstairs." Sofia had already started toward the door.

Alone with Reed Benton, Kate pressed her palm over the oozing wound in his shoulder and closed her eyes. Fate had not taken her dream, as she had thought, but had flung it in her face with a challenge.

She whispered a litany of frantic, silent prayers. *Saint Perpetua, please help him.*

Their life together was just beginning. She wasn't about to lose him now.

4

Kate was afraid to leave him, even for a moment. Afraid to look away from the big man stretched out on the crisp white sheets.

Her face had burned hot with the shy embarrassment of a silly spinster when Sofia stripped Reed of his boots and clothes and removed the useless, soiled bandage someone had wrapped around his shoulder.

The housekeeper worked with skilled and competent hands, never flinching, doing what had to be done to make Reed more comfortable. If she noticed Kate's discomfort, she made no comment as they worked side by side.

"How could this happen? Who would do such a thing to him? Why?" Kate cried as she held a wet towel to Reed's bleeding nose and then to his swollen lip.

"For five years, he has been a Texas Ranger, fighting to keep the frontier safe. Ever since his wife and child were taken from him."

Kate felt betrayed. Reed had led her to believe he was only a rancher. Why would he fail to tell her that he was also a Texas Ranger?

At last he had been dosed with laudanum, washed, and bandaged. There was nothing more they could do for him but wait for the fever to break.

When Sofia sat back and sighed, Kate admired her strength. The woman must have endured much over the last few hours, and yet she still appeared calm and collected, not a hair out of place. Her silk gown was crisp and for the most part clean, whereas Kate's drab beige outfit was smeared with Reed's blood.

She closed her eyes, thought of those frantic moments downstairs when she had pressed her hand over his wound, trying to will the blood to stop, terrified of its heat as it oozed from his shoulder beneath her palm.

Finally, Sofia stepped away from the bed.

"The minister should be here soon. Perhaps the doctor will come—but with him, one never knows." Sofia shrugged, and then her voice faltered. "People will gather from all over the ranch. We will . . . bury Reed Senior before sundown."

Kate saw something in Sofia's eyes: Here was a woman mourning much more than the loss of her employer, much more. "You loved him, didn't you?" Kate asked softly.

Sofia's eyes instantly flooded with tears. She made no attempt to blink them away.

"I have loved the señor since the day I first came to this ranch. I will love him until the day that I die. He was a great man. A man of pride and courage." She looked at the open window beside the bed where delicate lace curtains stirred with the shifting breeze, looked out toward the wide, endless rolling grasslands and beyond. "He was a man who would do anything, *anything* to see that this place he built from nothing survives. I did what I had to do to make the señor happy in his final days. I hope you can understand that, señora."

Kate offered, "You go and see to the mourners, and I will stay here." She wanted nothing more than to pull a chair up to Reed's bedside and watch him sleep. Her emotions were still in turmoil. To sit quietly beside him would surely be a gift.

Sofia acquiesced. "Stay if you wish, but I assure you, he will sleep for hours. You can use the room across the hall for now. Perhaps you wish to change and freshen up? The señor had a room built just for bathing. It is at the end of the hall."

Kate glanced down at Reed, who was still unconscious. She crossed the room and stepped into the hallway with the housekeeper; then she lowered her voice.

"Sofia, you *do* know that Reed and I are married, don't you? That we were married by proxy two weeks ago?"

Sofia looked down at her folded hands. "Yes. Yes, I know."

"Did his father know? Did he approve?"

The housekeeper's hands trembled. She took a deep breath. "Yes. He approved very much. Is there anything else?"

Kate nodded. Better to speak up than to let worry and doubt eat away at her. "Reed never told me that he was a Texas Ranger." What else might her husband have failed to disclose?

"Perhaps . . . perhaps he was afraid that you would worry about him. That if you knew, you would fear something like this happening. Perhaps . . . he was afraid you would stop writing to him." Sofia was growing more and more uncomfortable.

Just then, the hall echoed with sound as one of the men who had carried Reed upstairs appeared in the doorway. At least six feet and heavy-set, the older cowhand was sun-baked a nut brown. The hands that held his battered, stained hat were gnarled and scarred. His legs were bowed, his boots creased and dusty. He looked to be in his sixties. What was left of the grizzled hair at his temples stuck out in every direction.

His eyes were full of concern. Kate had watched this rough man and a younger cowhand lift and cradle Reed in their arms and carry him upstairs as gently as if he were a babe.

Now the man worried the hat in his hands, bobbed his head at Kate, and addressed Sofia.

"The preacher's here, ma'am. I tol' him to wait in the parlor with the rest of them that's gathered. Folks been pullin' in since you came up. Near t' ever'body who could get here on such short notice is come to bid Reed Senior good-bye."

"*Gracias,* Scrappy." Sofia turned to Kate. "Señora, this is Scrappy Parks, the wrangler. He has been here for years." Sofia paused as if making a decision, and then she said, "Scrappy, this is ... Katherine Whittington ... Benton. Reed Junior's wife."

Kate expected a polite nod of acknowledgment, perhaps an offer of a handshake, but not wide-eyed, slack-jawed astonishment.

Travel-weary, feeling out of place, and growing more uncertain by the moment, Kate forced a smile. She nodded at the old cowhand and murmured a polite greeting.

"You go on ahead. I will be right down," Sofia said, dismissing him.

But Scrappy Parks made no move to leave. "There's one more thing, ma'am. When Reed Junior rode in, he didn't come alone." His gaze flicked over to Kate, then back to Sofia. "He left a youngin' tied to the hitchin' post out front."

Sofia's hand went to her heart. *"Qué?"*

Kate thought surely she had misunderstood. "A child? Tied up outside?"

Scrappy bobbed his head. "Comanch'. Damn near tried to bite my hand off when I put him in a stall in the horse barn."

Kate glanced over her shoulder. Reed had not stirred.

She recognized the word *Comanch'*, a shortened version of Comanche. She had heard it often enough during the stagecoach ride to Lone Star.

"You hear about the latest Comanch' attack?"

"Worse than before the war."

"You'd think the government would help."

"Who needs them? Hell, this is Texas. We take care of our own."

She watched Sofia struggle in silent debate. Her eyes were shadowed, her rich, olive complexion pale. The woman was torn, but her first responsibility was to the mourners gathering downstairs, to see the man she had loved and served so long laid to rest.

Kate knew little of men, but she did know children, and she knew them well. How different could an Indian child be? As much as she hated to leave Reed now, Sofia had assured her that he would sleep for hours. Her decision was a simple one after all.

"You are needed downstairs, Sofia. If you think Reed will be all right alone, I'll go and see to the boy," she offered.

Scrappy shook his head. "Ma'am, excuse me, but I don't think—"

"I was a teacher at a girl's orphanage for eleven years, Mr. Parks. I think I can manage one little boy."

Scrappy waited for Sophia to respond.

She appeared distracted, and rightly so. "I think Miss . . . Katherine should see if there is anything she can do for the boy." Once he left them, Sofia turned to Kate. "Reed Junior will sleep until the laudanum wears off. After you tend to the child, please join us in the parlor." Then she seemed to draw on some inner strength, as if she had just come to terms with something that had been plaguing her. "As Reed Junior's wife, you should be at the burial, but I am not certain this is the time to announce to everyone that you are married. A marriage is an occasion for a grand celebration. This is a day to mourn. May I simply introduce you as a guest of the family from the East?"

The simple reaffirmation of her marital status helped ease Kate's mind. Sofia was right. This was a day to mourn Reed Senior. With her husband wounded, given all the turmoil, why not wait to announce the marriage?

She quickly agreed. After Sofia started downstairs, she gently closed the door to Reed's room and went to find Scrappy in the barn.

Pain ripped through Reed's shoulder like a white-hot poker, ate at his flesh and his nerves, hot and hard, cutting through the cobwebs in his mind. His pulse pounded in his ears.

He heard voices, smooth and warm. Women's voices. Not what he was used to in his world of men and war. Blood and guns.

There had been tenderness and caring in the hands that touched and ministered to him. The kind of touch he barely remembered.

There had been so little gentility in his life for so very long now that he had forgotten the feel of it, but certainly not all the pain that memories of it would bring.

Remembrance came to him in swift flashes of light, sound and fury. A bullet had torn through the fleshy part of his shoulder, barely missing bone. Another grazed his temple.

Horses had screamed as they went down around him. Women and children cried as they ran, terrified, seeking shelter where there was none.

There was nowhere to hide on the open plain. Nowhere to run to escape death. It rode over them. Trampled them down.

Pain splintered through him again. He tried to cry out, to move and relieve the stabbing ache, but those gentle women had done something to him, something that failed to obliterate the pain but numbed his mind, kept him from thinking clearly, from moving. Even from crying out.

Mercifully it made him oblivious to the deeper wound he had received in that last battle. A wound not of the flesh but of the soul.

His blissfully befuddled, drugged mind would not let him contemplate that at all.

5

"You locked him in like an animal?"

Kate stared at Scrappy Parks, wondering what kind of man could treat a child so abominably. Inside the cavernous horse barn surrounded by the sharp scents of horse manure and straw and the musty smell of cool damp earth, all was still.

Not a sound issued from behind the high, locked door of the stall where a boy had been imprisoned.

As they passed through the first floor of the house on the way out, she noticed the parlor crowded with people from all walks of life. Even a few children were present. The lane as well as the yard fronting the house was now filled with carriages and buckboards of all kinds. Benton House echoed with whispered condolences.

But in the barn, Scrappy was silent and frowning. Kate folded her arms.

"Unlock the door, Mr. Parks. Please."

"Ma'am, I don't think you know—"

She shook her head. "I know exactly what I am doing. That boy is no doubt frightened out of his wits. Let's not waste time arguing over this. Just open the door."

Edgy and tired, Kate had been through enough today. She was not about to back down now.

Scrappy mumbled something under his breath and threw the iron bolt.

When Kate first stepped into the stall, it took her a moment to make out in the far corner the small figure cowering in the shadows. He was small, perhaps no older than seven, eight at the most, seated with his back pressed to the wall, one leg extended, his arms crossed protectively over the tattered front of a faded red flannel shirt. His legs were filthy and bare. He wore a loincloth made of some kind of tanned hide and moccasins of the same material which were fancifully beaded with a decorative horse pattern, and very worn. His tangled, matted dark hair hung well past his shoulders and was littered with straw.

Tearstains streaked his dirty cheeks. In a flash of bravado, he sat up and glared at Kate. Taking stock of his condition, she was stunned by his thinness.

Despite an occasional scowl, he looked very small and very, very frightened.

She opened her arms wide, held her hands out in front of him to show she meant no harm.

"I'm Kate," she said softly as she slowly inched toward him. Straw rustled with every step. "I am going to help you."

She heard Scrappy snort and ignored him.

The child did not move a muscle. She continued to step closer, assuring him that she only wanted to help.

She felt confident and sure now, more self-assured than she had felt since she stepped into Benton House. When she was within arm's length of the boy, she bent closer.

Without a change of expression or hint of warning, he lunged at her, thin fingers curved like talons, teeth bared like a wild animal's.

She jumped back and crashed into Scrappy. The boy let

out a yowl of pain and fell back into the corner. Despite his pain, he continued to spit and snarl.

"I told you so," Snappy barked. He sidestepped Kate with a gun in his hand.

"Put that away!" She was frightened half to death by the sight of the firearm. "Don't you *dare* shoot that boy."

"I ain't gonna shoot him, for God's sake. I'm just gonna scare the piss and vinegar outta him."

Shaken, Kate refused to give up. Somewhere inside the pitiful little creature cowering in the corner of the stall beat the heart of a child.

"He's only a little boy. Just because he's an Indian doesn't mean you have to mistreat him."

"He's no Indian. He's white, turned Comanch'. That's even worse."

Kate swung around. "What are you saying?"

Scrappy nodded toward the boy. "I didn't notice at first either, but just look at them eyes."

She did look. The boy's eyes were as blue as the Texas sky. Brilliant blue and filled with pain.

"It doesn't matter to me what he is. He needs our help. He's badly hurt," she said.

"I figure his leg or his ankle's broke."

"I'm certain Reed would object to this treatment. I want him moved to the house immediately."

"Hell, lady, *Reed* tied him to the hitching post and Miss Sofia—"

"Sofia has her hands full." Kate could see that nothing she said would make a difference to this man until she established her authority. She forced herself to sound calm and controlled. "Sofia is the housekeeper here. I am Reed's wife. I want the boy moved."

"How come I ain't heard about no wife of Reed Junior's

before today?" He pronounced Reed's name as if it was all one word—*Reedjunah.*

"Perhaps Reed's father didn't feel it was *important* for you to know. Now, are you going to help me? Or do I have to go inside and disrupt a man's wake in order to get some help?"

Mumbling under his breath, Scrappy holstered his gun. During their exchange, the boy had not moved. He continued to watch them warily. When Kate tried talking to him again, he spat at her, thrashing and kicking out with his good leg.

"Got any fine ideas about how you think we ought to do this, teacher?" The cowhand did not try to hide his disdain.

Afraid the boy might further injure himself if they wrestled with him, Kate conceded momentary defeat.

"Maybe you're right, Mr. Parks. For the time being he is safe and out of the elements. Bring him some water and food and perhaps he will calm down. That leg needs to be set if it's broken or he'll be crippled for life."

"No sense in wasting any food on him."

Kate had suffered all of the man's ignorant intolerance that she could possibly bear. She whirled on him.

"How can you be so insensitive? Would you starve him?"

Scrappy tipped his hat up with his thumb until it rode the back of his crown.

"He won't eat. They been known to starve themselves to death when they're locked up."

She arched a brow. "They?"

"Comanches that are locked up. Even captives that have been with 'em too long starve themselves to death when they're taken back." He stared at the boy long and hard and then shook his head in resignation. "Sometimes the ones that's turned Comanch' suffer worst of all."

.   .   .

Wary of both white strangers, Fast Pony watched the woman carefully, trying to understand her. He already knew what was in the old man's heart. The old one would kill him if he had a chance.

But the woman was different. There was no hatred in her eyes, only curiosity and pity.

And flashes of anger.

The boy could see that she was mad at the old man. The angry sound of her strange white words and the way she stood, as stiff and straight as a lance, told him as much.

It took all his strength to keep from crying in front of them, all his courage not to rant and scream and tear at his hair. He had not seen any sign of his mother when the Rangers herded them together like animals.

Did she lie in the burnt-out shell of their tepee? Was she somewhere out in the open where the ravens and coyote and wolves would pick at her bones? Would he *ever* see his mother again?

He had to be brave, for he knew his father, Many Horses, would surely come for him soon. Many Horses was a great warrior. His father would track and kill the other Rangers and find the tall, cold-eyed one who had brought him here.

Until then, Fast Pony would watch and wait and find a way to escape.

6

". . . and so we commit Reed Benton Senior's body to the grave."

Kate stood among the throng of mourners assembled in a tight knot on a windswept knoll a half mile from the ranch house and watched as the plain pine coffin was lowered into a grave carved out of Texas soil.

The site was surrounded by people who had known Reed Benton Senior as friend, employer or both. Shoulder to shoulder, rough, weather-beaten cowhands of all ages, prosperous ranchers, dirt-poor farmers and settlers, a butcher, a dry goods store owner—all of them stood equaled by loss as they bade the founder of Lone Star farewell.

The wind whipped long, wayward strands of hair around Kate's face, wrapped her skirt against her thighs, revealed the high tops of her black leather shoes. Desperate to return to her husband's bedside, she thought about slipping away, but Sofia had again assured her before the burial that Reed would remain in a laudanum-induced sleep for quite some time.

There was so much she wanted to talk to him about, so much she wanted him to explain.

Why hadn't he told her that he was a Ranger? And what

of the strange child? Why had he left the boy tied to the hitching post? Why had Reed brought him home?

She felt a tentative touch just above her elbow, which shook her out of her reverie. Turning, she found herself looking into the eyes of Reverend Preston Marshall.

The preacher was near her own age, in his late twenties or early thirties, of medium height and build with light brown hair, pewter eyes, and strong, handsomely cut features.

Except for the white band around his throat, he was dressed entirely in black. The empty left sleeve of his jacket was folded under and pinned in place.

"Excuse me for interrupting your solitude, ma'am." He tipped his hat politely. "I thought I might walk back to the house with you, Miss Whittington." The discreet tone of his soft, Southern drawl soothed her.

Glancing around, Kate realized that while her thoughts had centered on Reed, the ceremony had ended and the crowd had already begun to disperse. Three cowhands lingered a polite distance away, shovels in hand, ready to close the grave. While a handful of folks tarried, speaking in hushed tones, others walked back down the hill toward the house.

"It's finally over." Kate caught herself. "I'm sorry. I . . . I'm anxious to get back."

She glanced down the hill. Benton House was separated from the ranch outbuildings, solitary, empty, and alone.

"I usually try to keep these things short, but Reed Senior cut quite a public figure around here. Many of us wouldn't be here if it weren't for him."

"How so, Reverend Marshall?"

He began to walk beside her as they headed downhill. Used to elderly priests relegated to saying Mass at the orphanage, Kate was surprised by the minister's youth and striking good looks.

"Reed Senior founded the ranch over thirty years ago and established the town of Lone Star smack in the center of it, hoping the ranch hands would marry and settle here. If they had a stake in the place, he figured that they would stay put through lean years and the threat of Comanche and Kiowa attacks.

"He started with a saloon, branched out to a dry goods store, brought in a butcher, and offered a free cabin to any man who wanted to marry and move in a family. When there were enough families to warrant it, he built a school. Two years ago, he built a church. That's why I came to Lone Star."

Her mind went to the child locked in the barn. The white child "gone Comanch'."

"It appears he was able to hold the Comanche back, at least from Lone Star." She took care walking. The ground was hard and uneven, pocked with prairie-dog mounds and tufts of buffalo grass.

"Things went fairly well—after his first few years." He paused to help her steer clear of a hole. "He gave the Indians occasional heads of beef when they needed it, and he was able to show plenty of firepower. There have been outlying raids along the borders of the ranch over the years, but it appears Lone Star's been left pretty much alone."

He continued to defy both her perception and first-hand knowledge of a man of God. "Do you have a family, Reverend?"

He paused, looked out across the open plain to where the sun was low in the afternoon sky. Clouds above the horizon had already begun to blush.

"I fought for the Confederacy. Even had a fiancée before the war started, but afterward—" He shrugged the shoulder above his empty sleeve. "—Well, let's just say things didn't work out. My only living relative is my maiden aunt. I brought her to Texas with me. If you get into town, I know Aunt Martha would love to have you to tea. She makes a creme cake that's the talk of the town."

They walked in silence for a few yards, Kate trying to understand everything that had happened since she stepped off the stage.

Reverend Marshall was the first to speak. "Sofia said that you are here visiting from the East."

Obviously, Reed had not told anyone other than his father and Sofia of his plans, and they had kept his confidence—just as she and Sofia had decided to tell no one Reed was injured, but that he was away on duty. What he had written assured Kate that he would have wanted it that way.

I'm a private person. No one really knows me.

"Actually I . . . I've been corresponding with Reed Junior." She smiled inside, reminded of that fall day when she first saw Reed's advertisement. "I'm from a small fishing village in Maine. Until a short time ago, I was a schoolteacher at a Catholic orphanage for girls."

"If you don't mind my saying so, you don't look like a teacher, Miss Whittington."

She turned to him and smiled. "You don't look like a man of God, Reverend Marshall."

His smile faded. "Because of my arm?"

"Heavens, no," she said quickly, embarrassed to think she had offended him. "Until today, the only men of God I've ever met have been priests, and all of them were very . . . old. None of them were han—none of them looked like you."

He smiled again. "I see."

They had reached the house. Kate glanced up at Reed's second-floor window. Although light shone from a few of the windows on the ground floor, the upper rooms were dark. The gloaming had thickened as twilight crept across the land. Miles and miles of darkness would soon engulf them. She looked out across the open prairie and shivered, suddenly feeling vulnerable, knowing they would be left in virtual isolation.

She was eager to get back to Reed, hated to have him wake up alone, in pain, in the darkness.

"It was nice to meet you, Reverend Marshall," she said.

He reached up and tipped his black hat. "I'll look forward to seeing you again, Miss Whittington." After a moment's hesitation he added, "Please feel free to call on me if you need anything while you are here."

She quickly assured him that she would, then bade him good-bye and walked up the wide steps beneath the portico.

As soon as the last caller drove away, Sofia went upstairs to rest, but Kate, unable to get her mind off the little boy in the barn, lit a lamp and slipped outside with it, balancing a blanket and a pillow from her own bed as she made her way through the gathering darkness.

The huge, hollow horse barn was pitch black until Kate stepped in with the light. As she stood on the threshold, the barn echoed with emptiness, the only sound a soft, mournful sobbing which stopped almost immediately as she stepped inside. Kate was halfway down the long central aisle between the stalls when Scrappy Parks walked in behind her.

"Saw you crossing the yard with that lamp," he said, eyeing her thoughtfully.

"I came in to see about the boy and to bring him these." She indicated the bedding and frowned. "You left him alone in the dark."

"Better than have him burn the place down."

"Do you honestly believe he could climb out of there?"

"It's my job not to take chances."

She looked around the barn, glanced up at the loft. "Why not hang a lantern way up there? He can't possibly climb in the condition he is in."

Scrappy craned his neck, followed her gaze. Then he shook his head no.

"I don't want him left alone out here in the dark," she re-iterated. "And I don't want to have to disturb Sofia about this. She's resting."

The wrangler let go a long-suffering sigh. "All right. I'll put a lantern up there, but if he burns this barn down with all the stock in it, then don't say I didn't warn you."

She refused to let herself doubt her order as she passed the many stalls and the beautiful horses in them, animals from the purest white to deep chestnut. There was even one warm-eyed, black-and-white pinto.

She shot the bolt on the boy's stall, found him just as she had left him, pressed against the wall and wary of every move she made. Easing close enough to gently toss the pillow beside him and then the blanket, she longed to be able to sit down beside him, to comfort him, perhaps lull him to sleep with a song or a story as she might have one of the girls at Saint Perpetua's.

For now, the simple offer of comfort would have to be enough. There was only so much she could do to relieve the suffering caused by the rending tear of separation from all he held dear. She knew that firsthand.

"Good night, little boy," she whispered before she left him. "I know how you feel. I truly, truly do. I hope you get some sleep."

Kate walked back to the house and went upstairs. Once she reached Reed's room, she lit another lamp and then paused to stretch and rub the back of her neck. When he suddenly moaned, the sound nearly frightened her to death. She dropped to her knees at his bedside.

He quickly became more restless, gripped by fever and pain, struggling with whatever demons they conjured. She pressed her palm to his forehead. Reed was burning up.

She brushed his dark hair back, worried by the dark shadows beneath his eyes. His head tossed from side to side as he mumbled something she could not understand. She leaned closer.

"Reed," she said softly. "It's me, Kate. I'm right here beside you at last. Please, fight this, Reed. Get well. We've so much to talk about. So much to plan."

As she leaned against the edge of the mattress, staring down at strong features drained of all color, she could not help but recall his written words. They were all she had of him now.

> I want a family again. I have been lost without a wife, without my child. I need a loving woman in my life who is willing to stand by me, willing to face life's challenges and share my hopes and dreams. A woman who can love this land.

"Reed?" She whispered. "Oh, please, Reed."

He stirred again and turned toward the sound of her voice but did not awaken. Kate sighed and leaned back on her heels, closed her eyes, and lowered her forehead to the edge of the mattress. She was exhausted but determined not to lose hope.

His arm brushed against her face and she felt his burning skin. A basin of fresh water and clean folded rags stood ready on the washstand across the room. She stood up and walked over to the washstand and dipped a rag into the tepid water, wrung it out and went back to Reed's bedside. Bone tired, she had no thought of leaving. Each passing hour spent alone with him was a gift. A precious, private, one-way exchange that allowed her time to know him in an intimate way.

Bathing him the way Sofia had done earlier, Kate found it almost impossible not to let her hand linger as she ran the damp cloth over his face and neck, across his strong shoulders, and down his arms. She drew the bedsheet past his chest, to his hips. Staring down at the crisp dark hair that covered his pectorals and trailed to his navel, she blushed fire.

I am touching a naked man.

She took comfort in the notion that he could not see the burning embarrassment of a once-cloistered spinster and tried to remind herself this wasn't the first time she had ever set eyes on a man's naked body.

As she studied the hard lines and angles, the muscular shoulders and arms, his size and strength became apparent and a bit overwhelming. Lying in the center of the double bed, he almost dwarfed it. There was barely any room left for someone else to lie there without being pressed against him.

She lifted his right hand, washed it carefully and gently, whispering all the details of her trip West, hoping to soothe and comfort him. Each finger was attended to with care. She turned his hand over, traced her fingertips across the lines and calluses that marked his palm, carefully laid his arm down, and then picked up the other.

As she studied his hand, she could not help but think about how, when he was well again, these very hands would one day touch her, fondle and caress her. She shivered and felt her face burn again. Still, she anticipated that day. *At least I know what to expect.* She had never forgotten all she had seen and heard those years she lived with her mother, had not forgotten the things that men and women did with one another.

The curtains billowed as the night wind lifted them high and let them sink back against the window frame. She looked outside, watched high, thick clouds slip across a full moon. In that instant, from somewhere deep inside the cobwebbed corners of her mind, came a recollection of her early years.

Twisted sheets on narrow beds. The pungent smell of aroused, sweaty bodies. The mystery behind the gruff sounds made by the noisy strangers her mother had taken into her body.

Meg Whittington had entertained men for money—for food and shelter. She had let them touch and taste her, couple with and ride her. If Mama hated those nights, if she had ever suffered shame, she had kept it hidden behind a brazen bravado. Kate refused to wonder if her mother might actually have enjoyed her work, if there was something in Meg that had made her want to whore with men.

Kate's hands began to shake. She set the washcloth aside and quickly drew the sheet up, covering Reed to the neck. She stared down at him, watched his chest rise and fall, memorizing the way his dark lashes—sinfully thick lashes— brushed his high cheekbones. He seemed to have calmed; his skin had cooled. He was resting comfortably. Kate decided to take advantage of the bathing room at the end of the hall, so she picked up the lamp, crossed the room, and gently closed the door.

7

Reed opened his eyes to darkness.

His head felt stuffed with cotton. His mouth was dry, his shoulder ached like a son of a bitch. He had been dreaming of Daniel, and in his dream he was running after his son— running as fast as he could, shouting his son's name.

But Daniel wouldn't respond, wouldn't stop running. Soon, the boy disappeared completely behind a dense wall of smoke.

Reed had been around Comanche long enough to have learned some of their beliefs. They took a lot of stock in a man's dreams. Had his dream of Daniel been some sort of warning?

He would have to remind Becky to keep a close eye on the boy.

He had dreamed of the old man, too. He'd seen his father dead, laid out in a wooden box in the window of the sitting room of his damn palace, Benton House. The place was a mansion suited for a city someplace back East, not the middle of the prairie. It looked like it had fallen out of the sky. His father used it to tempt Becky, to make her beg to move back.

Benton House was fit for a king, not a rancher.

Reed Benton Senior—the goddamn king of Lone Star Ranch. The man never listened to a soul, never cared about what anyone else wanted, not his son, not even his wife. Reed winced thinking of his mother, of the neglect she had suffered at the hands of his father, and of one thing she wanted that his father refused to give her—his love and attention. As far as Reed was concerned, her death was his father's fault. He would forever lay that on the old man's head.

His father might be the ruler of his domain, but he didn't wield enough power to dictate to him, or Becky, or Daniel. Not now, not ever. It would be a cold day in hell before he moved them back to Benton House to live under his father's thumb.

Becky knew he wasn't going to change his mind, either. He saw in her eyes that she hated him for not wanting to live the easy life, for not letting her enjoy the luxury of the big, solid house away from the frontier. She wanted Sofia waiting on her hand and foot while his father spent time trying to convince him to run for state legislature. The old man swore that he cast a long enough shadow that he could even buy his son an election.

Reed would never feel like a man, never be anything but "Junior" as long as his father was alive. At least living on the edge of the frontier kept him removed from the old man's grasp.

Reed opened his eyes and tried to sit up, but the bed beneath him began to spin, so he dropped back down.

Where in the hell was Becky?

He tried to call her, but his throat was so rusty that damn near gibberish was all that came out.

Just then the door opened and a shimmering halo of lamplight preceded her into the room. She had her hair twisted into a thick braid that fell like an auburn rope over her shoulder. He hadn't realized it nearly reached her waist. He loved her hair, loved to run his fingers through it.

Some men were of the opinion that if you told a woman you loved her too often, she would begin to take you for granted.

It seemed like a hell of a long time since he had held his wife in his arms. She stood in the doorway, not moving, just watching him. A circle of light played over her face, teased him with shaded glimpses of her features.

He tried to sit up, rolled to his side, decided to wait for her to come to him.

Damn, even as bad as he felt, just the sight of her had him hard as a rock.

He stretched out his arm, beckoned her closer.

When Kate opened the door and found Reed awake, struggling to sit up, she nearly dropped the lamp. Even now, as she stood there dumbstruck, her hand shook so hard that the flame threatened to go out.

The glow of lamplight spread before her into the room, far enough for her to see into his eyes. Reed stretched out his arm, beckoned her closer.

Her breath caught. Her knees began to tremble as hard as her hand. She hastily set the lamp down on the washstand. In half a dozen steps she crossed to his bedside.

With one hand pressed against the bodice of her nightgown, she watched him reach for her free hand. Slowly their palms met. A rush of heat shot through her, hard and hot as lightning.

He gently tugged until she sat on the narrow space between him and the edge of the mattress.

When the corner of his lips lifted into a half-smile, she almost dropped to her knees to offer a prayer to Saint Perpetua for interceding. His hand was too warm, his skin still radiated the last vestiges of fever, but he was conscious. He would recover. She knew her prayers had been answered.

No words came when he tried to speak, only a croaking sound. Kate reached for a glass of water on the bedside table, slid her arm beneath his head, cradling him so that he could take a sip. He swallowed half the contents before he raised his head again. When she lowered him to the pillow, he closed his eyes and sighed.

"Is . . . is the boy asleep?"

Hearing him speak startled her so that she nearly dropped the glass of water, but she smiled. It was fitting that his first inquiry be about the child, and that pleased her.

"He's sound asleep."

"Good. Good." Reed's lashes moved. His eyes slowly opened. "I dreamed he ran away."

"No. He's still here."

"I've been waiting for you."

Her heart swelled.

"I didn't know you were awake or I would have been here beside you."

"Your hair—"

Suddenly uncertain, she reached up and touched the part down the center of her hair.

"Let it loose," he whispered.

Reaching for the thin ribbon tied around the end of her braid, she tugged it and the bow unraveled. Staring into Reed's eyes, Kate ignored the scrap of ribbon as it sailed to the floor. She finger-combed her hair until it fell around her shoulders.

Reed reached up, wrapped his hand in her hair and with a gentle but persistent tug, drew her close, so close she was leaning against his chest. Her breasts flattened against him. He was surprisingly hard, unyielding where she was soft.

He urged her closer until she gazed into his eyes. Their lips met. His were surprisingly soft, warm and dry from fever. The kiss was a gentle meeting, an introduction, a chance to taste, to touch, to discover each other more intimately.

Her first kiss.

Something deep inside her slowly melted. Something she had guarded all her life, something she had once feared melted away. She loved him. She wanted him—wanted this night to go on forever.

"I waited so long," he whispered.

The past months of correspondence, the proxy marriage, the long trip west and anxious past few hours—she, too, had waited so long.

"I know," she whispered back. "I know, Reed. So very long."

Their lips touched again, then parted.

"Stay with me." His lips moved against her mouth.

"Yes. Of course."

She started to rise, to move the rocker close so that she could spend the night beside him.

"No." He protested the instant she began to pull away. His hand, still tangled in her hair, dropped to her shoulder. His thumb grazed her collarbone. He rubbed it back and forth. "Lie down. Here, beside me."

Stay with me.

She had mistaken his meaning. When her cheeks began to burn, she was thankful for the shadows.

So soon.

Her heart was pounding. His thumb continued to trace her collarbone. His fingers slipped across her skin. She shivered when they explored beneath the fabric.

She could not calm her racing heart. She thought that caring for him today would have helped her past this point of embarrassment, that she had grown used to him, to the *idea* of him and what being married to him meant. Now that reality was staring her in the face, she realized that she had been wandering around in a dream, unaware that this very night she would become his wife—in every sense of the word.

He was her husband. Their marriage had been recorded in Maine and Texas.

Reed slowly ran his hand down her shoulder and took her by surprise when he gently cupped her breast. She gasped, shocked at the intense sensation when his thumb found her nipple, teased it, stroked it. A moan escaped her, shocking her.

Wanting more, needing more, she pressed her hand over his. The fabric of her nightgown separated their hands, yet she felt the heat of his hand through the muslin.

"Take it off," he urged. His voice was low. Their eyes locked.

She took a deep breath to steady herself, tried to calm her racing heart. He wanted her to undress, to lie beside him, to give herself, her virginity to him.

To seal their marriage vows.

Outside, the moon was on the rise. Round, brilliant, obliterating all but one lone star beside it. It shone down and drenched the rolling prairie, the gentle sloping land.

As Reed reached up and stroked her cheek, he ran his fingers through her hair, patient. Waiting.

Kate stared out at the man in the moon.

She had made something of her life at Saint Perpetua's and then she had taken a chance on her dream.

She was no whore. She was not her mother.

She was a wife, and, determined to be the best wife a man ever had, Kate drew his hand away from her gown, clung to it as she rose to her feet. Then she gathered her nightgown in her hand and slowly drew it over her head. She let it fall across the arm of the rocker. Shivering despite the heat of summer, astounded by her own boldness, she stood before him in nothing but milk-white moonlight.

.   .   .

She was a dream wrapped in moonbeams. His wife. His love. Soft and gentle, warm as the ever-present breeze kissing the prairie.

He liked this newfound shyness in her. It gave him strength that may have otherwise failed him. She lifted the sheet and carefully slipped in beside him, somehow aware of the damn ache in his shoulder, even though the origin of it escaped him now.

He wanted his wife. Wanted to love her until she was certain she was his stars, his moon. The way Daniel was his sunshine, even on the darkest of days.

Her skin was smooth and silky. White as cream. Intoxicating. He drew her fingers to his lips, kissed them one by one, ran his hand up her arm and pulled her so close their bodies touched from shoulder to shoulder.

She trembled with excitement as he whispered love words against her neck, in the hollow of her shoulder, in her ear until she moaned. Then he placed his hand beneath her chin, brought her lips up to his. He brushed aside the fall of long hair and kissed her. He fell into the kiss, the heat and the wetness, and sucked her tongue.

Tonight, she kissed like a virgin. He took his cue from her, smiled against her lips and tried to roll to his side, but the dull ache became a searing pain in his shoulder.

"It hurts. . . ."

She went perfectly still. "If you would rather wait . . ."

"I would rather die than wait." He kissed her deeply. He would find a way.

"See how much I need you?" He took her hand, drew it beneath the sheet, across his stomach, until he urged her to curl her fingers around his arousal. "Take me inside you."

She gasped at his boldness, but she did not draw back. Nor did she let go. Instead, with a slow determination that bordered on torture, she began to trail her fingers over him, exploring by touch.

They had all the time in the world, and so he gave himself up to the sheer pleasure of the silky stroke of her hand, closed his eyes, let his senses gambol. A hint of roses swirled around her, reminding him of the old, red trailing rose his mother had brought all the way from Georgia before he was born. He had not thought of it in years.

Without letting him go, she shifted, drew her legs up until she was on her knees beside him. As the sheet slid down her body, the night breeze caressed their bare skin.

Reed slipped his hand between her thighs, unerringly found her dewy dampness. He pressed her mound, massaged her gently until she was softly panting. She leaned over him, her hands on both sides of his head, her long, auburn hair surrounding them until they were enclosed in a swaying, sensual web.

"I need you." He had waited so very, very long. He'd thought he would have to wait forever.

Her knee went across him. She settled there with her cheek against his heart. He could feel her breath against his chest, the moisture of tears was there, too.

"Are you crying?" he asked. "Why?"

". . . so happy . . ."

He felt the whispered words against his bare skin. He slid his hands to her hips, urged her to straddle him. Then he lowered her with measured slowness, spreading her gently as he inched himself inside.

She stiffened for an instant when he met with resistance, then gave a soft cry and enveloped him fully.

He lifted his chin, urged her to kiss him. It was a moment or two before she moved, and then she covered his lips with hers. They lay locked together. She melted inside and relaxed.

Her hips gradually began to move in a sensuous, rhythmic motion. She was tender, even tentative. She gave of herself, took no more than his injured, feverish body could give.

He wanted to add to her pleasure, wanted her to reach fulfillment with him, but with infinite, measured thrusts she coaxed him, milking him to a soul-shattering climax. A primitive sound tore from his throat when he came inside her.

With his release came a blessed peace, the likes of which he had not known for a long, long time.

She curled around him, gathered him into her arms. Replete, he slipped into a deep, contented sleep.

Not until Reed's breathing settled into a slow, rhythmic pattern did Kate even think of moving. When she did, it was with the utmost care.

She slid off him but did not leave the bed. Instead, she lay tucked against his side, savoring the hard masculine feel of him. She marveled at the wonder, the magic their bodies had made together.

Thank God she had taken a chance on happiness. Thank God that she had followed her dream. Now she had made the final step and what had once seemed mysterious and at the same time frightening had turned out to be more than magic. This first night with him would live forever in her heart.

All her thoughts drifted away when Reed stirred. His eyes were still closed when he softly whispered, "I love you, wife."

Tears smarted behind her eyes, though not the first she had shed on this glorious eve. As she let the words seep into her heart, she thought he had eased into sleep again.

Seconds passed. He gently nudged her calf with his knee. "Say it," he murmured.

She realized what he wanted. The words caught in her throat when she joyously echoed, "I love you."

It was the first time she had ever said the words aloud to anyone. The first time she had ever had anyone to truly love.

Reed settled into a deep sleep. The sheet was cool when she drew it over them, careful not to disturb him. She nestled beside him, unwilling to leave even though his seed and traces of her virgin blood were sticky between her thighs.

She thought again of what had passed between them, so different and yet the same as the acts she had witnessed as a child.

Kate could not imagine such a personal exchange occurring between two strangers. How had her mother done these intimate things night after night with men she did not know, even if it did keep Kate from starving?

Although she and Reed might not have exchanged more than a handful of words, he was no stranger to her. She knew his hopes and dreams from his letters. She had come to know every inch of him over the last few hours.

They were far from strangers. Legally, they were husband and wife. And now they were lovers, as well.

The moon crested. Its shimmering light poured over the bed, highlighting their bodies—Reed's heavier, darker form pressed against her pale skin, the bandage on his shoulder showed beneath the long strands of her hair. A pleasant breeze billowed the lace curtains. She looked out toward the moon, a milk-white stain on the rippled surface of the windowpane.

Not even the glow of the moon could disturb her tonight. Heady with the mysterious power only a woman in love knows, Kate turned her back on the smiling moonman's face, curled against her husband's side, and slept.

8

The gray light of dawn barely stained the room when Kate awoke beside Reed. Full of emotions she could not name, she lay there watching him sleep and then slowly, gently, rested her hand on his bare chest above his heart. He was still warm, but not feverish as before, so she was careful not to wake him. Closing her eyes, she imagined hearing his words again.

"I love you, wife."

Wife. She was indeed his wife now. In every way.

Finally, he stirred, shifted slightly, and ran his tongue across his lips. "Hurts . . ." he whispered.

She immediately slipped out of bed, grabbed her gown off the floor, and slipped it over her head. His fever was down, but he was obviously in pain. The bottle of laudanum was on the bedside table. She had watched Sofia administer the dose before, had seen her give Reed no more than a spoonful. She decided not to wait for the housekeeper.

She opened the bottle, filled the spoon, and then gently slipped her free arm beneath his head to cradle it while she eased his lips open with the spoon. Reed opened his eyes for a moment, stared into hers and slowly smiled.

Kate's heart took flight again.

He swallowed, closed his eyes. She tenderly lowered him to the pillow and drew back, smoothed a lock of his dark hair off his forehead.

She longed to sit beside him and watch him sleep, knowing that sleep would help him heal, but she needed to wash and change, uncomfortable with the idea of Sofia walking in and finding her in her nightgown. After pulling up the sheet and smoothing it across Reed's chest, she reluctantly stood up and left him.

As she tiptoed across the hall to the room where she had unpacked and laid out her things, she noticed that Sofia's door was still closed and was thankful that the woman was getting some much needed rest after all she had been through.

Within a quarter of an hour, Kate was dressed and brushing out her hair when she heard loud, rapid knocking on the door downstairs. Afraid the pounding would awaken Sofia and Reed, she raced through the house in the weak morning light.

The pounding came from the back of the house. She ran into the kitchen, opened the back door to Scrappy, who had a dark scowl on his face.

"The boy's gone," he barked.

"What?" She rushed past him, ran across the veranda, and headed toward the horse barn. The wrangler ran along behind her.

"I went to open up the barn and check on him, but he's not there," he explained.

"How did he get out?" Last night the boy hadn't been able to stand, let alone walk. She half suspected Scrappy Parks of setting him free just to be rid of him.

"He tipped over the water bucket and climbed out."

Kate recalled having seen a bucket of water in the stall, but had not thought anything of it at the time. The child needed water. She paused outside the barn doors.

"Did he take a horse?" Her mind raced as she scanned the prairie beyond the corral area. The land was bathed in morning light, the sky glowing pink.

"He didn't take a horse. I guess he couldn't work the bolts on the stalls or he would have."

Instantly, Kate calmed. "He couldn't have gotten very far on foot," she thought aloud. "Have you looked for him?"

"Ma'am, I just woke up, saw he was gone and went to the house. It was dark until a few minutes ago."

She started around the side of the barn, not knowing where to begin. Scrappy shouted a second later, and she backtracked.

"He went this way." He pointed at an impression in the dirt. The boy had dragged himself along, crawling, trailing his bad leg, headed northwest, away from the rising sun.

Kate's heart went out to him, trying to imagine the strength of will and endurance for pain the child must surely be suffering.

They found him far beyond the open corral area, sound asleep where the grass was thick, high, and beaten down where he had passed. He lay stretched out with his cheek cradled on his arm.

"What now?"

At the sound of Scrappy's voice, the boy came awake and pushed himself up. When he turned to face them, there was sullen resignation on his face. His eyes were swollen and red from crying, his hair matted and littered with grass and straw.

He looked like a pitiful, broken little scarecrow.

"We're going to have to splint that ankle," Kate said half to herself.

"Hell." Behind her, Scrappy spat.

"Please, refrain from cursing, Mr. Parks."

"Shit. There ain't no way to get near him."

She turned on him, hands on hips. "Would you *please* try to be just a bit more positive, Mr. Parks?"

"I'm pos-a-tively certain he ain't gonna let us get near enough to touch him, let alone set that busted leg—even if I hold a gun on him."

"You will do nothing of the kind." Kate frowned down at the boy, thinking as she twisted a stray lock of her hair. She watched the child's eyes dart from her to Scrappy and back again.

"Surely he's exhausted. We have to get him to the house."

Scrappy merely laughed at the idea.

"Go get Sofia," she said, unwilling to be swayed. "Tell her to bring the laudanum."

"You thinking of puttin' him out?"

"Please, Mr. Parks. Just go."

"You keep clear of him," he warned. "I won't be here to hit him on the conk if he jumps you."

"I'll be fine." Just to make certain, Kate took a step back. As long as the boy could not leap in her direction, she would be safe enough.

Once Scrappy was gone, Kate gathered her skirt and sat down in the grass. The boy seemed to relax a bit after the cowhand left and Kate retreated, but his expression remained wary. His huge eyes never left her.

"I am Kate," she said slowly. Then she pointed to her chest and said a bit louder, *"Kaaaate."*

Then she pointed at him and waited. When he made no response, she went through the motions again, pointing and repeating her name over and over.

From the look on his face, she knew that if the boy could curse, he was silently damning her to Comanche hell.

Next she tried eating motions. "Are you hungry? We'll take you inside and get you something to eat."

No response. The child merely stared back with blank, expressionless eyes and scratched his thin neck with grubby fingers.

Within minutes, Sofia came running with Scrappy lumbering beside her. Kate breathed a sigh of relief.

"I brought the laudanum." While Sofia paused to catch her breath, Scrappy shoved his hands on his hips and chewed on his bottom lip, staring down at the boy.

"He tried to escape," Kate told Sofia. "His ankle is either broken or very badly sprained. We have to get him cleaned up, but I'm afraid he's as wild as a barn kitten. I can't think of any way to get near him other than to drug him. Then we can move him to the house."

"You sure you want to take him *inside*?" Scrappy shook his head as if Kate had lost her mind.

"He's only a child, Mr. Parks."

"You don't understand the Comanche," the wrangler said.

"*Look* at him," Kate pleaded. "He's very young. And he's *not* Comanche. Even so, even if he was, I'm afraid I would have to insist on giving him the best of care."

Sofia, who had been concentrating on Kate, whirled around to look at the child. Her breath caught on a gasp. The sun had risen higher in the last few minutes. Full daylight now shone on the boy's face.

Despite the dirt, perhaps because of it, his eyes appeared more brilliant blue, wide and definitely full of loathing as he stared back at them. His hair was dark, faded by the sun to red-brown in places, not unlike Kate's own. His lips were full and pouting, his chin tipped defiantly toward them.

"*Ay, Dios mio.*" Sofia nearly dropped the amber bottle and spoon as she pressed one hand to her heart and reeled back a step. "This can't be. . . ."

"What is it? What's wrong?" Kate put her hand beneath the woman's elbow to steady her and watched, startled and uncomprehending, as the housekeeper's eyes flooded with tears.

"There has been so much . . . I have not been thinking clearly or I would have suspected, but . . . it *can't* be!" She began to whisper what sounded like a prayer in Spanish and then, in a show of anger, she turned on Scrappy. "You never told me that he was white!"

"What's wrong?" Kate looked down at the boy who appeared more frightened by Sofia's dramatic reaction than by either her or Scrappy. The housekeeper was staring at the child, openly crying now.

"Daniel?" Emotion choked Sofia's voice. "Is it you?"

"Daniel?" Scrappy was visibly shaken. His eyes went huge and then scrunched into a frown as he shook his head in disbelief.

"Who's Daniel?" Kate asked.

"Reed Junior's son." Sofia was trembling uncontrollably now. The silver teaspoon clicked against the glass medicine bottle in her hand.

"What are you talking about? How can this be Reed's son? Reed's son is *dead.*"

Sofia shook her head and wiped her eyes as she fought to collect herself.

"His son was either killed or *stolen* by Comanches the night his mother died. We never knew for certain. Reed Junior . . . ," Sofia could not take her eyes off the child. "I believe he preferred to think of him as . . . dead."

"He *preferred to think of him as dead*?"

Sofia nodded slightly. "The Rangers must have found him."

Kate shook her head. Was the woman trying to tell her that Reed had found his long-lost son and purposely left the injured boy tied to a hitching post?

How could Reed, wounded himself, have handled the

boy on horseback? Had the child been hurt before Reed found him, or could *he* have injured the boy?

Scrappy was mumbling something dark and unthinkable.

"*What* did you say?" Kate hoped she had not heard him right.

"I said this is worse than him dyin'." He sounded grave and thoroughly convinced the boy would be better off dead than turned Comanche.

Sofia looked at Scrappy in disdain. "Didn't you even suspect? Who else could this be?"

"Lil' Daniel's just a baby. This ain't him." Scrappy was horrified by the possibility that this wild boy could be Reed's son.

"He is not a baby now." Sofia indicated the boy on the ground with a wave of her hand. "He was three back then. He would be eight, nearly nine now."

Kate listened to their exchange. More than anything else, she wondered what kind of world she had walked into. More determined than ever to help the boy, she took the sedative and spoon from Sofia, who was still dealing with her own shock and doubt and was in no condition to help. Then Kate motioned Scrappy forward and kept her voice low and even as she issued instructions to Scrappy.

"You'll have to hold him down while I give him the laudanum. Try not to hurt him." Then she looked into the boy's eyes and said, "I wish there was some other way."

Fast Pony wished that his shame and humiliation would kill him. Maybe if he had gotten to one of the horses, his escape would have succeeded, but after he climbed out of the stall and hit the ground, he could not raise himself high enough to open a stall and steal one.

He wanted to scream at the pain in his ankle. It was swollen twice its size and had turned a dark, ugly color.

Instead, he fought to ignore the pain so that he could concentrate on the three white people staring at him.

He studied them carefully—the younger woman with fire in her hair—the one who talked to him the most and called herself Kaaaate; Hairy Face, the old man with hate and distrust in his eyes; and the newcomer, the tall, berry-eyed woman who cried when she looked at him.

What did the older woman see? Did she see more than he knew? Had she visions of his Comanche mother's death? Or maybe all the hurt he held inside caused her pain.

Was his fear and sadness a living thing that his eyes betrayed?

Afraid to see his own fear reflected in her dark eyes, he wanted to look away, but he had to watch all of them now, these whites who would soon pay for holding him here like a dog. The big, hollow house for horses was made of wood and full of dry grass. If they put him back in there, he would find a way to burn it down.

Burn it to ashes when they were all inside.

Soon he would do his part to drive the whites from Comanche lands and make his father proud. He would become a true warrior among The People, the Nermernuh.

The boy bit his lip to keep from crying out as the man with the rough white hairs growing out of his cheeks crouched low and began shuffling toward him. Hairy Face's mouth was set straight as an arrow shaft. Cold determination iced his eyes.

The younger woman looked about to cry. She started whispering to him.

Fast Pony knew he was about to die.

9

With Scrappy's help, Kate drugged the boy; then the wrangler carried him into the house where they placed him in the smallest of the spare rooms upstairs. Her heart broke for the child, so small and vulnerable, fighting to the last not to give in to them, struggling to be brave.

Once they had him inside, they stripped off his filthy, tattered clothing and had Scrappy burn them, then in the huge tub in the bathing room, they washed him, then dressed him in one of Reed Senior's cut-off nightshirts. After putting him in bed, they splinted his bruised and badly sprained ankle between two pieces of a cut-down broomstick and then Scrappy tied him into the narrow bed.

Beneath the white linen sheets, with his long hair combed back off his sweet face and his cheeks shining, he looked like an angel. But they all knew that he wasn't the angel he seemed, which is why Kate finally agreed to let Scrappy tie him to the bedposts.

She was now as convinced as Sofia that the boy was Daniel. Why else would Reed have brought him to Lone Star?

When they were through, she looked in on Reed, found him sleeping peacefully, his fever nearly gone, and then realizing that she was starved, Kate went downstairs.

.   .   .

As the sun crested at noon, Kate and Sofia sat at a small table next to tall windows at the end of the kitchen, lingering over cups of strong black coffee, which was nothing like the pale tea and honey Kate was used to at the orphanage. The two women had shared a late breakfast that included samples from the covered dishes the neighbors had brought with them to the funeral.

As she looked around the huge room, Kate recalled the pride Reed had expressed in his words to her about this room.

> I want to see my children and grandchildren living in this house, this grand tribute to all that is Lone Star. The kitchen is a wife's dream, with long windows to let in plenty of light, and a view of the horse corral. There's a new wood stove, too. Of course, you will have a housekeeper who cooks as well.

The kitchen was indeed warm and cozy, much larger than the entire shack Kate had shared with her mother. Sofia moved effortlessly, busying herself with things Kate knew little about. The nuns turned out well-educated young ladies, hoping for them to make fine marriages or become teachers or nannies. Experience in a kitchen was not as highly stressed as reading, writing, and the arts.

Within a few moments she felt at ease in the housekeeper's domain. Sofia allowed her time to get her bearings as new mistress, and Kate was grateful to have the other woman's help and expertise. If not for Sofia, she would never have known the boy upstairs was Reed's long-lost son.

She set her coffee cup down and covered her mouth when a yawn crept up on her. Then she folded her hands in her lap and watched Sofia pump water into one of two wash pans on the dry sink.

"Do you think either of them is awake yet?" As anxious as she was filled with nervous excitement to return to Reed's side, Kate stretched and collected cups, saucers, and spoons and carried them to the workbench.

Sofia answered without turning around. "I will finish up here. You look in on them."

With a dish towel wadded in her hands, Sofia reached for the handle of a kettle boiling on the stove and swung it over to two deep dishpans. She added steaming water to each, replaced the kettle, and then slipped the scraped dishes into the warm water.

Kate rubbed her brow, studied the woman's erect shoulders and the delicate, pale nape of her neck exposed by her upswept, tightly coiled hair. There was an enviable, exotic beauty that lingered in Sofia despite her age. She carried herself more like a queen than like a housekeeper. Her tailored black silk gown was worth far more than everything Kate owned combined. The woman had been welcoming and considerate to a fault, not outwardly concerned about her standing despite the arrival of a new mistress.

"Sofia, I hope you will forgive me for being frank, but there is no one else I can turn to."

Sofia's hands grew still in the sudsy water.

"What is it, señora?"

"First, please, assure me that Reed could not have hurt that boy."

Without a second's pause, Sofia turned and looked over her shoulder at Kate. In Sofia's eyes, Kate saw the truth.

"*Never*, señora. He would never do a child harm."

A weight lifted. Unable to sit any longer, Kate stood up and wrapped half a loaf of bread in a clean dish towel; then she set it aside. She took a deep breath and plunged in before she could talk herself out of asking any more.

"I entered into this marriage on blind faith, Sofia. Reed said in one of his letters that you have known him since he was a young man, so I hope perhaps you can explain to me why he would keep the fact that he was a Ranger from me. Not only have I learned that his child has been alive all these years, but in his letters, he always referred to his father in past tense, as if he was dead and not alive. *Why?*"

Sofia seemed to ponder the questions as she continued to wash the plates and serving dishes and set them on the waiter to drain. She was careful with each knife, keeping the hollow handles dry, slowly toweling each one, and laying them out in a row. Kate began to think that Sofia was not going to answer at all.

When Sofia finally rinsed her hands and turned around, her expression was grave. "Sit down, señora, and we will talk."

Kate sat in the chair she had used before. Sofia sat opposite. The already overly warm spring breeze blew in through the open windows, carrying the scent of grass and wildflowers. To Kate, so used to chilly winds off the coast, it seemed like heaven.

"Reed Junior's first wife's name was Becky Greene. His father never approved of her because he believed she was only marrying Reed for the wealth he would inherit when Lone Star became his. Reed Senior feared she was not in love with his son, which proved to be true.

"Reed Junior married against his father's wishes, without his consent. It was soon apparent that Becky did not really love him as much as she loved being a Benton. She fought the life that her husband had chosen—life on the edge of the ranch where he worked the cattle with the rest of the men. They lived here in this house when they were first married, but then Reed Junior insisted they move out to an old dog-run cabin, one built when his father first bought the land. But here, in this house, is where Becky thought she belonged.

"Young Reed naturally wanted her with him and insisted upon it. When Becky discovered she was having a child, she argued with him constantly. If he would not move back here, she wanted him to let her return alone. Finally, he agreed. Becky stayed here the last few weeks before Daniel's birth.

"A few months afterward, Reed Junior moved his family back out to the frontier. I think he realized that what his father had always believed was true. Becky did not really love him. Always, she flirted with other men."

Kate sat there feeling disconnected, as if listening to a tale about someone else, not the sincere, tenderhearted gentleman she had come to know through his letters. Reed had mentioned little about his first wife and son, save that he had married young, and had lost them both.

> I have had enough time to dwell on the past. My heart and my home are so empty now. I would hope that you would consider filling them with love and happiness.

Kate propped her elbow on the table and rested her chin in her hand. "Then Becky was killed and Daniel captured. How old was Daniel? How did it happen?"

Sofia shifted on her chair, obviously quite ill at ease. Kate sensed the woman might feel disloyal talking about Reed and things that he should explain himself, but even if Kate had to pull every word out of her, she was determined to try. She had to know the truth.

Sofia continued. "They had been living on the edge of the ranch for three years. On the night she died, Becky and the boy were alone. Reed had gone to the aid of some neighbors when their house was raided. When he got home, he found Becky outside, scalped, lying near the burned-out shell of the cabin. Daniel's body was never found. All the horses were gone."

Kate tried to imagine Becky, alone in the darkness. The image of a young woman ravaged, lying dead beside the remains of her home was horrifying. The accounts of Indian attacks Kate had read in the *Applesby Sentinel* did not actually describe gruesome practices of torture and bondage, but intelligent people could read between the lines.

"What she must have suffered at the last," Kate whispered.

"The Indians did not kill her, señora. It is believed Becky killed herself. She always swore that is what she would do before she let herself be taken. There is not a woman in Texas unaware of what happens to female captives. They are beaten, forced to submit. Some have returned to their families with their skin tattooed, their noses burnt off, their minds gone.

"Others, those with half-Indian children, refuse to stay with their white families even when they are finally rescued. Some cannot face the shame they suffer when they return. Others, like the boy upstairs, turn Comanche and cannot remember another way of life. Becky knew what would happen to her. She had one of Reed's guns. She was scalped, but died of a bullet through her temple. The Comanche would not have killed her outright."

Kate's nails cut into her palms. She opened her fists, pressed her damp hands against her skirt. "But . . . she left her little boy to the mercy of Comanche raiders," Kate whispered. Her thoughts spiraled back to her own childhood, to the night that she lay too sick to move, too sick to crawl after her mama when she left her on the steps of Saint Perpetua's.

She would never forget her mother's parting words.

"This is for the best, Katie. Someday when you realize that,

I hope to God you'll forgive me. I should have done this when you were born, so's you wouldn't remember. I've been selfish, Katie-girl, trying to keep you with me . . ."

Kate shook herself, remembering all too well the silent tears she had shed. Grief and fear had swallowed her just as sure as the sickness in her lungs. Her mother had turned her back on her and walked out of her life forever.

Hopefully Daniel was too young to remember anything of the terrifying night that his mother had taken her own life. Becky had abandoned him to the mercy of the Comanche just as surely as Meg Whittington had left Kate on the steps of the orphanage.

"Are you all right, señora? I'm sorry if I upset you, but you asked. This is what I know."

Kate looked up at Sofia, startled out of her dark memory. "Yes . . . I'm fine."

She vowed then and there that as long as she had anything to say about it, Daniel would never, ever feel abandoned again. Then she collected herself. "What happened afterward? After Reed found out?"

Sofia's eyes spoke of deep sorrow. "There was bad blood between them already. Reed blamed his father for his mother's early death. She hated Texas and longed to go back to Georgia. Junior thought that if his father had paid more attention to her and less to the ranch, that Virginia would have lived longer.

"The señor wanted so much for him, but Junior refused his help. Soon they fought over everything. If Reed Senior said it was day, Reed Junior insisted it was night. Time and again the señor urged him to bring Becky and Daniel back to Benton House. He wanted Junior to go into state politics, but Reed Junior loved ranching. He found joy in working alongside the men. He did not want to be a politician, nor was he ready to be a gentleman rancher.

"After Becky's burial, they had a terrible, terrible argument. I don't know what it was about, but Reed Junior left that very day and joined the Rangers. He never came back until he walked in the door yesterday."

Like pieces of a puzzle that *almost* fit, the story Sofia had just related left Kate with more questions than answers.

"If Reed and his father were estranged, how did you both know about our marriage? How did you know to expect me? Why would Reed have me meet him here in the first place? I could have joined him where the Rangers are, couldn't I?"

For the space of a heartbeat, consternation danced across Sofia's features, so briefly that Kate began to doubt that she saw it. Then the housekeeper slowly pushed away from the table, stood, and carefully replaced the chair. Reaching down, she brushed at an uneven fold in the tablecloth; then she cleared her throat.

"Reed was estranged from his father, but not from me, señora. I was the one who suggested that you come here first. Besides, a Ranger camp is no place for a new bride."

"And Reed agreed, even though he and his father were not speaking?"

Sofia looked away. "Yes."

"So, it was *you* who told Reed's father about me? About our proxy marriage?"

For a long, tense moment, Sofia said nothing. When she looked at Kate again, her eyes held only dark memories.

"The señor was as excited as a child, so looking forward to your arrival. He grew weaker by the day, but struggled to live long enough to meet you. He prayed that you could mend the trouble between them and bring his son home to Lone Star."

10

The sun was well up when Reed rolled over. He groaned as nagging pain shot through his shoulder, then opened his eyes, surprised to find himself in one of the upstairs rooms in Benton House at Lone Star.

Lone Star. His father's tribute to himself. A ranch that was bigger than some eastern states, with its own little town smack in the middle of it, and this house—a grand mansion by Texas standards. Money had bought the old man everything he ever wanted.

Everything but his only son's love. His father's money and power, his need to prove himself right, his stubborn belief that he knew what was best for everyone—those were the things that had driven Reed away.

He loved the land and in one respect, could appreciate all his father had done here, but living on the ranch came with too high a price. His father's devotion and one-sidedness to the place had drained his mother, left her neglected and alone, pining for her old life in Georgia. It was a way of life that was gone after the war, but nothing could dissuade her. On her final breath she had begged to be buried on Georgia soil.

Reed had seen this land suck away his mother's life. He

loved Texas, but he wasn't about to bend to his father's will and forfeit his own soul.

Bracing himself, he sat up and slowly swung his legs over the side of the bed. Flashing stars swam in front of his eyes until the pounding ache finally faded. He rubbed his eyes, then trailed his hand down his cheek and realized he was sporting more than a night's growth of stubble.

Not until he looked down at his bandaged right shoulder did it all come back to him, and he suddenly remembered why he was at Lone Star.

Everything else had been a dream.

Reaching for the half-empty glass of water on the bedside table, he watched his hand shake and the water slosh as he carried the glass to his lips and drained it.

Now he recalled that he'd had one hell of a nightmare. It had started with him walking in and seeing his father laid out in a coffin in the parlor and ended with Becky making sweet love to him.

A dream so vivid that even now he couldn't rid himself of the lingering memory of it.

Dream? Hell, must have been a nightmare if he had dreamed of making love to Becky. The longer he sat there thinking about it, the more he grew good and pissed at himself for having wanted her in that way again—even if it was only in a dream.

Thinking of Becky naturally called Daniel to mind, and in a blink of an eye, memory hit him as hard as a swift kick in the gut from an ornery mule. He remembered everything that had come to pass and the reason he had come back: The raid on the Comanche summer camp. The ambush. Hand-to-hand combat. Women and children screaming, running.

He had caught a bullet that hurt like hell, but luckily it

had passed clean through his shoulder. Another had grazed his scalp.

The worse pain had been inflicted when his friend, Capt. Jonah Taylor, had tracked him down at the medic's tent and told him that they had discovered a white boy among the renegades.

Even now, his heart tightened as he sat on the edge of the bed rubbing his shoulder, staring at his bare knees and long bare feet. He hurt deep inside again, the way he had when Jonah stood there looking down at him with undisguised pity.

Memory of everything that happened after that morning was a blur. The trip back had been a long, arduous ride while he tried to keep the squirming, kicking child on the horse. With every mile, fever took a stronger hold on him. The last thing he half recalled was tying the boy to the hitching post in front of the house.

Had that been part of his feverish nightmare, too? Where was the boy now?

Reed rubbed his temple. His forehead was warm, and his shoulder beneath the bandage ached. He was thirsty and hungry as a bear after hibernation. He figured he was going to live when the scent of bacon hit him and his stomach growled.

Hoping to spot his pants and shirt, he looked around the room. Sofia's touches were everywhere. Starched lace curtains hung at all the windows. The floors were polished to such a high gleaming shine that they appeared slick. There wasn't a speck of dust on the bedside table or the tall chest of drawers. His clothes were nowhere in sight, but his holster and guns were hanging on the back of a side chair by a window across the room.

He stood up, fighting dizziness as he wound the bedsheet

around his hips. He turned and tugged it free of the mattress. His gaze was immediately drawn to a smeared, coin-size bloodstain in the middle of the bed. He frowned and looked down at his bandaged shoulder, but the cloth was clean. There didn't appear to be any bleeding. He had not reopened his wound.

Then one of the floorboards creaked and was followed by the sound of a woman's voice. "You're awake," she said.

He turned in time to watch her gaze drop to the sheet he had wound around his hips, then shoot back up to his face.

At first glance, he was so shocked by her resemblance to Becky that all he could do was stare. She appeared just as stunned as he, but then she smiled, and the expression on her face scared the hell out of him. There was something in her eyes that he didn't want to name, something that held such shining promise, such admiration, almost as if he had hung the moon. Something he barely recognized anymore.

Something akin to love.

As she stood there apparently not knowing where to look, he noticed that his first impression had been wrong. In reality, she didn't look so much like his late wife. This woman was taller, long of limb. Her lips were fuller than Becky's. Her brown eyes were huge. Her hair, a deep, rich color, was vibrant with auburn highlights.

She was fresh-faced and glowing, the high color across her cheeks giving away her embarrassment. Was that because she knew he was naked beneath the sheet or because of his intent stare?

Before he could get a word out, she took a deep breath and focused on the tray as she bustled into the room.

In a prim, businesslike manner, one not in the least cold or unattractive, she set the tray down and began to fuss with a flowery little china pot, the silver cutlery, a covered dish—

all the time glancing over at him from beneath lowered lashes.

Reed kept a tight hold on the sheet. The smell of fresh bacon and eggs and hot coffee made his legs weak and his mouth water. He slowly lowered himself to the edge of the bed.

"Sofia thought you might be awake and hungry," she said. Her voice was low, smoky, arousing.

Sofia must have hired kitchen help. The woman certainly wasn't dressed any better than a maid. Her faded gown had seen better days. Even he, no expert on women's fashions, could see that.

She was definitely a handsome woman, and he was a man who had been without for a long, long while. Still, there was something about the way she moved, something in the sound of her voice, too, that left him feeling oddly satisfied.

As he watched her lean over and ready his meal, a feeling he couldn't dismiss continued to nag him. Something was missing here. She kept flashing him embarrassed, familiar glances, as if waiting for him to say something, and yet he had no recollection of her at all.

When he caught the scent of roses, something haunting and undeniable about her teased the edges of his consciousness. It teased him elsewhere, too. He glanced down to make certain the sheet was tightly wrapped.

"I don't know how you take your coffee." She sounded shy and preoccupied, almost as if thinking out loud rather than speaking to him directly. She had yet to actually meet his eyes again, though she hovered over the tray less than a foot away.

He could listen to her warm voice all day, for it was as potent as a caress. He watched her pick up the empty coffee cup, put it down, pick it up again. He studied her well shaped, pale fingers as they nervously moved over the flowered china.

He tried smiling. It had been a long time since he had been even halfway interested in a woman. "Do I know you, ma'am?"

She fumbled and dropped the cup. He made an instinctive lunge for it and was forced to grab for his sheet instead. He watched the cup slowly fall to the floor and shatter.

"Pardon me, but what did you say?" She stood there amid the broken china, ignoring it completely. Her eyes had gone huge and liquid and frightened. He wondered why.

"Have we met?" he asked.

She blanched. "Why, I'm . . . I'm Kate, Reed. Katherine Whittington." She pressed her palm hard against her midriff as if he'd punched her. "I . . . we're . . ."

"We're what?" He didn't like the break in her voice or the stunned look of utter betrayal in her eyes. He would have recognized the look anywhere—because he saw it deep in his own eyes every time he looked in the mirror.

He watched as she drew a calming breath, this Kate, this woman whom he had somehow wounded without intent, saw her square her shoulders and steady herself.

"We're married." Her lower lip trembled.

She had to be insane. Maybe Sofia had taken pity on a crazy woman and hired her. He didn't like the nagging suspicion that he did know her from someplace, the feeling that somehow, she did belong here. He reached up, touched his temple. The scabbed-over wound was tender. Maybe something had happened to his mind.

"Where did you come from? How did you get in here?" He glanced toward the door, then back.

"Surely, you remember. We . . . we corresponded for months. We were married by proxy three weeks ago."

As if a damn good explanation would make it all true, or

else to trap him in her lunacy, she kept talking. "You sent me money to make the trip out here." Her sultry voice had risen half an octave by the end of the sentence.

He shook his head, saw her eyes go wider. It was obvious his denial hurt her. "I don't know about any correspondence. I don't have any idea what you are talking about."

"I can *prove* it. I have all of your letters."

"I never *wrote* you any damn letters."

She spun away. The toe of her shoe connected with a piece of china. It skittered across the floor and smacked against the oak baseboard. Quickly kneeling, she began to gather up the shattered bits and cup them in her palm. Her hand shook as she set the shards on the tray.

She cleared her throat, her eyes suspiciously bright, but she spoke with more determination.

"I've kept all your letters. Every last one of them."

She was beginning to frighten him. Not *her* exactly, for even in his weakened condition she was no match for him, but he was completely unaware of what might have gone on here while he was unconscious.

"I don't know what you're up to. What day is it? What year?"

"May fifteenth, eighteen seventy. We were married by proxy."

She spoke slowly, carefully pronouncing each word as if *he* were the lunatic. The day and the date fit. He left the Rangers on the eleventh. It had probably taken him at least two days, if not more, to get here.

Married by proxy.

Suddenly he realized that this whole charade had the ring of one of his father's schemes. His last five years away had given the old man plenty of time to concoct something like this, time to dredge up a plan to keep him here.

The woman looked so stricken that Reed feared she was

about to faint. He had an oddly compelling urge to comfort her, to reach out and take her hand. She was either a pawn of his father's or she was a very good actress.

"Look, ma'am—"

"*Kate.* It's . . . Kate."

"Look, Kate. I'm sorry, but whatever it is you think I agreed to, whatever you were led to believe, well, it's all been a lie. I have no idea what you're talking about."

"But . . . it can't be a lie." When a solitary tear slipped and fell over the edge of her lower lashes to trickle down her cheek, she dashed it away with the back of her hand.

Something danced on the edges of his mind. The scent of roses, a vison of her long, dark hair, not in the pert little bun perched like a sparrow on her head right now, but rich skeins woven into a thick braid. He envisioned it loose, rippling to her hips. Reed shook his head.

"My father is behind this somehow. Just ask him," he said.

She blinked, and another tear fell. Something about her tensed, and she batted the tear away. Then she looked him square in the eye and said, "Your father is dead."

11

Her heart raw and bleeding, Kate had desperately wanted to inflict pain when she bluntly announced to Reed that his father was dead, but his expression never changed. Reed's eyes registered nothing—not shock, certainly not sorrow.

"He was buried yesterday afternoon," she added, "not long after you collapsed with fever."

Disconnected, she was utterly unable to believe that this was the same man who had held her so lovingly, had treated her with the utmost tenderness. The man who had told her that he loved her last night was now insisting that he had no idea who she was. She watched him tiredly rub his eyes as if to clear away the very sight of her.

If what he claimed was true, if he was ignorant of all the letters and the proxy marriage, if the entire long-distance courtship had been his father's doing, then all the questions that had plagued her could finally be explained.

He had not told her that he was a Texas Ranger, or about Daniel, or his father, or the fact that he did not even live at Benton House anymore because *he had not written the letters.*

But if she believed him, if she believed this was all part of a hoax concocted by Reed Senior, then last night she had consummated a union unsanctioned by law. She was not his wife.

Nor was she a virgin any longer.

Kate wanted to find a dark corner to crawl into, to curl up and hide just as she had done when her mother abandoned her.

She had expected too much. She had reached too high and now, even the dream had vanished. She had been reduced to something little better than her mother.

A few moments ago she had walked through the door to this room hoping to hear him say *I love you* again. She had been wondering how soon they would make love. Instead, he denied knowing her, denied their marriage. She had no reason to disbelieve his protest until suddenly, a faint glimmer of hope began to shine.

Perhaps the fever had somehow destroyed parts of his memory.

Yes, surely that was it. He was still suffering from the shock of his wounds and the power of the fever. Like the dark bruises beneath his eyes, the remnants of fever still clouded his mind. Certainly, the laudanum fogged his thoughts, too. After a good meal and some sound sleep, he would remember her and all his promises. He *would* remember.

Adrift, still frightened to her very soul, she did the only thing she could do. She forced a smile and uncovered the plate of bacon, eggs, fresh biscuits, and gravy that Sofia had prepared.

"Perhaps," she continued to speak softly, purposely keeping her voice smooth and even, "perhaps after you eat something and get some rest, you'll remember. After all, you've been very, very ill." She spoke slowly and clearly, as if he were one of her students, hoping to calm herself as well.

She glanced at the slivers of broken china remaining on the floor. "I really need to get a broom."

"I really need my clothes. And I need to get to the bottom of this. Where in the *hell* is Sofia?"

Kate snapped erect. "There is no need to shout." What if he became uncontrollable?

Thankfully, at that very moment, the door swung open and Sofia stepped into the room, cool and composed, her jet hair pulled back severely and fashioned in an intricate twist. Her expensive black gown was crisp, freshly pressed; a cameo brooch hugged her collar at her throat. But her composure was marred by her reddened eyes.

"Can you tell me what in the *hell* is going on here?" Reed turned on the housekeeper without so much as a hello.

Although Kate was unused to such explosive displays of temper, Sofia calmly folded her hands at her waist, seemingly unruffled by his outburst.

"If you will get back in bed and cover yourself properly, I will try to explain." She looked at Kate and added, "To both of you."

When Reed balked, the woman calmly insisted again that he get back into bed and cover himself.

Amazed when he actually did as the housekeeper asked, Kate turned her back when he began to unwind the sheet. As soon as he was comfortably seated in bed, Sofia crossed the room and helped him smooth out the bedclothes and then pulled the light woven coverlet to his waist.

Kate covered the plate of food. She wasn't quite sure how she managed it with her hands shaking so hard, but she even refilled his water glass for want of something to do.

Sofia offered her a seat in the rocking chair. When Kate declined, preferring to stand, Sofia sat down heavily, as if burdened by what she had to say.

Reed crossed his arms over his bare chest and pinned the housekeeper with an icy stare. "This woman claims we're married. And that the old man's dead."

"He is." Sofia nodded. Her eyes, unable to hold her sorrow, shimmered with unshed tears. "Your father was quite ill for the past two years. His heart was failing. He was desperate to have you come home and run Lone Star. Surely you knew that if you received his letters."

"I threw them out unopened."

"He came up with a plan to find you a woman, someone who would be a fitting wife. He hoped to use her . . . to entice you back." Her voice stumbled on the words, but she went on.

"With the help of his lawyer, he placed an advertisement in a few small-town newspapers in the Northeast, the area where his maternal grandmother was born. He received many, many letters in response."

Kate gasped. Sofia was discussing her as if she were not even there. Reed turned to stare, looked her up and down as if he was buying stock. It had been a deception, all of it. She had been part of a grand, horrific scheme, and worse yet, naive enough to believe she was the only woman to have answered the advertisement.

Sofia continued. "He was so excited. He began to look forward to getting up in the morning again. He could not wait for the mail to be brought in. Your father had not been so excited about life for a long, long time."

As if exhausted, she rested her head against the back of the rocker. "He asked me to help compose the letters because I would know better than he what was in a woman's heart, because I could say all the things a woman wants to hear. We worked on them together. I told him what to write."

All those letters Kate had waited for, the beautiful words and phrases she had memorized. All the hours of planning and dreaming, all the time and effort she took to compose her own letters to him, choosing each and every word as carefully as a mother chooses a child's name.

This Reed Benton, the man she thought she married, had never even read them. All of it had been a terrible lie. And she had been a desperate fool.

Sofia stared down at her clenched hands and then finally faced Reed. "I should not have done it. I knew it then, just as I do now, but I could not resist. Finding you a wife gave the señor a reason for living. He was so sad, ever since Daniel was taken and you refused to come home and run the ranch as you should have—"

"Don't try to put this on me, Sofia. You don't know the half of it. Do you really think he was about to step aside and turn this place over to me as long as there was a breath in his body?" Reed's eyes narrowed. "How did the old man think he was going to get me to go along with a marriage I knew nothing about?"

A knife might just as well have pierced Kate's heart at his words. What little was left of her pitiful hopes and tattered dreams crumbled like dried rose petals. She had reached too high and now the fall was going to break her.

"He asked them all to send pictures." Sofia began to slowly rock back and forth. "He spent hours going through them, laying them out on the desk like playing cards, studying each and every one carefully. When Katherine's photograph arrived, he knew that she was the right one the moment he saw her. She reminded him of . . . of your first wife."

Reed's expression darkened at the mention of his wife. His brow tightened; his mouth firmed. "Go on." He demanded that Sofia continue.

Kate had heard enough. She wished it were over.

"He chose Katherine Whittington not only for her looks, but because she was the most intelligent. She was a teacher. And she had no family ties."

When Sofia's image suddenly blurred and wavered, Kate turned her back and stared out the open window, seeing nothing. Humiliated, she listened to the sound of her own heartbeat.

No family ties. No one to protest should Reed Senior's little plan fall apart.

All those beautiful letters filled with lovely words of promise and hope, the letters that she had built her dream upon had not been a foundation for the future, as she thought, but a well-designed trap. They were not even the words of a man. They had been written by a woman, solely to appeal to another woman's heart.

She had lived locked away, safe and secure at the orphanage for far too long. She had become too trusting, too naive. Over the years she had wanted something so much that she had cast common sense aside and let herself be caught in the snare of a sick old man bent upon controlling his son's life.

Reed Junior knew nothing of her past, her hopes, her dreams—and she knew nothing of him except for what Sofia had written. Nothing at all. Who was he? Who was this man she had given herself to last night?

Anger and shame far worse than any she had ever suffered in her life clung to her now. She clenched her fists and spun away from the window to face them both.

"How could you?" she cried to Sofia. "How did you think you could *ever* deceive us both? Old Mr. Benton was ill, possibly confused. But you, Sofia? How could you do this to anyone? How could you play with someone else's life? Do you know what you have done?"

"How could I *not* do it, señora?" Sofia suddenly stopped rocking. Her hands lay in her lap, fingers entwined. "If you ever love a man the way I loved the señor, you will do *anything* for him. You will do anything in your power to see him live one more day, even one more hour. To see him draw one more breath. If you have to, you will bargain with the devil to keep him with you for as long as you can."

With a tortured look, Sofia sank back, let go a deep sigh. "The señor could not wait to meet you. I only wish he had lived a few more hours. That would have been long enough." The woman buried her face in her hands and coiled in on herself. Her shoulders heaved with silent tears.

Kate was no plaster saint. She was not moved enough to be merciful. "But, Sofia, after I arrived and he was already gone, you kept *on* deceiving me," she said.

"The moment I saw you, Katherine, I knew you would be good for Reed. I hoped there was still a chance, that somehow the scheme might work. When Reed walked in, when he actually came home, and then when he passed out, I prayed that he might be attracted to you. I hoped you two would get to know one another while you nursed him back to health. I did not think beyond that."

Reed had been watching Kate so closely that her shame made her turn away again. His stare was so palpable she knew without looking precisely when he turned his attention back to Sofia.

"I'd still like to know how you and the old man thought I would ever go along with this." He sounded tired, as drained as Kate felt.

She turned to hear what Sofia had to say.

The housekeeper's cheeks glistened with tears. "Once Kate arrived, I was going to send word to you that he was gravely ill, that you were needed here. By that time,

Katherine would have already arrived, and you two would have met." She shrugged. "We had not planned beyond that. The señor thought that Katherine, since she believed herself already married to you, would have no choice but to go along with his plan and would perhaps be willing to seduce you. I know how ridiculous it all sounds now, but you know your father. To him, nothing was impossible."

"I know how well he enjoyed playing God," Reed said.

"When I finally sent for you, it was to see him buried." Sofia wiped her cheeks with the back of her hand, then she smoothed her impeccable hair.

"I never received word of his death."

"Then why did you come home?" Sofia pushed up out of the chair.

"To bring the boy back."

The housekeeper drew a handkerchief from beneath the cuff of her sleeve and wiped her nose. "Ah, yes. Daniel."

Reed looked down at his hands. "Yes."

His cool, shuttered expression struck a chord in Kate, one that made her cringe. There was no love for the boy in his eyes, no tenderness at all in his expression, merely confusion.

Kate stepped forward. "Did you hurt him?"

"What are you talking about?"

"That child. Did you hurt him? He can't walk. His ankle is swollen. He's covered with cuts and bruises. You saw fit to tie him up like a dog outside the house, and you haven't even bothered to ask about him yet. *Did you hurt him?*"

"Who are *you* to ask me if I hurt him?" He turned away again, refusing to meet her eyes. "I didn't touch him. Besides, he's no concern of yours, anyway."

"As a caring adult, *any* child's welfare is my concern, Mr. Benton."

"I don't need a sermon from any sanctimonious spinster

so desperate for a man that she agreed to marry one sight unseen." He rubbed his chin, assessed her as if weighing her worth. "I'll pay for a ticket to wherever it was you came from so you can go back."

"I can't go back."

His easy dismissal fired her anger while the raw reality of her situation staggered her. There was no way she could undo what had been done last night. No way she could recover what she had lost in this room.

She was back where she had started, except that no decent man would want her now. "I can't go back," she repeated, summoning strength from an unknown reserve. She looked Reed straight in the eye. "The marriage has been recorded. Legally, I am your wife."

Reed sounded just as furious. "I haven't seen my father in five years. I sure as hell never signed any legal documents, marriage or otherwise." Reed looked to Sofia for yet another answer. "Who signed that proxy?"

The older woman closed her eyes and sighed. "Your father forged your signature. *That* I would not do."

Reed shook his head in disbelief. "This just keeps getting better and better." He pinned Kate again with his stare. "What will it take to get you out of my life? How much, Miss Whittington?"

Insulted beyond belief, Kate thought of the child down the hall. Daniel was the only thing that kept her from walking out the door and waiting for the stage to pass by. She wasn't about to abandon that child to this man yet.

She drew herself up, took a deep breath, and asked him, "How much is a woman's innocence worth these days?"

Finally, he reacted with something beyond anger. He shifted uncomfortably and went very still. He lowered his voice and avoided glancing at Sofia. "What are you talking about?" he asked softly.

Kate could see by the heat that flared in his eyes that he knew very well what she was talking about.

"You weren't trying to be rid of me last night when you begged me to make love with you."

"You're lying."

"Unfortunately, I am not."

Sofia drew their attention when she said, "I was troubled during the night and went downstairs for some water. Your door was not closed, Reed. I saw you asleep with Kate in your arms."

Reed's heart nearly stopped, but somehow he overcame his shock enough not to let it show. He knew Sofia well enough to know that she was not lying.

So, his hallucination about Becky had not been a dream. He *had* slept with Kate Whittington. He and the spinster had consummated the sham marriage. If that wasn't his bloodstain in the center of the bed, then it had to be hers. His father had bought him a virgin.

Reed shot his splayed fingers through his hair and cursed under his breath. He must have been only half conscious last night, and somehow the past had become enmeshed with the present if he had mistaken the woman for Becky, his dear, darling late wife. The woman who had not only betrayed him, but who had given up without a fight and abandoned Daniel to the Comanche.

12

The place where they kept him now was not the wooden lodge for horses. Fast Pony rubbed his eyes and pulled himself up until he was sitting in the middle of the big, too soft bed. Silly, thin coverings filled with tiny holes that let sunlight pour through hung at the glass-filled openings around the walls.

He faced the sun and prayed for his mother, Painted White Feather, prayed that she was still alive and that his father, Many Horses, was, too.

Last night in the dark, before he tried to escape, he had cried for them, for all his friends and family and everything they had lost when the camp was burned—all the meat his mother had stripped and dried, precious, woolly robes that would keep them from freezing in winter, beaded clothes and shoes, painted shields and feathered lances. Years of his mother's hard work had gone up in flames, destroyed in less than a morning.

Twenty scraped and cured hides had made up their tepee, the only home he had ever known. Now even that fine shelter was gone. So was the story of Many Horses' life that Painted White Feather had drawn around the outside. Fast Pony had fallen asleep trying to remember every bit of that story, every colorful event, so that he would never, ever forget.

As the sun gained strength, he vowed he would cry no more. Babies cried. Not strong boys like him.

He would find another way to escape. His ankle was still swollen, but the pain was not as bad this morning. It was time to begin to fool the white woman with hands as soft as new spring grass.

Today he would stop fighting them, even Hairy Face. He would eat and grow strong. And he would heal.

As soon as he could walk, he would steal a horse, maybe two, and leave this land of white devils behind. He would get away this time and go back to the Comancheria, find his clan's new camp, and return like a great warrior, like his father, Many Horses.

For many moons to come the Nermernuh would talk about his triumphant return around their campfires.

It felt good to have a plan.

He smiled to himself—a secret smile.

For the first time since the Ranger attack, he began to feel better, but then the silence was broken by the sound of voices raised in argument.

He recognized one as that of the tall Ranger with hate in his eyes, and he shivered. Maybe the man would kill him before his ankle had a chance to heal. Maybe they had been waiting to take him outside and torture him.

Tall Ranger was speaking in anger. The boy heard the women, too, and recognized Soft Grass Hands' low voice.

Had he been fooled into thinking he saw kindness in her eyes? Was she arguing for his life or his death? Maybe she was angry that Tall Ranger had brought him to this cold dwelling where even he, a stranger, could feel the loneliness.

It would be foolish to wait and see if Soft Grass Hands

won the argument. Fast Pony tried to untangle himself from the thin cloth covers and to untie the bonds that held him. He used his teeth and struggled with the knots in the cloth. Finally free, he scooted over to the edge of the bed. It creaked and groaned beneath him in the way a fierce storm wind whines through the branches of tired trees.

He looked over the edge. It was a very long way to the floor.

Kate was the first to hear Daniel's cry. She turned her back on Reed Benton, determined to run out of his room with a purpose and leave Sofia and him behind. As she walked away, she felt his stare.

"Whatever you were led to believe, it's all been a lie."

". . . a sanctimonious spinster . . . so desperate for a man that she agreed to marry one sight unseen."

Sofia had written the letters. Sofia!

The documents were forged. I am not Reed's wife.

Blinded by tears, Kate nearly stumbled as she hurried down the hall. She forced herself to think only of the boy.

Daniel needs me.

She struggled to gather the tattered remnants of her self-respect. Daniel was as lost here as she. Caring for him would give her steady ground on which to stand.

She opened the door, gasped when she saw him sprawled on the floor beside the bed. The too-big shirt had bunched up, revealing his thin, sun-browned legs and thighs. He levered himself onto his hands and elbows, slowly turned his face toward her.

She could see one eye peering at her through his long dark hair. In that blue, icy stare she immediately recognized his father. More than that, she glimpsed his deep hatred of her and of this place.

Like father, like son.

She reminded herself that he was small but strong, and if he had a mind to, he would take advantage of any carelessness on her part.

She stopped halfway to the bed and took a deep breath, tried to put what had just happened in Reed's room behind her for a few minutes, hoping an answer would come if she concentrated on something else.

"Good morning, Daniel. I certainly hope you haven't made your ankle any worse. It will never heal if you keep this up." She stepped within inches of him. "Let me put you back into bed."

With a quick turn of his head, he whipped his long hair back off his face. Although he was watching her with unflinching wariness, he did not move to strike.

Kate cautiously lowered herself until she was hunkered down beside him.

"Daniel, I'm going to pick you up now. It would be best if you cooperated."

Trying not to show fear, she reached for him with measured slowness. First touching him lightly on the shoulder, she brushed his long hair back. He supported himself with his hands, pushing the upper half of his body away from the floor.

Kate gingerly slipped her hands around him and lifted as she rose until he was standing on his good leg. Then with one hand she steadied him and used the other to draw back the sheet and coverlet and plump up his pillow.

"Very good, Daniel," she told him. "That's very, very good. Now, I'll help you up again." Carefully, half expecting him to bite or scratch or fight back, she lifted him onto the bed and arranged the bedclothes around him as he stared at the wall beyond her. She released the useless strips of cloth from which he had escaped and laid them aside. When she straightened away from him, she heard his little stomach growl.

"Are you ready to eat?" She kept smiling, but he refused to turn her way, so she reached for his chin and gently forced him to look at her.

"Daniel," she touched his chest lightly and then she moved her hand to rest over her own heart. "I am *Kate.*" Then she added, "I'm going to help you get better."

She longed to see him healed in mind and body, see him adjust to his new life. Surely that is what his mother would have wanted for him.

Helping this wild, lost little soul, even for an hour more, might keep her sane. She would help him for Becky, the mother who was no longer here.

What she didn't know was how to help herself out of the predicament she was in, how to make her heart stop loving a man who did not even exist.

13

Reed waited to hear something, anything that made sense from the woman who had helped usher him from boyhood to manhood after his mother died. Sofia had taught him how to dance, how to dress, and apparently, she had also helped his father bait a trap.

"What were you thinking, Sofia?"

"Only of your father. Of you and the future of Lone Star." Her eyes lowered; she shrugged. "I became caught up in it. I thought perhaps it would work, that if you came to love Katherine Whittington, your heart would finally heal."

Talk of healing a heart he no longer possessed made Reed uncomfortable. He looked down at his hands, scarred and callused from a life spent outdoors—riding, fighting, killing.

"I used to think of you as my friend, Sofia. I would never have seen this coming."

"You say you thought of me as your friend, yet you have not been home in five years. You have not written to me once. Sometimes people would speak of you when I went into town, and I knew you had been close by, yet you never came to see me."

He looked up, surprised when he heard her voice break. "I couldn't come back," he said quietly.

"Why not?"

The reasons were deep seated and obvious to him. Pride had forced him to keep them secret from everyone else, including her. "Because *he* was here."

"This hatred of your father is irrational, Reed."

"You know *nothing* of my hatred *or* where it comes from."

"I know you blame him for your mother's death."

He heard her sigh, saw her straighten and wipe a tear from the corner of her eye. She was hurting terribly. He was not surprised to see what losing his father had done to her. She had always looked at the old man as if she thought the sun rose and set in him.

Had his father ever even noticed?

Brisk, purposeful footsteps echoed in the hall. The spinster was heading downstairs. Sofia had not moved. Her unwavering, judgmental stare made him want to walk out.

"Does anyone else know about this? That she came out here as my wife?"

"Only Scrappy. We told everyone at the funeral she was visiting from the East."

"Seems you thought of everything. What are you going to do about her?" Reed asked.

"Nothing. I am leaving this afternoon when the stage comes by," Sofia said softly. "I cannot give any more years to you Bentons."

"What do you mean, you're *leaving?*"

Her eyes were so full of sadness that her pain threatened to reach him. He hated her for that more than all the rest put together. He didn't want to feel.

"I am going back to Santa Fe. To my family's rancho. After what I have done, you should fire me anyway."

"New Mexico?"

He had almost forgotten that Sofia once had a life beyond the boundaries of Lone Star, before she had been swept into the whirlwind of his father's life. He could not blame her. If he wasn't weak as a newborn foal, he'd be heading out, too. But Sofia had been instrumental in bringing the spinster here. He was not about to get stuck with her.

He shifted, trying to relieve the ache in his throbbing shoulder. "Before you go, do me one favor and send that woman packing, would you?"

Her eyes narrowed. Her expression darkened with anger she no longer tried to hide. "Katherine is the innocent one in all of this. A pawn, just as you were." Then she eyed him with a pointed, knowing look. "After last night, she is no longer my concern. She is yours."

"She can't stay here."

"Why not? What are you afraid of?"

Afraid of feeling. Afraid that if half of what he remembered from last night had really come to pass, that he was in danger of wanting the woman again, perhaps in danger of much more.

"Have you no heart left at all?" Sofia prodded.

"None." He wanted to keep it that way.

"You need a housekeeper, Reed. Someone to care for the boy. She was a teacher at a girls' orphanage. She knows how to deal with children. She can look after Daniel until you are able. Perhaps she can even cook."

Daniel. He had tried to forget.

"I don't want her here." *A girl's orphanage?* "I don't want him mollycoddled, either."

Truth be told, he wasn't sure he wanted anything to do with Daniel. Now that his father was gone, he didn't know what he was going to do with him.

Sofia slowly stood. In that one graceful movement, the years seemed to roll away. He caught a whiff of lemon balm, heard the rustle of starched fabric. She had come into their lives so long ago, a servant with far too much quiet elegance and pride. Born a Spanish don's daughter, she had overcome adversity and loss when her young husband died bankrupt. She had taken work that was beneath her after she met his father in Santa Fe, and Reed Senior had somehow convinced her that she would never be looked down upon at Lone Star.

Reed could tell by her stance she was not going to change her mind about leaving Kate Whittington's fate up to him.

"Before you send her away, you should know that the proxy papers were filed and that she has nowhere else to go, Reed. I believe that you are still legally married unless you protest the forgery."

"Seems to me that should be your problem more than mine," he grumbled.

She smiled, but the expression failed to reach her eyes.

"Kate is a problem I will leave to you to solve. You are a man long grown, Reed. Now you have a son to raise again and you cannot do it alone. She is intelligent and capable. She came here in hopes of having a home and family. Good marriages have been built on much less. I suggest you think about making this union legal, especially since you have already slept with her. Your son needs a mother. You could do far worse." One hand rested on the back of the rocker as she let him mull over all she had said.

"When are you coming back? I need you here."

She shook her head. There was enough pity on her face to make him squirm.

"You Benton men. It is always about you, no? About what *you* want. What you need. I do not know when or if I will ever return."

The idea that this woman who had been such a part of

his early life could turn her back and walk out and leave so
easily, hit him harder than he would ever have guessed.

He thought he knew her, but that was just another lie
that left him vulnerable to hurt. He should have remembered that she was a woman and that a woman would always betray a man to get what she wanted.

Determined to show indifference, to hide the hurt of
betrayal, he kept his expression blank, his voice cool. "Will
you send Scrappy up here? I need him to ride out to the
Ranger camp and tell Jonah that I'll be back as soon as I
can."

Kate hid behind caring for Daniel as long as she could, but
once the boy was fed, he ignored her and lay on his bed,
staring out the window.

She left him alone and escaped to her own room, tiptoe-
ing down the hall so that Reed would not hear her moving
about. Numb, she sank to the edge of the bed and folded
her hands in her lap. Where her heart had been, there was
nothing but a yawning, empty space in her chest. Where
her dreams had been, there was only a bottomless chasm in
her soul.

The cold, hard realization of what had happened left her
floundering. She could not even summon enough strength
of will to offer an appeal to Saint Perpetua.

Kate started when she heard a soft tap at the door. Half
afraid it might be Reed, she hesitated until she heard Sofia
call out, "Katherine, I wish to speak to you."

Anger returned. On her feet in an instant, Kate hurried
to open the door. Sofia stood on the other side holding an
old covered basket in her arms. Her face was expressionless.
Drained of color, her olive skin appeared sallow. The
woman's misery did much to dampen Kate's temper.

"Come in." She stepped back to admit the housekeeper

to her room and for a moment the two of them stood there in silence, the tension in the air so thick it stifled conversation.

"I am leaving for Santa Fe this afternoon," Sofia said without preamble. "Before I go, I wanted to give you this."

Kate stared at the timeworn basket.

"No, thank you." She forced herself to meet Sofia's eyes. In them, unspoken sadness and regret mingled with silent apology.

"I thought that perhaps these things might help you to help Daniel."

"Help Daniel? I would like nothing more, but how do you expect me to help him when I'll no doubt be leaving very shortly myself?"

Sofia forced the basket on her. "Until Reed is on his feet, there is no one else to care for the boy. Surely you won't abandon him."

Any other argument would never have moved her to stay one more hour, but how could she abandon the boy? She would just as soon take him with her as leave him here with Reed Benton.

"I'm sure Reed will object to my staying."

"He has no choice at the moment but to let you stay."

"He *said* that?"

"Not in so many words."

"Then he still wants me out of here." There was no question. He had said as much.

"He is a man. He doesn't really know what he wants. The boy needs to be fed and tended to. So does Reed, for that matter."

"Surely he could send to town for someone."

"He may do just that, but Lone Star is a town of families. There are no single women there who would take the position, at least none of good stature. If you care about Daniel, you will find a way to stay."

She hated the thought of walking out on Daniel as much as she did facing Reed again. What happened last night still made her cringe.

Kate sighed, the basket in her arms growing heavy.

Sofia gestured toward the bed. "Set that down, and I will explain the things inside."

Kate sat and Sofia lifted the lid. On top was a small, neatly folded quilt made of calico fabric stars. Kate reached in and drew the piece out. Mostly navy and red, not much larger than an oversize towel, it was the perfect size for an infant. It was faded in places, well worn and puckered from many washings.

"That was Daniel's. He took it with him everywhere. It was found near the burned out cabin the night his mother died."

Holding the quilt close, Kate peered down at the rest of the basket's contents as Sofia began to draw them out, one by one.

"This is a wooden horse that Scrappy carved for him." She turned a fire-scorched and scarred toy over and over and then set it aside. "This silver cup is engraved with Daniel's name." The tarnished cup joined the wounded toy on the bed.

Kate realized she was hugging the quilt, and she quickly set it aside, too.

Finally Sofia withdrew a closed silver case that fit in the palm of her hand out of the bottom of the basket. She opened it. Inside was a photograph. Without a word of explanation, Sofia handed it to Kate, who found herself staring at the image of a young woman with long brown hair and dark, unreadable eyes. The similarity in size and coloring between Kate and the woman in the picture was undeniable.

"That is Rebecca Greene Benton, Daniel's mother."

"Reed's wife." Kate couldn't take her eyes off the likeness.
"Yes."

"This is why Reed Senior chose me." Sorrow welled up inside Kate again. The deception came rushing back to her.

"He chose you out of all the others—"

"Because I looked like her."

"Because you *reminded* him of her, but in truth, you are far lovelier. I only hope that when Daniel sees that picture, he will remember his mother."

Kate doubted the boy would remember. He had been so young when he was captured; besides, he had most likely seen his mother die. What child's mind would want to be awakened to such hideous memories? What adult's would, for that matter?

"After Daniel was gone, I cleared out the extra nursery that was here. I stored these few things that Scrappy recovered without telling Reed or his father. This basket has been in the attic, waiting for the day Daniel returned."

"You never gave up hope, Sofia?"

"I am foolish enough to believe in miracles. This is the first time one has ever come true." The woman raised her chin, showing her determined willfulness. "What of you, Katherine? Do you believe in them?"

Kate set the silver case down alongside the other silent, poignant reminders of Daniel's past.

Miracles? Sainthood was bestowed on those who worked proven miracles. There were more saints than anyone could name, but did she truly believe?

"I don't know what I believe anymore. I let myself be taken in by your scheme because I *wanted* something so badly that I threw caution to the wind. The only thing I am certain of is that I can't trust my own judgment anymore."

Sofia reached for Kate's hands and held on tight, even when Kate tried to pull away. "Everything you dreamed of having is still here for the taking, Katherine. If you are strong enough. If you are determined. Daniel needs you. Reed needs you, too, although he doesn't see that right now. Here is a home for you, a family, everything you wanted, everything you believed you were getting when you signed those proxy papers."

"*Forged* papers." Kate felt her insides clench. "I believed a lie."

"Make your own miracle. Make it all come true. You are a teacher. Teach Reed to love again. Teach him to love his little boy again. Bring him and Daniel together. Fight to stay. Who knows? Perhaps you will all find love."

Kate thought of the cold detachment in Reed's eyes and shook her head. "Why did he do it, Sofia? Why did he sleep with me?"

"He was feverish. He thought you were Becky."

I love you, wife. "What chance do I have with him now? He hates me. After what you and his father have done, how can he ever look at me and forget that deception?"

Sofia squeezed her fingers to get her point across. "I read your responses to those letters, remember? I know what is in your heart. I know how badly you want a home and family. How much you wanted this marriage to work—"

"Stop saying that! There *is* no marriage. I don't even know that man in there."

"Get to know him. Fight to save your dream."

Without another word, Sofia let go and walked toward the door. Then she paused. "One more thing, Katherine. If it turns out that marriage to Reed is what you want, then *do* fight for it, but not forever. Try, señora, but do not waste your life waiting for Reed Benton to fall in love with you. Do not make the same mistake I did."

Shaken, Kate found herself staring down at the little quilt, the scorched wooden horse, the tarnished silver, and the silver frame spread out on the bed. Pieces of Daniel's past. Of Reed's, too.

Everyone but Sofia had given up hope, but by tucking these things away, the woman had kept faith in the boy's return.

Now she expected Kate to make her own miracle.

14

Wobbly as a newborn colt, Reed sat in the rocker and studied the bed. How was he going to make it back?

Sofia had come in once more, changed his sheets, told him good-bye, and left him the letters the spinster had written to his father. He told her he didn't want them, but she tucked them in the bottom drawer of the dresser before she walked out.

Scrappy had already left for the Ranger camp to let Jonah know he would be laid up for a few more days. Finally, Reed had gotten up, determined to dress.

He made it as far as the dresser, where he found his underdrawers washed and neatly folded inside. Struggling to get them on, he felt so faint that it was all he could do to get to the chair before he hit the floor.

There he sat, light-headed, trembling, damning his weakness, trying—by sheer force of will—to gather enough strength to walk back to the bed, when he heard someone pause outside the door.

There was only one person left who could be hovering on the other side. He wished to God he could simply ignore her, but he was starving and cotton-headed, and as much as he hated to admit it, Kate Whittington was the only one who could help him right now.

He didn't try to keep the resentment out of his tone when he yelled, "Come in."

There was more hesitation before the door slowly opened and the woman stepped into the room. Shock registered on her delicate features when she noticed his empty bed.

She whirled around and her warm dark eyes found him immediately. A blush crept across her cheeks and down her throat when she realized he was sitting there in his long white drawers.

He thought for a minute she was going to bolt, but then had to give her credit when she squared her shoulders and marched across the room to where his pants lay in a wad. Ignoring him, she picked them up, shook them out with a snap and draped them over the top of the chest of drawers.

"Are you all right?" she asked.

"Do I look all right? I tried to get dressed and almost passed out cold. Now I can't even get back in bed."

Her forehead wrinkled in a deep frown. She looked everywhere but at him and finally wound up staring hard at his bare toes.

He glanced down and realized he had not yet done up the four buttons down the front of his damn wool drawers. There was a yawning gap in the material over his privates.

"No need to be embarrassed," he said as he fought the stubborn buttons with fingers that were worthless. "Nothing down there you didn't see last night."

After a gasp she said, "There is no need to be crude." The retort was issued in little more than a whisper. Except for two bright spots of color on her cheeks, her face blanched white above the high collar of a sorrowful mud-brown dress.

A long, strained silence followed before she volunteered, "Let me help you back to bed."

The offer surprised him. It meant she would have to move closer, even touch him. An unwanted image flashed into his mind, one of Kate with her long hair flowing free, cascading down her back. He could almost feel it swaying to the rhythm of her movements as she straddled him, riding him to fulfillment.

He closed his eyes, shook his head. Now surely *that* was no more than a fever-induced hallucination. No virgin, no untried schoolmarm would have ever been so bold her first time.

He caught the scent of roses. When he looked up again he found her beside him, waiting to help him to the bed.

"Can you stand up?"

Trim, but not overly thin, she did not look strong enough to lift him to his feet. "I think so. Just steady me."

He hated like hell to be dependent upon anyone, but most especially her, this woman who had been his father's choice, the bait to lure him home. Sofia had claimed Kate innocent of his father's scheme. If she was so innocent, why the hell had she climbed into bed with him?

Without hesitation, she reached down and slipped her arm around his waist, rose with him as he pushed himself to his feet. When the room started to whirl, Reed found himself leaning more heavily on her shoulder.

Her strength surprised him. She bore his weight without complaint as he forced himself to shuffle toward the bed, afraid that he would black out before they made it.

The dizzying journey seemed to take forever, but eventually she was propping him up against the pillows and tucking him beneath fresh sheets.

From all outward appearances, Katherine Whittington was all business, from the efficient way she turned down the top sheet and smoothed it across his chest, to the careful, measured way she poured another glass of water and handed it to him without his having to ask for it.

Their fingers touched as he took the glass, and Reed was shocked at his body's involuntary reaction to her. An arousing warmth coursed through him after the brief connection.

He reminded himself that they had shared a bed last night. As he sipped the water, he wished the memory of it would come back to him in more than bits and pieces of recollection. She waited in patient silence to take the glass. He was careful to avoid touching her as he handed it back.

His empty stomach growled louder than a bobcat when the water hit it.

Kate carefully set the glass down on the precise spot where it had been. Absently, she stroked the tabletop and then looked at her fingertips, inspecting for dust.

"Are you hungry?" she asked over her shoulder.

"I'm starved."

Initially she was silent; then she walked over to the rocker and perched herself on the edge. With her knees pressed together beneath her skirt, ankles touching, she primly rested her folded hands on her thighs and looked him in the eye.

"Sofia left an hour ago. The way I see it, you have three choices, Mr. Benton. You can lay there and grow weaker, you can try to get up and feed yourself *and* Daniel, or you can hire me to stay on and run this house until you find a suitable replacement."

Scrappy wouldn't return until tomorrow night at the earliest, and the way he felt now, he might very well starve. By then his intestines would be gnawing through his backbone.

"You surprise me, ma'am. Blackmailing a sick man with food."

"I have no option, I'm afraid."

"I told Scrappy to look for a housekeeper in Lone Star on his way back."

Let her chew on that.

Her face clouded over, but rather than feeling pleased with her reaction, he felt oddly guilty.

"What about Daniel?" She sounded confident, but her bravado had noticeably slipped a notch. There was a telltale quiver in her smoky voice.

"What about Daniel?"

"He can't walk. He certainly can't care for himself any more than you can right now. I think he's beginning to respond to me—" She stopped abruptly, as if loath to argue too strongly.

Reed sighed and rubbed his shoulder. His damn stomach growled again, giving him away.

He wished she hadn't brought up the boy. He didn't want to think about Daniel yet. The dirty, sullen creature he had fought with all the way home wasn't his sweet little son anymore. Daniel was exactly what Reed had feared he would become if captured. Still, the woman was right. The boy needed care, and Reed wasn't in a position to give it.

Kate Whittington had him over a barrel, but if she knew it, it didn't show on her face. He left her on pins and needles, wishing he had read some of her letters as he tried to recall everything Sofia had told him about her.

She had given up everything to come to Texas. Supposedly she believed she was his wedded wife when she climbed into his bed last night, but she could have been aware of his father's scheme when she stepped into his hallucination as Becky. By sleeping with her, he had unwittingly fallen into their hands. Still, in his mind he had every right to send her packing as soon as help arrived.

So why did he feel so guilty considering it?

He studied her from head to toe as she waited, white knuckled, for him to decide. His gaze lingered a bit too long on her breasts, and when she looked up, she caught him staring. Her face and neck blushed crimson.

Reed sighed. He *was* starved. Weak as a kitten, too. His body felt as if he had been dragged twenty miles behind a runaway wagon. He definitely couldn't do much for himself yet, let alone care for Daniel.

"Looks like you win for now, Kate Whittington. You can stay until help arrives."

"Thank you." If she was relieved, she did not show it. "I'll get you something to eat."

"Don't bring me something you would feed an invalid. I don't want any damn broth or runny gruel. I need real food so I can get on my feet." Maybe with something in his stomach, he would be able to stand up without seeing stars.

"I understand."

"Beef. Fried potatoes. And plenty of 'em."

"Yes. All right." She frowned, deep in thought.

"Something wrong?"

"Well . . ." She paused and tapped her thumbs together above her folded hands. Tap, tap, tap, without speaking.

"You don't cook, do you?"

She cleared her throat. "That's not exactly true. At the orphanage I helped cook, but not often. Everyone took turns in the kitchen, preparing food, cleaning up. But one of the nuns always did the actual cooking."

"Have you ever put out a meal by yourself?"

He thought for a second she would lie, but she obviously knew her own limitations when it came to deception.

"No, not really." Then she brightened a bit. "There are still some covered dishes left over from the burial. And I have brought along a book on housekeeping and a few recipes."

"That's a relief." Dry leftovers would be better than nothing, he reckoned.

She pushed herself up out of the chair. The rockers tapped against the bare wood floor until the sound and motion slowly died.

"I'll go down and fix a dinner tray for you. It won't take but a few minutes."

Armed with purpose, she bustled out of the room. Reed stared out the open window, across miles of yellow grassland baking beneath a warm June sun.

He had grown used to living with men, used to action, not forced inactivity. Life in a Ranger camp was rugged. They lived in tents, hunted, fished, scouted renegade Indians, and chased down bandits. He doubted he could stand being laid up very long, doubted he could ever live on the ranch again.

Reed Senior had hired an expert crew. Early on, he had divided Lone Star Ranch into quadrants and given the responsibility of each section to four experienced foremen he had lured away from other, more established ranches. The cowhands working under them were every bit as loyal and hardworking as their bosses. His father made certain of that by establishing as safe an environment as he could for the families in the small town he had created almost overnight. Because he had raised beef for both sides during the war, Lone Star was virtually untouched by the fighting.

So, although his father was gone, Reed really had no responsibility to the ranch yet. He would be more than willing to turn everything over to his father's lawyer's keeping, step out of the way, let the place run itself.

He already felt the confines of his father's house.

As he stared out at the prairie, Reed hoped that Scrappy would return sooner than later. Before the leftovers ran out.

15

Fast Pony smiled to himself as he sat alone in the too-soft bed, watching the stars appear far beyond the opening in the wall. He was waiting for Soft Grass Hands to come back, to sit with him in the yellow glow of lamplight.

She had been with him almost all the time, talking to him, bringing him food, sitting beside him until he fell asleep. He knew that he shouldn't look forward to her visits, but it was better than sitting in the room all alone. He ate whatever she offered, but refused to say any of the words she urged him to speak, even the name she called him. She had no idea what he was really thinking, or that he was growing stronger, planning to escape.

Earlier she had insulted him by giving him an old fire-blackened horse made of wood. It was a toy that might have pleased a baby, but not the son of Many Horses, the great Nermernuh warrior.

Before the raid he had owned a real horse of his own, a strong spotted horse that ran fast as the wind. Like all of The People, he learned to ride long before he could run. He could hang from his pony's mane and scoop up small objects from the ground at full gallop.

To please Soft Grass Hands, he had taken the toy from

her anyway and felt oddly comforted when the worry lines on her forehead disappeared.

He gave her a false smile and held on to the old thing for a while, just so she would think that it made him happy, but it didn't. A bad spirit dwelled inside it. One that made him feel sad whenever he looked at the wounded wooden horse.

She called him *Dan-iel* over and over as if trying to make the name stick to him. But he knew in his heart that his true name was Fast Pony, the name his mother and father had given him, and he would never, ever forget it.

He glanced over at the mute wooden horse with its terrible blind eyes and straight stiff legs. Stretching across the bed, he squeezed its fetlock. Soon his own ankle would be just as strong as the hard wood. Soon he would be able to walk, and then run. Then he would escape, and this time they would never find him.

He heard the woman outside his door and lay still so that she would not suspect how much easier it was for him to move now. The door opened and she walked in carrying a large woven basket in her hands. As usual, she was smiling and talking gibberish.

He settled back, biding his time, waiting to see what she was up to now.

Time could be as mercurial as the weather.

It crawled past when Kate had lived in Maine anticipating the trip to Texas. Now that her situation here was tentative, it flew by.

She could not decide whether the three-day reprieve she had survived was a blessing or not. She had taken over care of the house, of Daniel, and of Reed, but her mind was full of the haunting notion that Scrappy could return any day with a new housekeeper in tow.

Her feelings vacillated as she did the best she could for Daniel, as she concentrated on putting together simple meals for him and Reed and tried not to think of what she would do if a replacement arrived.

For now, it was enough that she was still here with a roof over her head. She would take one day at a time.

"Hello, Daniel." She shifted the basket in her arms.

As usual, he watched her but did not speak or smile. His wooden horse stood neglected on the bedside table. Because her time with him could end at any moment, she had decided to show him all the items in the basket tonight, including the photograph of his mother, in hopes of prodding his memory.

Kate sat on the edge of the bed. He had been remarkably calm over the past few days, almost as if he was finally resigned to his fate.

"How are you this evening, young man? Sleepy yet?" Setting the basket on the bed behind her, she reached in for the small piece of patchwork first. Slowly, she unfolded the blanket and held it in front of him.

"Do you like this? It was yours when you were just a little baby." Shaking out the quilt, she spread it over his lap and smoothed out the puckered red, white, and blue stars.

Daniel watched her closely, his glance falling to the quilt and then back to her eyes.

"I wish you could talk to me," she said. "I wish you could tell me what you are thinking. I wish I could tell you that your heart will heal, even though you will never forget the family you left behind."

She went on to explain that someone had made the quilt, most likely just for him. She wished she had thought to ask Sofia who had taken such care to cut and stitch the countless small pieces together.

Daniel did not move, although he stared down at the quilt for so long that she wondered if perhaps he remembered the bright colors and star patterns. She let him study it a while before she drew out the silver cup and held it out to him.

Slowly, he reached for the inscribed piece, turned it over and over and then looked at her questioningly.

"That was your cup. Daniel's cup," she said, pointing to the name on the silver piece before she handed it to him. When he lost interest and offered it back, she carefully set it beside the horse on the table.

The only thing left in the basket was the small silver case with the photograph of him and his mother. She took a deep breath, arrested by the image of the young woman who had taken her own life rather than stay with her son, no matter the outcome.

Becky was smiling a wistful hint of a smile. What had she been thinking as she stared into the camera's lens?

Daniel, dressed in a long white gown, was perched on his mother's knees. Around two years old, his features, though pudgy with baby fat, were virtually the same as now. There was no denying he was the child in the picture—but would he recognize himself? Kate set the basket down, hoping that if Daniel did remember his mother, that it would not overly upset him.

He watched her intently, waited expectantly for her to show him the object in her hands.

"This is a photograph," she told him, turning the case so that he could see it better. Lamplight reflected off the surface of the glass inside. Kate held her breath as the boy took the silver case shaped like a small book into his own hands. He bent over it and stared for a long time.

Then he touched his forefinger to his face in the photograph and afterward, through a shock of hair that fell across his face, he looked up at Kate questioningly. Without thinking, she brushed his hair back and tucked it behind his ear.

"That's you. That's Daniel." She pointed to the photograph and then to his chest. "And that's your mama. Can you say *Mama*?"

He glanced down, then back up at her with a quizzical expression on his face. He squinted hard at the glass and then quickly pulled back.

"*Mama.* That's your mama. Do you remember her?"

Relieved to find that after a few days of rest his head had cleared and he was able to dress by himself, Reed paused in the doorway of his room, drawn by the seductive pitch of Kate's voice. Down the hall, lamplight spilled out of the boy's room. Both the enticing sound and the light beckoned him.

He was already sick to death of being laid up and forced to eat some of the worst food he ever tasted while Kate had hovered in his room, anxious to see if he would eat or not, busying herself straightening and dusting, fussing and fluffing.

More times than he liked to admit, his gaze had sought her out as she worked. Sometimes he caught her watching him with undisguised hope and unrealized dreams in her eyes—hopes and dreams that silently spoke of home fires and family, of traditions and trust—the kinds of things that made a man like him want to ride out and never look back.

Every morning she would come in fresh-faced and glowing, ready for each new day. No matter how businesslike she tried to appear, the high color in her cheeks and her shy glances gave away her embarrassment.

She never stayed long in his room, just long enough to

serve him a meal and putter while he ate. When she wasn't
there, he would hear her down the hall talking to Daniel, or
downstairs, rattling pans in the kitchen below.

That afternoon he had pulled himself over to the edge of
the bed and tried standing. Able to walk to the window, he
had stood there in the nightshirt she had insisted he wear,
watching her hang out the wash. She stretched up on tiptoe
to reach the high line, and each time she did, the breeze
would mold her skirt to her long legs, her bodice to her
breasts. Then she would bend over the laundry basket, pull
out another piece, and repeat the process.

At one point, as if she sensed someone was watching, she
paused and looked around. As she turned her head to look
up toward the window, he quickly stepped back so that she
would not see him. He stood there beside the window
frame with his back pressed against the wall, his heart beating like a racehorse's, feeling like a randy, inexperienced
youth.

Now, moving toward the light, he leaned against the door
jamb when he reached the boy's room where she sat on the
edge of Daniel's bed. Lamplight ignited the auburn highlights in her hair, a sharp contrast to her faded powder-blue
robe. Only the hem of her white nightgown showed where
it teased her bare feet. He could hear her speaking in low,
warm tones to Daniel. The sound of her voice was haunting, unforgettable.

It was a homey picture—warm and cozy—the woman
and the boy sitting with their heads together, looking at
something Daniel held in his hands. It was the kind of scene
in which he had always longed to see Becky with their son,
but she never had an instinct for mothering any more than
she had for being a wife.

As Reed watched Kate, he tried hard to forget that it was

he who used to tuck the boy in at night, he who told his son bedtime stories, sang him songs and kissed his tender cheek.

As he strained to hear Kate's soft words, he pitied her in her efforts. Didn't she know that no matter how well she scrubbed him, no matter how nice she dressed him, that Daniel had a Comanche heart now?

Given half a chance, he would cut their throats.

She could pamper him and coddle him, but the shuttered sullenness in Daniel's eyes would not disappear until he returned to the people he believed to be his true family.

A weathered woven basket stood on the floor, tucked beside her bare feet. It yawned open and empty. Reed took a good look at the things on the bed and table, felt his heart jump to his throat and stick there like one of her bad biscuits. He was appalled by a sudden, fleeting ache to have the years roll back when his gaze touched each object again. The wooden horse. The silver baby cup. The star quilt that had once been his own. Chunks of the past resurrected. Painful memories come back to haunt him.

Memories he thought long buried, along with painful images of Daniel toddling across the floor, dragging the quilt behind him. Recollections of the night he had gone outside to search for the lost horse so that the little boy would stop crying and go to sleep. The day Daniel was born, his father presented them with the engraved cup.

The memories hit him harder than the bullet he had taken in the shoulder.

Kate, still unaware of his presence, spoke a little louder to the boy, and Reed heard her.

"*Mama.* That's your mama. Can you say *Mama?*"

When Reed realized Daniel was holding a photograph, he stopped breathing.

Without warning, the boy erupted and threw the picture

case across the room where it hit the wall. The glass shattered, and the front of the case broke off its hinges. Daniel started shouting, cursing at Kate in Comanche. His face turned scarlet with anger as he shook uncontrollably.

Reed crossed the room before he even knew he had moved. Both the woman and the boy jumped at the sound of his voice. "What in the hell were you thinking?"

Kate leapt to her feet. Reed sidestepped her, picked up the pieces of the photograph case, glanced at the likeness of Becky and the boy, and then tossed it on the bed. Daniel moved his good leg and kicked everything to the floor.

Kate stood perfectly still, unwilling to give ground. "Sofia gave me some things she had saved for Daniel. Some of his baby things. I was just showing them to him."

Reed glanced down at Daniel. No longer the sweet innocent toddler in the photograph, he had melted back against the huge pillows. His posture betrayed his fear, but there was still simmering anger in his blue eyes. In them, Reed saw the hatred and defiance he had shown his own father.

"I thought that seeing these things might help him remember," she said.

"Remember what? The night his mother blew her brains out?"

The spinster was shaken but not deterred. "His life before he was captured. His things. His mother. And . . . and you. Or don't you care if he remembers you?"

"What I care about is none of your business."

He had cared once, about everything, and all that had brought him was hurt.

He wished she were wearing one of her worn, shapeless brown dresses instead of the nightgown, wished that the essence of roses wasn't filling his head, calling flashes of memory to mind, confusing the situation. He wished he weren't standing close enough to feel the warmth emanating from her, to see the pulse point beating at the base of her throat.

He let his gaze wander to the opening of her robe, watched her full breasts rise and fall beneath the white cotton gown.

When he looked into her eyes again, he was afraid of falling into them, of losing himself. Her eyes were wide and guileless, openly staring back, filled with uncertainty and confusion. More than that, he saw her bottomless hope—hope that things would change, hope that she would awaken to find it had all been one great lie, that everything was really the way she believed it would be when she boarded the train in Maine.

Involuntarily, his hand closed over her arm. He had to get away from Daniel, with his long Comanche hair and the haunting familiarity of his eyes. Before he could change his mind, he pulled Kate into the hall.

"I don't want you getting close to him," Reed told her once they were by themselves.

"If I didn't spend time with him, he would be alone all day. You certainly haven't made any effort to be with him, to help him adjust."

"Until tonight I couldn't even put my pants on by myself. You don't know Comanches, Miss Whittington, but I do. That boy's been with them so long that all he wants is to go back. He won't let anything stand in his way—not you, not me."

"He's just a little boy!"

"He's Comanche now. He'd just as soon slit your throat as not if you stand in the way of his escape."

"I'll *never* believe that child capable of killing."

"Then you don't have the sense God gave a goose. I've

been fighting Comanche and Kiowa for years. I've seen just
about every kind of nightmare you can imagine. Do you
know what he said in there? He cursed you and all your an-
cestors. He cursed your spirit to wander the earth forever
when you die."

"You understood him?"

"Enough."

"Why, then, you can talk to him! You can help him understand what is happening to him and why."

"I'm not speaking Comanche in this house."

Bright spots of color stained her pale cheeks. Her breath
was coming hard and fast, her anger barely contained. She
had far more spirit than he would have ever credited to a
spinster teacher from some orphanage school. In her anger,
her loveliness was only heightened.

An unbidden image flashed through his mind. One
of her straddling him, easing down on him, taking him inside her. He closed his eyes but failed to dim the memory of
a throaty cry of pleasure-pain.

Impossible if she had been a virgin. What would she
know of such uninhibited lovemaking? The dream must
have confused her with Becky in his mind. No innocent
woman would be so brazen her first time with a man, except
perhaps one who was desperate enough, greedy enough to
try to make herself unforgettable to him. A woman like
Becky.

He couldn't shake the notion that Kate had been part of
his father's scheme all along. Had she intentionally seduced
him that night? He wished he had not stubbornly talked
himself out of reading her letters.

The night wind whipped across the prairie, came snaking
down the long upper hallway, ruffled the lace at the open
collar of her nightgown.

How far would she be willing to go now that she was no longer a virgin?

A little cry escaped her when he grabbed her by the upper arms and roughly drew her against him. Before she could cry out or pull away, he lowered his head and pressed his mouth to hers.

At first she was stiff as a war lance. Her lips remained locked, her mouth a hard line against her teeth. Slowly he flicked his tongue over the seam between her lips, coaxed her until she thawed, and then he deepened the kiss.

Lost in her scent and taste, he slipped his right hand between them and gently cupped her breast, surprised that her clothing hid her full figure so well.

She moaned and leaned into him, then pressed her palms hard against his chest and shoved. Even in his weakened state, she was no match for his strength, but he let her go.

She stumbled back. He reached out to steady her. She pushed his hand away and caught herself. The pins had fallen from her hair. Now a long, rich strand dangled over her shoulder. Breathless, they stared at each other in shock.

Reed damned himself for wanting her again—this woman his father had handpicked for him.

Embraced by the shadows in the hall, Kate blessed the semi-darkness. Although it could never erase her mortification, it could at least mask it from him.

Dear God, he had kissed her shamelessly, touched her breast, pressed her so close that she had recognized his arousal through her thin nightclothes. From the minute the kiss had begun, she had wanted it to last forever. She would be a fool to try to deny that her body had understood and answered of its own accord.

Outside the ring of lamplight spilling from Daniel's room,

she stared up at Reed with her mind and heart racing, her body aching to feel him inside her again.

Perhaps she had inherited the heart of a whore. Perhaps her blood ran hot because she was Meg Whittington's daughter. Her wanton nature came naturally. Her need was definitely physical. Her heart was still pounding so hard that her blood rushed in her ears.

His touch had rekindled all the wonderful feelings of the night that had passed between them. His kiss had ignited the same fire in her, one she never realized existed before, one that made her want him again—even though she knew he hated her for being here.

She had opened Pandora's box the night she had given herself to him, and now, no matter what she told herself, no matter how tenuous her position here, her traitorous body still wanted him. She could never take back what had happened that night. She could never go back to what she was before.

Nor would she ever forget. Now that he had kissed her, she knew for certain that not only her mind, but her body would never let her forget either.

She forced herself to think, to move, to act as she clutched the edges of her robe together at her throat. Her alternatives were to run like a scared rabbit or go back to Daniel as if nothing had happened.

She did not want to feel like both a whore *and* a coward, so she raised her chin a notch and stood her ground. "I am going to ignore your lack of manners, Mr. Benton. Now, if you will excuse me, I'm going to tuck Daniel in."

"I take it you aren't putting any store into my warning about him." He offered no apology, not that she had expected any.

"I have my own convictions, sir. He's a child, hurt, alone, confused. I'll do what I can for him for as long as I can."

"You go right ahead and do that, but don't say I didn't warn you."

Finally, after a long, measured look, he stepped aside and let her go to Daniel. But as she passed by, Kate realized it was not Daniel she needed to fear, but Reed Benton's power over her body and her badly bruised heart.

16

Reed couldn't get the taste or the feel of her out of his mind. He walked back to his room, found the letters Sofia had left in the drawer, locked the door, and then sat on the bed to read them.

Opening the first one in the stack, he noted the date, last October. Kate wrote in a fine hand, the letters even, the lines straight. He absently rubbed his thumb back and forth along the edge of the page as he read.

Dear Mr. Benton,

I suppose you might wonder what kind of a woman would answer your advertisement, but the truth is that I am wondering what kind of a man would place one in a paper so far from his home.

For twenty years I have lived in an orphanage in Applesby, Maine—first as an orphan, and for the past eleven of those years as a teacher to the girls who lived here before the place recently closed.

I will not lie to you about my background. My mother left me at Saint Perpetua's Orphanage when I was nine years old. I feel that if we are to consider forming a matrimonial bond, that you must know all, so I will not spare the dark details of my past.

My mother was a woman of ill repute who sold her favors on the street. We lived together in a one-room shanty until she abandoned me on the steps of the orphans' home. Now I realize I was fortunate that she chose to give me up, for I have gone on to live a decent life.

I write in answer to your advertisement because once, long ago, I dreamed of having a home and family of my own, but alas, I have let the years slip away. If our correspondence succeeds, I would be delighted to move to Texas, to begin a new life with you and realize my dreams.

Reed rested the letter in his lap and stared down at the written page. *A home and family of her own.*

It seemed little to ask for when he saw it there in black and white on paper. Between the lines he found an explanation for the fragmented images that had haunted him since the night they had been together. If she had seen her mother with men, if she had witnessed the woman plying her trade in the one-room shack—or granting favors, as Kate had so politely put it—then although she might have been a virgin that night with him, she was a woman raised by nuns who possibly knew as much as a practiced harlot.

He thought about what he already knew of her, which was not much. She had a gentle, caring nature, but her stubborn side had shown in her determination to stay on despite what had happened and in her concern for Daniel. She was well spoken and educated. A horrible cook. Desperately in need of new clothes.

And she had kissed him back tonight, this orphan who had never left the orphanage except to come West, carrying her hopes and dreams and childhood wishes.

He read on.

When I lived with my mother, I always wished for hot food and clean sheets. When she left me, I suddenly had both, but not in the way I had dreamed. That experience taught me early on not to wish for too much. Fate has a way of giving you what you ask for, but not exactly the way you had pictured it.

If nothing else, Reed, I am loyal. I stayed at Saint Perpetua's for eleven years after I was hired to teach there. Now I find myself twenty-nine years old, a little old for a bride, I know, but none the less, I am sincere and would honor an agreement between us.

She was a year older than he, but what difference did that make in the long run? He would be lying to himself not to admit that he found her downright striking. As he sat there thinking about her, he realized he had not seen her really smile since that first morning he had laid eyes on her. Nor had he heard her laugh out loud. Then again, what did she have to laugh or smile about now? Once again, fate had been fickle.

He recalled the way she had looked the morning she had walked into his room like a bright promise unspoken. The glow in her eyes when she looked into his that very first time had scared the hell out of him.

He had taken her virginity the night before, and all he could say was, "Do I know you? Have we met?"

Shock, disbelief, and then an incredible expression of loss had come over her. It was a shattered look that he would never forget.

After reading a few more letters, his eyes ached from straining to see by the weak lamplight. Too weary to stay awake any longer, he refolded the letters and then shoved them all beneath his pillow.

.   .   .

Reed blamed what he had read as much as kissing Kate for a night of tossing and turning. Up and dressed again by the time the sky was barely washed with gray light, Reed hankered for a cup of strong black coffee—the kind the spinster never served.

Careful not to make a sound as he walked down the hall, he paused beside Daniel's door, took a deep breath, opened it, and looked in. The boy was still asleep but uncovered, lying crosswise in the bed. His bandaged ankle dangled over the edge.

He sighed and lingered, watching the child, this boy who'd looked at him through sullen eyes. There was no way of knowing what Daniel had endured during his early days of captivity, but Reed knew that once captives were adopted into a Comanche family, they were treated well. So well, in fact, that most recovered captives eventually found ways to escape back to the Comancheria.

Daniel stirred in his sleep and Reed almost closed the door, but when the boy did not awaken, he lingered, and his thoughts harked back to the night Daniel was kidnaped.

Sick of the constant battle of wills with his father, he had moved Becky and the boy out to an abandoned cabin on the far western border of the ranch.

Raids occurred beneath the full moon so often the settlers had taken to calling them Comanche moons. That night, a full, soft summer moon hung low in the sky.

For years before the war, Texas border lands had been more secure from Comanche and Kiowa attacks, but with the state's secession from the Union and the withdrawal of troops from nearby forts, raiding warriors took advantage of the Tejanos' weakened defense.

During the winter months, renegade bands would return to the reservations to live off rations, but in the spring and

summer months when the weather was warm, the grass
long, and buffalo plenty, hostilities would begin again. Like
his father, he believed that since wandering bands were invited to take Lone Star cattle when times were hard, the
ranch was safe from attack.

When he and Becky had argued heatedly that warm summer night long ago, he knew he would never forget the way
she had looked at him, as if he were the lowest man on
earth.

She was diminutive and beautiful, with dark hair and
eyes, a woman who would seem forever youthful because
of her size. He had fallen in love with her at first sight,
had wanted to marry her despite his father's protests to
the contrary. Becky's parents were farmers who had moved
from Illinois to Texas. They weren't dirt poor, nor were they
rich. Reed Senior had wanted him to marry a well-educated
woman with powerful connections. Becky was neither.

She had been insistent upon his taking her back to live at
Benton House the next day. She had told him so in no uncertain terms that night after Reed had tucked Daniel into
bed. "I won't stay out here in this old cabin one more day,
Reed. I won't do it, and you shouldn't expect me to. It's not
fair to me or to Daniel. We're Bentons now. I grew up in an
old, run-down cabin like this. It wasn't what I had in mind
when I married you, you know. This is no place to raise the
grandson of a prominent landholder, the grandson of a man
as rich and powerful as your father."

She demanded he take them back to live with Reed Senior in the big house, but he had refused. She thought the
old dog-run cabin on the edge of the ranch was beneath her.

"There are no conveniences out here, Reed. We don't
even have a well or a pump. And I need more help with
Daniel."

Because he still loved her, because, no matter what she said or did, he believed he always would love her, he didn't remind her that Daniel's care fell to him most of the time already.

"I know life out here is harder on you than it is on me," he told her, "but I love the frontier as much as I despise my father's attempts to push me into public office."

"I think he's right," she told him, brushing aside his hand when he tried to take her in his arms and kiss her out of her dark mood. "You're not livin' up to your full potential."

Pushed to the limit, Reed reminded her that his father's opinion of her was not the highest. Becky assured him that no matter what he decided about running for office, his father would do anything to have them all under his roof again, especially Daniel.

The argument intensified until Becky finally threw a dish at his head. Reed ducked and came up laughing until she saw that he was not taking her seriously and became vicious.

"Don't you laugh at me, Reed. Don't think you can kiss me and make this all go away. If you think I love you enough to put up with this anymore, think again." Suddenly she grew very still and coolly calm. She looked him straight in the eye and said without pause, "You want the truth? Daniel isn't even your son. I'm leaving here tomorrow whether you want me to or not, and I'm taking Daniel with me."

She went on to reveal, in stomach-churning detail, exactly how she had cheated on him and with whom. What she confessed to that night had been inconceivable, but there was only one way to discover the truth. He would take her back to his father's house as soon as it was daylight.

They had fought before, but never like that night. Shaken with rage and doubt, Reed had stormed out into the dark, marched to the barn to see to the stock. He was furious.

Everything his father had tried to warn him about Becky—including that she was a loose woman with the morals of a stray cat—backed up her claim.

As he walked out of the barn after securing shutters and filling feed bins, he noticed a brilliant red glow on the far horizon, and his blood had run cold.

The Comanche were on the move.

The closest settlers living off the ranch were across a far ridge, two brothers from Tennessee who had settled their families in the rich bottomland along the Brazos. Reed raced back to the house, slammed in the door. Inside, Becky was packing her things.

"The Williams place is on fire." He kept his tone even as he strapped on a Colt, took up his rifle, and gathered ammunition. "I'm going to ride over and see if anyone is still alive."

He would forever remember how her eyes had filled with fright, the way her skin had gone pale and ghostly, her face a pallid oval framed by long dark hair.

"Are you just going to *leave* us here?"

"You'll be safe. Turn out the lamps, bar the shutters. Here." He gave her one of his handguns. "That's loaded. Keep it close by. Lone Star's never been raided before, and it won't be tonight. Besides, the Williams place is already burning, which means the Comanche have moved on. They would be here by now if they were coming this direction."

She had raced around the table and grabbed his sleeve. He had to pry her hands off his shirt.

"You *know* what they will do to me if they come here."

War with the Comanche had been going on nigh onto thirty years. Everyone in Texas knew what happened during a raid. Men were tortured, staked out, and butchered, women were raped and murdered on the spot or worse yet, carried off and forced into slavery. Some were made to take Co-manche husbands. Some lost their minds. Those too weak to survive the trip back to the Comancheria were killed along the way.

Older children fared little better. Those too small to protest were quickly adopted, raised Comanche, and soon they forgot they were ever white at all.

He had known very well what *could* happen that night, but they were on Lone Star land. He was as arrogant as his father in his belief that they were safe. Like Reed Senior, he was convinced they were untouchable.

Truth be told, as he stood in the hallway now, watching the savage boy his baby had become, Reed wondered if deep in his heart something more than arrogance had made him leave them there alone.

He faced questions he had not dared ask himself since that night. Had he wanted Becky to suffer? Had he left her so that she would have to sit there alone and taste heart-stopping fear until he returned? Had he wanted to terrify her for all the soul-shattering things she had told him, for the doubt and disgust she had inflicted on his heart and soul?

Even now, years later, he couldn't say for sure. He hoped to God he had not done it on purpose, but his conscience would haunt him until the day he died.

17

Mother Superior had always claimed that an idle mind was the devil's workshop and that there was nothing like a long walk to clear one's head, so Kate left the house shortly after dawn, head down, determined to walk off her frustration and keep the devil at bay.

If Reed had a heart of stone, then hers—already bruised and vulnerable—was in terrible jeopardy. Thoughts of him had her so riled up that she believed she might have to walk forever. She smiled at the idea of Reed having to take care of his own son for an hour or two.

She had been so certain she could help Daniel until last night when she had terrified him by showing him the photograph. She was still loath to believe there was no help for him or his father. Reed Benton definitely had a heart of stone, but his body, and hers, were different matters.

After the liberties he had taken last night, after the way he had molested her right there in the hallway, not to mention the way she had responded to him, she could not afford to ever let down her guard again.

Away from the confines of the house, the open land was even more intimidating with its raw beauty and desperate loneliness. She stopped to watch a hawk circle overhead.

When she started walking again, she heard hoofbeats pounding behind her.

Instantly aware of how vulnerable she was, she thought of everything Sofia had told her about the Comanche and glanced over her shoulder, afraid of what she might see. Then she groaned in frustration when she recognized Reed.

He rode so close that she was nearly nose to nose with his horse. She had no idea if he was angry at her for leaving or not, because his eyes were half hidden beneath the shadow of the wide brim of his hat. She let her gaze drift over his face. He was clean shaven, and there was a crooked half-smile on his lips.

Still in the saddle, he raised his thumb and forefinger to the brim of his hat, gave it a tug, and nodded.

"Miss Whittington."

"Mr. Benton." She crossed her arms and looked out over the prairie.

"Going someplace?"

"I was thinking about it. How far is Lone Star?"

"Far enough." He pointed over his shoulder in the opposite direction. "Back that way."

She reckoned he was starving or he would not have come looking for her.

"You shouldn't be out here alone."

"What I do is no concern of yours."

"You work for me now. If anything were to happen to you on your little stroll, I'd be responsible, wouldn't I?"

"Nothing is going to happen to me." She wished she sounded more convincing. "I am responsible for myself."

"Scrappy rode in just as I was leaving. I left him with Daniel."

She knew Daniel was terrified of Scrappy, and she tried not to panic at the thought of the two of them alone together.

Reed must have sensed her concern, for he immediately tried to reassure her.

"The boy's still sound asleep. Are you ready to go back?"

"Did Mr. Parks find my replacement?" She was afraid to hear, but had to ask.

He squinted, scanning the land around them. "Nope. Looks like you'll have to stay. Same terms we agreed on before, room and board, twenty-five dollars a month, and you'll look after Daniel."

"For how long?"

He squinted toward the morning sun. "Why don't we say three months?"

"Can I look after him the way I see fit?"

"As long as you never trust him completely. Don't let him outside alone."

She almost laughed. Her worry wasn't Daniel. It was Reed. She wouldn't trust Reed Benton as far as she could carry him.

"Turn your back, and he'll be gone," he warned her. "There's one other thing. You need to learn to cook."

Over the past few days, cooking had proved to be a very messy mystery best left to someone with a talent for it, but she would certainly keep trying.

"Fine."

"We shouldn't stand out here in the hot sun all day."

Kate sighed. A stiff, hot breeze had already started to roll across the open land. She was thirsty.

"I'll go back with you on one condition."

"Let's hear it."

"I would like an apology for last night."

He opened his mouth and quickly shut it as if he had thought better about what he was going to say. "Fine. I'm sorry."

"It won't happen again?" The moment she asked, she wasn't sure she wanted him to agree. She looked down, brushed at a burr near the hem of her dress, and waited for him to answer. When she looked up again, she discovered him staring at her mouth.

Reed shook his head. "I can't promise you that."

"What are you saying?" Her words were barely audible, but he heard them.

"We might have been tricked into this situation, but I'm a man, and you're a woman. And we've already shared a bed, Miss Whittington. Things are bound to be . . . a bit strained as long as we're together."

Strained? She would grant him that, but she thought that after what his father and Sofia had done, the last woman he would want was her. She couldn't imagine him having anything to do with her, but here he was talking about his being a man and her being a woman and things being a bit strained.

Did that mean he was attracted to her? Was that what he was saying? She had no experience with men, no way of knowing how to take what he had just said.

Sofia's advice came back to her. *Fight for what you want.* Perhaps there was a chance that he was attracted to her after all, unless he was just a man who found himself alone in a house with a woman he had already made love to and he, like her, couldn't help wondering what it would be like to make love again.

Her heart skipped a beat when he swung his leg over the saddle and dismounted.

"What are you doing?" She backed up a step. Alone with him in the yawning open prairie, she felt as vulnerable as ever.

I don't know him at all.

He's not the one who wrote to me.

He took a step closer and said, "I'm going to help you onto my horse. We'll ride back together."

"No, thank you."

"Come here, Miss Whittington, and give me your hand."

"I would rather not, Mr. Benton." Kate headed toward the house on foot.

Leading his horse, Reed caught up with her in two long strides and fell into step beside her.

"I'd rather you call me Reed," he said.

"Then call me Kate."

"This is ridiculous, you know," he said. "It's a long way back."

"I don't mind walking."

"Is it the horse, or is it that you don't want to ride with me?"

She looked over at the huge, coal-black beast he rode. "It's not the horse."

It was the fact that she could not trust him—or herself, but she wasn't about to give him any ideas by explaining. She stared straight ahead and kept right on walking.

"If you're worried that I might kiss you again, Kate, I give you my word that I'll mind my manners this morning."

She stopped dead in her tracks and slowly turned, hoping to freeze him with an icy stare, but he didn't even look chilled. She started walking again, head high and shoulders straight.

Within seconds he was walking beside her. "Tell me about Maine," he said.

She stopped walking. "When did I mention I was from Maine?"

He looked surprised. "Sofia must have. Look, Kate, I'm trying to make pleasant conversation here."

"It must be quite a challenge for you."

"I don't do this very often; you could do me the favor of helping out. Tell me about Maine."

"It's cold."

"All the time?"

"Most of the time."

"What did you teach?"

"History and elocution."

As they continued on in silence, she realized she had been more at ease when he wasn't trying to be congenial. She had never had a beau, never flirted with a man, let alone carried on any lengthy conversation with one. She stared down at the dust on his knee-high boots, watched a dirt clod go flying as he kicked it aside.

Daring to slide what she intended to be an unseen glance his way, she discovered he was watching her. Their eyes met and held.

And then Kate stumbled over a prairie dog mound.

Reed reached for her arm when he saw she was headed for a fall, caught her in time, but momentum forced her into him as he grabbed her, and she wound up in his arms. Time stood still as he held her, his senses alive and totally aware of her, the feel of her, the scent of her hair. Like him, she had gone perfectly still. Seconds ticked by. In the distance, a hawk circled its prey. Beside him, Kate drew a deep breath, steadied herself, and straightened.

Reluctantly, Reed let her go. Being around her twenty-four hours a day wasn't going to be easy.

If she had been Becky, he would have suspected her of pretending to trip to wind up in his arms. His late wife had been a consummate flirt. Even marriage had not tamed that side of her. If Kate knew how to flirt, if she was aware of any seductive ways to lure a man into her arms, she had not tried them on him yet.

The awkward moment over, they started off again, Kate taking care to watch the ground with every step. Failing to start a conversation, Reed gave up and walked along in silence.

"How did you meet your wife?"

The question, coming from her, surprised him. "Why?"

"No particular reason. I was trying to make conversation." Kate negotiated a low spot in the ground. She had her head down, but there was a hint of a smile playing on her lips.

"We met at a barn dance in a little town north of Dallas. I was on a cattle-buying trip for my father. Do we have to talk about my wife?" The last thing on earth he wanted to talk about was Becky.

"I'm sorry. I didn't mean to upset you."

He looked over, and Kate blushed fire red. She was staring at the ground.

The words of another of her letters, one she had written after accepting the proposal, came to mind.

> I've never been to a dance, never even been to a dinner party. The things you have described in your last letter, the things you have told me of the life that I will partake in as your wife will all be new to me. I've never even ridden in a hired carriage, let alone a train. Every single thing about my new life with you will be a grand adventure. I look forward to it with excitement.

Knowing that she would have none of it now, that her grand adventure had vanished made him too uncomfortable to try to strike up a conversation again.

The house was still a good distance away. He didn't think she meant to, but she had him in knots anyway. Unused to feeling so awkward, afraid that he was beginning to shoulder the guilt for what his father and Sofia had done, Reed was tempted to get on his horse and ride the rest of the way alone. He wondered if they would ever get there at this pace.

Once they were back at the house, Kate washed her face and hands and combed her hair, and then she hurried to Daniel's room.

Down the hall, she found Scrappy seated on a ladder-back chair just inside the door. The air was filled with strained silence as the old man and the boy matched wits in a staring contest. The pieces of the photograph case were scattered on top of the dresser.

Daniel was as embittered as she had ever seen him. When she smiled, he looked away.

"He don't look half bad now that he's cleaned up, does he?" Scrappy reminded her that he was still in the room. "I saw that pi'cher over there, the one of him and his ma. Sure makes a fella think, don't it? Never know what life's gonna give you, do you?"

Two weeks ago she had been a new bride packing for her trip West. "The only thing that's for certain in this world is that we don't know what life has in store for us," she said.

He nodded in agreement and stood. "If you don't·need me, ma'am, I'll be going."

She paused to consider him. He had dug the keepsakes out of the ruins of Daniel's life and turned them over to Sofia. Perhaps he wasn't as hard-hearted as she had first believed.

"Thank you, no. We'll be fine, Mr. Parks. Thank you."

Fast Pony watched Hairy Face leave and felt better right away, though he did not let the woman see his relief. He had awakened to find the old man guarding the door and knew he had angered Soft Grass Hands by cursing her last night, but he thought he could trust her, that she was not like the others. Now he knew she was as evil as the rest.

Last night she had tricked him with the terrible charms in the basket. Looking at them had made him feel sick in the pit of his stomach, so sick he had wanted to cry. Finally she had showed him the terrible, flat likeness of himself pressed between glass and metal. It was bad medicine—his face on the body of a baby dressed in a long white robe, the white woman holding him upon her lap. His face was pale as a ghost, as white as the gown. Stiff and unsmiling and flat, they were probably dead beneath that glass. Spirits frozen in time.

Once he had seen a dead girl lying in the snow, a captive of the Nermernuh. She had been foolish and willful and tried to escape, only to become lost in a harsh winter storm. Her lips were blue, her skin whiter than the snow. She had been as stiff as wood.

The creatures he had seen under the little glass reminded him of death. So much so that he had thrown them away and revealed his weakness to Soft Grass Hands and Tall Ranger by shouting and crying. A warrior showed bravery, not weakness. The purpose of a warrior's life was to raid and to hunt. A true warrior would never have cried over some white woman's weak, evil magic.

Determined not to listen, he refused to look at her. Then the old man came back and spoke to Soft Grass Hands in the jabber of the Tejanos.

She said something back and then they both walked out of the room. A soft click sounded behind them, and he knew they had locked him in.

He did not care, for he was better off alone. He would be very wary from now on. Even of Soft Grass Hands.

18

The kitchen was quiet as a dead cow in a snowstorm.

Reed sat across the table from Capt. Jonah Taylor and the girl he had brought with him from town, wondering what was taking Scrappy so long to fetch Kate.

Though he tried not to stare, time and again Reed's gaze wandered back to the battered young blonde seated beside Jonah. Purple swelling had closed her left eye. Her thin shoulders curled inward protectively, as if to make herself disappear. Her long, tapered fingers clenched and unclenched the remnant of the torn, red ruffled silk of her gown's low-cut bodice.

Looking heavy on her thin frame, Jonah's brown wool jacket hung across her shoulders, an extension of the man, protectively touching her in a way Jonah would never dare.

Reed knew her only as Charm. She had curly blond hair, a pert nose, pouting lips that were too full for her face, and breasts that were too large for her thin frame. She had the kind of body that a man couldn't help but admire even if he wasn't interested, but plenty of men were interested in Charm. She was one of the favorite whores at Dolly B. Goode's Social Club and Entertainment Emporium in Lone Star.

Reed Senior, forward thinking and a true business man, had established a whorehouse and saloon in Lone Star early on. When the settled folk he recruited to populate his new town had taken umbrage to what he called a "social club" on Main Street, he quickly reminded them that there were plenty of single cowboys around, not only those working the ranch, but also others passing through as they pushed cattle north.

Randy men spelled trouble. If the townsfolk were smart, Reed Senior had argued, they would avoid it at all costs by leaving Dolly and her girls.

Reed's gaze slid away and lit on the stove. "Want some coffee?" he offered lamely.

Where in the hell were Scrappy and Katherine? He had the feeling she would know just what to do for Charm. Between her and Sofia and a bottle of laudanum, they had gotten him through the fever. He only hoped she had empathy for someone in Charm's position and was not too straitlaced or above herself now to help a whore.

"No. No thanks." Jonah shifted in the chair and glanced down at the top of the girl's head. "You want some coffee, Charm?"

A slight shake of her head brought a wince.

Reed watched the muscle in the other man's jaw tighten, and he knew exactly what Jonah was thinking. There was a man out there somewhere who needed a taste of his own medicine.

Jonah was the epitome of a Ranger, outside and in. He had been a part of the ranging companies protecting the Texas frontier for fifteen years. Like Reed, he favored knee-high boots and the wide-brimmed hat, and he carried a knife and a pistol in a belt worn high on his waist. He preferred the great outdoors to a sedentary life inside, fought on the side of right as Texans saw it, and used any means necessary to track down offenders and deal with them, be they raiding Indians, rustlers, or bandits.

Inactivity was a stranger to both men. Neither was comfortable sitting around wringing his hands like an old woman.

Reed pushed away from the table just as Kate entered the room followed by Scrappy. He watched her as she halted inside the door, saw her consider the two strangers sitting there.

She blanched when she noticed the damage to Charm's face, then visibly gathered her wits while she smoothed her hands down the front of her skirt. Her expression hid nothing, but Reed could tell she had assessed the situation in one sharp glance. She then crossed the room, headed for the stove.

"I'm Kate Whittington," she said before he could introduce her. She opened the stove and added a piece of split wood from a nearby basket. Then she set the kettle full of water on the stovetop. She glanced over at Reed. "I'm Mr. Benton's . . . housekeeper."

Jonah contemplated her curiously, flashed a look at Reed, but didn't say a word. Reed introduced the Ranger and then Charm to Kate.

"Charm Riley," Jonah added her last name.

Kate acknowledged both with a polite nod.

Reed tried to read her, frustrated when he could not tell what she was thinking.

"Jonah brought Charm out here hoping Sofia could help her, but since she's gone—" He let the unspoken question linger.

"I'd be happy to do whatever I can," Kate told them.

When she immediately walked over to the corner of the table, and stood beside Charm, Reed felt his insides settle.

Then Kate looked down at Charm and gently brushed hair away from the girl's ravaged face and examined her swollen eye. He wanted to jump up and hug her when she said softly, "Can you walk, Miss Riley?"

"Yes," Charm whispered. "Of course."

It pained Reed to watch Charm talk around her split lip.

As the girl stood, Jonah shot to his feet and pulled her chair out for her. Kate stayed by her side, although she was looking at Reed when she said, "When the kettle boils, I'll need a pitcher of warm water, a basin, and some clean towels."

Jonah slipped his jacket off the girl's shoulders before the women crossed the room. Charm hesitated in the doorway as if loath to leave him.

Reed let go a pent-up sigh he hadn't even known he was holding when Jonah gave the girl a silent nod of assurance. She followed Kate out of the room.

Kate had seen the look that passed between Charm and Jonah Taylor. The captain was a good twenty years older than Charm Riley, but he gazed at her with such love and longing, such deep concern, that Kate's heart contracted just watching them.

She took Charm by the arm and led her up to Sofia's room. Then she hurried to her own room, grabbed her robe, and carried it back down the hall.

"I'll leave you alone to undress," Kate said as she handed her faded blue robe to the girl.

"Don't go!" Charm panicked but quickly calmed. "I'll need your help to get this dress off."

Kate walked over to where the girl stood uncertainly beside the bed. As gingerly as she could, Kate helped Charm slip her torn gown off her shoulders.

She was determined not to stare at Charm's deep black

lace corset, but as soon as she caught sight of the welts and bruises across the girl's shoulder blades, the scandalous cut and color of the seductive undergarment was forgotten.

Kate seethed inside, furious that anyone should suffer such a beating, let alone someone as young and defenseless as Charm.

Though no one had told Kate what Charm did to earn her keep, it was written on the girl's face, evident in the immodest cut of her red ruffled gown and the telltale black corset.

Beatings came with the occupation. There had been nights when things had gone terribly wrong for Meg Whittington, too. Occasionally a man would turn mean, furious over what her mother always said were "his own shortcomings." Afterwards, her mama would bitterly try to explain it away to Kate.

"It's my fault, Katie darlin'," she said, "for not seeing the signs. Some men aren't right in the head. I just hope to God that you don't ever have to learn that the hard way."

Kate draped Charm's ruined red gown over an overstuffed upholstered chair and then helped her slip on the robe.

There was a knock at the door. Kate answered to Scrappy standing outside, his arms full of the things she had requested. Keeping his eyes averted, he crossed the room and set the basin and water pitcher on a washstand, then laid out a pile of clean towels and rags. Kate thanked him and asked him to watch Daniel as he tried to duck out of the room.

She poured warm water into the bowl, dipped in a thick towel and twisted the excess water out. Charm still stood beside the bed.

"Sit down, Miss Riley," Kate instructed softly.

"Please, ma'am, call me Charm."

"Only if you will call me Kate."

Charm sat on the edge of the bed as Kate pressed the

rag gently against Charm's blood-encrusted lip and held it there. The girl closed her eyes. Her tears slowly leaked from beneath gold lashes.

Kate gently moved the cloth over her face, returned to the basin to rinse it out and then let Charm hold it over her swollen eye.

"Thank you, Kate."

"It's nothing."

"It's everything," Charm said with a catch in her voice. "A fine lady like you, helping the likes of me."

"Fine lady?" Kate smiled as she folded back the top sheet and bedspread.

She took up another cloth, held it against Charm's bruised back and shoulders, debating whether to tell her about her own past. She had come West to begin again, hoping no one but Reed Benton would know the truth. Now the only Benton who knew everything about her was dead, and Sofia was gone. No one knew. Her silence would keep the past secret, but looking at the lovely little blonde, able to recognize and feel the shame in her eyes, Kate knew she had to tell Charm the truth.

"My mother was a woman of the streets. We lived hand to mouth, one step ahead of starvation most of the time. I know what you are and what you do all too well, believe me."

A weak smile twisted Charm's swollen lips. "Life isn't as bad as all that at Dolly's place. We get plenty to eat."

Kate sat on the bed beside the girl, hoping to put her more at ease.

"How old are you, Charm?"

"Eighteen. I've been working at Dolly's for three years."

Kate wanted to rail at the injustice of a world that allowed a girl of fifteen to give her body to any man with enough coin. She decided then and there that she had to do all she could to rescue Charm Riley.

"How long have you known Mr. Taylor?"

"Almost since I came to Lone Star," Charm said.

"I see."

"It's not what you think, ma'am. Jonah's never been with me in that way. He's the kindest man I've ever known. He always chooses one of the others for . . . you know, but he brings me candy sometimes and once, he even gave me a pretty gold locket." Her eyes filled with tears. "The chain got broke last night, and I lost it."

"Maybe someone will find it and save it for you."

"Maybe." She looked doubtful.

"Would you change your life if you could, Charm?"

"Change my life?"

"Would you do something else?"

"I don't know how to do much else. Besides, nobody's going to marry me now. It's a little too late to think about finding a husband and having babies. Working at Dolly's is all right, I guess."

Kate wished she could argue that a husband and children weren't out of the question for Charm, but she had been entertaining the same thoughts about herself since she had slept with Reed.

Charm sighed. "It's too late."

"It's never too late." Kate was suddenly inspired with a plan. "Can you cook, Charm?"

"Sure, I can cook. My family used to own a hotel in Saint Louis. All my twelve brothers and sisters worked. I started cooking when I was tall enough to reach the stove. Why?"

"I was just thinking out loud." Kate stood, eager to go speak to Reed. "Why don't you slip into bed and try to rest for a while?"

Charm hesitated, uncertain. "I didn't plan on staying here, ma'am. Bringing me here was Jonah's idea."

"I insist." Kate was ready to argue. The girl appeared to

be on the verge of collapse. "I'll go down and tell the men that you are staying. I won't take no for an answer. You'll feel better after you get some sleep."

"It is a far sight quieter here than at the Social Club." She looked around at the unmarked paint on the walls, the glowing wood floor, the freshly laundered lace curtains. "A far sight cleaner, too. Are you and Reed engaged or anything?" Charm asked.

Or anything? Kate tried to hide her surprise.

"Absolutely not."

Charm moved the towel over her eye. "I thought maybe you were, from the way you two look at each other."

Kate was amazed by the observation. Was she that transparent? Did Reed really look at her in an admiring way?

"You're not from around here, are you, Kate?"

"No . . . that's a long story that I will tell you another time. Right now, you relax, and I'll look in on you in a bit."

Charm slipped beneath the sheet. Kate turned to go.

"Ma'am?"

"Yes?" Kate paused and smiled at Charm.

"Could you just sit with me for a spell until I fall asleep?"

19

Reed watched Jonah pace the confines of the kitchen. The Ranger paused, picked up a bread-slicing box off a sideboard, and turned the wooden object over and over in his hands.

"I'm going to hang the bastard who did this to her, Reed."

"You know who it was?"

Jonah nodded. "A drifter riding with four ruffians from Kansas. They left Dolly's sometime before dawn, but not before cleaning out her cash box. Hurt some of the other girls, too, but none of them got it as bad as Charm."

"You been carrying a torch for her for three years. Why don't you marry her?"

"Me settle down?" Jonah looked incredulous.

"Other men have done it." Reed knew what was going through Jonah's mind. The sky was their roof. The saddle their home. It would be as hard for Jonah to give up rangering as it would be for Reed.

"I'm too old for her, anyway."

"You're not forty."

"Damn right I'm not. I'm forty-two."

Reed hid his surprise. "She'd be lucky to have a good man like you."

Jonah steered the conversation back to the robbery of

Dolly Goode. "If I get back to camp before tomorrow's gone and round up a few men, we can ride after them before the trail's cold."

"I'm going to give this one more week's rest, and then I'll be back." Reed rubbed his shoulder.

Jonah eyed him carefully. "You really feel up to it?"

It still hurt, and it would pain him no matter where he was, but he was hesitant to leave so soon. At least getting out of here as quickly as he could would keep him from listening for Kate's footsteps all day, wondering what she was doing and making excuses to run into her.

"No, but I'm going, anyway. It won't do me any good to laze around getting soft."

"No worry about that. Summer's heating up, and the Comanche are getting bolder by the day. There'll be plenty to do no matter when you come back."

Trusting his friend to keep his confidence, Reed briefly told Jonah about Kate, who she was and how she had come to be there. He also told Jonah that he was fairly convinced that she was innocent of his father's scheme.

"Are you leaving so soon because you're running away from her or Daniel?" Jonah asked.

"Both, maybe."

Jonah locked his hands behind his head and stretched, contemplating. Reed sipped his coffee. Talking about going back had him thinking about the last raid, wondering if his passion for revenge hadn't cooled now that he had Daniel back. How long had it been since he had really thought about why he was fighting Comanche?

After a bit Jonah suggested, "Maybe Kate could find work in Lone Star. She's a looker. Couple days in town, and she'd probably come up with some cowboy's proposal soon enough."

Although it would get her out of his life, there was something about the idea that didn't quite sit right with Reed.

"You said she signed proxy papers. Maybe she's still legally married to you. If not, maybe she's legally your pa's widow," Jonah speculated. "Wouldn't that beat all?"

"Sofia said my father signed Reed Benton Junior. I had Scrappy stop by to see our lawyer in Lone Star, and to top it all off, my father conveniently sent him on a trip to Europe, probably to keep the man away from Kate and from finding out what he'd been up to. I'll have to wait until Jeb gets back to have him untangle everything. For now, I've hired Kate to take care of Daniel and the house. She thinks she can help him. Thinks just because she was a teacher at an orphanage back East that she can tame him."

"What do you think?"

"I think she means well, but she's got about as much chance as an icicle in hell. He'll never be the same. You know it as well as I. Lord knows, we've seen them like this often enough." Things crowded in on Reed so hard he found it difficult to breathe.

"Maybe she's right. Maybe it's not too late," Jonah said.

"Yeah. And maybe someday cows will bark. I think she's plum loco."

"You won't get me to speak unkindly of her, not after the way she didn't bat an eye when it came to helping Charm." Jonah looked up at the ceiling. "I wonder what's going on up there?"

"She likes to hover. It about drove me crazy, her fluffing pillows and shifting trays all the time I was down."

"She's a good-looking woman, Reed. You could do worse."

"That's what Sofia said, but I know by now that it isn't looks that count. I'm not looking for a wife. Besides, you know I'm not a good judge of women. I was burned once, and I don't intend to go through that again."

"Maybe this Kate is different."

> As I've never been a wife, I can't promise you that I'll be perfect, but I will certainly give my all.

Thinking of what she had written, keeping his own council, Reed hooked his arm over the back of the chair. There was no doubt in his mind that Kate was different from Becky, but that didn't mean they would suit each other. Besides, as he already told Jonah, he wasn't looking for a wife. Before he had come back here, the idea had never even entered his mind.

He was about to say that she was stubborn enough to put up with him and Daniel, and that's all he could ask for right now. Not a moment too soon, Jonah flashed him a quick warning nod and Reed held his tongue.

A second later, Kate breezed back into the room. When both men stood, she blushed and looked flustered.

Reed pulled out a chair and she sat down. "Want some coffee?" he offered, relieved just to have her there and know she had been of help to Charm.

"Why, thank you. Yes." She looked surprised by his offer.

He took down a heavy pottery mug and filled it to the brim with the thick, steaming brew. His camp specialty. Careful not to slosh it on her, he set it on the table and eased into the chair beside her.

She gave him a sideways glance from beneath her lashes; then she concentrated on Jonah. "Charm's asleep, Mr. Taylor. I have invited her to stay here and rest." Then she turned to Reed. "I hope that's all right with you."

"It is."

He had the feeling it didn't matter to her in the least what he thought, for she had already made up her mind. She was merely being polite by asking. Again, her tenacity surprised him. He would do well not to underestimate her.

Her kindness to the girl surprised him, too, until he realized it *was* possible that she might not have the vaguest idea that Charm was a whore. From all she had said so far about nuns and orphans, Kate had led a sheltered life in Maine after her mother abandoned her.

He watched her take a long sip of coffee. Her already huge eyes went wide over the rim of the cup. She swallowed, coughed, and quickly set the mug down.

"What *is* that?"

Jonah laughed.

Reed acted insulted. "It's coffee. Real coffee, not that watery excuse you've been giving me for days."

"Reed makes the best coffee around," Jonah piped up in defense.

Kate looked at them both in turn as if they had lost their minds. She pushed the cup a little farther away and said without warning, "I would like Charm to stay on indefinitely."

Both men openly stared. She focused on him.

"You said we need a cook. She can cook. I would like to offer her the position. Anything would be preferable to what she does in Lone Star."

She knew. She knew what Charm was, what she did, and yet Kate wanted her there, anyway. Reed was so stunned it took him a minute to recover.

"You think she would stay?" Jonah sounded as if the idea was too good to be true.

"I believe she would," Kate assured him. "What do you think, Reed?"

He thought perhaps there was much, much more to Kate Whittington than what he had already learned from her letters. He also realized he liked hearing her say his name. He rubbed his hand over the ache in his shoulder. "I think it's a fine idea. If you can talk her into it, you and the boy might not starve after all."

20

The kitchen grew progressively warmer as morning melted into high noon. A hot wind from the south assaulted the house, baking the grass on the gently undulating hills and valleys around it.

Kate made eggs and burned some fried potatoes for the midday meal and served them up to Reed, Jonah, and Scrappy, and then she fed Daniel. Having men around the table was nothing at all like the sedate, orderly meals served in the dining hall at Saint Perpetua's. Here the talk was loud, oftentimes boisterous. She had the feeling that if Charm had not been asleep upstairs, the men would have been even louder as they related some of the legendary jokes the Rangers played on each other in camp.

More than once she was startled when they forgot themselves and let slip a word not fit for a lady's ears, but then they apologized profusely.

The meal gave her a glimpse of how it might have been if she and Reed had met under other circumstances. As she watched his easy exchange with Jonah and Scrappy, as the men laughed and talked of times past and adventures they had shared, she saw a side of Reed that was far different from the bitter man he had been for the last few days. She wished she knew him well, wished she could forget how he purposely avoided Daniel.

Above all else, she wished she could forget that he had only made love to her because he mistook her for Becky. *I love you, wife.*

Up to her elbows in soapy dishwater, Kate remembered the way Reed had pulled her close after they made love, tucked her beside his fevered body and held her tight.

She tried to concentrate on what he was saying to Jonah.

"I ought to be able to go join you at camp in another week."

A plate slipped from her hands, hit the dishpan, and splashed water over her and the sideboard. Her heart skipped a beat. He was going back to the Rangers. Just like that, he was leaving his father's house and his son in her care without a backward glance. She had known eventually he would leave, but not so soon.

She spun around, ignoring the damp bodice of her faded gray gown, and wiped her hands on her skirt. "You're leaving in a week?"

Jonah took one look at her face and pushed back from the table. Scrappy quickly followed suit. Both of them thanked her for the meal and were out the door before Reed decided to answer.

"When will you be back?" she asked.

He shrugged. "I haven't even left yet. All you need to do is what you've been doing. Look after Daniel. Fuss with the house. Scrappy will be here. He'll get whatever supplies you need from town."

He looked as if he was going to walk out without another word, but then he paused in the door to the hallway. "Jeb Cooley is my father's lawyer. He's not in Lone Star right now, but I'll make certain that you get paid each month.

Charm, too, if she stays on as cook. Anything you want—food, clothes, whatever you need for yourself or the boy, or Charm—tell Harrison Barker at the Mercantile, and you'll have it. I'll stop and leave credit instructions with him." He looked at the damp bodice of her gown. "I mean it—don't hesitate to buy whatever you need."

Kate was too stunned to speak as he walked out into the hall. She rushed after him, caught him by the sleeve. "Reed, wait."

He frowned down at her hand. "What is it?"

She let go. "Will you be well enough to leave in a week?"

His hand went to his injured shoulder. "I'll heal no matter where I am."

"What about Daniel? Are you simply going to walk out on him? He needs you right now more than the Rangers do."

"You seem to be doing all right by him."

"But, it's not the same. I'm hired help. He needs *you*. You're his father."

Reed's expression immediately shuttered. His eyes iced over.

What terrible pain lodged in his heart kept him from wanting to be with his son after all these years? She fought to reach him. "I didn't just teach at Saint Perpetua's. I was raised at the orphanage. My mother left me there and walked out of my life. I'll never forget that night as long as I live, the emptiness I felt, the bottomless fear. I blamed myself. I thought that if I had only been better, if I hadn't gotten sick and slowed her down, that she wouldn't have done it. Don't abandon Daniel just because he's been with the Comanche. None of this was his fault."

She had hit a raw nerve. His hands curled into tight fists. He hesitated before he spoke, stood with his forehead creased in thought, his expression darkly fierce. He drew a long breath, slowly let it go. "I'm giving you leave to do with him as you see fit," he told her. "You think this is easy for me, to see him the way he is now? To know what he's been through? It's my fault he was captured that night. I left him and his mother alone in a cabin on the edge of the ranch in what had become hostile territory."

Kate waited, sensing he had more to say, stunned by his startling admission of guilt.

The wind howled across the prairie, sighed beneath the eaves of the house, breaking the strained silence, echoing his shame and deep-seated pain. He bowed his head, stared at his boots. Then he met her eyes with raw, unflinching honesty. "I don't know that Daniel's my son."

"But . . . he looks exactly like the child in the photograph."

"I don't mean that he isn't the same boy stolen from Becky and me. What I'm saying is that I don't know that the boy she gave birth to was *my* own flesh and blood."

Kate's hand went to her throat. "What?"

"The night she died, Becky told me that Daniel wasn't mine. She claimed another man fathered him."

"Oh, Reed."

Resurrected pain left an indelible brand on his features, haunted his eyes. Compelled to move closer, she stepped up to him. She tried to imagine what he must have gone through after Becky's terrible revelation. Any man would have been devastated. His only son had been taken from him by his wife's confession of adultery, then captured by Comanche raiders. The light of his life had been taken from him not once, but twice that night.

The weight of his words hung heavy on the air around them in the empty hallway. Kate wished there were something she could do or say to ease his pain. Had he been a child, she could have held him, rocked him, told him everything would be fine. But what could she possibly say that might ease his guilt and pain? Especially if he *was* guilty of leaving them to their fates.

There were no words, no answers. Without thinking, she reached for his hand, expecting him to shrug her off. As if numb to her touch, he didn't even react. She held on tight, giving him the only thing that she could give, silent understanding.

She wondered how his wife could have betrayed him, wondered with whom. "Did you know him?" Her question was hushed, barely uttered.

"Yeah. Yeah I knew him." He swallowed, stared straight at the opposite wall. "It was my father."

Reeling, Kate closed her eyes. Daniel looked like Reed, but then, Reed favored his father, too. She had mistakenly thought that his father had been the man in the photograph she had received.

"Your father?" She still couldn't believe it.

"That's what Becky claimed. After we were married, we lived here at the house. She told me they had been lovers off and on since that time. She said I wasn't half the man my father was, and that Daniel was his for certain. A few minutes later I left to go see if I could help the neighbors, but only after convincing myself that Becky and Daniel would be all right that night—but they weren't."

He was holding her hand so tight, squeezing so hard it was growing uncomfortable, but she didn't pull away.

"She shot herself outside the cabin door. I wasn't certain what happened to Daniel at first. His body wasn't there. I didn't know if Becky might have killed him to keep him from being captured. I nearly went crazy. Do you have any idea what it's like to sift through the ashes of your home looking for what might be left of a three-year-old? When I never found a trace, I started tracking the war party.

There had been four homesteads attacked that night, so the Rangers were called in to take up the chase. I joined up then and there. We never found Daniel."

"What about your father? Did you ask him if what Becky said was true?"

"Of course, but he denied it. Claimed she only said it to hurt me, to drive him and me farther apart. I told him that I thought he was capable of it and that he would have slept with her just to prove that he had been right about her in the first place. He said if it would change my mind about her that he would have. We argued. I left to join the Rangers and never saw him again."

"But you brought Daniel back to Lone Star. Why?"

"For the same reason I was so hellbent on rescuing him right after he was captured. I wanted my father to swear on Daniel's life, to tell me to my face that he never touched Becky. That there was no chance in hell Daniel was his."

He looked down, realized he was rubbing his thumb across the back of her hand. It settled him to talk to her, calmed him. She was listening to him with rapt attention. Her expression told him that she cared about what he had to say, that his story greatly disturbed her.

He paused, leaned back against the wall, empty, hollowed out by hurt and betrayal. "When I walked back into this house that day, I thought I would finally learn the truth."

"But your father was dead."

"And now I'll never know."

Her intense anger surprised him. "I'm glad he's dead. I'm glad that I never met him face-to-face. When I think of what he did to me, of how he tried to use me to lure you home, it makes me furious. After everything you just told me, I can understand how you could believe he might have fathered Daniel, and I know how much you could hate him, and me—or anyone else connected to him. But please believe me. I would *never* have agreed to such a twisted plan."

"I know. I've read your letters."

She went perfectly still.

"You *what*?"

"I read your letters. The ones you wrote to my father."

"My letters?" She tried to pull her hand away. "You read them all?"

"Sofia gave them to me before she left."

Kate was shaken to the quick.

He knows.

He knows all about my mother.

He knew about the desperation that made her begin her correspondence in the first place. Again, she tried to take her hand back, but he wouldn't let go.

"I know that's why you befriended Charm so easily, when any other woman in your position would not have and why you don't hold what she is against her," he explained. "You took to Daniel because you know better than most what he must be going through, what it feels like to be a child alone in strange surroundings."

She finally managed to wrest her hand from his grasp, but she didn't walk away. He knew all of it. He knew about her and her foolish dreams. All the reasons she had given for answering his father's advertisement. He knew her childhood fancies of a home of her own, a place she could care for and cherish. A safe haven where she had hoped to raise children. "It's not fair, you know," she said aloud.

"What's that?"

"You know all about me, but I know next to nothing except what they chose to tell me about you. I only know what your father wanted me to know."

"I just told you how it was with me and Becky. There's

not much else to tell." He rubbed the back of his neck and glanced back into the kitchen when someone knocked at the back door.

"That'd be Jonah." Reed sounded as tired as he looked.

"You need some rest. I need to see about supper."

"Kate, I'm sorry I ruffled your feathers, but—"

She held up a hand and stopped him cold. "I'd thank you not to refer to me as some sort of fowl."

Jonah knocked again. Reed stepped around her and headed for the door. "Hell, Kate. Those letters were addressed to me. I'm the one you thought you were writing to, so where's the harm?" He swung the door open.

Jonah was standing there with his hat in his hand, looking sheepish, ready to ride. "Well, I'll be going," the captain told them, glancing from one to the other. "Just in time, too."

"Bye, Jonah. I'll see you soon," Reed said.

Jonah nodded and then bobbed his head to Kate. "Adios, ma'am."

"Good-bye, Captain. It was nice to meet you. Don't worry about Charm. She'll be fine."

"No, ma'am, I sure won't. Thank you, ma'am." He told Reed good-bye and walked away.

Reed closed the door, and they were face-to-face again.

When Kate noticed the dark circles of fatigue beneath his eyes, she felt like a shrew. "Why don't you try to get some sleep before supper? This is the first time you've been up all day. I'll wake you when it's ready."

"I'm sorry about the letters. I didn't think you would mind."

"If you really thought that, you would have told me you read them before now," she said softly.

He closed the space between them until they were standing toe to toe. She caught her breath, afraid he was going to kiss her again, knowing she did not have the will to resist.

It took every ounce of waning fortitude that he had not to kiss her.

Reed found himself wishing he had ridden off with Jonah and taken himself out of temptation's way. Now he was going to have to live with it. He was going to be under the same roof with Kate for at least another week.

She was right. He had a feeling she would resent his reading her letters, which is exactly why he hadn't told her before. Reading them had made him feel like he was peering into the windows of her soul without permission. He didn't know which bothered him more, his intrusion or the look of betrayal on her face.

First his father and Sofia, now him.

"I'm sorry," he said again. He really was. "Would you like to have them back?"

"What?" she whispered, staring up into his eyes.

"Your letters."

She shrugged and sounded sad. "What does it matter now? I don't want them anymore. They'll only remind me of something I would rather forget."

She had come to Texas with stars in her eyes, and her hopes had been dashed. He felt bad enough about what happened right now to see if maybe those stars were still there, banked like embers that, with a little attention, just might flare to life.

But he wasn't a man to start something he couldn't finish, so he forced himself to step away.

"I think I'll go take that nap you suggested," he told her.

He couldn't tell if she was relieved or disappointed when he turned and walked away.

21

There were still three days left in May, but Texas nights were already so hot that Kate found it hard to sleep. She wondered how she would ever survive July and August.

She had taken refuge in her room with all her windows raised; a book of poetry she had found in the parlor bookcase rested open on her lap. About to give up and turn down the light, hoping that darkness might make the room seem cooler, she was reaching for the lamp when she heard Daniel yell.

Without taking time to grab her robe, she whipped open her bedroom door and started running down the hall. The deep flounce around the bottom of her nightgown billowed. Her long braid swayed like a pendulum against her back.

Loud, angry Comanche words echoed down the hall. She was about to rush into Daniel's room but stopped on the threshold the minute she realized that Reed was already there.

Reed, in fact, was the target of the boy's curses. Kate's hand went to her throat. Daniel had somehow gotten out of bed and managed to crawl, hop, or drag himself over to one of the open windows. He was clinging with his arms looped over the sill, half in and half out.

Reed had the tail of the boy's nightshirt in his fist and appeared willing to let Daniel vent his rage. "Go ahead and holler all you want, you're not going anywhere," Reed told the frustrated child. "I don't think you really want to fall out on your head anyway. This is all for show."

Kate's first instinct was to step in and help him calm the boy but seeing Reed finally trying to deal with his son kept her from reacting. Knowing that she was running out of time, she had tried all week to get him to sit with Daniel, to carry a meal up to him, or to read to him the way she had started to do—but Reed had either refused outright or found some excuse not to be with the boy.

Fearing Reed would see her, she stepped back into the hall and let him handle Daniel's rage, even though it appeared that his solution was to let the boy yell his lungs out. Every now and again Daniel would try to kick Reed away with his good leg while still clinging to the sill.

Charm came running down the hall half-naked with her curly hair standing out around her head. Kate took one look at the short black chemise that barely covered her breasts and at the girl's long, bare legs and was speechless.

"What's wrong?" Charm whispered, trying to peer around Kate into Daniel's room.

"It's all right," Kate whispered back. "Reed's with him."

Charm rubbed her eyes and smiled a sleepy smile. "Good. It's about time." She turned around and headed back to her room without giving the situation a second thought.

Reed waited, not so patiently, until the boy slowly quieted, then Kate saw him reach down and pick Daniel up by his waist and none-too-gently deposit him on the bed. Then he went over to the open window, closed and locked the bottom pane. With a bit of pulling and banging on the frame, he got the window to open from the top, where Daniel could not reach it.

While Reed was moving from window to window in

Daniel's room, reaching up to open them and then lock the bottom halves shut, Kate stepped farther away from the door and waited for him in the hall.

She hoped that Reed would stay and talk to Daniel now that the boy was calm again, but almost as soon as the pounding stopped, he stepped out into the hall. He closed Daniel's door and turned the key in the lock.

"Is everything all right?" Kate tried to act as if she had just come moseying down the hall.

One of his dark brows arched. She could tell that he knew very well that she would not have waited to see what was bothering her charge.

"Everything's all right now. I found Daniel hanging out of the window. He had a fit when I tried to pull him back in, so I let him get it over with. He's back in bed but not very happy about it. I opened the windows from the top so he can't climb out."

She was tempted to go in and see if Daniel was indeed settled, but she wanted Reed to have the last word this time.

Reed glanced back at the door. "We can't keep him locked up forever."

"He's changing, Reed. He really is. Slowly, but surely."

"Yeah? Well, I don't see it."

"Because you aren't with him enough. He lets me read to him. Charm sits with him and bakes him cookies, which, by the way, he loves. You would know that if you spent some time with him."

He walked down the hall to the room at the end, one that had been his father's office. She followed him, bound and determined not to let him ignore her this time. As he strode inside, Kate lingered in the doorway, watched him walk over to the massive wooden desk that shared stacks of papers and receipts with a fine crystal cigar humidor and a matching inkwell. A sterling letter opener lay amid the clutter.

She had come in once to dust, taken one look at the desk, and decided not to disturb anything and closed the door. Reed walked over to a tea cart beneath the window, where a collection of crystal decanters was gathered along with an array of glasses. He picked up a bottle of amber liquid, carefully laid the top aside, and poured himself half a tumbler full.

Kate watched him as he raised the glass to his lips and took a sip. He was still dressed, and from the looks of it, he had been seated in the deep leather chair, working at the desk earlier. He wore his hair long enough to tease his shirt collar. It was neatly trimmed, thick and dark. She found herself taking in every detail, from his height to his confident stance to the way his strong hand dwarfed the crystal tumbler.

Over the past week they had trodden carefully around each other. Over time she had grown used to being near him, used to the differences of living with a man as opposed to a houseful of women.

His footsteps were always loud and firm, filling the house with sound whenever he was about. His temper was mercurial. While recovering from his wounds, he spent his time lost in deep thought, his mind taking him places he was not willing to discuss.

Except for the attempts she had made at bringing him closer to Daniel, she had left him pretty much alone, but she was ever aware of where he was and what he was doing, whether he was here in the office or out in the corral with Scrappy.

"How did you know he was trying to escape?" she asked, still hovering in the doorway.

Reed turned with a startled look on his face, as if he had forgotten she was still there. Then he looked down into his drink as if the answer might be there. "I went to look in on him."

"I'm glad." Knowing he had made the effort lightened her heart.

He walked closer. "I've gone in to see him every night after he's fallen asleep."

"Thank goodness you were there tonight."

"I meant what I said, Kate. You can't keep him locked up in there forever."

"I don't intend to. In fact, I think we should try taking him downstairs tomorrow. He's been here almost two weeks. If it was you or I, we might have tried to jump out of the window by now, too."

He actually smiled.

"What are you thinking?" she asked.

"That I'd like to see you climbing over that window ledge in your nightgown."

She gasped and looked down, felt herself grow hot with embarrassment, and crossed her arms over her breasts even though the gown was not transparent.

A modest, serviceable nightgown is a girl's best friend.

Mother Superior had made certain every girl had two.

"I don't think you need to worry about your modesty in that thing, Kate. You're covered from neck to toe."

"But . . . it's my *night*gown," she whispered, appalled at herself. Mother Superior's hair would be standing out around her head if she could see her now.

"I've seen women in *dresses* that show more than that thing shows. Some women sleep in a lot less." He tossed back the rest of the drink and set the glass down on the desk.

She thought of Charm and blushed again.

"Before I went to see about Daniel, I was looking through my father's papers for a copy of the forged marriage document."

"Did you find one?"

"No. I'm sure that his lawyer must have one, but Jeb's out of the country. I'll make certain that as soon as he's back, he'll start clearing things up."

And then the marriage, even if it is false, will be over.

She was not fooling herself. There was nothing to bind them to each other now save a night of lovemaking that he could not recall and a stolen kiss, and yet, at times she found herself hoping that there could be more between them, wishing that he would stay and not go back to the Rangers.

Her gaze dropped to a nearby book stand where a small daguerreotype stood upon a stack of receipts. A woman's face stared up at her. It wasn't Becky's. The woman was thin, almost gaunt, with light eyes that gave her a ghostly look in the picture.

"Is that your mother?" she guessed.

He nodded. "Her name was Virginia. She was from Georgia."

She had learned as much from his father's letters, but since Reed was opening up at last, she let him talk.

"She died when I was thirteen."

"Was she ill?"

He shook his head. "Not that I could see. I blame my father for her death."

She realized then that the burden of hatred he carried for his father was a far heavier one than she had first thought, that their troubles started before he met Becky. It was far too heavy a load to tote around now that the man was dead.

He continued without her having to question him. "She

hated Texas. She was spoiled, a planter's daughter who always had everything she ever wanted. My father, when they met, was quite poor. Her family thought she married beneath them and told him so. Later, my father loved to tell folks how after the War, her family lost everything and how he had become one of the richest men in Texas."

"But if you were only thirteen at the time, then she died well before the War."

"Thankfully, she died without knowing what happened to her family. She had four brothers, all strapping Irishmen— that's what she liked to call them. I tried to write to them after the War, but I learned they were killed fighting for the Confederacy." He shook his head, his mouth in a grim line. "I'm glad she didn't live to see it."

She leaned back against the doorjamb, content to let him talk, wanting to know more about him, about his life.

"She knew my father was making a place for himself here, so she never insisted that he take her back to Georgia, 'back to the home place,' as she called it. She had wanted 'a passel' of children, but she wasn't a strong woman. She only had me.

"My father was devoted to one thing in his life, and that was Lone Star. When she finally came to realize that, it broke her spirit. She told me once that her love for me was the only thing that kept her alive. Eventually, she developed what my father called 'female trouble.' She was sad most of the time, real quiet. There was no one in town she ever considered on her social level, so she had no close friends. She spent a lot of time alone, staring out at the prairie. One morning she up and disappeared. Later one of the men found her hanging in the back of the barn."

"Oh, Reed." She didn't know what else to say. He had lost the two women most important to him to suicide.

"Unfortunately, she had done a poor job of trying to kill

herself, and she lingered for a day in agony. Her last wish was to be buried in Georgia."

"Was she?"

"Of course not. My father buried her out by the old dog run where they first lived when they moved here."

The old cabin that Reed had loved before the Comanche burned it to the ground. The very place he had later moved to with his wife and Daniel.

Kate realized then that he had a sentimental side after all and that he had suffered from more than guilt because of Becky's loss and betrayal. His mother had left him, too.

She looked up, found him watching her closely.

"I don't usually talk about her," he said.

He walked over to the desk, stared down at the papers lying there, but she could tell that he was not concentrating on them.

"Is there much work here?" She indicated the desk.

He shook his head. "No. Not until Jeb gets back from Europe. I'm content to let things go on just as they did before and let the foremen run the ranch."

"Surely there will come a time when you'll need to be here to take care of things."

He shook his head, drowning the spark of hope that he might stay and take over.

"I can't stay here, Kate."

"I understand why you would feel that way, but—"

"You still don't think I should leave."

"Your father's gone, but Daniel's back. He's just a child. A little boy who needs a home and a family. He is either your son . . . or your half brother—"

"Don't." He held up his hand.

But Kate refused to be ignored. The boy's welfare, his future were dependent on his relationship with this man. If she was going to do all she could for Daniel, she needed

Reed's help. "You can't turn your back on him. He's family, one way or another."

"You don't want to take care of him now, is that it?"

"That's not it at all. I'll stay as long as he needs me, but he's *your* responsibility. He is the innocent one in all of this. He's still the little boy you thought of as yours for three years, the boy you called your son until Becky put doubt in your mind. Can't you find it in your heart to love him again?"

Her challenge went unanswered. Reed ran his hand over the back of his neck, wiped the sweat off his brow with his shirt cuff. The room was stifling, the night air still as death.

"I'm leaving day after tomorrow," he said with finality.

How could she ever bring him and Daniel together if he left?

"If anything comes up, Scrappy knows where we'll be camped for the summer."

The summer. The whole summer.

"This isn't going to help things between you and Daniel. You'll have to start over with him when you come back."

She could see by the look on his face that he had no intention of coming back. If he did, it certainly wasn't any time soon.

"He hates me for what I am. I was there at the raid on the Comanche encampment."

"Why keep him here if you don't want him? Why not let him go back to the Comanche? Obviously, he had people who cared for him there. People he loved." She was pushing too hard, and she knew it, but there was no time left.

"Don't think I haven't been asking myself that same question, Kate, but I know if I send him back that sooner or later he's likely to resist and be killed. I won't condemn him to that. In a while we'll have ended their way of life completely. Those that aren't killed outright will be left to die on reservations. At least here, Daniel will have a chance to survive."

"Raised by a housekeeper? Ignored by his father?"

"But, I may *not* be his father, damn it."

She shook her head, sorry for him, sorry for the burden of hate he carried. "But what if you are?" she whispered. "Do you really think that he can survive without love?"

He crossed the room until he was close enough to touch her. He stared down into her eyes for a long, silent stretch of heartbeats. Then he said softly, "I've lived without it for years."

22

His last day at Lone Star, Reed realized that he should have left without telling Kate. The woman was bound and determined to celebrate.

"We're planning a special supper for you," she announced that morning over coffee.

He was still half asleep. It was the time of day he usually liked to be alone with his thoughts, but with Kate around, that was impossible. "Don't go to any trouble on my account," he mumbled.

Charm, who was rolling out pie dough across the room, turned around. The crestfallen look on her face had him backtracking.

"Whatever you're planning will be fine." He shoved his face back into the coffee cup.

"We'll be eating in the dining room." Kate went on as if he hadn't objected. She already had her mind made up about how things were going to be.

They had been eating all their meals in the kitchen, and that was all right by him. There he wasn't reminded of the times he and Becky lived here and the way his father liked to reign over the long dining table. The way the old man would entertain Becky and Sofia with every detail of his latest business coup.

"I've got some things to do today." He made his announcement before Kate could work herself up and start in about wanting him to spend time with Daniel.

It was clear the boy hated him. For his part, Reed hadn't a clue as to how to make things any different. He had just about convinced himself that leaving the boy alone with Kate might help calm him down.

"We've planned supper for two." Kate had opened the back door and was standing there with a broom, ready to sweep the veranda.

"I'll be out in the barn if you need me," he said.

He hid all day, spent the time with Scrappy, working the thoroughbreds, realizing they were all his now, as was all the rest of it. At one point he found himself staring at the house, wondering if he could ever feel content living there. Just then, Kate had walked out the back door, her steps clipped and determined as she hurried around the house carrying the laundry basket to the clothesline.

Despite the deception that brought her here, she seemed content, a part of the household, perhaps because she truly seemed devoted to Daniel's care. Her mind held no dark memories of this place.

He found himself thinking that fate was fickle and he was lucky she was here. Leaving the boy with someone else might not have been as easy.

He avoided the flurry of activity in the house as much as possible. He went in once to get his spurs and found Kate sweating over an ironing board, pressing the wrinkles out of a starched linen tablecloth. Charm was bustling back and forth to the stove. The heat it emitted made the already overly warm kitchen nearly unbearable, but the heavenly aroma of a huge pot roast and onions mingled with the mouthwatering smell of warm fresh bread.

Another time he went back for some water and was

treated to the sight of Kate standing on a chair, reaching for the good china on a high shelf in the kitchen pantry. He was there a spell without her knowing, admiring her trim waist and the tempting swell of her hips, all the while trying to convince himself that it was only what any red-blooded man would do and that he wasn't attracted to Kate.

His life was too unsettled to complicate it any more. Just because he liked looking at her didn't mean that things between them would ever go any further.

She glanced over her shoulder, caught him staring, and nearly lost her balance. He stepped up and made a grab for her, meaning to steady her until she found her footing, but wound up bracing his hand beneath her derriere. She blushed beet red. He quickly gave her a slight shove that put her feet back square on the chair seat.

"Can I help?"

Kate turned around and stared at the china in the cabinet. "Thank you, that would be nice." She didn't move.

"You'll have to let me help you down."

He heard her sigh. When she turned around and held out her hand, she was still blushing.

"I didn't do that on purpose, Kate."

"I know."

"Then what's wrong?"

"Nothing."

He knew damn well when a woman said there was nothing wrong that she definitely had a bee in her bonnet, but he wasn't about to go down that road. They switched places.

"Which plates do you want?"

"Four of everything. Plates, cups, saucers, salads, bread and butters."

He hadn't seen the china in years. Tiny dogwood flowers stood out against an ivory background. The scalloped edges were trimmed in gold. The fragile legacy had been his mother's, given to her on her wedding day by her mother. Reed Senior had offered it to Becky one night at dinner, but she shook her head and refused.

"I want to choose a set of my own." Reed could still remember the way she said the words, the hard edge to her voice. She tossed him a look and added, "*If* we ever get to move out of that old cabin and live in a decent place like this."

"Reed?" Kate's voice brought him back. He had been staring down at the bread and butter plates in his hand. When he gave them to Kate he noticed how carefully she held them, as if they were a precious treasure.

"Those were my mother's," he told her as he stepped down off the chair.

"That makes them twice as special. They're very beautiful." She cradled the pieces in her arms, waiting to set them out on the dining table with the others she'd already put there. "The dishes we had at the orphanage were plain white and so thick that they almost never broke, even when one of the girls dropped them."

She looked away, busied herself at the long dining table covered with the freshly ironed linen cloth. At each place there was a pressed and folded napkin.

"Is that all you need?"

"That's all," she told him without looking back him. "Thank you."

He hurried off to the barn, eager to get back to the horses. At least they were predictable, and if he accidently touched one on the behind, it didn't get out of sorts.

Kate listened to the fading sound of his footsteps as Reed went out through the kitchen. She couldn't bear the thought of him leaving in the morning, and not just because of Daniel.

She was beginning to know him as something other than a Texas Ranger, or Reed Senior's son. She understood why it was so hard for him to accept Daniel, and she knew what doubt and pain plagued him.

Since he had opened up about the past, she had discovered a gentler soul and a wounded heart beneath his hard exterior. Despite his discomfort around Daniel, he was a man worthy of love who believed he didn't need it because he was afraid of the hurt it would bring.

She would be a fool to deny her growing attraction to him. Perhaps because of her memory of the night they made love, perhaps because she was getting to know him better, whatever the reason, she knew it wouldn't be hard to love him. Not hard at all.

Reed thought she would be happy that he had dressed for dinner. He had found an old white shirt of his in the upstairs wardrobe that still fit. When he went downstairs a few minutes before five, Kate started to greet him, paused, and then, embarrassed, glanced down at one of three faded, worn gowns he had seen her in many times. This one was a particularly drab brown, the color of dried mud.

Suddenly, he realized that neither she nor Charm had anything nicer to wear than what he had already seen them in. Charm's gown was not only mended, but she had altered it by sewing what looked like a plain white kerchief across the low-cut bodice to cover her cleavage.

Trying to put Kate at ease, he said, "I decided that since you two have worked so hard on supper that I'd clean up a bit."

"You look . . . wonderful," she said, smiling up at him.

Her compliment didn't make him feel much better so he added, "You be sure and send Scrappy into town for whatever it is you'll need for some new outfits for you and Charm."

Too late, he realized he had put his foot in his mouth again. Kate primly folded her hands and continued to smile uncomfortably.

His shirt collar was suddenly too tight, so he stuck his finger between it and his neck and tugged. "When do we eat?" He glanced toward the dining room.

"As soon as we bring Daniel down."

"Daniel is eating with us?"

"It's your going-away dinner. He should be here."

"He has no idea what kind of a dinner it is. You told me two days ago that he was finally doing better just eating off a tray."

"Which is why I think including him is a good idea. The higher our expectations, the more he will achieve."

Reed shook his head. "That approach didn't work for my father where I was concerned."

She ignored him and headed for the stairs. "I'd appreciate your help. He can't walk on his own, and I certainly can't carry him very far."

He could tell by the look on her face that arguing would get him nowhere. Without another word, he walked past her and headed up the stairs.

Daniel proved to be more cooperative than Reed had guessed. Kate signed as if she was eating, pointed down and told him that they were taking him downstairs to eat. The boy was listening in earnest. Reed could only guess what he was really thinking. Kate reached for Daniel's hand and held it, smiling encouragement as Reed picked him up.

The child stiffened but let Reed carry him downstairs.

Kate opened the dining-room door with a flourish, and Charm was standing beside the table expectantly, obviously ready to serve. She couldn't hide her excitement. By candlelight, the remnants of the bruises on her face were barely visible.

The room had been transformed, not only with candles glowing in the brightly polished silver candelabra, but by a huge bouquet of Texas wildflowers that stood in a tall crystal vase on the sideboard.

Both women seemed to be expecting something. He looked from one to the other.

"It looks real good in here. Real pretty."

He set Daniel on a chair. Once it appeared he was going to stay put, Reed quickly took both the fork and knife from the boy's place setting and handed them to Kate.

"My expectations still aren't high enough to let him have any sharp objects," he said.

The plates were soon filled with succulent Lone Star beef and potatoes smothered in gravy, carrots with butter and cinnamon, and plenty of onions. Despite all the compliments Reed lavished on her, Charm was nervous as she set the meal down in front of him. Daniel started to reach for his plate, but Kate held up her hand and shook her head no.

"Reed, you are closer than I. Will you hand him his spoon?"

Reed did. Daniel held it clenched in his fist like a spear.

"I think we should say grace," Kate announced.

Charm looked uncomfortable. Reed's stomach growled.

Daniel tossed the spoon on the floor, grabbed the thick slice of pot roast off his plate and began to gnaw at it.

Reed started to come up out of his chair, but Kate laid her hand on his arm. He slowly sat back down. By now, gravy was smeared all over both Daniel and the formerly pristine tablecloth.

Charm's eyes were huge; Kate folded her hands and bowed her head. Despite the smacking sounds Daniel made as he stuffed and chewed and tore at the pot roast dripping in his hands, Kate said grace as if his behavior were nothing out of the ordinary.

Then she raised her head, sweetly smiled at Reed, carefully lifted her fork, and said, "Shall we begin?"

Reed began to doubt not only her methods with Daniel, but her sanity.

23

After Reed left, it was the land that slowly seduced Kate with its ever-changing, endless sky and supple golden grass dancing on the wind. Cloud shadows rolled across the land. Summer showers would surprise them with lightning and thunder and move on. Rainbows arched across the sky, shimmering prisms that echoed all the colors of the wildflowers blooming in mass profusion.

She spent at least an hour a day walking outside with Daniel, and sometimes, when her work was through, she was tempted back outside to sit on the veranda alone, to think about Reed and the impossible situation she was in.

What of him? Could he ever trust her or any other woman after what Becky had done to him?

Even though he was gone for now, she still had her mind set on bringing Daniel and him together somehow. Did it really matter anymore if Daniel was Reed's son or his father's? Reed Senior was dead. The boy was a Benton. He belonged here on Lone Star, on this land. Maybe Reed wanted to turn his back on his father's legacy, but the least he could do was see it survive for Daniel.

In the passing weeks, Kate, Charm, and Daniel melded into a family of sorts, not the kind Kate had imagined on her way West, but they gradually settled into a whole.

Neither Kate nor Charm ever talked about the impermanence of their situation, because it was so tenuous. Kate tried not to dwell on the future. Instead she awoke to each new day content with the routine of life they had established.

The big white house seemed to settle more comfortably around them, embracing them all.

Charm's considerable homemaking talents lent themselves to making the place a home. Not only was she a talented cook, but she proved to be a creditable seamstress, too. Kate took Reed at his word about funds and sent Scrappy to Lone Star to buy fabric. Since she had no idea whether Charm would actually succeed, she told him to purchase an inexpensive bolt of white muslin.

Instead, he had returned with yards and yards of robin's egg blue silk and a bolt of colorful calico, insisting that was what Reed would have wanted him to buy. "No sense in you ladies looking like inmates in an asylum," he had said.

When she wasn't baking or putting meals together, Charm would disappear into Sofia's room with paper and scissors and thread. Within a week she had completed a modest gown for herself and then set to work on one for Kate.

Even Daniel benefited from Charm's enthusiasm. She was all smiles the day she proudly presented him with a long-sleeved blue silk shirt that matched their gowns. Soon he had one of calico, too.

Charm healed faster than Daniel. Early on, Kate had explained to her how she came to be at the ranch. Then, one day while peeling carrots for dinner, Charm asked a personal question.

"Have you ever kissed Reed?"

Kate blushed, giving herself away.

"You have!" Charm laughed.

Kate shook her head thinking, *if she only knew.*

"He kissed me."

"Did you like it?"

Setting the paring knife down, Kate sighed. "Actually, I was frightened."

"Of Reed? He seems like a real good man. Jonah always speaks highly of him."

"No, not of Reed. Of myself. I . . . I'm afraid I could very easily lose control of my emotions and let things . . . go too far."

She could never explain everything to Charm. She would die of embarrassment.

"When he gets back, let him know you are interested. Surely you must know what it takes to seduce a man," Charm said.

Nothing her mother had done had anything to do with seduction. It hadn't been like that in the dingy old shack. She was visited by sailors and fishermen with fistfuls of coins who wanted relief, pure and simple. There was nothing magical or seductive about it.

"I didn't learn anything from my mother," she admitted, picking up the knife again and turning her attention to the carrots. "I wouldn't even know where to begin."

"When you're ready, I'll tell you everything I know."

Kate wasn't certain she would survive the telling.

Although she spent hours reading to Daniel, talking to him, naming objects from around the house, day after day he disappeared further inside himself.

Scrappy came to the rescue and surprised Kate when he knocked at the back door one morning and handed her a crutch made of a long willow branch padded with ticking on top.

"Thought we ought to get that boy up and walking," he said by way of explanation.

Kate noted the care the cowhand had taken with the crutch. It was sanded smooth, polished to a high shine.

"You've quite a talent as a woodworker, Mr. Parks. This is not only useful, it's lovely."

"If it's too long, I can cut it down," he said, looking everywhere but at her. "If you think it'll be all right to give it to him, that is."

His sudden shyness moved her to smile and ask him to come up with her to Daniel's room and give it to the boy himself.

"I'm worried about him," she admitted as they walked upstairs together. "He's grown so pale and listless. He eats, but not really enough for a growing boy. I know he's desperately unhappy, but I have no idea how to help him."

"He's not used to bein' inside. I thought if he could learn to use the crutch, at least then he could move around some, maybe get outside."

"Reed told me he would try to run away the first chance he got."

"I'll help you keep an eye on him."

Kate had paused outside Daniel's room, handed the crutch back to him so Scrappy could give it to the boy. Over the past few weeks he had volunteered to sit and watch Daniel whenever she had work to do. She had come to realize Scrappy Parks's grousing and grumbling hid a soft heart.

"I'm glad you've set aside your feelings of animosity toward him, Mr. Parks." She wished Reed would have stayed and devoted as much time to the boy.

"Well, ma'am, I can't help but think of the old days whenever I look at him. They lived here for a time, you know, Reed Junior and Becky and little Dan'el. Used to carry him around on my shoulders when he was a little 'un."

They showed Daniel the crutch. First Scrappy and then

Kate demonstrated how to use it. Although Daniel gave no outward indication that he understood, his eyes lit up, and he straightened away from the pillows.

It wasn't until Scrappy actually handed the boy the crutch and Daniel held it in both hands across him like a weapon that Kate realized they may have underestimated him. She and Scrappy stepped back, and after a tense moment or two, Daniel laid the crutch on the bed beside him and scooted over to the edge. Then he eased himself to the floor onto his good foot and placed the padded top beneath his arm.

He teetered at first, shoved aside Kate's hand when she reached out to steady him. Trying to work the crutch, he frowned in fierce concentration. He was the image of Reed as he slowly negotiated the empty floor space around the bed. Within minutes, he was moving about with ease.

"I don't know if this is such a good idea." Scrappy shook his head as the boy hobbled faster and faster around the room.

"Oh, but just look at his face. It's the first time I've seen him smile," Kate laughed, relieved. "Of course, we'll have to be vigilant now that he's up and moving, but that smile is worth the extra effort, don't you think?"

Scrappy did not look very sure at all.

With Soft Grass Hands close beside him, Daniel lay on the ground relishing the warmth of the sun on his face. Until a few days ago, he thought his spirit would leave him if he did not get out of the prison where they kept him. Then Hairy Face had brought him the walking stick and given him back a piece of his freedom.

They let him go outside with Soft Grass Hands who would sit beside him with a faraway look in her eyes as she was doing now, staring across the land in wonder, touching the flowers, running her hands over the grass. She seemed to be amazed by everything he pointed out to her. Natural, everyday things that she would never have seen if it hadn't been for him.

Slowly he sat up and watched the ground to the right of them. The woman turned, waiting expectantly. He patiently pointed until she squinted and finally saw a fat badger that had poked its striped gray head out of a hole in freshly dug earth.

When she smiled in surprise, he felt a swell of pride. Silly woman. She would never have known the badger was so close by without him.

It could have been a rattlesnake, or a stealthy coyote. Soft Grass Hands would not survive more than a few days on the prairie alone.

He had never seen such a lazy or talkative woman in his life. His true mother, his Comanche mother, was always busy from dawn to dusk, scraping hides, carrying water, cooking, making clothing. Thinking of her now, wondering if she was dead or alive, choked him with sadness.

He looked over at Soft Grass Hands. The delicate white woman seemed to have no responsibility other than to spend her days sitting with him. Sometimes she would point and name useless things around the house but he ignored her, refusing to learn the white man's words. He would not need them where he was going.

Other times, she stared at tiny marks on papers bound together, talking and talking. But the best part of the day came when she would set aside the bound pages and smile. Then they would go outside to walk the land as they were doing now.

While she watched huge white clouds float across the

blue sky, he slyly studied the Tejano buildings where the horses were kept.

Soon, he promised himself. Very soon he would be strong enough to slip out alone, steal one of the many fine horses, maybe even two or three, and ride back to the Comancheria in triumph.

The woman beside him said something and then sighed softly before she stood up and shook the folds of her brown dress. It was time to go back.

That she might be hurt if she was alone on one of her walks after he left should not have been his concern. But as they walked back to the big dwelling together, he found himself thinking of all the dangers that might befall her once he was gone. Though he tried not to let them do so, the thoughts made him sad.

Encouraged by the way she and Daniel could communicate without words, Kate walked slowly beside him as they made their way back to the house. When they had almost reached the back door, Charm stepped outside, taking care to close the door without letting it bang.

She wiped her hands on an apron as she hurried over to Kate.

"What is it?" Kate could tell by the girl's face that something was definitely wrong.

Charm kept her voice low. "We've got callers. Scrappy's got them out on the front porch. They're asking to see Daniel."

Kate shot a sideways glance at the boy. Although his attention was focused on the stable, she could tell by the way he had stiffened at the sound of his name that he knew they were talking about him.

"Who are they? Where are they from?"

"Their name is Greene. From what I heard, I think they were Reed's wife's parents."

Reed's wife.

Was it just a few weeks ago that she had thought of herself as his wife? That she had washed his fevered body and dreamed of the day he would recover and their life together would begin?

"Kate?" Charm had touched her arm, calling her back.

"Yes, I'm sorry. Reed's wife. Becky."

"They heard Daniel has been found and want to see him."

"Scrappy's with them on the veranda?"

Charm nodded. "He saw them drive up and stopped them right there. Told me to find you quick. He didn't have to say it, but I could tell he's not pleased to see them."

Kate turned to the boy, reached out, and touched the sleeve of his new blue shirt. He remained silent as always.

"Come with me." She crooked her finger. Then she turned to Charm. "Put on some coffee and slice some of that wonderful chocolate cake you made yesterday. Daniel's grandparents have every right to see him."

Charm hurried away. Kate matched her steps to Daniel's slow uneven ones as he hobbled along with his crutch.

She imagined the imminent reunion. How thrilled the Greenes must have been when they received word that he had been found.

As they crossed the yard in back of the house, she realized how much a part of her life Daniel had become in so short a time. She devoted hours of the day to him, trying to teach him English, trying to get him to respond. But he was more at home on the land. That was evident in the way he sniffed the air, listened to the wind and the birds, and drank in the sunshine. There was so much he could teach her if only they could communicate in words. So much she would miss if he were not here, but she told herself to be happy that he had blood relations.

These people, the Greenes, had as much right to the boy as Reed. If they wanted him, if they would love and cherish him, then despite her own feelings, it would be best for Daniel to be with them.

Again, she looked at the child walking beside her. His long dark hair swayed with every uneven step. He had gained weight since Charm began plying him with delicious sweets, but he was still small, so vulnerable and so stubborn.

But he *was* making progress. Even Reed, if he were to return today would see it, but there was so much further to go.

You have no real claim to him.

This is what you wanted for Daniel.

Kinfolk. Blood relations who care about him.

Family to love him.

Even after so short a time, it hurt to think that she might no longer be a part of his life.

24

Gideon and Winifred Greene were self-proclaimed God-
fearing folk who had immigrated to Texas from Illinois.
Even in the heat of summer they wore black wool from
throat to toe; the couple finished each other's sentences
and addressed each other as Ma and Pa. They sat ramrod
straight on the edge of the settee in the Benton parlor as if
relaxing might seduce them to sin.

The frontier had eroded a mass of lines and creases on
Winifred's long, thin face. Her hands were hard and callused on her palms, the backs spattered with noticeable
brown spots. Gideon still had a head full of white hair and
sported a narrow, carefully trimmed white beard that outlined his firm jaw. His thin lips were set in a harsh line that
gave him the appearance of a man who had forgotten how
to smile long ago.

After witnessing their initial encounter with Daniel,
while they stood a good six feet away from him, staring,
without even trying to disguise their shock and disapproval
or touching him at all, Kate took an immediate dislike
to them.

"We heard the news from a tinker traveling close to
Willowbrook that Daniel was rescued." Gideon Greene

balanced a good china teacup in a saucer on his bony knees and looked straight into Kate's eyes without blinking once.

"We live two days' ride from here. We're staying with some friends not far away. Nobody from Lone Star saw fit to tell us about Daniel or—"

"To invite us to Reed Senior's funeral," Winifred finished. She had refused cake altogether but was on her third cup of coffee.

Kate wondered why Sofia had not contacted them.

"As I was saying," Gideon cleared his throat, "we see the boy's return as our God-given chance to make up for failing with Rebecca, who—"

"Was always a willful, headstrong girl," Winifred went on. "Wild at heart, that one. Pa here couldn't even beat the stubbornness out of her."

"I never spared the rod, that's for certain," Gideon added.

Charm, uncomfortable joining them in the first place, was there at Kate's insistence. She made an abrupt excuse to go back to the kitchen, and Kate enviously watched her leave.

Mother Superior had always been stern but fair. As far as sparing the rod, the only physical punishment any student endured was a slap on the hands with a wooden stick.

Kate had the distinct feeling the Greenes' form of discipline went far beyond hand-slapping. She glanced over at Daniel, who fidgeted uncomfortably at a side table, swinging his legs back and forth beneath the chair.

He had eaten a piece of cake with his hands. There were crumbs on the table, his lap, and the floor, not to mention a smear of white frosting down the front of his silk shirt.

Kate smiled at him reassuringly, but if he noticed, he did not let on as he watched the Greenes through slitted eyes.

Winifred helped herself to more coffee. "Did we mention we came to Texas in 'thirty-six?"

"Three times." Kate smiled politely and took another sip.

"We knew the Parkers. Elder John Parker and his family. They were from Illinois, too. Baptists."

"She might not have heard of them, Ma, if she's not from around here." Gideon's head jutted out on his neck like a strutting hen.

"Actually, I'm from Ma—"

"Everybody's heard of the Parkers," Winifred said. "Their fort down on the Navasota River was raided in the spring of 'thirty-six. Some of the men were killed, two of the women and three children were carried off by the Comanches. Those poor women were beaten and raped time and time again. Why, Rachel Parker—she married into the Plummers, you know—she lived long enough to be rescued and tell the tale. Saw her babe strangled and dragged behind a horse. I tell you, the very devil rides the plains in the guise of those heathens." Slowly, Winifred looked over at Daniel.

Gideon turned his way, too. "There's evil in that boy's eyes. I can see it. Can't you, Ma?"

"I do, Pa. The devil will be hard to drive out of him, that's for certain, but with God's help it will be done."

Gideon carefully set his cup and saucer down and nodded to Kate as he stood. "Thank you for the coffee, ma'am. But if it's all the same to you, we'd best be going. We've a long way to go."

"Maybe I can help you get the boy's things together?" Winifred followed suit, putting aside her own cup and saucer.

Kate, still thinking about poor Rachel Plummer and the devil being beaten out of Daniel, nearly dropped her cup before she set it beside the china coffeepot and delicate cake plates piled on a tray. "His things?" Kate found Winifred waiting for a response.

"We'll be taking him back to our place, of course." Winifred turned to Gideon, who nodded in agreement.

"That's right. The sooner the better," he said.

Kate quickly grasped at the only straw available. "I can't let Daniel leave without Reed's permission."

"If Reed Benton cared about that boy, he would be here now, wouldn't he? If he'd been with Becky that night, if he had protected his family, our girl would still be alive, wouldn't she?" There was no sorrow or loss in Winifred's tone, only condemnation.

"He's still Daniel's father," Kate said. She had no idea if the Greenes knew anything of their daughter's professed adultery with Reed Senior.

Gideon grew red around the collar. "We know Reed's off in the Frontier Forces, or whatever the Yankee government is calling our Rangers this year. If he cared about the boy, he'd be here," he said.

"Besides, this isn't any of your concern at all, is it? You're only the housekeeper here." Winifred looked down her nose at Kate.

Kate's mind was racing. She saw herself having to barricade the door to keep the Greenes from taking Daniel and knew she would do it if forced. As if he sensed her fear, Daniel slowly edged off the chair, balanced on his good leg, and adjusted his crutch. Then he skirted the settee, slowly making his way toward her. His eyes were huge pools of worry. The crutch thumped along beside him.

He had suffered enough in his young life. Far too much to have to bear adjusting to yet another home. Far too much to have to face life with people as stern as the Greenes.

"I'm afraid you are mistaken about my position here." Kate drew herself up, refusing to give in to them. "I am not just a housekeeper. I'm Reed Benton's wife."

Winifred and Gideon couldn't have been more shocked if Kate had shot a gun off in the room.

"What do you mean, you're Reed's *wife*?"

Only Scrappy and Charm, and perhaps by now, Reed's lawyer, knew about Reed Senior's duplicity, which still would not help, for they all knew the marriage was a sham. She needed someone these people would believe.

"Ask Reverend Preston Marshall in Lone Star." She prayed they would do no such thing, not until she could speak to the man herself.

"Lone Star is a hellhole. A cow town where liquor runs in the streets and fornication spreads the devil's pox." Gideon shook his finger at the ceiling.

Winifred sniffed and crossed her arms beneath her bosom. "I say we take the boy now. If Reed wants him, then he can come and get him. He knows where we live."

Before Kate could say a word, Gideon grabbed Daniel's arm as the boy limped by.

The crutch clattered to the floor, knocking a milk glass plate off a side table. The piece shattered with a resounding crash.

At the same time, Daniel let out a bloodcurdling yell a second before he sank his teeth into Gideon Greene's wrist. The man howled in pain, raised his free arm, and smacked Daniel away as if the boy were a vicious dog.

Daniel hit the floor and pitifully began to scoot toward Kate's skirt, dragging his injured leg. She nearly stepped on him in her attempt to shield him.

"Oh, Pa! You're bleedin' like a stuck pig!" Winifred cried, rushing to her husband's side.

The front door banged open. Spurs chimed as Scrappy rushed into the room brandishing a pistol.

He had no sooner barged in than Charm burst in from the hallway wielding the heavy wooden beetle she used to pound meat. Daniel grabbed hold of a chair to help himself to his feet. Half hidden behind Kate, he clung to her skirt, trembling.

"I would thank you both to leave. Now." Kate spoke with as much dignity and confidence as she could muster. "I refuse to let you take Daniel anywhere until I have a chance to speak to Reed. Scrappy will see you to your buggy."

Thankfully, the Greenes did not care to argue with an armed man. "Don't think we won't be back." Winifred Greene had not budged, although Gideon had already started for the door with his hand pressed to his bleeding wrist.

"Come on, Ma." The white cuff of Gideon's shirtsleeve was tainted with a widening bloodstain. As he passed by, he glared at Daniel. "We had best get home and pray on this. He's not only turned Comanche, he's Becky's boy. Maybe he's as rock-headed as she was, bless her soul. Maybe he's already too far gone to save."

Shaken, Kate felt her lips tremble when she smiled her thanks to Scrappy. The old cowhand acknowledged her with a nod and followed the Greenes out the front door.

Charm rushed to Kate's side and set the heavy beetle down on the settee. With her hands on her thighs, she bent over and peered around Kate at Daniel.

"You can come out now, Danny-boy. Come on." She offered her hand and tried to coax him out, but Daniel did not move an inch.

To Kate's amazement he looked into her eyes and then after a moment's hesitation, he grabbed her hand.

"Well then," she said softly, her heart swelling. She tried to keep her tone even, tried not to let on that she was greatly moved and make him shy away.

She helped him balance as she handed him the crutch that Charm had retrieved.

"He's taken a shine to anything with sugar in it," Charm whispered to Kate. "Bring him in the kitchen, and I'll give him some more cake. He'll forget all this ruckus in a minute or two."

Far from relieved, Kate walked with Daniel as they followed Charm into the kitchen, where she helped him sit at the table. Then Kate hurried back to the front door and walked out onto the veranda. She refused to let the Greenes leave thinking they had intimidated her.

They definitely saw her standing there in the shade of the veranda as Gideon turned the buggy around in the yard and headed down the lane.

Scrappy, as spry as she had ever seen him, with his pistol tucked in his waistband and a broad smile of accomplishment on his face, climbed the steps to stand beside her. Shoulder to shoulder, they watched the buggy bounce down the road in a cloud of dust. Out on the far horizon, buzzards circled in the hot dry air.

"Reed should ought to be here," Scrappy grumbled. "You shouldn't ought to have to be the one defendin' his boy."

As the buggy grew smaller on the horizon, Kate let go a sigh of relief and then smiled.

"I wasn't exactly alone, was I? I knew they were going nowhere with him when you rushed in waving that gun, and I truly feared for their lives when Charm came charging in holding that beetle over her head. It's heavier than she is."

The old cowhand chortled. "I guess we gave 'em somethin' to chew on."

"We sure did, didn't we? Thank you for your help, Mr. Parks."

The confrontation had only been a skirmish. Kate intended to win the war. She had given them plenty to think about, telling them she was Reed's wife. If the Greenes wanted Daniel, they would be back, and unfortunately, they might even go to Preston Marshall.

"You know where Reed is, don't you, Scrappy?"

"You want me to go after him? Tell him we got an emergency here?"

Lord, she was tempted to call him home. Tempted to see him again, too. But Reed had left her in charge of his house and his son. It was up to her to face the challenge and manage on her own.

"No. I want you to go into town. Can you get to town before the Greenes?"

He nodded. "Hell, yes."

"Then ride into Lone Star and invite Reverend Marshall to dinner."

"The preacher?"

"Yes. And do whatever it takes to convince him to come back with you."

Scrappy scratched beneath his hat. "The preacher."

"Please."

She watched him sigh and shake his head, but he didn't argue. He quickly left her standing alone in the shade of the wide veranda. Out in the distance, the vultures had disappeared. The sky was clear and blue, the breeze soft, warm, and even.

She had to talk to Preston Marshall in case the Greenes sought confirmation of her and Reed's marriage. Somehow, she had to enlist the minister's help, which meant that she would have to think of a way to convince a man of God to bend the truth.

25

It was early morning and already far too hot when Reed walked through camp in no mood to talk to anyone. A week ago Jonah moved them all farther up the Brazos, strategically placing scouts along the river in hopes of intercepting raiding parties forced to stop for water on their way across the prairie. Last night they had recovered over fifty stolen horses and pushed the renegade warriors back with no casualties on their side.

Reed rubbed his hand over his eyes, ducked through the opening of his tent, seeking relief from the sun. In the shadowed interior, he sat on the edge of his cot, rested his arms on his knees, and stared down at his dust-coated boots. His silver spurs from Chihuahua caught the sunlight that oozed between the edges of the opening.

He had tried for weeks to forget about Kate Whittington, but she haunted his thoughts day and night. His shoulder ached, he was short-tempered and testy, and he knew it, but he couldn't seem to do a damn thing about it. It was easiest to blame Kate for his being out of sorts and downright discontented: Not only was he haunted by bits and pieces of memory of the night they had spent together, but he kept wondering how he would have felt about her if he had met her in some way other than through his father's scheme.

On his way back to camp, he had stopped in Lone Star to leave Jeb Cooley a letter of explanation instructing the lawyer to clear up the legal ramifications of the forged proxy papers and ask Jeb to contact him when he returned from Europe. So far he hadn't heard from the man.

While he was in town, he had left credit for Kate at Lone Star Mercantile and Dry Goods; then, as he was walking out of the store, the image of her face had unexpectedly come to him. He remembered the troubled way her dark trusting eyes had looked the morning he had ridden away, the way she had stood there at the veranda rail and waved good-bye. As time passed, he found himself feeling more and more like an ass for the way he had treated her and Daniel.

He had brought her letters with him, worn them around the edges by reading them so many times that he had memorized almost all of them. Reading about her life and her dreams and expectations in her own words kept him dwelling on her and the unsettled situation at the ranch, which did nothing to improve his disposition. He never took himself for a man who would walk out on responsibility, and it didn't sit well with him now.

He heard riders coming, stretched, and left the tent. Across the campground, two new recruits dismounted and then hobbled and sidelined their mounts. Laughing and talking, they crossed the campground. It was hard to miss the excitement and pride on their faces, not to mention the relief. They had just completed their first real duty, put their eager young lives on the line for forty dollars a month.

Reed couldn't remember ever being that young or dedicated to the Ranger cause. He had joined up to seek revenge and to give his intense anger and betrayal a place to spend itself. Back then, being a Ranger had given him a reason to go on living—and, if he chose, a way to die.

He crossed the campground and joined Jonah, who was waiting for the new men near the picket rope.

"Find anything, gentlemen?" Jonah asked them.

Tommy Harlan bobbed his head. "Thought we saw a Comanch' with a lame pony up near the bend in the river, but it turned out to be a Mexican trader."

"Damn near blew his head off 'fore we realized our mistake," the shorter one said with a chuckle. "Other than that, nothing."

"I think there's still some beans and bacon left from breakfast if you want it." Jonah watched them walk away and then turned to Reed. "Your shoulder been bothering you? You don't seem yourself lately."

"It's not my shoulder. It's my mind."

Jonah smiled and shrugged. "That's never been right to begin with."

Reed gave a short laugh but quickly sobered. Since his return he had slowly begun to realize that his passion and intensity for the job were waning. Maybe it was because he had compared his own ebbing enthusiasm with the company's five new recruits. Their zealous dedication to the cause was boundless.

"Anything you want to talk about?" Jonah asked seriously.

"It's a lot of things," Reed said. "My shoulder for one. The damn thing still hurts." The pain had gone on for longer than he had expected. The fever and his time at Lone Star had taken him back to places in his mind where he had not been in years. "Finding Daniel's brought a lot of things home to me. I keep thinking about what could have happened to him the day of the raid when we took that camp. He could have been killed. Hell, I might have shot him myself. I find myself wondering what we're doing out here."

"We're fighting for Texas and for the hundreds of settlers who have been murdered. For the frontier folks that come to us because the government has turned its back on them. Washington could take care of the Comanche if it wasn't for all the softhearted do-gooders back East. What do they know about what's going on out here? They're sitting back there reading books about noble savages and whitewashed newspaper accounts. Nobody would dare print what really happens out here.

"I would think that what Daniel's become would make you want to fight even harder, but I get the feeling that's not the way you see it." Jonah shoved his hands in his pockets, scuffed his toe against the knob of an exposed root on the ground.

Reed said, "Somebody took care of him all these years. Kept him safe. He'd rather be with them than me, that's for sure. It makes me wonder why both sides are so hell-bent on killing each other."

He didn't know how Jonah could understand the direction of his thoughts when he didn't understand himself lately. The Comanche were different in many, many ways, but were the differences so great that they should have to die? Was there no way to have a lasting peace?

"Maybe it's time you went home," Jonah suggested. "I don't want you out in the field if you don't know why you're here."

"Are you telling me I can't do my job?"

"Not at all. I think that's what you're telling me." Before Reed could comment, the captain walked away.

It was Jonah's way to give a man time to think. Reed

leaned back against the trunk of a pecan tree. Somewhere off in the distance a turkey gobbled to its mate. Game was plentiful in the field where the hills and valleys teemed with wild turkey, antelope, and deer. Thousands of buffalo roamed the open plains. Rainbows of wildflowers bloomed all spring and summer, one kind after another, changing the color of the plains like the cloud shadows that brushed across the land. Plenty and beauty were everywhere, but the abundance and magnificence of the land was deceiving.

It was the time of the soft summer moon again.

He had no sooner settled himself beside the central fire and poured a cup of lukewarm coffee than a call came from one of the armed guards on the south end of the camp. More scouts were coming in, shouting, agitated, riding hard.

Another band of renegades had been sighted.

Reed swallowed half the cup of lousy brew that had no doubt been sitting since before dawn; then he chucked the rest. Within seconds the dark coffee was no more than a stain on the thirsty soil. Reed set the tin cup on a rock near the fire ring and went to collect his rifle and ammunition.

It was time to ride.

26

The preacher accepted her invitation.

With her hair coiled in a neat chignon, and wearing the simple blue silk dress that Charm had made, Kate ushered Reverend Marshall in the front door and led him into the Benton parlor.

"Thank you for coming on such short notice, Reverend," she said over her shoulder as he followed her to the settee placed opposite the huge stone fireplace.

"I rarely turn down an invite to dinner," he said with an easy smile. "Although Scrappy hinted that you were not about to take no for an answer. He also alluded to the fact that you need my help."

His slow Southern accent was soothing, although not nearly enough to quiet her nerves. As he lowered himself to the settee, Kate noted his smile was open but curious.

"Would you care for some tea or coffee, Reverend?"

"Nothing, thank you." He shook his head and centered his low-crowned black hat on his knee.

"Well, then." Kate let go a nervous sigh and took a chair opposite, hard-pressed not to feel as if she had just entered a confessional. She had been baptized Catholic the week she entered the orphanage and was certainly no stranger to confession.

When she was nine, the act had been terribly frightening, the whispering of secret sins in the dark confines of an airless little box, the cloying scent of incense heavy on the chapel air.

She could still recall the old priest, Father Timmons, who had not a single hair on his head and yet had no trouble sprouting it out of his ears. During mass, his square bald head reflected the light of the altar candles.

A wooden screen had separated them in the confessional, but she could always make out his profile through the grate as he leaned against the wall, his eyes closed.

The same trepidation and guilt churned in her now as she faced Reverend Marshall. He was no more than a few years older than she at best, and very handsome. He looked directly into her eyes, smiling encouragement.

Bless me, Father.

She took a deep breath, forced herself to meet his sincere, steady gaze and plunged right in.

"I need the help you so kindly offered the day of the burial. And I need you to keep what I tell you strictly confidential." She was talking too fast, but couldn't slow down.

"Anything I can do, Miss Whittington. You can count on me."

"When we met, I told you that Reed Benton and I had corresponded, but not that we were married by proxy before I came to Texas."

His smile faded. "You *married* Reed Junior by proxy?"

She fiddled with the ruffle on the cuff of her gown. "As it turns out, there was some misunderstanding, more of a misrepresentation, actually. And not exactly some, but quite a lot." She sighed, realized she was twisting the silk material as much as the story and stopped. There was no way around the truth. "It is really a long story, but as it turns out, Reed and I were both duped by his father. I was already here when I discovered that we were not married at all. But you see, I thought that I was—married, that is. That's why I came to Texas."

Kate felt her skin burning and wished his gaze were not so intent.

"Go on," he urged.

"Reed's father was writing to me, courting me through correspondence in Reed's name. Unbeknownst to Reed . . . Junior . . . he had forged the signature on the marriage papers. After Reed recovered and returned to the Rangers, he stopped by his lawyer in Lone Star to start the process of clearing things up. So, you see, I am sort of married, at least on paper, until things are straightened out. It all sounds very confusing, I know. . . ."

"The signature was forged?"

"That's right. But the papers were filed."

When there was no disapproval, no condemnation on his face, relief swept over her. She relaxed a bit and unknitted her fingers.

Preston Marshall leaned closer. "I'm glad you feel you can confide in me, but how can I help?"

"Reed's son, Daniel, was recovered from the Comanche. He is in my care now."

"I was told about Reed Junior's wife's death and his son's kidnapping when I moved here. Naturally, Lone Star is a close-knit community, and Reed Senior is quite legendary in these parts." He stretched his arm over the back of the settee. "I can't believe he did such a dastardly thing to you, let alone his own son."

"I think that, in his mind, he meant well."

"Not many people would be as understanding. I commend you."

"There isn't much else I can do, is there, Reverend, but

forgive? The reason I need your help is that Daniel's maternal grandparents came here today. They wanted the boy. They actually wanted to take Daniel with them when they left, but I couldn't let them without Reed's approval. When they questioned my authority, I told them that I was more than the housekeeper here, that I was Reed's wife. When they didn't believe me, I . . . I suggested they go into town and ask you."

"That's why you called me out here, why Scrappy insisted I come."

She shrugged. "I didn't want them to catch you off guard."

She had expected disapproval and rejection. At the very least, she thought that he surely would see her as a desperate, penniless spinster now.

But he surprised her completely when he shook his head and said, "How terrible for you, Miss Whittington."

"It's Kate. Please, call me Kate."

"Only if you call me Preston." Again, he smiled sympathetically. "You must have been deeply hurt by all of this. How are you holding up?"

It was the first time in all these weeks that anyone had asked how she felt, how she was doing. Sofia's apology had held no compassion. Reed had had enough troubles of his own.

She had stepped in and taken care of Daniel, of Charm, and of the house. No one ever asked or cared how she was faring, let alone how she must feel in the wake of what had happened.

Now this man, this kindly stranger had said the one thing that threatened her fortitude. Her eyes smarted with tears, and suddenly Preston Marshall's image wavered.

"I'm sorry, Kate. I didn't mean to make you cry." He

quickly pulled out a starched and ironed handkerchief, a reminder that he lived with his maiden aunt. "May I?"

She nodded. He wiped a tear from the corner of her eye and then handed her the kerchief. Wadding it in her hand, she sniffed and cursed her weakness.

Not now, Kate. Pull yourself together.

Her mother always said that crying was a waste of time and water.

"Now that you know the truth, I suppose you will be honor-bound to tell the Greenes if they come to town asking about me."

Preston sat in silent contemplation. Then, like the sun on a cloudy day, his smile dawned again.

"You're still Reed's bride of record and will be until the proper papers are signed and filed, I assume. So, I really would not be lying if I assured the Greenes that you are, indeed, married to Reed Benton."

Emotion had drained her, but her fear was quickly whitewashed by relief. "You will never know what your understanding and kindness mean to me," she said.

She thanked him as Charm walked in from the kitchen and hesitated just across the threshold. Kate could see by the look they exchanged that Charm and the minister were no strangers to each other. Preston stood to greet the girl.

"Hello, Miss Riley," he said with a nod. His tone and expression were not only devoid of censure, but they carried a hint of compassion as well.

"Hello, Reverend."

"Charm is our cook," Kate quickly explained when an awkward silence spread.

Preston looked relieved. "I commend you, Miss Riley. It appears Kate has been successful where I was not when I made an argument for change outside the Social Club."

Charm smiled Kate's way. "You did try, Reverend. All the girls thought you looked real grand up there on that wooden box preaching and giving us the what for. Kate's just a very special lady," she said softly.

Kate blinked rapidly as her eyes teared up again. Quickly, she changed the subject. "This is my day to learn to make fried chicken," she told him. "I hope you will stay regardless, Reverend. Until Charm started tutoring me, I was a terrible cook, so I make no guarantees."

Preston remained standing as he smiled down at Kate.

"Scrappy tempted me out here with the promise of a meal, remember? I'm not going anywhere, except into the kitchen to help. What you don't know is that I happen to be one of the best one-armed cooks west of the Mississippi."

Fast Pony sat at the table staring daggers at the smiling man with one arm, wondering if he lost it in battle, wondering if that was why he did woman's work now. Fast Pony had watched him laugh with Soft Grass Hands as they cooked over the big metal pot-on-legs in the room where the yellow-haired girl prepared food.

The man had even spread the white cloth over the table for Soft Grass Hands and set out the shining pieces of silver they used to carry food to their mouths. Fast Pony refused to touch the shining silver. Instead, he grabbed his food by the bone and tore fiercely at it, trying to eat as much and as fast as he could without choking. He could see that Soft Grass Hands was very disappointed in him, just as Painted White Feather would have been if she could see the way he was acting, but he refused to let them change him.

The People never ate birds or turkey unless they were starving, just as they never ate dog or frog or other water creatures. But he had come to love the juicy meat of the fat white feathered birds that Soft Grass Hands sometimes let him feed, and he liked the crunch it made against his teeth when he ate it. His father, Many Horses, would surely forgive him for eating birds. After all, he did so only to stay alive.

He wiped the back of his hand across his mouth and then started to rub his greasy hands on the leg coverings they made him wear, but Soft Grass Hands moved as fast as lightning, came up out of her chair, and grabbed him. She bent down until her nose was almost touching his.

She spoke slowly and firmly, but she did not yell as she held both his wrists in one hand and picked up the small white cloth near the pile of bones on the table and wiped his hands and fingers with it. When she was satisfied that he was clean, she let go.

He glared at her. She glared back and shook her head. It was a game they played every time he ate.

Yellow Hair ignored him. When he looked at One Arm, the man quickly looked down at his food. The stranger's hand was soft and white, his eyes the color of rain clouds. But it wasn't his soft white skin or his missing arm or even his cooking that made Fast Pony hate him. It was the way the man looked at Soft Grass Hands, the way he smiled at her so much, that worried Fast Pony.

What if the white man with rain clouds in his eyes offered a bride price for Soft Grass Hands?

As far as Fast Pony could tell, she had no man, no husband of her own, unless it was Tall Ranger, but he was never here. If the one-armed stranger offered for her, then she would have to leave and go with him to his own clan.

For reasons that he did not understand, the notion of Soft Grass Hands leaving made Fast Pony feel sad, which in turn made him angry enough to want to hit something. She was the only one here who cared about him, the only one who ever took him outside and walked with him, the only one to wash and dress him.

If there had been no Soft Grass Hands, he most likely would still be locked in the house of horses. Maybe when she left, they would put him back there.

He slid down on the chair bottom until he was half hidden by the edge of the table. Quiet as a butterfly, hopefully forgotten, he watched them all: Soft Grass Hands, One Arm, Yellow Hair.

They talked and talked and laughed. More than anything, he was amazed at the change in Soft Grass Hands. He had not ever seen her smile this much before One Arm came. At least, not inside the house. Sometimes she would smile whenever they were outside and he showed her something special, but she rarely smiled inside this place. It was almost as if the dwelling itself made her sad.

Before tonight, before One Arm appeared, she had *never* laughed aloud.

There was much here to worry about, he decided.

Maybe much to fear.

27

Two good things happened over the next few weeks. There was no further sign of the Greenes, and Preston Marshall became a fixture at Sunday supper. Kate began to look forward to his visits, to the open, caring manner he extended to all of them, to his delightful conversation and company.

On just such a Sunday, after she and Charm had cleared the dishes, scraped away the remains, and carefully slipped the last of the Benton china into a dishpan of sudsy water, Kate looked out the window above the dry sink and saw a rider in the stable area behind the house.

At first her heart skipped a beat when she thought the man wearing a tall white hat and knee-high boots was Reed. Then she realized it was not him, but the Ranger captain, Jonah Taylor, and her excitement immediately turned to worry.

"Captain Taylor is here," she said aloud, afraid something had happened to Reed.

When Charm suddenly dropped the bread and butter plate into the dishpan, splashing them both, Kate remembered that Jonah was Charm's knight in shining armor. Kate had jumped back, but not before soap suds splattered across her bodice. Charm was as still as a marble statue as she stared out the window. Scrappy came trotting out of the bunkhouse, greeted the Ranger, and took his horse.

As the captain started toward the back door, Charm riveted her concentration on the dishes. Kate dried her hands and touched Charm reassuringly on the shoulder.

The girl turned to Kate with despair and hope, desire and fear in her eyes.

"Dry your hands and smile," Kate urged. "I'll bet he has come to see you."

"Oh, Kate." The girl sighed.

Kate knew the fear of reaching too high, of dreaming impossible dreams, but even knowing how hard the fall might be, she hoped that Charm would at least try.

She also prayed that no harm had come to Reed as she opened the door before Jonah knocked.

"Is Reed all right?" she asked.

Jonah doffed his hat. "He's fine. Kind of quiet since he came back, but otherwise he's all right. Hello, Miss Riley." His gaze immediately sought out Charm and slipped away again.

"Hello, Captain Taylor," Charm said.

Kate sensed the girl's tension, knew that even though Charm hadn't done more than glance his way, that she was aware of every move Jonah made.

Kate ended their misery. "Charm, why don't you dish up a plate of supper for the captain so that he can eat while we all have dessert and coffee? I'm sure he has some interesting stories to tell us." Then to Jonah, "Reverend Marshall is here for supper, too."

Jonah shuffled his feet, looking uncomfortable. "I was just passing by and stopped to say hello. I didn't expect food, ma'am, but if you're offering, I won't turn it down."

It was a far piece to come just to stop to say hello, but

Kate did not comment. He followed her into the dining room and cordially greeted the reverend who was engaged in a staring contest with Daniel. Kate introduced the men and went back to the kitchen for a place setting for the captain. Charm still had not moved.

Kate grabbed a plate from the pantry and hurried over to the stove. Pan lids clanged, ladles and spoons clattered as she quickly dished up pot roast, carrots and potatoes, and then some wilted greens for the captain. She went back to where Charm stood watching her.

"Here." She shoved the plate into the girl's hands. "Take this in to the captain."

"I can't," Charm whispered.

"Why not?"

"I just can't."

"Yes, you can. He's here to see you."

"He *said* that?"

"Not in so many words but . . ."

"Then how do you know?"

"Charm, this house is in the middle of nowhere, miles from nothing. No one just *passes* by. If he had come with word from Reed, he would have said so. The poor man is here to see you but he's not about to admit it. Now—" She turned Charm around and gave her a light, encouraging shove. "—go."

Charm went, head high, her steps slow and careful.

Kate readied a tray with coffee cups, cream and sugar, and a plate of cookies and joined the gathering in the dining room. She hoped the captain would tell her more about Reed without her having to ask.

Reed may have turned his back on them, but he was never far from her mind. She often chided herself for dwelling on him and then asked, how could she not? She was living in his house, caring for his son. They had made love, and afterward, he had kissed her. She had come to know him better before he left and often found herself wishing he would return and wondering how things would be between them when he did.

The arrival of the captain was just another strong reminder of her weakness where Reed was concerned.

She told Preston and Jonah not to stand when they tried to show off their manners. Fighting to hide her nervousness, she poured coffee with cream but no sugar for Preston, just the way he liked it and then asked Jonah how he took his.

"Black." His eyes cut to Charm and back again. He picked up the cup, smiled at Kate. "Thank you, ma'am. Everything's wonderful."

He ate a heaping forkful of beef, chewing and swallowing with gusto.

"Thank Charm," Kate said, and watched Charm blush crimson. "She is a wonderful cook."

We really are a pair, Kate thought. A spinster warmed by the sight of this odd assembly of souls gathered at the table and her only friend, an eighteen-year-old whore too scared to speak to the man who owned her tainted heart.

Nothing Kate had learned at the convent could have prepared her for what she was experiencing in Texas.

Preston was courteous and kind as always, thoughtful to ask the captain about his duties and news of the frontier. Captain Taylor responded between mouthfuls, his gaze riveted on the preacher, on Kate, even Daniel. Anyone but Charm.

At the far end of the table, Daniel shoved sugar cookies into his mouth with both hands. When Kate caught Jonah frowning at the child, she hoped he wouldn't tell Reed about Daniel's manners. After the atrocious way Daniel had behaved at the going-away dinner, Reed might decide there was no hope for the boy.

"Table manners seem to be our battleground. I'm certain he understands perfectly well what I expect of him, but so far he refuses to cooperate."

"I think it's a miracle you have him in the chair at all, if you ask me." Jonah ignored Daniel again.

Preston set his coffee cup down, and Kate refilled it. The preacher said to Jonah, "Kate has actually done a remarkable job with Daniel. He goes to bed without a fuss and usually does whatever it is she asks of him. He has adjusted to using his crutch, too."

"He can't walk yet?"

Sadness crept into Kate's heart. "I'm almost afraid he'll be crippled for life," she said softly. "His ankle was badly damaged."

"I doubt a limp will slow him down," Jonah commented, nodding at Daniel again. "You still lock him up at night, don't you?"

"Regretfully, yes," Kate admitted. Like Reed, the captain probably knew too much to trust a former captive. "I lock him in his room at night, but only because Reed was so adamant about it."

She sighed, wished she could believe otherwise, but it would be hard for a blind man to miss the look on the boy's face whenever he stared out across the prairie. There was such an intense longing there that she could almost feel it. Lately she found herself wondering if it might not be better just to let him go, but that was not her choice to make. She was caring for Daniel in Reed's stead, keeping him here so that he would survive. Despite the circumstances of his birth, Daniel was without a doubt a Benton. Lone Star would one day be his.

What the child needed most in his life was Reed. But she didn't know how to get the man to come home and take responsibility for his son.

Preston set his cup down again, and when Kate started to refill it, he thanked her, but declined.

"It's time I head back to town," he said. "Aunt Martha will be looking for me. Kate, as always, I thank you for including me. Charm, the meal was delicious." He pushed away from the table and then said to Jonah, "Captain, it was good to see you again. Take care of yourself."

Finally, Preston walked over to Daniel's chair and hunkered down so they were eye to eye. "Bye, Daniel. I'll see you again soon."

Daniel met the preacher's eyes, stared into them without blinking.

As Preston rose, Kate noticed Charm staring down into her untouched coffee and decided to give her time alone with the captain.

"I'll see you out, Preston," she said, rising from her chair. Accompanying the preacher out of the dining room, she left Charm and Jonah alone with Daniel.

The front entry was lit only by the fading light of a summer's eve as Kate and Preston stepped out onto the veranda. Twilight was a purple hush over the land. There was no hint of a breeze tonight. A barn owl hooted somewhere nearby, a salute to the full, buttery moon.

"Please bring your aunt out for dinner next Sunday," Kate said, then immediately apologized. "I'm sorry, Preston. I shouldn't assume that you will be coming out here every Sunday."

She saw his smile even in the gathering darkness.

"And here I was hoping that I wasn't wearing out my welcome. As for Aunt Martha, she doesn't like to leave town.

The thought of her coming all the way out here in a buggy is more than she wants to contemplate these days."

"I hate to think of her sitting there alone for Sunday supper."

"Someone from the congregation always invites her over. She would love to have you come to break bread with us sometime soon, Kate. Naturally, I've told her all about you and Daniel. I'd be more than willing to drive out and get you both."

"What about Charm?"

Slowly, he shook his head. "Surely you understand why I cannot invite Charm into my home."

"And yet you take supper with her here every week. You've never shown her anything but kindness, Preston."

"Lone Star is a very small town. People would talk."

"And say what? That their reverend is not above forgiveness?" It was hard to forget the shame of her own childhood. She could not help but defend Charm.

He sighed, a long frustrated sound that lingered heavy on the hot summer air. "Please understand. Don't hold the image I must maintain against me, Kate."

What would he say if he knew her own mother had been a whore? How might that alter their friendship? "I do understand," she said softly. "But I don't have to like it."

"Will you come to dinner?"

She shook her head. "No. Under the circumstances, I cannot. I won't leave Charm behind. To do so would be a slap in the face."

She had no warning before his fingers gently enfolded hers. Her breath caught in surprise.

What will I do if he takes a step closer?
What will I do if he tries to kiss me?

But when he made no further advances, Kate was relieved, for she had no idea how she would have reacted if he had kissed her, no idea if she would have responded to him in the way she had to Reed.

His fingers moved against her palm. "Let's just leave things as they are for now, all right? I would miss your company too much to jeopardize our friendship by pressing the issue. You will meet Aunt Martha someday."

"Thank you," she whispered, stunned by his overture.

When he let go of her hand, she could still feel his touch. "Good night, Preston."

He lingered a moment longer before he promised, "I'll see you next week."

Kate watched Preston ride into the night, and then she walked back inside. She found Daniel alone, kneeling on the floor before the kitchen door with one eye plastered to the keyhole.

Without a word, she walked over and knelt down beside him.

When he realized she was there, he started, his eyes growing wide with surprise. He grabbed hold of the sideboard next to him and pulled himself to his feet.

"What are you looking at?" Kate whispered, still on her knees.

He crossed his arms over his chest. He glanced toward the door and then back at her expectantly.

Kate was tempted to peer through the keyhole, but was half afraid of what she might see.

"Why don't I take you up to bed?" She got to her feet and extended her hand, expecting him to take it. He didn't budge.

"What's wrong?"

His eyes cut to the keyhole and back, his meaning perfectly clear. She went back to his chair, collected his crutch, and carried it to him. The act of shoving the padded top beneath his arm had become second nature to him. He looked up at her, silently insisting she open the door.

She knocked and called out Charm's name before she walked into the kitchen. Since she had expected to find Charm and the captain together, Kate was surprised when Charm was all alone, finishing up the dishes.

"Did Jonah already leave?"

The girl nodded but said nothing.

"Charm?" Kate crossed the room. Daniel followed close behind, silent as a shadow. The only sound in the room was the splash of dishwater and the thump of Daniel's crutch against the floor.

When Charm turned her head, Kate put her hand on the girl's arm. "Charm, look at me."

Charm shook her head. Kate heard her breath catch on a sob. She slipped her arm around the girl's shoulders. "Did he hurt you?"

Charm shook her head no.

"Tell me the truth, please."

"He didn't hurt me," Charm whispered.

"Then what happened?"

Finally Charm turned, soapy hands and all, and threw herself into Kate's arms. She gasped out something unintelligible.

"What did you say?"

"He—he—asked me—to—m-marry him!" Charm burst into soul-racking sobs on Kate's shoulder.

For a moment Kate was too stunned to speak. She rubbed Charm's back, held her tight, and then finally eased the girl's hair off her tear-soaked cheek.

"He gave me a new—locket and he—he asked me to— marry him."

"Do you love him?"

Charm nodded yes fiercely.

"Did you accept?"

"I—told him—no. Because I don't want to—to ruin his life."

"Captain Taylor is a grown man, Charm. He knows what he's doing. He knows what you were, but he can also see the woman you have become. He sees what I see when I look at you, someone with so much love to give, someone who deserves a second chance. If you love him, you should be with him." Kate saw the shining gold locket on a fine chain around Charm's neck. She glanced toward the back door.

"Did he leave?"

Charm wiped her face on the backs of her wrists and hiccupped another sob. Daniel thumped over to the kitchen table and slipped a cookie off a platter.

Charm sniffed. "He's gone. He—said he knew he was too old for me. He thinks that's why—I said no—because he's too old. I tried to tell him that wasn't true, but he didn't believe me."

Kate grabbed the dish towel and used it to mop Charm's streaming tears.

"Oh, Kate. You should have seen his face. I know I hurt him, but I had to do it. I—can't be—responsible for ruining his life. He's so good. So honorable. What would folks say if they found out that he married a whore?"

Another woman might have tried to dissuade Charm from thinking the worst, might even have offered platitudes, but Kate knew exactly what people would say.

The insults that sprang from the tongues of the righteous and narrow-minded were as sharp and deadly as the mightiest of swords.

28

Day had already dawned when a party of settlers rode into the Ranger camp, three men dazed and shocked, one wounded. Their outpost on the Brazos had been attacked by a raiding party, their cabins burned to the ground. Female captives were stolen along with all the outpost's horses.

As second in command, Reed had readied the men and ordered a supply mule loaded, then he had stalled, waiting for Jonah to get back. For some reason the man had insisted on accompanying the sutler into Lone Star for supplies. At first Reed thought maybe government money allocated to the Rangers had been reduced again and that Jonah had gone in to haggle over prices. Then he remembered Charm was out at the ranch, less than an hour's ride from town.

It was nearly nine in the morning now, and there was still no sign of Jonah.

New recruit Tommy Harlan, the youngest of eight strapping Harlan boys and the only one to leave the family farm and join the Rangers, left the picket line where the other men were sober as they tied gear and weapons to their mounts.

"The men are ready to ride, sir. Any sign of Captain Taylor yet?" Overenthusiastic, young Harlan did everything but salute.

Reed wanted to give Jonah another ten minutes. He would have led the men out long before now if they weren't tracking a party of fifteen warriors and twice as many horses. With so many tracks cutting a wide swath across the prairie, the trail would be impossible to miss.

"Tell the men to mount up. We can't wait any longer." Reed slapped his hat against his thigh then shoved it on and tapped it down. His gut was knotted tighter than a short belt around a fat man's belly by the time he saddled up.

The men were silent, intent on what they had to do. He gave orders, told them that captives had been taken, warned them to stay together and wait for his commands. Then he sent two scouts on ahead. Just as he was about to issue the order to ride, the sutler's supply wagon came rumbling over the rise with Jonah riding beside it.

When the captain saw his troops mounted, he spurred his horse and quickly rode up to Reed, who gave the signal for the column of riders to head out. He and Jonah rode side by side.

"Comanche war band hit south of the Brazos before sunup," Reed explained. "The settlers tried to hold them off. They sent for help, but the rider didn't make it through. Three of them came in this morning for help. Two farmers were killed, four captives taken along with about twenty head of horses. I sent the men back to their families. The raiders slaughtered a few head of beef and left them to rot. They weren't after food."

"How much time do they have on us?"

"Three, maybe four hours."

They rode in silence for a quarter of a mile before Reed decided Jonah wasn't going to tell him voluntarily why he had suddenly taken it upon himself to go into town with the sutler.

"Mind telling me why *you* had to go for supplies?" The

minute the question was hanging on the air Reed wished he hadn't asked it.

Jonah's mouth hardened into a tight line. When he turned to Reed there was a bottomless ache in his eyes. "I stopped by the ranch to see Charm."

Reed's gut cinched another notch. They rode on a piece, Jonah's silence eating at him until he was raw. "Everything all right there?" Reed finally asked.

"Oh, yeah. Just fine. Better than fine from what I could tell." Jonah went stone silent again.

"Mind telling me what 'better than fine' means?"

"Well, they've got a preacher coming for Sunday suppers. He was there when I arrived. It wasn't the first time, either. Both women were gussied up in matching blue dresses. Even the boy was cleaned up, sitting at the table."

Reed strained for a scrap of memory that would help him recall what the Lone Star preacher looked like. He remembered hearing about a church starting up a couple of years back and something about the man being a war hero. The church building was being framed on one of his infrequent trips into town, and he had seen the preacher, but just now he couldn't put a face to a name.

Jonah smoothly guided his bay around a prairie dog hole. "Nice and cozy."

"What did you say?" Reed thought he had heard right. Heard plenty of resentment in the tone, too.

"I said, they looked nice and cozy. Laughing and talking at the dinner table. Charm's been teaching Kate to cook. The boy's using a crutch to get around. Still looks wild around the eyes, to me, but it appears he listens some to Kate now." A flash of a smile flickered across Jonah's mouth but didn't come near to touching his eyes. "Still eats like a Comanche, though."

Reed wished his imagination wasn't working overtime but with credible ease he remembered Kate, all prim and proper, seated at the dining table presiding over a fine meal. Now she could smile at some whey-faced preacher with soft hands and a kindly, practiced smile.

It was harder to imagine Charm breaking bread with a preacher, but any man in his right mind would be hard-pressed to turn down an invitation from not one, but two such good-looking women. The ranch house was far enough from town for the preacher to avoid gossip, too. Anything could go on out there, and no one would be the wiser.

"You all right?" Jonah was watching him closely.

"About as right as you." None of it sat well with Reed. He could see that it didn't with Jonah, either.

As he let his friend mull things over, he soon spotted their scouts high on a swell on the open prairie. One of the men raised his rifle in the air. They had picked up the trail.

The women forgotten for the time being, Reed and Jonah urged their horses on, and the column followed. Once they reached the knoll, the wide-open prairie spread out in every direction. There was no sign of the raiding party, but that didn't mean a hell of a lot. Comanche could be anywhere, below a rise or riding along a creek bottom. Everyone was quiet, the teasing banter, the jovial exchanges that usually filled the campground had been left there.

Hunting down Comanche was a cold and dangerous business. Young or old, there was not a man among them who didn't know that. One wrong move, one misjudgment, and a man would be making the ride back slung across a saddle and carried home to be buried.

The sun was slinking across the afternoon sky, and tensions were as high as the temperature. The Rangers were trying to circle ahead of the Comanche trail in order to head them off in a narrow river bottom.

Jonah called a halt on a ridge and sent a scout out.

Reed shifted in the saddle, heard the familiar creak of leather beneath him. "Sundown is going to catch us out here in the open," he told Jonah.

Reed's concentration had been scattered all day, plagued by what Jonah had told him about Kate, Daniel, and the minister dancing attendance on the women at Lone Star.

Kate had sent no message, not even word of Daniel. A woman like her, someone as conscientious as Kate surely would have thought to send some news—unless maybe she had gone starry-eyed over the preacher.

All worry over what Kate might be doing fled as Reed watched Tommy Harlan come streaking across the landscape riding low over his horse's neck. Not so much as a whisper whipped through the ranks as Harlan galloped up and reined in.

"Small Indian encampment, sir." The young recruit reported to Jonah. "This side of the river, out in the open. Got close enough to see women and young'ins moving around."

Jonah squinted. "Looks to be a ravine cutting across the open plain following the creek bed. The raiders would be able to hide the horses there, and they would be easy enough to collect when they are ready to move on. Any sign yet?"

Harlan shook his head. His freckled cheeks glowed pink with sunburn. "None. Although there's a small stand of trees along the riverbank. Could be working their way back through there, but I didn't see or hear any sign."

Reed shoved his hat to the back of his head. "How many in the camp?"

"It's a fairly small number. Just a few tepees spread out along the river. Cook fires lit."

"Any sign of captives?" Jonah raised his hand to shield his eyes against the sun.

Tommy shook his head. "None that I could make out. That's not to say there aren't any down there."

By taking the women and children hostage they would have leverage with the bucks when they returned and could easily barter for the release of the white captives and the horses. It would mean avoiding more bloodshed, but they would not be able to ride in without the occupants of the village retaliating. Even the women and older children would put up resistance.

The full moon was already chasing the sun, the sky still a brilliant liquid blue without a wisp of a cloud in sight.

"Harlan, pass the word that we're going in. I want every man armed and ready. Tell them to fire in the air and don't shoot to kill unless it's in self-defense. I want as many taken alive as possible. Is that clear?"

"Yes, sir." Harlan took his assignment seriously. Solemn as a judge, he began to move down the line, spreading the word. There was barely a sound as the men unsheathed their rifles.

Sweat trickled down Reed's temple. When he swiped at it with the back of his arm, his shoulder wound gave a twinge. He took a deep breath, closed his eyes. Unbidden, Daniel's image flashed through his mind.

Jonah was riding along the line of troops, repeating over and over, "Ride slow, stay low, and fan out until I give the signal—then we ride fast and hard and take as many prisoners as we can." He pointed out a holding area and assigned four men to hang back and act as guards.

"I got a bad feeling about this," Reed told him when they joined up again.

Jonah's expression was intent. "If you aren't feeling right about this, tell me now and stay back with the guards. No one's gonna blame you, not after what you went through before, but I can't risk having you with us if you aren't up to it."

Reed thought of the settlers who had been killed, of the terrified women who had already spent hours in Comanche hands. He wasn't about to back out, even if his mind and heart were unsettled.

"Let's go."

Jonah waved the men on, and the Rangers fanned out along the upper slope of the plain, moving in a slow, single file toward the tree line along the river. Before the encampment came into view, they separated into two columns, Reed leading one, Jonah the other.

Somewhere in the camp, a baby cried but was quickly quieted. Smoke spiraled from campfires; the smell of burning mesquite did little to alleviate the stench of curing hides and rotting bones scattered around—evidence of a recent buffalo hunt. When an encampment went too sour, the Comanche simply moved on. Reed had smelled worse.

Down the line of troopers, someone's horse whinnied and tossed its head, fighting the bit. Jonah waved the men into a charge, and, as one, thirty Rangers spurred their mounts across the shallow water of the running stream and up the slight embankment, directly into the Comanche camp.

When the firing began, startled women, children, and old men ran for cover and for weapons. Cooking paunches filled with simmering food were dumped; fires were scattered in the melee that ensued. The Rangers followed Jonah's orders, firing over their heads, kicking away attackers when they could, knocking them out with their rifle butts instead of shooting, but in many cases there was nothing to do but kill or wound the enemy.

Within seconds the Comanche were able to get their

hands on weapons—spears, war axes, knives, pistols, even rifles. Smoke filled the air as the Rangers began torching tepees and summer shelters made of boughs. Reed was dead center in the middle of the encampment when, screaming like a banshee, a woman came running through a screen of smoke. Even though an infant hung in a carrier on her back, the woman charged him with a war ax raised over her head.

His horse reared, and she dropped the ax, fell back, and rolled on the ground. At first her eyes went wide with terror then dark with resignation. She expected death, was ready to face it. Reed shouted at her in broken Comanche, ordered her to surrender.

Then came a flash of movement to his right. Reed turned in the saddle, saw a boy no older than ten years running toward him with an old percussion pistol.

Reed raised his rifle, looked down the barrel.

And imagined Daniel's face.

29

When Reed heard Tommy Harlan holler at him to shoot, he looked away from the Comanche boy with the pistol and watched Tommy jump his horse over a low campfire, riding down on them. Detached, Reed froze, unable to move, unable to shoot the boy aiming at him as he tried to protect the woman.

Rifle at the ready, Tommy closed in, screaming, "Shoot, Reed! Kill him! He's going to fire!"

Reed knew the Comanche boy had one shot and knew he would take it. Suddenly, without warning, the boy whirled and fired at Harlan. Tommy was nearly knocked out of the saddle as his body reacted to the impact of the bullet. A red stain flowered across his shirtfront as shock and surprise registered on his face.

The Comanche boy looked as surprised as the young Ranger when Tommy's eyes glazed over and he fell to the ground.

Distinct within the volley of shots fired around him, Reed heard another, this one fired at close range. He saw the Comanche youth's body arch, his thin arms flail the air. The old pistol flew out of his hand. He fell forward and hit the ground facedown. A ragged bullet hole ravaged his back.

Reed swallowed bile.

The young mother-sister-wife on the ground screamed and scrambled to her feet. She took off running for the shelter of the trees along the river as Reed looked past the fallen boy to see who the shooter was.

His eyes met and held Jonah's. In that instant Reed saw concern, disappointment, and resignation. Then Jonah turned his horse and charged after an old man hobbling for the stream.

Reed kicked his horse, rode down the woman with the babe. He dismounted and tied her hands together, forced her to follow him as he rode over to the holding area. In the distance, sporadic firing faded into silence.

It was high summer, the time of long days. Sunlight held until the Comanche braves rode into the creek bottom with the stolen horses. When they saw the smoking remains of the camp and realized what had happened, they were more than willing to trade the four white captives—two women and two young girls under fifteen, as well as the horses, in exchange for their wives and children.

A full moon lit up the night sky as Company J set up their own camp for the night a few miles away. Doc saw to the wounded. The only life lost had been Harlan's. Jonah ordered guards to watch the body. It was covered by a tarpaulin and draped over his saddle, the horse picketed away from where the women could see it. No one forgot it was there.

In self-imposed exile, Reed sat alone a good distance from the cook fire, staring at the moon, seeing nothing, feeling little more. Jonah had not been the only witness to Tommy's death. Word had quickly spread that Reed was responsible. It wasn't long before he had become a pariah.

Somewhere off in the distance, a coyote pack set up raucous howling. Seated on the ground, his legs drawn up and his rifle alongside him, Reed shoved his hat back and rested his arms on his knees.

He heard footsteps rustling the grass but did not bother to pick up his rifle. If death had come for him, he was ready.

But it was only Jonah.

The man said nothing as he lowered himself to the ground, pulled out a rolled smoke, a case of matches. Once the tobacco was lit and he had taken a drag, Jonah finally spoke. "You cost a man his life today. You could have lost your own."

"You don't think I know that?" Reed asked.

"What happened?"

What happened?

Daniel happened.

Daniel with his long Comanche hair, his defiant eyes. Whether Daniel was his own child, or his father's, like Kate had said, he was a Benton. The boy was back in his life and so were the memories of what Daniel had meant to him once, long ago.

What happened today?

I stopped seeing Comanches and saw a child.

A boy like Daniel.

Someone's son. Someone's brother.

I saw a mother, a babe.

Not just Comanches.

He had left himself open and vulnerable and had gotten Tommy Harlan killed as sure as if he had pulled the trigger on that old percussion pistol himself.

Deep inside, he guessed Jonah was perfectly aware of what had happened out there today, but the man wanted him to admit it.

"I couldn't have shot that boy today any more than I could shoot you," Reed admitted.

Jonah took a long pull on the cigarette. "But I could have been killed by your inability to act in the heat of battle the same as Harlan. You're through as a Ranger, Reed. You know that, don't you? I can't have you out here, a danger to yourself and the rest of the men.

"Go home, Reed, and put your life back together. You've been hiding out here for years, you and I both know that. Revenge and hatred can get real old."

Jonah dropped what was left of the tobacco and snuffed it out with his boot. "This war has gone on way too long with too many lost on both sides. I don't see an end to it without one side or the other leaving Texas altogether, and I know it won't be us. Like I told you before, I'm doing this for the people of Texas. If you aren't, then it's time to get out. You know we'll always be friends."

Since there would be years of bloodshed to come before the Comanche either went peaceably to the reservation land or died fighting, Reed had never much thought past being a Ranger. Before this afternoon he never could have imagined having this conversation.

Once he assumed his father would live on for years to come, but now Lone Star was his. He could run it as he saw fit and live on the ranch without battling his father's will.

In his heart, he knew where he belonged, just as he knew there was no avoiding Daniel or his responsibility to Lone Star any longer. He already had Tommy Harlan on his conscience. He didn't need Daniel and Kate there, too.

Jonah was right. It was time to go home.

30

Kate sat on the settee in the Benton parlor watching Charm laugh over a bad checker move in a match against Preston.

Wearing a red-and-white striped shirt and denim pants that Charm had just finished the day before, Daniel sat at the opposite end of the plush upholstered piece, his little legs and feet sticking out over the edge, his crutch propped beside him. It was the first time he ever sat so close to the rest of them. His usual haunt was a chair at the far end of the room where he could observe without being part of the group.

Another Sunday supper had just ended. Another pleasant summer afternoon lazed on. It cheered Kate to see Charm laugh with such a light heart. The girl was more at ease with the minister, too. It had been two weeks since Jonah Taylor's proposal, and neither Kate nor Charm had brought up the subject again. Although Charm never said a word about it, Kate could tell that she was suffering from a broken heart.

Wishing there was something she could do, it suddenly dawned on Kate that Charm had become a good friend. As had Preston. Dear friends. Something she had never had before.

Preston won the checker game, and Charm conceded defeat. Kate thought about fate and how it had brought three such unlikely souls together to share each other's company. Over and over she tried to remind herself that her time and position here were only temporary, that circumstances could change as quickly as the weather.

She had come to care for not only Charm, but for Preston, and of course, for Daniel, who was trying so hard not to slip into their way of life, fighting to remain what he had become during his captivity.

"Kate, recite something for us, would you please?"

Drawn out of her musing, Kate saw Charm smile expectantly, seated across from Preston, elbows on the table, her chin in her hand. The day that Jonah had proposed, Charm had been so upset that Kate had recited two humorous pieces, trying to cheer her. The girl had begged for more every evening since.

"You do recitations, Kate?" Preston leaned forward on his chair. "I would love to hear one."

Kate felt her color rise. "I used to teach elocution."

"What's echo-lution?" Charm asked.

"*Elocution.* According to the Latin, the word means 'to speak out,' from *e* meaning out and *loqui* meaning to speak."

"Whatever you call it, Kate is wonderful at it," Charm assured Preston. "As good as an actress I saw once in Saint Louis."

"Oh, I'm not anywhere near professional," Kate insisted.

"Please," Charm urged. "For me."

"And for me." Preston smiled encouragingly, his gray eyes intent, filled with something Kate did not dare to name. Her life was uncertain enough.

She stood and shook out her skirt, let the bright calico fall into place.

"I've never performed for a man," she told Preston, too nervous to begin.

"Then what if we both recite? Do you know any Shakespeare?"

Kate was tempted to deny it, but the thought of actually delivering a dramatic recitation with someone else was something she had never experienced. The idea intrigued her.

"I know a few passages from one or two of his works."

"Then we may be in luck. Do you know anything from *A Midsummer Night's Dream*?"

"Part of Act One, Scene One, was my older students' favorite."

"The scene between Lysander and Hermia?"

"Yes." Kate stood. "It's not very long and is easily memorized."

"I happen to know it, too."

Charm came to life and clapped her hands.

Daniel, aware that something was about to happen, sat up straighter. Kate tucked his long hair back behind his ear.

Ever the Southern gentleman, Preston offered, "I would be happy to join you, if you are willing to give it a try."

Kate nodded, and they stood together before the huge stone fireplace, a fitting background with the bucket of wildflowers Charm had set inside it.

Kate stood erect, pressed her hands firmly together and began to slowly inhale and exhale. The guide to elocution stated that the chest was a sounding board that gave strength to the voice. Beside her, Preston stood tall and straight and very, very close. Within seconds of his opening, his strong voice and lilting Southern drawl made him a wonderful orator. She was certain he was capable of delivering rousing sermons.

Too late she realized that this particular scene was entirely the wrong one to perform with a preacher.

Lysander and Hermia were lovers.

It had been two weeks since Reed had left the Rangers, two weeks since he'd gotten Tommy Harlan killed and Jonah had thrown him out of the company.

He had spent most of the last few days lost in a bottle of whiskey, holing up at one outpost or another until he had wound up in Lone Star last night, passed out at Dolly B. Goode's.

None of the girls would have done him any good, at least not with all the liquor he had consumed flowing through his veins.

Dolly, cheerfully assuring him that he looked like death warmed over and that his father would rise up out of his grave if she didn't do something, saw to it that he had a good night's sleep, a close shave, and a bath before he left her establishment.

Now, as he rode into the stable area behind the Benton House, Reed was thankful the robust madam had insisted on cleaning him up.

If he had arrived looking the way he had last night, he most likely would have scared Kate half to death.

As it was now, he no longer reeked of whiskey or self-pity. Hopefully, he had left them behind.

Scrappy was waiting for him as he rode in. The old cowhand had seen him the minute he came over the rise and had waved his hat over his head in greeting. Reed rode up, swung his leg over the saddle, dismounted, and handed the wrangler his reins.

" 'Bout time you decided to come back," the old cowhand said.

"Yeah. I guess so." He wasn't about to tell Scrappy what had happened. The afternoon sun beat down on them both as Reed glanced at the back door. There was no sign of life behind either of the long kitchen windows.

"The women are in the house," Scrappy told him without being asked. "So's the preacher."

Reed frowned. Hell, if it wasn't Sunday. Then he remembered it had been the damn church bell ringing that had shocked him out of a deep sleep this morning and set his head pounding.

Scrappy opened his mouth, then shut it without a word.

"What?" Reed looked into the old man's eyes.

"Nothin'."

"Come on, I can see you bustin' to say something. Out with it."

"Welcome back."

Reed knew that wasn't what the old man was going to say as sure as he knew it wouldn't do any good to push the stubborn old coot.

"Might as well go in and get it over with," Scrappy said as he started to lead Reed's horse away.

"Yeah, might as well."

Now was as good a time as any. Besides, he was curious to see for himself if the pretty little picture Jonah had painted for him of Kate, Charm, and the preacher was anywhere near true.

He let himself into the house without a sound, hung his hat on a rack near the door, and stopped at the stove to dip his finger in a pot of mashed potatoes. They were still warm as he scooped out a taste and then closed his eyes over the creamy delight. Bacon, beans, rice, and fresh-killed game could fill a Ranger's stomach, but there was nothing like a pile of mashed potatoes and a plate of golden fried chicken to warm his heart.

The sound of voices carried from the parlor. He walked out of the kitchen and entered the windowless hall. A breeze sneaked through the house from front to back along the hallway, a pleasant touch he had missed while living in a stifling tent.

He walked without making a sound, intent upon Kate's voice; then he heard the preacher's baritone. He stopped short of entering the parlor, lingered inside the double door to the entry hall, intrigued by a scene he could view without being seen.

Across the long room, framed in front of the fireplace, Kate stood beside the preacher. She was playacting, her voice growing stronger and more certain with each word.

Dressed in a calico dress that modestly covered her bountiful cleavage, Charm sat at the table watching in rapt wonder, her bright eyes shining. In a glance Reed noticed the girl looked younger and prettier than ever.

Daniel sat alone, paying close attention, though there was a look of scorn on his face. But even though he looked mad enough to spit worms, he was very still and watched intently.

Reed shook his head. Damned if Kate hadn't succeeded in pulling them all together somehow, this odd little band—preacher, whore, spinster, and wild child.

She had done what his father had wanted. She had brought life into this cavernous house, given it a family—not exactly the one his father had imagined, but a gathering of souls who shared laughter and meals and left their loneliness at the door.

Unnoticed as he stood alone watching them, Reed felt like an outsider, an intruder in a place where he had never intended to be again.

The preacher was taking a turn now, dramatically gesturing toward the east, going on about ". . . a widow aunt, a dowager of great revenue, and she hath no child."

The speech sounded pretty, but having missed the beginning, none of it made much sense to Reed. It was hard to concentrate on the minister's words, for he was arrested with Kate, with her glowing complexion and the fact that Texas agreed with her. If not Texas, then something or someone definitely did.

Her eyes were wide, dark and shining. Her hair was wound up in a loose, indifferent way that tempted a man to reach for the pins and let it fall around her shoulders.

I have missed her.

He hadn't realized how much until now.

He settled his shoulder against the door frame and crossed his arms, content to watch. It nagged at him like a burr in his sock that they made such a handsome couple— the preacher and Kate—and as he stood there watching, all his initial suspicions about what might be behind these little gatherings came back to him.

From the look on Kate's beaming face, he wouldn't doubt that she had already set her cap for the preacher. She had set out to get a husband when she answered his father's advertisement. Maybe the preacher would serve.

Suddenly, for the very first time ever, he saw her smile, really smile.

His insides turned to water.

Her entire countenance changed. She lit up the room.

The preacher noticed, too, and was winding up with a flourish. His stance and cadence changed as he took a step closer to Kate. Then he reached for her hand.

That's when Reed pushed away from the doorjamb.

". . . To do observance to a morn of May, There I will stay for thee," the reverend said.

Kate turned to the preacher. As he held her hand, she continued to smile up at him. Her cheeks were bright pink, her voice was as sultry and sensual as Reed remembered.

"I swear to thee by Cupid's strongest vow, By his best arrow with the golden head, By the simplicity of Venus' doves, By that which knitteth souls and prospers loves, And by that fire which burned the Carthage queen, When the false Troyan under sail was seen, By all the vows that ever men have broke, In number more than ever women spoke, In that same place thou hast appointed me, Tomorrow truly will I meet with thee."

Reed had heard enough.

31

He stepped farther into the room, his footfalls loud enough to turn heads.

He had no idea how Charm, Daniel, or the preacher were reacting to his surprise appearance. He was too intent upon Kate to notice.

As for her, all color drained from her face. Her lovely smile instantly faded.

It wasn't until he crossed the room and stood before her, staring into her shocked, upturned face, that she finally managed to speak. "What are you doing here?"

He hadn't expected a warm welcome. Nor was he about to explain how Jonah had kicked him out of the Rangers. He turned to the preacher, a tall, good-looking man with pewter-colored eyes, and dressed like a gentleman in black, straight-cut trousers and a jacket with bound edges. Despite the heat, he appeared perfectly comfortable in the suit jacket. Reed felt trail-worn and dusty in his wrinkled brown shirt and denim pants.

"Mr. Benton, I'm Reverend Prescott Marshall. Kate has been kind enough to invite me to join her and Miss Riley for supper on occasion." Marshall offered his hand and a warm, friendly smile.

"Call me Reed." He shook the minister's hand and nodded, wondering just how many other occasions there might have been. Noting Marshall's empty left sleeve, he finally remembered what he had heard.

The man had been a war hero in the South, once quite wealthy. He had moved to Texas after he lost everything but his faith. He looked like a good enough sort, but not the kind of man Reed would have ever associated with. But there he was, standing in the middle of the parlor.

My parlor now.

Charm put the checkers into a small, carved wooden box and carried it with the painted game board to a bookcase across the room. She paused, looked at Reed, and gave him a nervous smile.

When Reed's gaze touched Daniel, he saw that the boy had not moved. Like Kate and Charm, Daniel looked far healthier than before and had even put on some weight. After less exposure to raw sunshine, his skin had faded and he looked less like a Comanche.

If it weren't for his long hair hanging almost to the middle of his back, there would be no outward sign of his years of captivity left at all.

Then Reed noticed the crutch resting against the arm of the settee and felt an unexpected pang. He tried to shake it off, but it clung to him like a burr on wool.

"How's his ankle?" He trusted Kate to be frank and not pretty up the truth.

"It's better, but I'm afraid he's going to keep that limp." She smiled reassuringly at Daniel. It was certainly not the same charming smile she had given the preacher during the performance, but it held concern and warmth nonetheless. Daniel did not smile back.

The reverend cleared his throat, a reminder that he was still there. Grudgingly, Reed gave him his attention.

"I'm sure you and Kate have a lot to talk about, so I'll be

going now. It was a pleasure meeting you, Reed, and I'll look forward to seeing you again soon," Preston said.

"You are more than welcome to come back next week if you can," Kate urged. Reed realized she did not think she needed to ask his permission or his opinion on the matter.

Reverend Marshall thanked Kate and Charm for another wonderful meal. Reed told him good-bye and was not surprised when Kate walked the man to the door and led him out onto the porch.

He was straining to hear what they were saying through the open window when Charm walked over to him. Her fingers were knitted together. She seemed so nervous he was sure that if he said *boo* she would jump.

"Mr. Benton?"

"Charm. You call me Reed, too." He tried to make it easy on her. "What is it?"

"Is . . . is Captain Taylor all right?"

Reed saw everything Charm had not said on her face—the worry, fear, and deep concern for Jonah. The man had been her savior, perhaps the only person besides Dolly, and now Kate, who had ever really cared about her. It was no wonder she had feelings for his friend.

"He was just fine two weeks ago. I haven't seen him since then."

She looked relieved by his answer, but not by much. She thanked him and then asked if she could fix him a plate of leftovers.

"Thank you. I'd appreciate it," he said.

"Will you watch Daniel?" She must have seen the hesitation in his eyes. She added: "We don't ever leave him alone downstairs."

He glanced at the boy while trying hard to ignore the rise and fall of Kate's voice on the breeze, the snatches of conversation, which were not enough to actually piece together what was being said, just enough to make him damn curious.

It's none of your business, he reminded himself.

None whatsoever.

Daniel had not moved a muscle. Reed walked to the settee and sat at the other end. He draped his arm over the curved wooden back and watched the boy. His father's boy. Perhaps his own.

Alone with Daniel, Reed felt awkward and out of sorts, as if he had been tossed into a deep pond with his hands tied behind his back. When the child had been little, Reed had known just how to make him smile, just where to tickle him. The boy would squeal with laughter whenever he rubbed beard stubble against Daniel's smooth skin.

Becky had never minded that he wanted the boy with him all the time, or that he took him everywhere. He carried him around the homestead on his shoulders, let him play close by while he worked.

Daniel had been his constant companion. The apple of his eye. Now he didn't know if the boy could even understand one word of English yet or not.

"Daniel?"

There was no response. Daniel kept staring intently at the window, as though he was listening to Kate's voice. Whenever the good reverend spoke, the child frowned harder.

"Something you don't like about him?" Reed asked in a hushed voice. Daniel stared at him for a moment, then looked out the window again.

Just as stubborn, Reed wasn't about to use any of the Comanche words he had picked up over the years—or any Spanish, either, though it was likely Daniel had been exposed to the language.

So they sat side by side, stiff and silent, stoically ignoring each other as they waited for Kate.

Mere inches lay between them, yet they were worlds apart.

After Preston bade her good-bye, Kate silently closed the front door and lingered in the entry where Reed could not see her. She needed time to gather her wits, to calm her racing heart.

Reed was home. But for how long? A night? A few days?

Jonah had not mentioned Reed would be returning so soon. His appearance had caught her unaware. She reached up and patted her hair to see if the loose top knot on the crown of her head was still in place. Flushed and bothered, she was perspiring along her hairline and tried to blot the edge of her damp forehead with her fingertips.

Charm was rattling pots and pans in the kitchen. Outside, Scrappy was hammering something. Now and again, the heady scent of wildflowers floated in on the breeze.

Reed was back. How long did he intend to stay this time?

She had been in the middle of her final speech as Hermia when she sensed someone watching her. A chill arched down her spine long before Preston had taken hold of her hand, almost as if she had known Reed was there. Without seeing him, she had sensed that he was in the house. When he had stepped into the room and she had turned toward the sound of his footsteps, when she saw him walk in with that dangerous air about him, she was reminded of that very first day.

She had fallen in love with him before she had ever met him, in love with the word pictures Sofia had so falsely painted, in love with the bundle of letters she had kept with her constantly. She had fallen in love with the man in the photograph they had sent her.

But the man waiting for her in the parlor now was not that man at all. There *was* no such man. The real Reed Benton was another breed all together—a man who could turn his back on his family and his past, a man who had been deeply hurt and convinced that he needed no one. He was stubborn and so hardened by tragedy. And yet he was the same man she had given her virginity to so willingly, a man who wanted to love his son but didn't know how.

She knew nothing of his kind. Before him, before Lone Star, her world had been one of cloistered nuns, of babies and girls and properly trained, well-educated young women on the verge of making their own way in the world. Bells had summoned her to prayers, to Mass, to meals. She had virtually lived the life of a nun without the spiritual benefits.

What did she know of dealing with a man as hard and scarred as Reed Benton?

By the time she finally pulled herself together enough to face him, another five minutes had passed.

She took a deep breath and slowly walked back into the parlor.

Reed was slouched down, nearly hugging the arm on one end of the settee. Daniel was jammed up against the opposite arm. Each stared straight ahead, ignoring the other.

When she walked in, both of them turned her way, but neither smiled. They looked like two peas in too tight a pod. If the scene hadn't been so pitiful, she might have laughed at their matching expressions.

How was she ever going to get the two of them together?

And when she did, how was she ever going to walk away from them with her heart unscathed?

Fast Pony never thought he would be so glad to see the tall, angry man return, though he was not about to let Tall

Ranger see his relief. If anyone could keep Soft Grass Hands from going off with One Arm, this man could.

He had dared to slide his gaze over to watch Tall Ranger while they waited for Soft Grass Hands. From what he could see, Tall Ranger did not like One Arm talking to her any more than he did.

The woman had started acting strange when Tall Ranger walked in earlier, and now that she was back, she seemed content to stand and stare at Tall Ranger. When Fast Pony realized she was also watching him, too, he wondered if she was up to some kind of mischief. Then a terrible thought came to him.

What if One Arm had named his bride price outside? What if she had come to tell them good-bye?

Wouldn't One Arm have to offer Tall Ranger some horses for her? Maybe that was what the two men were talking about.

He felt desperately confused, not knowing all the ways or the words of the whites. Since they had brought him here, he never knew what was going to happen next, which was a very unsettling way to live.

Soft Grass Hands looked very scared. As scared as he felt.

The two grown-ups talked in short clipped tones, hoarding their words like precious winter stores. Soft Grass Hands had stopped smiling, but Tall Ranger seemed to relax the longer they spoke.

Fast Pony heard them say his white name, but he acted as if he did not know they spoke of him, wondering what was going to happen next.

Soft Grass Hands took his hand and led him back to the room that was not the cooking room, but where they ate whenever One Arm came to join them.

The girl, Yellow Hair, carried in a plate of steaming food

for the Ranger. When he sat down to eat, Soft Grass Hands spoke softly to Fast Pony.

He recognized the word *outside* and felt relieved. They were going to leave the dwelling. They were going out to walk across the land, just as they did every afternoon.

It was all he could do to keep from smiling, knowing Soft Grass Hands would leave Tall Ranger eating alone to take him outside.

She said something more to the man and then opened the door to the kitchen. With the aid of the walking stick under his arm, Fast Pony moved quick as a sidewinder, hoping to impress the Ranger with his speed.

It was good for one warrior to admire the skill of another. Even if they were enemies.

32

There were still a few good hours of the clear, sunny Sunday afternoon remaining as Kate and Daniel leaned against the horse corral watching a pinto filly run toward them.

A few days before, Scrappy had introduced Daniel to the leggy little foal and now, every time they went for a walk, Kate made certain she had sugar lumps, a carrot or an apple in her pocket to lure the horse over to them.

Resting her arms over the rail, Kate watched Daniel's slight smile as he fed the young pinto.

"You have a good friend there, Daniel, but she's a greedy little girl, that's for certain." Kate sighed and watched the boy prop his crutch on the fence rail and slowly climb to the top, where he could sit and watch the filly gambol around the corral.

Kate instinctively stepped behind him, tempted to hang on to the back of his shirt lest he topple off the fence. Despite his injury, he was incredibly agile, but she stayed behind him just in case.

"Quite a surprise we had today." She had grown used to carrying on one-sided conversations. She had no idea whether or not Daniel was surprised, but she had certainly felt the ground drop out from under her when she saw Reed standing in the parlor.

Reed had told her in the dining room that he had come back because his heart wasn't in rangering anymore. He planned to stay on, even meet with the foremen, and he fully intended to run Lone Star now that his father was gone. She didn't know whether to be relieved or not.

Daniel held out his hand and made kissing sounds as he tried to lure the filly back to the fence. Kate smiled.

"No matter what he said, I think he really came back because of you," she said, thinking out loud. "He would never admit it, even to himself. But just you wait and see. I'm sure that before long, you and he will be doing lots of things together. He is going to see what a wonderful boy you really are, just the way I do."

Daniel was already climbing down again, so Kate stepped back. He picked up his crutch and, wielding it deftly, hurried around to the other side of the corral where the filly was rubbing her head against the rail.

Kate followed slowly, watching him closely, at the same time thinking of the picture of Becky. Knowing how it had upset Daniel, she kept the photograph hidden in her dresser drawer. Since then, she had not tried to force him to remember his past, but she was still torn, hoping that she was doing right by him.

Raising a child, especially one injured in spirit, was a far cry from educating one. She had no books to help her, no mentor, and certainly no memories of a loving mother. Meg Whittington had been far from a glowing example of motherhood. The nuns, although firm and fair, had never done the little things Kate had sometimes seen other mothers do: cuddle and kiss and tease, dry tears, give praise.

She wanted all those things for Daniel, but was it fair to lavish love on him, knowing that her time here depended on Reed and on what he wanted for the boy?

What would *Becky* have wanted for her son? What advice would she give if she were here?

See to him as if he were your own. Make sure he is happy and healthy. Teach him to laugh again. Love my boy, my baby. Please. That's all I ask.

She had no idea if the words echoing in her heart were her own or Becky's. All she knew for certain was that she already cared deeply for the boy.

What would happen to him if she left?

By now Daniel had lost interest in the filly and was walking with his head down, searching the dirt—a pastime he seemed to thoroughly enjoy, especially when he found something for her, like a pretty rock, an iron nail, or some other treasure.

She wanted to come up with ways to get Reed and Daniel to know each other again. She had no idea how she was going to do it, but she was bound and determined to have Reed spend time alone with the boy.

Inside, Reed finished his meal and thanked Charm.

"Kate and Daniel are out by the corral. He sure loves horses." She took his plate and deftly shoved it in the dishpan and soaped it off.

Of course he does, Reed thought. A Comanche lived his life on the back of his horse. Entire villages were moved by horse travois. Boys learned to ride as soon as they could walk. Horses were trained to hunt. The animal was a symbol of Comanche wealth, live currency that bought brides and settled debts. Some warriors acquired vast herds.

Charm was watching Kate and the boy through the window over the dry sink. He thanked her again, complimented her cooking, and walked out of the kitchen. Unobserved, he sat on the veranda rail and watched.

Kate appeared to be talking to the boy, stubbornly refusing not to give up on him. He watched her stand protectively behind Daniel as he climbed the fence rails, saw her reach up and smooth out the wrinkles on the back of his shirt.

She was good for him, no doubt about that. There was something in Kate, perhaps her gentleness and patience, that were traits Becky never possessed. Becky had been incredibly selfish, maybe even incapable of loving anyone but herself.

He had discovered that shortly after they were married. She had been beautiful, outgoing, and an incorrigible flirt. He had loved her the moment he saw her. Once they were married she had him heart and soul, but she never had the life that she thought the Benton wealth should have afforded her.

Back then, he had been naive enough to think that if he could get her away from all the trappings and things his father's money could buy, that she would love him for himself.

He saw the old dog-run homestead cabin on the edge of the ranch as a private place, a romantic, rustic spot where the three of them could really become a family.

Becky saw it as a run-down shack. A trap. She thought he was punishing her by depriving her of all she ever wanted.

It was hard to admit that his father had been right about her. She had never really loved him at all. She had loved the Benton money, the vast holdings, her status in town as a Benton's wife.

Reed watched Kate help Daniel down. When she turned away, the boy continued to watch her. Reed couldn't help but notice that Daniel watched Kate with something more than respect in his eyes. There was acceptance, perhaps even a bit of admiration there, too. Daniel was starting to care for Kate. There was definitely a bond between them now.

Kate had made so much progress with Daniel that Reed was moved. He stood up, walked over to the stairs. Beneath the shade of the overhang, he watched as they walked around the corral.

What if Kate suddenly took it in her head to leave? There was absolutely nothing to stop her. The papers Jeb Cooley had drawn up were in his saddlebag. Legal documents that, once signed by both of them and filed, would render the forged marriage license null and void.

They would both be free. Sooner or later Kate would recover from the shock of his father's deception. Sooner or later she would want a life of her own.

Hell, maybe she was already dreaming about marrying the damn minister.

Could the old man have been right about Kate? Had his father somehow sensed that she would be good for Lone Star? She would make any man a good wife. Was she the right mother for Daniel?

The boy bent over and picked up something small from the dry ground and handed it to Kate. She held it in the palm of her hand and studied it carefully. They stood there for a time, heads together, looking at whatever it was.

Reed could almost hear Kate lavishing compliments on Daniel. The exchange surprised Reed more than anything he had seen yet today. For Daniel to share a gift with Kate, no matter how insignificant, was a great step.

Maybe she will consider staying on permanently.

Maybe the marriage does not have to be dissolved.

For Daniel's sake, maybe we should stay wed—in name only.

Shaken by his train of thought, Reed dragged his fingers through his hair. He was in worse shape than he figured if he was even *considering* the possibility.

As he watched Kate and Daniel walk back to the house, he knew that she would be an easy woman to love, if he let himself. He wanted her on a physical level, for she was lovely and definitely moved him in that way. She was also warm and sensitive, and as she had said herself, loyal. But she had been hurt and embarrassed by what had happened between them. Was she willing? It was hard to say.

Even if she was, he didn't know if he could put his past behind him. All he had to do was think of Becky, of all the ways he had tried to make her happy and how he had failed, of her betrayal, and he was pretty damn sure that he never wanted to take a chance on love again.

But as Kate walked across the open area behind the house, as he watched the graceful, easy sway of her hips and heard the low, provocative sound of her voice, his attraction to her made contemplating a closer relationship with Kate very, very tempting.

The boy was the first to notice him and stopped immediately in his tracks. His gaze locked on Reed's guns.

Kate touched Daniel lightly on the shoulder, urged him toward the house. When he balked, she looked up. Her eyes met Reed's, and his hand tightened on the porch rail.

After a noticeable pause, she took Daniel's hand and led him forward as if there was nothing wrong, but the look on the boy's face, his hesitance to approach, told Reed there was still no love lost there.

Once they crossed the porch, Kate opened the door for Daniel, took his chin in her hand and forced him to look at her. She leaned close and spoke slowly.

"Go inside, and Charm will give you some cookies."

She made certain her voice carried to the kitchen where Charm was still working. The girl immediately came to the door, smiled in assurance, and Kate knew without exchanging a word that Charm would look after Daniel.

Reed began to wonder if his sudden return would upset the applecart. Things seemed to be running smoothly enough without him.

Kate lingered instead of going back inside. Reed was glad. "Does he understand you?" He stepped back, leaned a hip against the rail again, and settled his weight. Despite his attraction, she had a calming effect on him.

"I think so. I believe he's just too willful to speak."

"Why haven't you cut his hair yet?"

She looked startled at the suggestion. "Because it's all he has left of his old life. We've taken away the rest. You can't imagine what that's like." There was a deep abiding sadness in her voice.

He could tell her thoughts were drifting back to her past, the life he had read about in her letters.

. . . abandoned on the steps of an orphans' home . . .

He did not remind her that he, too, knew what it was like to have his life snatched away in an instant, to have to go on. His life had been taken from him one night beneath a Comanche moon.

He looked down at the new dress she was wearing, the fabric covered with the tiniest of printed flowers. It wasn't fancy, but it fit her well, outlined her curves and hollows and was an improvement over the worn, somber, spinster's garb.

"What about you, Kate? Do you miss your old life?"

She tilted her head, stared at the corral, deciding. "Sometimes I do. I miss the girls. I miss the cold. And the forest behind the orphanage. Things seem much closer there, the buildings, the streets, the trees are all gathered together. It was almost as if nature held everything together. And I miss the sea." She looked beyond the veranda, toward the horizon. "I've never seen such wide open sky before as here, and there weren't these winds to contend with, either. Texas makes me feel ... lonely, I guess." She shrugged. "Alone against the elements."

"Some folks go crazy out here. The wind and the loneliness drives them right out of their heads."

She smiled. "I'm not going out of my head," she assured him. "I just miss the East sometimes."

He moved away from the rail. Took a step closer. "Are you really lonely, Kate?"

Their eyes met. She looked thoughtful for a moment, and then a wistful smile tipped the corners of her mouth. "Sometimes, but I don't know why. Charm is wonderful company, and there's Daniel, too."

Another step, and he was close enough to touch her. "People need more than friendships, Kate." He spoke softly, so that only she could hear him. "That's only natural."

He watched the tip of her tongue slide across her full lower lip as she contemplated his words. Small lines appeared between her eyebrows as she stared back at him, frowning. "Is it?" she whispered.

"Is it what?"

"Natural. To want more."

He could see the idea disturbed her. She had, after all, been raised by celibate women.

"Yes." He was tempted to show her how natural it was, tempted to cup her jaw, turn her face up to his, and taste her soft, full lips. Instead, he made himself step back, walk over to the rail, and look out over the land until he'd gotten control of his emotions again.

When he turned back around, she was rubbing her thumb over something she held in her hand.

"What's that Daniel found for you?"

"Were you watching?"

"Yeah."

She smiled again, a small triumphant smile, and opened her palm. "It's an arrowhead."

She handed it to him. A pointed obsidian flint glittered in his hand.

"The ground is full of them," he said.

"We find something new almost every day. Daniel has taught me so much."

"Without talking?"

"People don't need words to share what's in their hearts."

He shrugged. "I guess not."

"I can see what's in yours, Reed. It's reflected in your eyes."

"And what is that, Kate?" If she could really read his mind, she would be blushing ten shades of red.

"You wish that you could do more than stand in the shadows and watch your son. You would like to know how to talk to him, what to say to help him realize that he is home. That he is safe. That you don't intend to lose him again. You want to start over."

Daniel again. His jaw felt tight. His heart ached. "You need glasses," he said.

"You wish you could make him understand that you are his father. You want to love him, but you don't know how."

He stared at the arrowhead until the edges blurred, and he silently damned her for saying such things to him—then he damned himself letting her poke around the hardened corners of his heart.

Without a word, he handed it back and headed for the dark interior of the barn, where a man could think without somebody peering into the dark, secret places of his soul.

.   .   .

Reed wasn't alone long before Kate walked into the barn dragging Daniel with her. The boy was scowling.

"Charm is trying on a new dress she's made and wants me to pin up the hem. I was hoping you wouldn't mind watching Daniel for a few minutes."

He knew what she was up to, but he had a strong feeling it wouldn't do him any good to refuse. "It's Sunday. I thought God-fearing folk didn't work on Sunday," he said.

She blinked twice. "Well, sewing is more of a hobby for Charm than work. A pastime, really." Then she took Daniel's hand and drew him closer to the stall where Reed was currying one of the horses.

"He loves them," she informed him.

"So Charm said." He didn't tell her that if the boy ever managed to actually get on a horse, he would probably be gone.

"I'm sure you can find something for him to do. I'll be back in no time at all," she said.

Reed watched her sashay out of the barn. So did Daniel. Reed couldn't help but notice the smoldering anger on the boy's face. His savior had just betrayed him. Delivered him right into the hands of the enemy.

Reed took a deep breath and let it go, shook his head as he looked down at Daniel. "This was inevitable, you know? She's a stubborn woman. It looks like we're stuck with each other until she decides otherwise."

Daniel ignored him. Reed held the curry brush out to him.

The boy looked up, then back down at the brush. Reed indicated the horse with his hand, then held the brush out to Daniel again.

"You want to brush him?" Reed demonstrated, making a few even strokes down the horse's flank. "Do that."

This time Daniel reached for the brush, but slowly, as if it were a snake that he was afraid might strike, but he took it anyway.

Reed's heart tightened when Daniel propped his crutch against the side of the stall, but he didn't seem to need any help as he slowly limped over to the horse's side. He used the animal for support and hesitantly began to apply the brush.

The only sounds in the barn were those of the horses moving about in their stalls and the rustle of doves nesting high in the rafters.

A sudden, unexpected feeling of serenity stole over Reed as he watched Daniel work, a feeling of peace the likes of which he had not known in years.

The need to touch the boy was overwhelming. He raised his arm, held his hand above Daniel's glossy hair for a moment and then dropped his arm. Too soon. Too soon to leave himself open and vulnerable to more heartache. Daniel was here only because Kate had marched him out to the barn. Reed couldn't risk touching him, igniting his hatred again, but he ached to turn time backward, to make things different. He just wished he knew for certain how to go about it.

Uncomfortable with such raw new feelings, he shoved his hands in his pockets and glanced toward the barn door, wondering exactly how long it would be before Kate returned, refusing to be lulled into thinking that their troubles were over.

Peace was only temporary, at best. He had been a Ranger far too long to believe any different.

33

Thirty minutes later Kate walked into the kitchen on her way to get Daniel and came to a sudden halt when she discovered Reed and the boy already seated at the table. Her heart turned over. She had forgotten what it was like to have him around, how her pulse sped up each time she saw him.

Then she took in Reed and Daniel together. They were ignoring each other. Daniel concentrated on the cookies he had lined up on the oilcloth table cover while Reed sat slumped in a chair, his arms crossed over his chest, his long legs extended, boots crossed at the ankles.

When he realized she was there, he straightened.

She pasted on a smile, hoping she had made the right decision leaving him and the boy alone. For the most part, they looked none the worse for wear.

"I'm sorry that took longer than I expected. Was he any trouble?"

"None."

She knew better than to expect details. He gave her a look that told her he knew she had contrived to leave them alone. It wouldn't do to press her luck.

"Well, that's good. Thank you for watching him."

She walked over to the cupboard, took down a cup and

saucer and poured herself coffee from the pot warming on the back of the stove. She offered some to Reed, but he refused.

Kate sat at the opposite end of the table. In moments like this, when he seemed so distant, she found herself wondering if the night they had made love had ever really happened at all.

"What started the preacher coming around?" Reed asked without warning.

Coffee sloshed over the rim of her cup. Collecting herself, she took a sip. "Do you mean Reverend Marshall?"

"You have *more* than one preacher coming around?"

She had no idea if Scrappy had already told him why she had sent him to town after Preston, but she had no reason to hide it. She had fully intended to tell Reed about the Greenes' visit, but she wanted him to settle in first.

"I sent for him because I needed his help."

He sat up straighter, leaned his elbows on the table. "What for? What happened?" His dark brows knit in concern as his eyes became even more intense.

"Your former in-laws came to see Daniel."

The boy looked up at the sound of his name and then quickly concentrated on the mess he was making with the cookies. There were crumbs and sugar sprinkled all over the table in front of him. He licked the tip of his index finger, dabbed up crumbs with it and licked them off.

"Why didn't you send for me?"

"You left me here to handle things, so I did."

"What happened?"

"They wanted to take Daniel home with them, but I will be completely honest with you. I didn't like them. They were far too stern. They thought Daniel would be fine if they just beat the devil out of him. I didn't want to let them take him, so I told them I couldn't consider it until I spoke to you."

He nodded, waited for more.

"When they questioned my authority, I . . . I told them that I was not just the housekeeper . . . but that I was your wife."

His brows shot up. He cleared his throat. "My wife."

"Yes, but they didn't believe me. I told them to ask the minister in Lone Star. I sent for Pres—the minister to tell him what I had done."

"And he came running."

"In a manner of speaking, yes. I told him about the Greenes and explained . . . the rest . . . that we weren't really married . . . but, well, I told him about everything. Well, most of it anyway."

He was watching her with an unreadable expression. She found herself shifting under his cool stare. "So the good reverend knows everything?" He hadn't moved an inch.

"Yes. He does, except for . . . except the personal things." Embarrassment forced her to look down at her hands. "He promised to keep my confidence."

He was silent so long that she finally looked up. He was still staring at her.

"Have you spoken to your lawyer? About the papers?"

"I did," he said.

"And?"

There was another long pause.

"We'll both have to sign an affidavit swearing that my signature was forged and that you were tricked into the proxy marriage. After he files them, the marriage will be null and void."

It will be over.

She thought back to that day in Maine, of how hard it

was to find two witnesses in town who would stand up for her. A traveling salesman had finally agreed, for a small fee, to step in as proxy. He had been wearing a musty-smelling checkered suit, a bowler hat and bow tie, but she wouldn't have cared if he had had two heads. The salesman had only been a stand-in for the man she had fallen in love with, a substitute for her groom. She had held Reed's photograph in her hands.

Now, as soon as Reed's lawyer presented them with papers to sign, the marriage would be null and void.

So simple. So final.

Tell him you don't want to sign.

Tell him you wouldn't be opposed to an agreement, see what he says.

Go to Charm and ask her how to seduce him.

Had she imagined the warmth she had seen in his eyes an hour ago? Or had her own desire been reflected there?

Reed was still watching her. Daniel was kicking the leg of the table and squirming around on his chair.

Afraid Reed would turn her down, she left everything unsaid and changed the subject. "It's time for Daniel's bath."

"I'll bet he's never bathed so much in his life." Reed shook his head.

"He's actually beginning to like it, I think. Who wouldn't in that room your father built?"

He was staring at her speculatively now, almost as if he could see her in the huge tub.

She felt herself go crimson.

"I'll pump some water and put it on to boil," he offered, surprising her.

"Thank you."

"Don't mention it." He stood up. The chair legs protested

with a sharp squeal against the floor. He shoved his fingers through his hair and looked down at Daniel. "Did the Greenes say they would be back?"

She shook her head. "No, but I don't think we've seen the last of them. They ... claim you don't want to keep him, that if you did you would have been here."

Kate realized she was holding her breath, waiting for him to say something, anything reassuring.

"Yeah, well, I'm here now." He looked away from the boy. Nodded at her. "You did the right thing."

Reed watched them leave the room, listened to the sound of Daniel's crutch against the wood floor and Kate's voice as she chatted all the way down the hall.

She continually surprised him. She had faced down the Greenes—formidable foes, he knew. Becky had little love for them. He suspected her parents were the reason she had married him so soon after they had met. She told him outright that she wanted to get away from them, to be free of their overzealous beliefs and unbending rules.

Kate had done right by Daniel in his stead. He would never have agreed to let them take the boy, even if he had decided not to keep him. No child deserved that.

Reed picked up a pail beside the stove, took it over to the pump, and set the bucket beneath the spout. He primed the pump, and started working the handle up and down.

No wonder the minister was dancing attendance on Kate every Sunday. He probably felt sorry for her after hearing her long, sad tale. As much as he didn't want to admit it, Reed figured the reverend would make Kate a fine husband. She deserved someone that polite and well mannered. A true gentleman.

Anybody would make a better husband than me.

The affidavits were in his saddlebag. Once Kate signed, she would no longer be his concern. If she and the preacher married, her future would be secure.

But what he kept coming back to time and again was the notion that until those papers were signed and recorded, until the proxy marriage was declared null and void, Kate was legally bound, and she would stay at Lone Star.

34

It was Saturday. Clouds were gathering in the southwest; the air was close and thick. Even the horses in the corral were affected by the weather, too lazy to do more than swish their tails with their heads hanging.

Kate and Daniel were seated at the library table in the parlor where she was trying to teach him to copy the letters of his name when she looked out the window and saw a buggy coming over the rise like a little black spider crawling across the land.

She watched the driver negotiate the dry rutted road up to the house and as the buggy drew closer, Kate recognized Preston and wondered if Reed had seen him yet.

She heard footsteps overhead on the second floor in Reed's office. For the past week he had met with each of the four Lone Star foremen and afterward spent hours alone poring over ledgers and accounts.

She took the pen from Daniel, picked up a rag, wiped the steel point, and placed them in the pen case. Then she began to dab at the India ink on the ends of his fingers.

"We have a guest, Daniel. Shall we go out and greet him?"

Daniel used his crutch to limp over to the window and

together they watched Preston tie his horse to the hitching post. Kate motioned for him to follow her outside.

When she reached the veranda, Preston had already cleared the steps. "Good morning, Reverend. This is a nice surprise. What's brought you out here on such a hot morning?"

"How are you, Kate?"

"Doing quite well, despite the weather. I feel as if I might melt and run down into my shoes."

"You certainly don't look it. You look fresh as a daisy."

The screen door banged behind them, and Reed stepped out onto the porch. Daniel moved so close to her that he was pressed against her hip.

"Reed." Preston acknowledged Reed with a friendly nod.

"Preacher." Reed wasn't smiling.

"Would you like some lemonade?" Kate offered. "I believe Charm just made some." She tried to make up for Reed's less than enthusiastic welcome.

"I would love some." Preston smiled again. Reed stepped aside, and Kate led the way to the door.

"The church is having a Saturday afternoon social today, and I've come to invite all of you." Preston followed Kate down the hall.

Charm was in the kitchen rolling out pie crust. Preston sat down at the table. Reed walked in but continued to stand, and Daniel went straight to Charm and pressed close as a baby chick.

Kate poured the preacher a glass of lemonade as Preston went on to explain about the social.

"There'll be a dessert auction, plenty of home-cooked food, games. The town band will perform, too. I thought you might want to bring Daniel so that he could meet some other children."

Daniel was standing nose to crust with a hot apple pie that Charm had put on the dry sink. Kate realized how far he had come, but with his crutch, a headband around his forehead, and his hair halfway to his waist, she was afraid that other children would tease him unmercifully, especially in a place where animosity toward the Comanche was a way of life.

As if he could read her thoughts, Reed interceded. "It's too soon for him to go to town." His tone brooked no argument. Then he glanced over at Kate and added, "Children can be mighty cruel."

Secretly she wished that there were some way she could go. In over a month she had yet to see anything of the ranch except this house and the land immediately around it.

She had never been to a church social, never walked along a street where she had not been treated with scorn or curiosity.

"Perhaps later, when Daniel is more . . . settled." She tried to keep the disappointment out of her voice, then she remembered that Charm had mentioned wanting to go into town to pick up the things she had left behind at Dolly B. Goode's. Although Charm certainly would not want to attend a church social, Kate knew she would appreciate the chance to see her friends and collect her things.

Kate caught Reed watching Daniel limp over to the table where Charm had set out a piece of pie. If she and Charm left for the day, Reed and Daniel would have hours alone together.

"Aunt Martha was looking forward to meeting you," Preston was saying. There was no mistaking his disappointment.

"Actually," Kate said quickly, "Charm has been wanting to collect some of her belongings, and I have not seen Lone Star yet. Perhaps the two of us could ride back to town with you for the day. Scrappy can drive in later and bring us back."

Reed was looking at her as if she had just sprouted green hair.

She crossed the room until she was no more than a few inches from him and lowered her voice. "You don't mind, do you? I haven't had a day to myself since we made our agreement."

She could see that he wanted to say no, but with Preston waiting for an answer and Charm looking hopeful as a new spring morning, she knew he could hardly refuse.

"What about Daniel?" Reed looked at the boy. He was busy stuffing apple pie into his mouth.

"Why he's no trouble at all. He'll just follow you around outside. Maybe you can let him help with the horses."

"They'll be back before dark," Preston assured him.

Reed looked uncomfortable, almost trapped. Kate tried not to smile too triumphantly.

"Fine." He finally agreed, but grudgingly. "Go ahead and have a good time."

For Reed it became a long, quiet, boring day that went from bad to worse as more dark clouds gathered on the horizon.

He waited on the veranda with Daniel as Kate and Charm got themselves gussied up and loaded into the preacher's buggy.

As soon as the buggy turned around and headed down the drive, Daniel had bolted off the porch, struggling to run with his crutch beneath his arm, trailing behind the carriage as the dust swirled up and blinded him. Kate and the others rode on, unaware Daniel had tried to follow.

Reed had to literally drag him back to the house, assuring him over and over that Kate would be back after supper, but Daniel was so despondent, Reed figured he was just wasting his breath. Eventually he fell silent and forced the boy to sit in his office while he worked. He gave him a lead pencil and some old ledger paper and showed him how to draw, but

Daniel refused to do anything except stare out the window and watch the empty road.

Finally, Reed took him outside. Afraid Daniel might get the best of Scrappy, he stood by idle while the boy helped the wrangler feed and water the horses.

Reed couldn't help but feel pride creeping up on him when he noticed the easy, natural way Daniel had with horses. A huge white Andalusian his father had imported was Daniel's favorite, and Reed knew why. Among the Comanche, white and pinto horses were the most valued of all.

"Didn't think I'd ever see it, but he's comin' along just fine." Scrappy walked over to where Reed was leaning against an open stall, watching Daniel pour feed into a trough.

"Kate's bound and determined to see it."

He had been thinking of her every other minute since she had waved and rode off neatly tucked in between Preston Marshall and Charm in the cramped buggy. She had changed into her blue silk gown and combed her hair up real fancy. In fact, both women had changed so fast he had been amazed. Becky had never gotten ready for anything in her life in under two hours.

"She's one of the most hardheaded women I ever seen," Scrappy mumbled.

Reed nodded in agreement. She was almost as stubborn as he. He would have liked to go along, liked to show her a good time, see her enjoy herself, but he couldn't imagine taking Daniel into town and subjecting him to ridicule. Even the Benton name wasn't big enough to prevent that, not now, not with the boy acting Comanche.

"They leave you anything to eat?" Scrappy asked.

"There's plenty in the kitchen. Want to join us later?" Things might go easier if he wasn't all alone with Daniel's brooding silence.

"Naw. Just gonna offer you some chili and beans. Course, if I left now, I could mebbe eat somethin' decent at that sociable."

There was no missing the hint. Reed sighed and found himself chuckling again. It didn't feel half bad, either. "Go on, then. It looks like it may rain tonight, so you best leave sooner than later."

Scrappy rubbed the gray stubble on his jaw. "You know what they say—"

"Fools and strangers predict the weather in Texas."

"Yep. Well, I guess I'll be going. If I get there in time I can get the week's supplies from the Mercantile, too." Then Scrappy looked at Daniel. "What are you gonna do with him for the rest of the day?"

Reed watched Daniel's long hair sway against his back as he limped around the stall and then stopped to rub noses with the Andalusian mare.

"I was thinking that with the women out of the house, maybe it's time to do a little barbering."

Fast Pony did everything Tall Ranger wanted, but he moved slowly, with the heaviest of hearts. Soft Grass Hands had put her arms around him, brushed her hand over his hair the way his mother always did, then she had spoken to him very softly before she left him, but she had left him just the same.

Now she and Yellow Hair were both gone. Both taken by One Arm who had not given one single horse in exchange for two women.

He hated Tall Ranger now, worse than before. His hate smoldered so deep that the time had come for him to leave. Trying not to draw suspicion, Fast Pony fed and watered the horses and whispered to the huge white mare that soon they would both be free of this place. Free to ride the prairie and find his people again. He promised the white horse that she would be happy at last because she would carry him, a great warrior, home. He would make her proud when he rode into the center of the village and told his tale.

He closed his eyes and pressed his cheek to the horse's soft muzzle and hoped that he would find his mother and his father both alive. He wanted to slip into his old life again and forget that this terrible thing had ever happened to him.

Now that Soft Grass Hands was gone, there was no reason to stay.

When he finished feeding and watering the horses, Fast Pony followed the Ranger back to the house. He didn't know why the man wanted to keep him anyway. Until today, he had not been expected to do any useful work, at least not anything Daniel considered to be of use.

Soft Grass Hands never expected anything of him except to listen and sometimes make the black D-A-N-I-E-L marks on paper. He still refused to speak. Whenever he was tempted to repeat words the way she wanted him to, he remembered his vow never to let the white man's words live in his mouth.

Tall Ranger stopped in the cooking room and pointed to a chair. Fast Pony decided that the man was going to feed him, so he sat down. After all, he needed to eat so that he would not get hungry on the trail. The band may have moved farther north and it could be a very long ride back to the Comancheria.

He tried not to appear to be watching as Tall Ranger picked up one of the white cloths hanging on a hook across the room. Soft Grass Hands used to tie one around his neck before he ate, and now Tall Ranger was doing the same thing, so it didn't alarm him. Tall Ranger covered Fast Pony's shirtfront, his shoulders, and smoothed out the white cloth.

Then he stepped back and was rattling things in the place where the dull silver knives and other eating tools were kept.

When Tall Ranger stepped close behind him, Fast Pony was tempted to look over his shoulder, suspicious of the big man, but he refused to let Tall Ranger see his fear.

Then, before Fast Pony knew what was happening, the man gathered his hair into a bunch and held it tight in his fist. With a swift sawing movement, he cut it off.

Fast Pony cried out in horror and twisted around on the chair. He yelled Comanche curses, calling terrible evil down on Tall Ranger as he stared in horror at the long clump of dark brown hair clutched in the man's hand.

Tall Ranger looked as shocked as Fast Pony felt, and for a heartbeat, the two of them stared at one another. Then Fast Pony ripped the white cloth from around his neck and threw it on the floor.

He was still yelling curses when Tall Ranger put aside the cutting tool and the hair and began to yell back. Fast Pony tried to jump off the chair, then he grabbed hold of the edge of the table. Tall Ranger reached for him, picked him up and held him tight against his shoulder.

Fast Pony started kicking and beating the man about the head with his fists. He could feel the air on his neck where his hair used to be, felt the ragged edges brushing against his earlobes and suffered deep, abiding shame.

He continued hitting Tall Ranger over and over with his fists as the man carried him up to the place where they made him sleep.

Reed took the stairs two at a time, kicked open the door to Daniel's room and tossed the ranting, raving, kicking, spitting boy onto his bed. When he hit the spread, Daniel's eyes widened, and he grew silent as he lay there panting, his chest heaving, staring daggers.

"You might have those two women wrapped around your little finger, but not me." Reed lowered his voice, reined in his temper, and with his hands on his hips, leaned over the bed.

"When you simmer down and act human, I'll let you out, but not a minute before."

Turning on his heel, Reed stalked out of the room, closed the door hard, and flipped the key in the lock. He pocketed it and went downstairs without looking back.

If the boy was going to be part of this household, he was going to start now, today, to learn to behave.

Reed walked back into the kitchen, picked up the long hank of hair he had left on the table and carried it to the trash box. He stood in the open doorway damning the gathering thunderclouds and the heavy smell of rain on the air and hoped Scrappy made it to town before the storm hit.

Then he thought about the tears shimmering in Daniel's eyes just before he had turned his back on him and walked out of the room.

35

They dropped Charm off in front of Dolly B. Goode's Social Club and Entertainment Emporium, which was situated close enough to the rest of Lone Star so that it could be seen, but far enough away so that the tinny sound of piano music that played night and day couldn't be heard.

Charm waved good-bye and was quickly enfolded into the arms of Dolly's lovely soiled doves lined up along the porch rail; standing together, they all formed a rainbow of satin and lace. They smiled and waved and threw boisterous, lip-smacking bare-armed kisses at Preston. He studiously avoided them all as he drove away.

Kate slid over to the far edge of the seat and concentrated on Lone Star as they neared the main part of town. From a rise a half mile away, the identical whitewashed houses and store buildings had looked like eggs nestled together in a basket.

As they drew near, she noticed that the majority of the places were two-room, single-story dwellings, built to house the cowhands' families, much like mining camp houses she had seen in the east from the windows of the train. Oak, maple, and poplar trees had been planted here and there behind and between the buildings on both sides of the street to give the town a more settled feel, but the trees appeared as uncomfortable and out of place as the houses.

Besides the homes, there was a dry goods store, a butcher shop, a boarding house that advertised meals, as well as the two-story church that Preston told her housed the town school upstairs. The only other business in town displayed a shingle proclaiming it was Jeb Cooley's place of law and real estate office.

The lawyer, Preston informed her, had returned from Europe but had left for Houston on business. Kate was secretly relieved that she wouldn't have to meet him.

I won't have to sign the papers yet.

The notion that she was thankful for the reprieve came to her unbidden and so did an image of Reed and Daniel alone at the kitchen table.

She shook herself and concentrated on the event in progress. The air was filled with the luscious aroma of a smoking barbecue pit, and the church social was already under way when they arrived. Many folk crowded around the preacher's buggy to greet Preston and meet Kate.

At first she felt shy, certainly like an impostor among people who knew each other so well, people who believed she was just a visitor from Maine, but they were all cordial and friendly, full of good humor and out to have fun. As far as anyone but Preston knew, she was the guest of their employer, and Sofia was still living at the house. Soon everyone's enthusiasm put her at ease.

Preston led her over to the dappled shade of an oak, where a smiling older woman with milk-white skin and hair to match sat fanning herself with a decorative fan covered with faded blue feathers and seed pearls. The fan, like the woman herself, must have been quite lovely once.

As they approached, the lady's eyes began to twinkle

mischievously with the glow of familiarity, and Kate knew in an instant that this had to be Preston's aunt Martha.

"I'm so pleased to meet you at last, dear." The woman spoke in the same thick Southern accent that colored Preston's speech. "Why, I declare, I thought Pres would never bring you to town."

Embarrassed, Kate blushed and complimented Aunt Martha on her fan.

Spry as a young girl, the older woman stood up and took Kate by the arm. "Come on, dear, let me introduce you around and show you what goings-on we have here in Lone Star."

She chatted unceasingly while holding on to Kate's arm, almost as if she were afraid Kate would bound away at any given moment. Pulling her into the church, Aunt Martha led her to the back room, where a few of the older ladies had set up a quilt rack and were working on a lovely, perfectly stitched patchwork piece, a wedding quilt for a young cowhand and his bride-to-be.

Kate declined taking a turn, claiming her stitches were far too uneven to be included on such a fine piece of work. A fussy quilter in charge of the group looked relieved. Kate and Martha wandered back outside where young people were dancing to lively fiddle tunes beneath the trees.

Martha watched them for a while and then tugged on Kate's arm until she bent closer. "They can really cut the pigeon's wing, can't they? Why, we were never allowed to do such forward dances in my day, but then, that was decades ago, honey. Let's go on over and take a look at the food they have laid out, then, after that, it will be time for the Lone Star Cowboy Marching Band to perform. We don't want to miss that." Then she burst into gales of laughter.

Kate's head was filled with sights and sounds and smells she had never experienced before. The Cowboy Marching

Band proved to be, if nothing else, loud. The bass drum nearly drowned out two off-key trumpets and one French horn, which was probably for the best. As for marching, the cowboys were not able to walk and play at the same time, but seeing a band decked out in mismatched shirts, wearing chaps and spurs, gun belts and John B. Stetson hats was a pure delight.

Preston stayed with her as much as he could, but everyone wanted to talk to him, to confide in him and draw him aside. She soon realized what a demanding job it was to be the only preacher for miles around. He baptized and buried, and if he were to stay here a lifetime, would see some of these folk from cradle to grave.

After finishing a plate of supper from food laid out on long tables covered with white sheets and platters of turkey, pork, venison, pies, cakes, chicken, eggs, butter, and preserves—more food than Kate had ever seen in one place in her life—Preston asked her to walk off supper with him.

They strolled along the storefronts, lingered in front of the dry goods store. For so remote a place, it seemed very well stocked. Preston glanced back toward the picnic area at the far end of the street.

"Kate, there's something I want to ask you, but I hesitate to jeopardize our friendship in any way."

"I wouldn't worry about that," she said softly, noting that he had suddenly grown very serious. She couldn't imagine what he might say that could possibly threaten the congenial bond between them.

"You have come to mean a lot to me, Kate, even in the short time I've known you."

Startled by the turn of the conversation, she looked down and shoved a pebble between the cracks in the boardwalk with the toe of her shoe.

She had no idea how she should return his compliment.

Certainly she cared for him as a friend, but what exactly did he mean that she "meant a lot" to him?

"I'm glad we are friends, too, Preston. I'm glad that I confided in you."

"With Jeb Cooley back in Texas, I'm sure that everything will be cleared up sooner rather than later."

"What would people think of me if they ever found out?"

"Jeb values his job, so I'm sure that he can be trusted not to tell Benton secrets. What Reed Senior did to you wouldn't surprise many people here, though. He was a tough man, Kate, a hard man. He had to be, in order to hang on and survive out here. You shouldn't be ashamed. You are the innocent one in all of this."

Innocent?

Shame washed over her. She had spent a night in Reed's bed. She was no longer innocent.

"Do you love Reed, Kate?"

Do you love Reed?

He asked the one question she had been afraid to ask herself. She took a deep breath and let go of a sigh.

"I was just getting to know him when he went back to the Rangers." She threaded her fingers together and twisted them back and forth.

"So, you're saying you don't know him enough to love him."

"I know he seems to be a hard man on the outside but . . . ," she stopped, knowing there was no way she could begin to explain Reed Benton, even if Preston had wanted to listen.

Preston seemed to understand. "Reed couldn't do what he's done all these years or seen the things he has seen and not be hardened by them. You don't ride into battle and not lose another piece of your soul every time." He lifted his shoulder above his empty coat sleeve. "Believe me, I know."

He is a good man, she thought. Good enough to try to explain Reed.

Preston sighed, looked back toward the picnic grounds again. Folks were gathering up their baskets and children, folding tablecloths, loading wagons.

"Could you love him? What is it you want from life, Kate?"

Could she love Reed? Yes. She could. Perhaps she already loved him a little. More than a little.

Two months ago she thought she knew what she wanted out of life: a real home, a family of her own. Her dreams had blown away like the dust on the prairie.

She did know what she wanted for the man and the little boy at Lone Star. "I want Reed to love his son again. I want to see them make peace with each other."

"There's no one here like you, Kate. You're refined, well educated."

"You don't really know me, Preston." She wished he would stop.

"I know enough. These past few weeks have been wonderful for me. I've found myself counting the days until Sunday comes along, looking forward to my life in a way that I haven't for a long, long time."

"I'm glad that you feel that way, I—"

When he took her hand, she was too stunned to move. "I want you at the head of my table, Kate. I want to marry you and raise children with you. You don't owe Reed Benton anything. Leave the ranch and move to town."

"But, how would I live?"

"Marry me."

"Oh, Preston, it's too soon."

"I understand. You certainly don't have to decide right away, but I can get you employment at the Mercantile if you want to leave Lone Star. I don't blame you for not want-ing to jump from the frying pan into the fire, but I love you and I don't believe in beating around the bush."

She thought of Sofia's parting words.

"Fight for what you want, but not forever. Do not waste your life waiting for Reed Benton to fall in love with you. . . . Do not make the same mistake I did."

A place to live. Employment in Lone Star, away from Reed. Away from Daniel, too.

"Kate?"

"Yes?"

"Think about everything I've said, but promise me one thing."

"What's that?"

"That you will give me a chance to win your heart."

36

For Kate, it was a long, reflective ride home in the Benton buckboard that night.

Though heat clouds had gathered on the horizon all day, there had been no rain. All the way back, miles off in the distance, lightning bolts sparred between the clouds.

She had to poke Scrappy in the ribs twice to keep him from dozing off and letting go of the reins while Charm fell sound asleep in the back of the wagon.

Despite the bumps and jolts, the girl slept deeply, slumped over her retrieved trunk with her head cradled on her arms. Having hoped to hear something of Jonah while she was in town, Charm left disappointed. No one at Dolly's had seen or heard from him.

But Charm's predicament was not foremost on Kate's mind on the ride home. Over and over she thought about Preston's asking her to give him a chance to win her heart.

Until the moment he proposed, she had no idea her heart was any kind of a prize.

The wagon rattled and rolled into the corral area just as the last light of the long summer day faded from the sky. Scrappy pulled the team close to the back door and climbed down. He was tying the reins to the hitching post when Reed came out the back door.

The lamplight escaping the kitchen windows gilded sparkles of water droplets in his hair. His shirt had been hastily donned and was still unbuttoned at the throat. Kate's breath caught. She stared at the bare skin showing beneath the hollow of his throat. When she looked up, she knew that he had been watching her.

Thankfully it was too dark for him to see her blush when he offered her his hand. She hesitated for a heartbeat and then accepted.

When his fingers closed around hers, hard and strong and confident, an unexpected thrill shot through her. She had forgotten just how electric his skin felt against hers.

How simple a thing, the touch of a man's hand, and yet the contact immediately set her heart pounding. The very idea that such innocent yet intimate contact could evoke such a physical reaction gave her pause.

Preston had taken her hand that day, too, to help her out of his buggy. All day he had lightly rested his hand at her waist as he escorted her around the social, yet his touch had not evoked more than feelings of friendship and trust.

On solid ground, Kate brushed road dust off her skirt, and then she smiled at Reed.

He, on the other hand, was not smiling.

"Did you have a good time?" He stood aside while she glanced over her shoulder. Scrappy had already awakened Charm and was unloading the girl's trunk.

"I wish you and Daniel could have come," Kate told him. "Everyone was so nice. The food was delicious. Preston's aunt sent along some cream cake and half a dozen delicious buttermilk biscuits for both of you."

Collecting the cake gave her an excuse to put space

between them. She moved around to the back of the buckboard, reached for a small tin bucket of carefully wrapped and layered baked goods, and handed it to Reed.

He took it without a word, and they started back toward the house together.

The air was close and still. Rolling thunder headed toward them, growing closer with every peal. She glanced up at the dark second-floor windows.

"Is Daniel already in bed?" She picked up her skirt, careful not to trip on the uneven ground. They had reached the veranda steps before he responded.

"He's in his room."

There was something in his voice, something more guarded than usual. She stopped on the second step and looked back at him.

"What's the matter?"

"Let's go inside first," he said.

"Reed—"

He was stubbornly silent as he walked past, opened the door, and waited for her to step inside.

Everything appeared fine in the kitchen, right down to the clean dishes laid out on a dish towel to dry.

He set down the bucket. She wanted to give him the benefit of the doubt, told herself that nothing was wrong. She even smiled.

Until he looked her straight in the eye. There was a hint of a challenge in his stare. "I cut off his hair," he said.

"You did what?"

"I cut off his hair."

"What did he do?" Her palm went to her midriff. She found it hard to speak.

"He threw a fit. Started hitting me, kicking, generally raising the roof. I locked him in his room until he settles down." Reed hooked his thumbs in his waistband and stood there daring her to object.

She was tempted to run upstairs and comfort Daniel. Instead, she forced herself to stay calm. She licked her lips. Swallowed.

"Is he all right?"

"Do you still think I would hurt him?"

She let her silence demand an answer.

"He's fine. Just madder than a hornet."

The air inside the house was growing thick as custard. The temperature had risen since she walked in. Kate ran her fingertips along her damp temple.

"I'll just slip in and tell him good night." She started to leave.

Reed was beside her before she had taken three steps. His hand closed over her arm, stopping her in her tracks. She looked at it and then unflinchingly met his gaze. He let go.

"You can see him tomorrow. I want him to learn he can't act that way around here anymore."

She glanced toward the stove. "Did you give him any dinner?"

"I took him some."

"Did he eat it?"

"I don't know. I didn't go back in."

"Oh, Reed . . ."

"Look, Kate. You've been hounding me to act like his father. Now that I have, you want to step in. It won't hurt him to miss a meal if he's that rock-headed. He won't starve overnight. By tomorrow he'll be over it, and he will know he can't throw a fit and kick or spit whenever things don't go his way."

Suddenly, her head was pounding. She ached all over from the jolting ride in the buckboard. She felt gritty and tired and more than a little overwhelmed by everything that had happened.

Now this.

She sighed heavily and tapped her foot for a second while she thought things through.

Reed leaned a hip against the kitchen table. "I suppose your preacher wouldn't have handled Daniel this way."

"He's not *my* preacher. He's my friend. I don't know why you have taken such a dislike to Preston."

"Your *friend*? I'll bet he'd like to be a hell of a lot more than that." He was tight-jawed and angry—at Daniel, or her, or both, she couldn't tell.

He might as well have set a match to both her cheeks after mentioning Preston like that, hinting that the preacher might want more of a relationship.

How does he know?

"I'm right, aren't I?" He came away from the table and took a step closer, crowding her.

She tried to step back but came up against the edge of the table. "It's no concern of yours what Preston Marshall thinks or what he wants from me. You are my employer, Reed. You are *not* really my husband, nor do you own me."

She drew herself up, stepping forward until they were nearly nose to nose.

"No, I don't, do I?"

He was staring at her mouth. Standing so close that she could see herself reflected in his eyes. She stared at his lashes, made the mistake of glancing at his lips.

Kiss him.

She could almost hear Charm urging her on. Kate closed her eyes, told the voice in her head to stop tempting her. When she opened her eyes, something in his had softened. He was as shaken as she.

Reed stepped back. "Hell, Kate. I don't know what I'm doing."

Instantly her anger cooled, but more than ever she wanted to take him in her arms, to comfort and reassure him.

"It's not easy," she said softly. "Neither of us knows exactly how to help him."

"You're better at this than I am." He sounded reluctant when he admitted, "I don't know what I'd do if you weren't here."

If she wasn't here, he would have to take charge. Daniel would be entirely his responsibility then, unless he found someone else willing to take over.

"You would do just fine." She gave a deep sigh. "I'm going up to wash up and go to bed. You're right. I did ask you to act like Daniel's father, and now it seems you have taken things into your own hands. I'll do as you ask and wait to see him in the morning."

She hoped to goodness that he hadn't undone everything she had accomplished so far.

Reed watched her go, shoulders stiff, skirts swishing behind her. Life on earth might be a hell of a lot easier without women.

Her chiming in was not what he needed tonight. He had already berated himself all afternoon for what had happened. Maybe he should have taken more time, maybe even tried to sign to the boy or tell him what he was going to do in broken Comanche instead of lopping off Daniel's hair without warning.

It was too late for *if only*. He had almost settled it in his mind—then Kate had come back. He had even come to terms with her going into town with the preacher. Now she had more than his temper all stirred up.

In the glow of the lamplight when he had walked out to greet them, he had seen a smile in her eyes that reminded him of the morning after they made love. A smile full of promise that reminded him that she had burrowed way under his skin since that day. Lately he had begun to think of her as much more than a housekeeper. Much more.

Earlier, there had been something in her touch that he couldn't deny, as if she had come home pleased to see him—until he told her what he had done.

He walked over to the dry sink and dipped out a ladle full of water from a stoneware crock and glanced out the window. Heat clouds were drifting closer, the sky wild with distant lightning. The land was dry, the summer grass yellow. There would be hell to pay if a prairie fire started tonight.

He drained the glass but got no relief from the heat, inside or out. Between the oppressive temperature and the thunder—not to mention the emotional storm playing itself out inside the house—he wondered if he would get any sleep at all.

Upstairs, Fast Pony knelt by the open window watching the lightning race closer. His walking stick stood in the far corner of the room and there it would stay.

He did not need it.

He barely limped at all anymore and hadn't for weeks. Using the walking stick, pretending to be crippled had been his sly way of tricking the whites.

Soft Grass Hands had come home. So had Yellow Hair. At first, he had been so relieved to see the women that he thought maybe he should stay a while longer.

Then he missed the feel of his long hair on his neck and remembered what Tall Ranger had done to him. He waited for her, but Soft Grass Hands did not come in to see him. He wanted to see her one last time, to have her sit beside him. He wanted to hear her speak softly to him the way she did every night before he went to sleep.

He had waited for her, but she had not come.

He was leaving tonight, and she would never see him again.

She would never know what Tall Ranger had done to his hair—unless the man already told her. Maybe she did not care.

Fast Pony opened his hand and stared at the little metal stick that kept the door from opening. All the thin sticks were exactly the same. He had discovered that one day when Yellow Hair had been cooking, ignoring him as he played with the door.

Sly as a coyote, he had stolen the little locking stick long ago.

He smiled at the lightning and waited for the hollow sound of thunder. Tall Ranger thought he had him trapped, but the white man did not know how cunning he was.

He sat on the floor beneath the window and waited as the house grew quiet. The lamplight went out in the little dwelling where Old Hairy Face lived. Soon everyone would be asleep, and it would be time to go.

He closed his eyes and whispered a soft chant, thankful for the rolling thunder that would cover any sound he made when he slipped away.

37

Reed had tossed and turned all night, too hot, too unsettled to get any sleep. He worried about Daniel and had been riled by his reaction to Kate. He kept thinking about her trip to town with the preacher and wishing it didn't bother him. Wishing he didn't care.

By morning, he was more exhausted than when he had gone to bed. It still hadn't rained. There had been no blessed relief from the building heat. He dressed and found Kate in the kitchen with Charm, putting a tray of food together for Daniel. She looked as if she had slept no better than he.

They nodded in silent greeting. She dismissed him, a sure sign of which way the wind was blowing this morning.

"Morning, Reed." Charm distracted him by handing him a cup of hot coffee, but absent her usual smile. "Your steak and eggs will be ready in a minute." When she turned around and started breaking eggs against the edge of the skillet with sharp, purposeful taps, he knew he was getting the freeze from both of them.

He pulled out a chair at the kitchen table and sat down. Kate asked for the key to Daniel's room. When he gave it to her, she picked up Daniel's tray and left without even glancing at him.

She wasn't gone three minutes before there was a loud crash overhead. Reed was on his feet the instant he heard the tray hit the floor. Charm was right behind him. He met Kate coming down the stairs.

Her face was stark white, her eyes huge and frightened. "He's gone." She closed the gap between them, reeled down three more stairs. "He's *gone*, Reed! My God, he's not in his room!"

She was shaking so hard he feared she might tumble the rest of the way down. He took her arm, led her back up to the landing. "Did you look in the other rooms?" He charged down the hall, banging doors, opening armoires, throwing back bedspreads, bending to look under beds.

Kate followed in his wake, repeating over and over, "He's gone. He's run away."

Reed searched Daniel's room, trying to decide if the boy had taken anything. He went down on his knees, looked around under the bed, telling himself Daniel had to be hiding someplace, that he was scaring them on purpose, paying him back for the haircut.

But in his heart he knew the truth.

When he turned around, Kate was clutching Daniel's crutch. Oddly enough, she was smiling through her tears. She even raised the crutch like a trophy.

"Without this, he couldn't have gotten very far." She sniffed and wiped the back of her hand over her eyes, took a deep breath and glanced out the window. "I'm sure we'll find him close to the house. Maybe even in the barn." She swallowed a little sob. "I should have thought of that already. He's with the horses. He's probably there right now."

Reed knew better. He wasn't about to offer false hope. If the boy had made it as far as the barn, if he had gotten to the horses, then he was long gone.

He hurried past Kate. When he heard her racing after

him, he slowed his steps. She had suffered a shock and was still unsteady, so he waited at the top of the stairs, taking her arm as they walked down together.

She was still hugging the crutch.

Reed tried to leave her in the kitchen, hoping to spare her the bald truth for a few more minutes. "Wait here. I'll look outside."

"No, I—"

He had his hand on the back door when it opened from outside. Scrappy was there, his face lined with sleep, creased into a puckered frown. Charm was right behind him.

"The Andalusian's gone. Somebody stole him last night."

"The boy's gone, too," Reed told him.

"Shee-it." Scrappy spat on the veranda, wiped his mouth with the back of his hand. "Damn it all. You sure?"

"He's not in his room." Reed stepped outside. Kate and Charm followed close on his heels.

"The horse ain't in the stall." Scrappy shoved his hat down tight. Reed stepped off the veranda with all of them trailing behind.

Head down, his gaze swept the ground around the corral. It was covered with horseshoe prints and wagon-wheel impressions. Hundreds of them. To find the boy, they would have to circle the property, pick up a trail that led off on its own. He glanced up at the leaden sky, prayed the rain would hold off.

"Reed, what are we going to do?" Kate was racing beside him, one hand holding her skirt out of the dirt, the other still hanging on to Daniel's crutch.

"I'm going after him."

It wasn't until he had said it that he realized he was not about to let the boy go again. Not as long as there was a breath in his body. He had lost Daniel once. He wasn't going to lose him again.

He looked into Kate's frightened eyes, tried to assure himself as well as her and the others. "I'm going after him. I'll get him back."

"I'm going with you." Kate handed the crutch to Charm, who was crying like a baby.

"Don't be ridiculous. You'll only slow me down. We have no idea how far of a head start he has on us. Besides, I'm not taking you into Comanche country. What if I get killed? What do you think will happen to you out there alone?" He didn't want to think about it.

"That's a choice I'm willing to make. If you don't take me, then I'll leave on my own after you're gone."

"If you're really worried about Daniel, you wouldn't be begging to slow me down."

"But you're the reason he left. Even if you find him, do you think he'll come back with you?"

"Hell, no. I'll drag him back like I did before."

"Listen to yourself, Reed. You're furious. You'll frighten him to death. Let me go with you. At least he's not afraid of me." She grabbed hold of his sleeve and held on. "Even if you tie me down, sooner or later, I'll be free. I'm going no matter what you say."

She was the most bullheaded creature he had ever seen. No other woman would be begging to go into hostile territory with him.

He watched her stew, saw her making her own plans in silence. If he left her here, she would be harebrained enough to try to follow him. Knowing Scrappy, the old man wouldn't let her go alone, and they would both end up getting killed.

As much as he hated to admit it, he would be better off taking her than leaving her behind.

She never thought he would agree.

"Can you even ride?" He yelled it at her before he started

firing orders at Scrappy, telling the old wrangler which horse to saddle, what supplies he'd need for the trail.

"Of course, I can ride." Kate dogged his steps around the corral area.

It was a white lie. She had ridden some, but not often. The nuns kept an old swaybacked mare named Sweetie in a crumbling brick stable, and every spring they brought in a woman who taught the girls the rudiments of riding sidesaddle. Every year Kate tried to set a good example for her students, but each time she had to overcome the fear of sitting so high off the ground on an animal with a mind of its own.

The minute Reed realized she was not going to back down—against his own judgment, he let her know—he acquiesced. Charm immediately grabbed Kate's hand and dragged her into the house and up to her room.

"If you aren't ready to go when Reed is, it'll just give him an excuse to leave you behind," she told Kate. "Believe me, I know how men think."

Kate watched as Charm tore through a camelbacked trunk at the foot of her bed. She had never seen so many ruffles and feathers, so much satin and lace—and every bit of it in bold, provocative colors. Curious, she reached down to touch a deep violet chemise.

"Of course! My lucky chemise," Charm cried. "Take it."

Kate let go as if scorched. "Oh, my—no. I couldn't."

The girl was grabbing clothes right and left. Kate tried to dissuade her from what appeared to be a mad mission. "I really appreciate this, but I don't think—"

"Here!" Charm pulled out a pair of Levi Strauss pants, which had seen better days. "Wear these and you won't be slowed down by petticoats."

"Pants?" Kate's face was afire. "You want me to wear a pair of men's pants? What in the world are you doing with these, anyway?"

Charm whirled around and held them up to Kate's waist. "You don't really want to know." She adjusted the pants, shaking her head. "They're too long, but you can roll them up."

Then she rummaged around a bit more and tugged out a huge, deep purple satin poke bonnet with a great black feather that was bent and broken in three places. Charm jerked the feather off the hat. It fluttered like a disjointed bird and settled on the floor between them.

"This will keep the sun off your face. Now, do you have a shirtwaist?"

Kate shook her head. "No, but . . ."

Charm threw the pants on the bed and raced out of the room. A minute later she was back with an overlarge print shirt that she tossed at Kate.

"Wear this, too. If you're worried about your modesty, it'll come well past your waist and cover the crotch and seat of the pants."

Crotch? Modesty? Despite her early years with her mother, she *had* been raised by nuns. Modesty was her middle name.

"Where did you get this?" Kate suspected that she already knew.

"I stole it out of Reed's closet." She handed Kate the pants that lay crumpled on the end of the bed, the hat and the violet chemise as well. Then she shoved her toward the door. "Get dressed. He won't wait."

Kate hesitated. To wear pants . . . to ride astride . . . Mother Superior would advise countless novenas.

And Preston. What would Preston and all the upstanding townsfolk she had met yesterday think of her riding across the prairie like a madwoman sporting a man's pants and a whore's lucky chemise and bonnet?

Charm crossed her arms beneath her ample bosom. "You

won't have time to worry about a skirt flapping in the wind or your ankles showing. And what about . . . well, *private* things? You can't give Reed one single solitary excuse to leave you behind. Besides, you might be gone for days. Days and nights on the trail, Kate. How are you going to manage out there if you are all gussied up to the gills in a dress and petticoats?"

She hadn't thought of any of that. She hadn't thought of anything but Daniel and the stricken look on Reed's face when she told him that Daniel was gone.

Days and nights on the trail alone with Reed.

She couldn't—wouldn't—stop to think of the ramifications of what it would mean to her newfound reputation if anyone found out. Nor did she dwell on how terrified she was to ride into hostile Comanche territory.

Charm paced back and forth, chewing on her thumbnail. "Daniel needs you, Kate. You *have* to be there when Reed finds him. Now you get dressed. I'll go downstairs and wrap up some cookies for him." She suddenly burst into tears sobbing, "You know how he loves his sweets."

Despite the life she had led, Charm had a heart the size of Texas. She deserved to be happy. As Kate hurried down the hall to change clothes, she swore that once they were all back together safe and sound, she would find Jonah Taylor, and she wouldn't rest until Charm was married.

38

You should have known better.

Walking away from where he had picketed the horses for the night, Reed cursed his lack of judgment. He had been loco to agree to bring Kate along: Just as he thought beforehand, he spent every minute worrying about her. Not only that, but she was definitely slowing him down. Even though she hadn't once complained, he could tell she was saddle weary and exhausted. Not to mention upset.

At one point when they stopped for water, he found himself trying to reassure her. "We'll find him." He wished he had faith in himself, in his words.

Kate had been standing beside a small creek where barely a trickle of water ran this time of year. She turned full circle, tipped her head back so she could see out from beneath the wide brim of the satin poke bonnet.

Her gaze scanned the sky, followed the flight of a brown hawk before she turned to him with tears shimmering in her eyes. "I can't bear the thought of him riding around alone out here. My God, Reed. How can he survive?"

"I'm sure the Comanche taught him well. He's grown up on horseback. He knows how to live off the land."

"He showed me so much," she said softly. "He was always

pointing out flowers and animals to me, little things that I would not have seen if not for him. Sometimes even big ones that were practically under my nose." She tried to smile, even brightened a bit afterward.

Seated on the little brown mare, wearing oversize baggy pants, his shirt, and the ridiculously huge ruffled bonnet, she was more than a sight. Added to her outlandish outfit was the gun and holster he had strapped on her after one rudimentary lesson in how to fire it.

They covered plenty of ground that first day, pushing their horses and themselves. Whenever he asked if she needed to stop, she said no. Dusk had enveloped them when he finally insisted they get some rest, not for himself, but for her.

Her tears came and went so freely that he almost envied her being a woman at a time like this. His heart had been numb so long that it only knew how to ache in silence.

Cloaked in darkness, Reed walked back to where Kate lay sound asleep on a thin blanket near their saddles. She had been too exhausted to eat more than a few crackers and an apple. It was still light out. Still overly warm.

He picked up his rifle, sat close beside her, and leaned back against his saddle. He laid the weapon across his lap, wondered if Daniel had found his clan yet. If so, they would have welcomed him back with open arms.

The way I should have done.

I should have left his hair alone.

I should have stayed home and not gone back to the Rangers once I found him again.

No matter what Becky said, no matter what the truth might be, it's dead and buried now.

He's my son.

Mine.

After suffering a deep case of the shoulds, the conviction

came to him so strong, so clear, that it would have knocked him to his knees had he been standing: Daniel deserved better than what he had given him.

He swore to himself that from this day forward he would think of Daniel as *his*—the way he had before Becky ruined all their lives with her bitter words.

He heard Kate groan when she rolled over on the hard ground. Slowly, she came awake, appearing startled by the growing darkness.

"I'm right here," he said softly.

She sat up, wiped her eyes, and stretched.

"I feel as if I've been trampled by a herd of buffalo," she whispered.

"Want some water?"

Barely more than a shadow against the night sky, she shook her head no and shifted until she was more comfortable. "I'll keep watch. I can wake you if I hear anything," she offered.

By the time she heard anything, they would be dead. Besides, he doubted she would use the gun.

"I'm all right. I can't sleep anyway," he admitted. He knew she was tired.

"Thinking of Daniel?"

"Yeah."

When she moved closer, he silently admitted to his loneliness for the first time in years when he realized that he welcomed her companionship. He found himself eased by her presence; the sound of her voice became a soothing balm. He had lived in a world of men for so long that he was rusty around a woman.

"Earlier, you convinced me that he'll be all right," she reminded him. "I believed you."

Reed sighed heavily. "A million and one things could happen to him out here."

"You told me he knows the land."

"It's not the prairie I'm worried about."

The Comanche had far more enemies than just Texans. Any of them would be happy to get their hands on the boy, not to mention the expensive white Andalusian. Reed only hoped Daniel was still wearing the clothes Kate and Charm had given him. With his hair cut off, he looked more white than Comanche, which just might save his hide if a troop of Federal soldiers or a Texas Ranger outfit found him first and he resisted.

Kate shifted closer. Reed was shocked when she reached through the twilight and slid her hand atop the back of his. "We'll get him back."

The giving, supportive touch surprised him, opened a raw spot, and left him vulnerable. He wished that he had the courage to put his feelings into words the way she did— to tell her that he truly wanted his boy back, that he was ready to try to be the father Daniel needed, to give him the love he deserved. He didn't want Tommy Harlan to have died for nothing. Something good had to come out of what happened to him that day.

"If anything happens to Daniel now . . ."

Kate reached up, pressed her fingertips to his lips. "*Nothing* is going to happen to him."

He took her hand, held it away from his mouth but didn't let her go. "If he gets to the Comanche first . . ."

"We'll get him back."

We . . .

He was holding fiercely to her hand now. Suddenly, she had become a lifeline to all the feelings he had denied for so long.

"You know those things you said to me about why I really left the Rangers? About how I came back because I wanted to start over with Daniel? You were right. I wasn't able to do my job because all I could think about in the middle of a raid was Daniel. Because of my inability to act, one of our men lost his life. Everywhere I looked in that Comanche camp, I imagined Daniel and . . . I couldn't bring myself to shoot."

"We'll find him," she said again.

"I should have listened to you. I would never have cut off his hair if I had known it would push him into running."

"You had no idea. We both know that. You told me in the beginning that he would run if given a chance. I really thought he was settling in, getting used to our ways. I had hoped that he was long past wanting to leave us."

"I'm sorry for the things I've said to you, Kate. For the way I've treated you."

"What a shock it must have been for you to wake up one day and discover you had a wife you never met . . . or wanted."

The growing darkness gave him the ability to focus on the sound of her voice, sincere, yet tinged with regret. "You didn't deserve what my father and Sofia did to you, not to mention what I put you through, but you stayed even though I made an ass out of myself time after time. I know that you've stayed because of Daniel."

They were as alone as if stranded on one of the countless distant stars above them.

She said, "I asked you once what you wanted, Reed, what you dreamed of, and you didn't know. If you wished on one of those stars up there, what would you wish for?"

"Wish for?" For so long he had merely existed from day to day. He didn't really know what he wanted beyond getting Daniel back. Wasn't it enough that he was alive and for once sitting under the prairie stars without aching with loneliness? He had stopped dreaming after hard experience taught him that it brought only heartache.

Kate still hadn't moved. She waited for an answer.

"I'd wish to find Daniel safe. To take him home and keep the ranch going on my own. My father cast a pretty big shadow, one I'm not sure I can live up to."

She lifted her head and looked into his eyes. "All he really left behind besides a prosperous ranch was doubt and deception. You can do much more—for Daniel and for Lone Star, if you want to."

He doubted it, but he didn't want to think of Lone Star right now. Not with her sitting so close.

Her voice was seductive, low, and as smooth as honey. She sat very still, watching him, as if waiting for him to kiss her. There was only one way to find out if she would object this time.

He reached out, slid his hand beneath her hair, pulled her closer. She rested her palm against his shirtfront, a gentle touch, one without resistance. Beneath her hand, his heart beat faster.

Lowering his lips to hers, he gave her the softest of kisses, one that lingered rather than teased, one that he hoped told her he was truly sorry for what had been and that he would like to start over.

When he lifted his head, he heard her sigh. Without another word, he pulled her close, until her head rested where her hand had been.

An owl flew overhead, its heavy wings making soft whispering sounds as it skimmed along on the still night air. Reed stared up at all the stars that filled the sky.

There was no raiders' moon out tonight.

Lack of moonlight just might save their scalps.

Kate had been quiet for so long that he wasn't surprised to discover she had fallen sound asleep. He pulled her closer, surprised at how familiar she felt within the circle of his arm.

As the night deepened and the warmth of her cheek

seeped into his chest, he wondered if his heart wasn't beginning to thaw just a little.

Kate blessed the darkness and feigned sleep. Her mind held only one thought.

Reed just kissed me.

She had no idea why or what the morrow would bring, but she did know that she had loved him before he even knew she existed, that she had fallen in love with the promise of what they could have shared together.

She had loved the idea of him then.

Now she loved the man.

39

Kate woke up alone shortly after the first light of dawn. She looked over and saw that Reed had already saddled up the horses and was waiting. She wondered if she had dreamed of falling asleep in his arms.

As the sky turned pink they headed out. Reed was close and guarded all morning, as if he regretted what had happened last night. Kate tried to convince herself the kiss had been spontaneous, born out of the solitude of the trail and their mutual concern for Daniel. She told herself that nothing had changed between them and wished that she believed it.

Reed looked as worn as she felt. Dark circles tinted the skin beneath his eyes. A full day's growth of beard shadowed his jaw. She didn't know how he could make out any kind of trail on the hard, grassy soil. The ground all looked the same to her, but he claimed to be following the Andalusian's shoe prints. Now and again he would lose the trail, but they kept heading northwest, and he would eventually rediscover it, almost as if he were following Daniel by instinct.

She marveled that the landscape had not changed in two days and was lulled into the notion that the prairie rolled on forever. She tried not to picture them as two lone, vulnerable specks adrift in a sea of dying summer grass.

She concentrated on Daniel, reminding herself that he was riding across the same lonely stretch of prairie all by himself.

Was he afraid or rejoicing his escape with every mile? When she thought of all the hours she had spent reading to him and trying to teach him to speak English again, or how willing Charm had been to spend hours sewing for him, of all the cookies and treats the girl had baked to please him, it nearly broke her heart. When she remembered the quiet hours she spent trying to establish a bond between them, she could hardly bring herself to accept the fact that he had been planning this escape all along.

She had been foolish not to believe Reed's warning.

The farther they rode, the more she wondered what would become of Daniel if they took him back by force. Knowing how sorely he wanted to escape, she wondered if there was any way to reach him or if all they would initiate was more heartache.

Fast Pony had ridden into the camp at dawn when no one but one of the old men guarding the village was there to witness his return. He did not care that there was no crowd to hail him as a hero, for he was too tired to boast, too exhausted to do more than mumble when No Teeth Left took the prize white horse from him and pointed him toward the teepee of his uncle, where his mother now lived.

At first he was so happy to hear that his mother was alive he did not realize she was living in his uncle's tepee because his father was dead. The truth hit him as he stepped through the opening and looked around the dusky interior. Gone were many of the things that usually hung around the walls. There was no decorated shield, no medicine bag, no hide backrests. The dwelling looked as if it had been stripped of all but a handful of necessary items.

His mother was sitting near the cook fire stirring a stew bubbling in a buffalo paunch. He smelled wild onions and turnips, and his mouth watered. Her long shining hair was gone, shorn because she was mourning. When his mother did not look up from her task, her sadness introduced itself to him. She sat with her shoulders bowed, huddled in upon herself. The corners of her mouth drooped sorrowfully. There was a distant, lost look in her eyes.

One of his uncle's wives glanced up and shrieked with gladness. His cousins and aunts soon surrounded him, and his heart leapt with joy. He had eyes only for his mother, Painted White Feather. She looked at him as if seeing a spirit.

He had prayed and planned this homecoming for so long that it seemed like a dream unfolding. He wanted to be as brave as his father. He wanted to hold his head high. As he started toward his mother, he walked straight and tall without showing any sign of his faded limp.

But when his mother rose to her knees and held her arms out to him, he no longer wanted to be brave. He ran to her, not as a warrior, but as her son. He let her enfold him in her embrace. Then he cried.

Later she took him outside and together they walked to a nearby stream to collect water. They sat side by side as she spoke to him of his father, of how Many Horses had died bravely during the same raid in which Fast Pony had been captured.

She told the story in great detail, of how she had saved

herself by running and hiding behind a smoldering pile of buffalo robes. She risked death by crawling beneath one very close to the burning heap. The Rangers left without finding her. Later, as the survivors crept back to the ashes of what was left of their encampment, she had found his father's body. When she did not find Fast Pony and realized that he must have been captured and not killed, she rejoiced.

He told her of Tall Ranger, the one who had taken him away to live in a huge wooden dwelling a long ride away. He spoke of how he planned his escape and of the fine white horse he had stolen.

Boasting, he recited all the white man's words he knew: *cookie, chicken, cake, eat, water, horse.* And his favorite, *chock-o-late.* Laughing, he described all the sweet foods they had given him, but then he felt bad, thinking of all his hollow-eyed cousins.

Times had not been good among the Nermernuh, his mother said. Many of the warriors were dead now or imprisoned at Fort Sill. The raids between the Tejanos and their people had been many. The blue coats were paying for the return of captives, so the warriors raided more, taking captives and turning them over to the blue coats for money—money they turned around and used to buy guns from the Comancheros. Guns for taking more captives.

Fast Pony laughed at the stupidity of the whites.

They sat in silence for a time, happy in each other's company. His mother did not seem to mind at all that Tall Ranger had cut his hair. She stroked it just the way she used to and held him close.

Then she began to ask him many, many questions about Tall Ranger. She asked what the man looked like and about the woman, Soft Grass Hands. He admitted that, other than cutting off his hair, they had treated him very well, for a prisoner. They never beat him or cut or burned him, either, even when he was bad. He thought of the way he had fought and cursed and the terrible way he grabbed and ate their food.

His mother sat in silence, her thoughts far, far away. Then she grew very still. When he looked into her face, he saw tears glittering in her eyes.

"What is it, Mother? Why do you cry?"

She wiped her tears and tried to smile, but her lips were trembling. Even a baby could have seen that she was very, very sad. "Do you know the way back? To the home of the Tall Ranger?"

"I think so. Yes, I could find it again."

He threw back his shoulders and stuck out his chest. Perhaps she was going to send him back to steal more horses. He pictured himself leading a raiding party back to the Tall Ranger's land to bring back more of the fine stock. This time he would claim the spotted mare and her foal as his own.

The look on his mother's face quickly dampened his joy. He had never seen her so sad. He thought he knew why. "Are you thinking of Father?"

She hugged him close, kissing the top of his head. "No, my son. I am thinking of *you*. I want you to go back." She took a deep breath and shivered, as if she were freezing cold, even on such a hot, dry day. "I want you to take your fine white horse and go back to Tall Ranger."

"To steal more horses?" He felt her trembling beside him and grew frightened.

She shook her head. "No. I want you to go back . . . to live with the Tall Ranger again. I want you to stay with him forever."

If she had struck him with a war ax, he could not have hurt any worse. He tried to understand. Perhaps losing his father had left her confused.

"Why do you want me to go back there? I hate them."

She took hold of his hand, studied it as if she had never seen it before. She turned it over, traced his palm with her fingertip. Then she looked down into his eyes and the sorrow he saw in hers made him afraid.

"Listen to me and listen well, Fast Pony. You are my son as surely as if you had come from my belly, but you were not always my son. Many Horses stole you from the whites when you were little more than a babe. He gave you to me, for we had no children of our own." She looked off across the stream, toward the embankment. "I think maybe you once belonged to this Tall Ranger. Perhaps that is why he took you to his dwelling. Because you were his son long ago."

"But I don't want to be the son of a white man." He spat on the ground beside him to rid his mouth of such horrible, frightening words.

"You are a white man's son by blood. You have the eyes of the whites."

"You told me my eyes were different because the Great Spirit made me special. That I am not like the others because my father was a great warrior and his son was not like other little boys." He was furious at her for saying such things to him, for lying.

"In your heart you will always be Nermernuh, but you are truly white, and I am afraid for you if you stay here. Our people are dying faster than the summer grass withers. Your father is gone. Soon we will all have to go onto the reservation to survive, and when we do, those adopted into our clan will be sent back to their white families."

She took his face in her hands. "You will be taken from

me, and I will not be able to stop them. Tall Ranger and his people treated you well. You say he has many horses, that he can take care of you. He can give you all I cannot anymore. Without your father here to protect us—"

He jumped to his feet before she could say any more. "I can protect you! I won't go!" He pounded his fist over his heart. "I am *Nermernuh*."

She grabbed his wrist, kept him from running away. His tears shamed him now, tears that betrayed his weak and broken heart.

His mother held him by the shoulders, gently shook him, and made him listen to the terrible things she was saying. "I want you to live, Fast Pony. I want you to grow up safe, away from death and sickness. With a full belly. To send you away is like tearing out my own heart, but it must be done. You have always been the best son a mother could ever want, so do not argue with me now. Make me proud of your bravery. I only want what is best for you."

"What is best for me is to stay here with you, with all my cousins and friends."

He wiped his runny nose on his arm. Despite the warmth of the day, his teeth were chattering. He was frightened to death. He felt as if the earth had fallen out from under him and he was hanging over a deep, dark, bottomless pit.

His mother wanted him to leave her and go back.

"No!" he shouted, turning away from her, running back toward the camp. "I will *not* go! You cannot make me go back there!"

He dodged children and dogs. Little Badger, a boy of twelve summers who always taunted him, shouted his name. Fast Pony ran on, blinded by tears. He was halfway through the encampment when the terrifying sound of the blue coats' horn raked the air.

He stopped running, too confused to move. Was he dreaming or was it really happening all over again? He turned, started to run back to where he had left his mother by the stream.

The first shots were fired when the blue coats came swarming out of the wash. He was running back the way he had come when he tripped and fell headlong onto the hard ground. His knee was skinned, his palms, too, but he jumped up and kept on running.

An old woman ran past him. She screamed and fell. Fast Pony nearly tripped over her body. He kept running. The blue coats were everywhere at once. Through the noise and smoke he saw his mother racing toward him, saw the fringe on her doeskin dress flying, her arms outstretched.

She screamed his name.

By midday, Kate was already trail weary and tired of tasting dust when they stopped in a sparse grove of trees along a river bottom. Since Reed was loath to light a fire, they ate a cold meal of hard cheese, apples, and biscuits.

She washed her face and hands in the trickle of water. Kneeling in the dirt beside the stream, she blessed Charm for convincing her to wear pants. A dress never would have survived.

Pushing herself up, she walked to where Reed held the horses, watching her. His deep-set eyes never betrayed his thoughts, but today there was something in them that made her blush. Though she could not define it, she felt it. Every so often she caught him looking at her in ways he never had before.

She found herself thinking about last night and the hint of tenderness, a certain closeness, between them.

He held her horse while she hooked her foot in the stir-rup and then settled in the saddle. She admired his easy grace as he mounted up. Soon they were clearing a gentle rise that brought them out of the creek bottom.

Then, without warning, Reed suddenly pulled rein. His horse danced back into hers. Kate tightened her grip on the reins and held the little mare steady. When she looked over at Reed, he was staring off into the distance. His face slowly drained of color.

Terror gripped her hard. The realization of where they were and what they were doing came slamming back. "What is it? Reed? What's happening?"

Suddenly she was all too aware of the heavy gunbelt she had tried to ignore. Black smoke billowed up from the ground, snaked like separate writhing arms against the sky. The usual stillness was broken by the popping sound of gunfire.

"Get back down into the gully and wait for me by the creek."

Was her heart *trying* to shatter her rib cage? "Are you insane?"

He edged his horse close enough to grab her arm and forced her to look into his eyes. "Calm down, Kate, and listen to me. There are no settlers this far out. That has to be an encampment going up in smoke. That has to be where Daniel was headed. I've got to get to him before . . . before anything happens."

Though his hand had tightened on her arm, she was numb to everything but fear. "I can't stay here. I won't." She would die of fright before anything else. It was better to face the unknown than to wait for it to find her.

"The army or the Rangers are trying to drive the Comanche out. I'll be looking for Daniel. I can't be worried about you, too."

Comanche. So close. Suddenly she was too scared to cry. "Go." She croaked the word, her throat so tight she could barely speak. "Go after him."

"You'll wait here? Promise?"

"Go!" She wasn't about to wait. She couldn't bear not knowing what had become of him, not knowing if the Comanche were about to come upon her in their flight, but she couldn't tell him that. Not now. Not when Daniel might be in danger.

"Get down in the gully." He wasn't about to leave before she did.

She turned her mare and started down, but then stopped to watch him spur his horse and ride toward the distinct patches of billowing smoke. Just in the last few seconds, more and more fires had bloomed on the horizon.

Unable to look away, she watched Reed ride toward the inferno.

Reed did not have to see what was happening to know that he was riding into hell.

He leaned over his horse's neck and spurred it on, knowing the raid would be over within minutes, yet each and every one of those minutes would seem like a lifetime to those involved in the conflict.

He was still too far away to hear more than gunfire, but the sound of battle was etched in his memory. Screams of humans and horses, babies bawling, men shouting orders. The smell of fear and death that tainted every thought.

Common sense, fairness, even sanity withered in battle. On both sides, brutality reigned until the dust cleared and the living were left to count the dead. Reed pictured Daniel in the midst of the confusion and hoped to God that he wasn't too late.

40

It was all over by the time Reed rode in.

Here and there bursts of gunshots tolled as the army rounded the survivors and killed off the last of the resisters.

He recognized Capt. John Davis, out of Fort Sill. The veteran officer had been stationed in Texas ever since the war. As Reed rode up, Davis was twisting the waxed end of his long, dark mustache, thoughtfully surveying the smoking remains of a small Comanche clan's campsite. They exchanged greetings from horseback.

"What are you doing here, Benton?" Before Reed could answer, Davis went on. "We were out on reconnaissance and came across them just after dawn. I decided to round these people up and take them back to the reservation."

Reed stared at the carnage. "Looks like you did a little more than that."

"Yeah, well, that happens. Damn Comanche have been taking captives right and left lately, turning them in for rewards. They're even bringing in scalps and demanding payment. How in the hell am I supposed to tell my men not to avenge the lice-ridden, battered children and women who've been tortured and then returned?"

Davis's men weren't his concern. "I'm here looking for my son."

The captain stared at him long and hard, then shrugged with grave doubt in his eyes. "I hope you find him."

Reed worked his way slowly through the camp, guiding his horse past knots of Comanche prisoners, ignoring the sullen stares of some, the hopelessness in the eyes of others. Most were women and children and a few old men. They would be marched back to Fort Sill, which they would no doubt leave again as soon as they could.

His hope of finding Daniel alive sank with every prisoner he passed, every twisted, maimed body he saw bleeding in the dirt. Pausing beside a fallen cavalry horse, he gazed through the smoking ruins. His gut clenched. A few feet away, facedown, lay the body of a child.

His mind emptied like a broken pitcher. He slowly dismounted and led his horse toward the body. The world narrowed down to the boy lying there with arms outstretched, his cheek pressed against the earth. Reed did not start breathing again until he realized the boy's hair was waist length. He remembered the weight of Daniel's long, shining hair in his hand.

Rubbing his hand over his eyes, he let go a ragged sigh and turned, willing Daniel to be alive. Suddenly the hair on the back of his neck stood up. A strange sense of knowing settled over him. With it came a quiet calm as he stood beside the dead child. He turned full circle.

Smoke drifted like fog, then slowly cleared.

He saw him then. His son. Daniel was sitting on littered ground not far away, staring into the distance. His expression was as empty as a blank page.

As Reed started toward him, he began to take in the entire scene and realized Daniel was not alone. A young woman lay beside him, her buckskin clothing riddled with crimson-stained bullet holes. As he walked toward his son, he saw the boy lift the woman's lifeless hand and cradle it tenderly before he pressed it to his cheek. When he let go, the woman's arm fell limply back to the ground. Daniel sat there stroking her raggedly hacked hair over and over, his eyes vacant, his soul empty.

When Reed reached him, he hunkered down on his heels. He was afraid Daniel might run until he saw the emptiness in his eyes. For a time at least, Daniel's mind had sought refuge deep inside itself, his emotions deadened by all he had seen, by the death of the woman he had called mother.

Though he ached to do so, Reed did not immediately reach for him. He merely squatted beside Daniel until he could not stand the pitiful, utterly lost look on the boy's face any longer.

"Daniel? Come on, son. Let me take you home."

Kate wished she had listened to Reed. Wished she had waited in the gully the way he had asked.

Instead, when the shooting had finally stopped, she rode toward the smoking remains of the Comanche settlement.

Two minutes after she arrived, she vomited.

Death as she knew it had always been something quiet and serene. She had attended more than her share of funerals at Saint Perpetua's because the girls' choir sang at every funeral Mass. Death meant the pungent scent of incense in the old church. Hymns. Chants. Flickering candles.

A quiet slipping away of life. A journey to the next world.

Here, where blood seeped into the Texas prairie, death was brutal, cold, and ugly. Something not caused by disease or old age, but something horrible done to one man by another. And not only to men, but to women and children, young and old alike.

One or two of the army enlisted men noticed her, but dressed as she was in the baggy pants with the oversize poke bonnet hiding her face, they did not give her a second glance, except perhaps as an oddity. The rest of the troop had its hands full with the prisoners.

She asked one young man if he had seen a civilian among them, praying that Reed had not been wounded or killed during the skirmish. He pointed toward the center of the camp.

Smoke was heaviest there and stung her eyes. She raised her fist to wipe away tears. As she lowered her hand, she saw Reed kneeling beside a fallen woman. Kate nudged the mare forward.

Daniel was sitting on the ground in front of Reed, unmoving as he stared with unseeing eyes at a point in the distance. His fingers were threaded through the fallen woman's hair.

She stopped her horse, slid off, and leaned against the mare, oddly taking comfort in the solid feel and warmth of the big animal.

Her first inclination was to go to Daniel and see if he would respond to her, but Reed was speaking softly to him. If they were to become father and son again, she had to let Reed have this moment. She prayed he would succeed.

Finally, Reed reached out for Daniel and slipped his hands beneath the boy's arms. Daniel did not protest when Reed stood and held him close against his shoulder. Reed closed his eyes and embraced Daniel, one hand protectively pressed against the boy's back.

She gave them time alone before she finally led the mare over. "Reed?" she said softly.

He turned slowly. If he was surprised or angry to see her there, he gave no indication.

"Is he hurt?"

"His heart is broken." He looked toward the fallen woman. "She must have been his mother."

Kate could not bear to do more than glance down, take in the blood-soaked buckskin and long dark hair. She did not have to see more. As it was, she might have nightmares of this day for eternity.

Daniel stayed in Reed's arms, his head on the man's shoulder.

"Mount up, Kate. I want you to hold him. There's something I need to do."

She did as he asked without question; then Reed walked over to the mare and handed the boy up to her. Daniel had no more life than a rag doll. She pressed him against her, tightened her arm around his waist, and negotiated the reins.

Reed went back to his own horse, untied the rawhide strips that held his bedroll behind his saddle, shook out the striped blanket, and covered the Comanche woman with it. Then he gently rolled her over and tucked the blanket around her entire body.

To Kate's amazement, he tenderly lifted the woman's shrouded form and carried it over to his horse where he draped her across his saddle.

Daniel had not stirred since Reed set him up in front of Kate. She continued to hold him close, hoping that her love and caring might translate itself through touch. As Reed began to lead his horse toward the outskirts of the camp, Kate slowly followed on the mare.

They traveled away from the smell of smoke and the sound of soldiers barking orders, back to the gully where Reed had told Kate to wait. Once there, he took Daniel's Comanche mother off his horse and gently laid her body on the bank above the creek bed.

When he pulled open the edges of the blanket, exposing her face and neck, Kate looked away. A few seconds later he had the blanket secured again.

As Kate sat there holding Daniel against her, she was amazed at the time and care Reed took to dig out a shallow grave with little more than his bare hands and a flat rock. After he had positioned the woman's body, he gathered more rocks from along the streambed until the grave was well covered and safe from animals.

Reed remained beside the cairn with his head bowed. Deeply moved by what he had done, inspired by such a giving gesture toward the woman who had cared for his son, Kate whispered a silent prayer of her own.

Moments later, Reed mounted up and walked his horse over to her mare.

"I'll take him now," he said. "It's time to go home."

He reached for Daniel. Again, the boy was indifferent to whatever they did. Her heart melted as she watched the big man tuck the boy in front of him and cradle him so tenderly.

If she had not witnessed what Reed had done this afternoon, the care he had taken with the Comanche woman and his gentleness with his son, she would not have believed him capable of it.

She tucked the memory away in order to concentrate on the journey ahead. The sky was still clear, the air surprisingly calm as they turned their mounts toward Lone Star.

A few miles later she spotted the white Andalusian on a rise, magnificent, like a fanciful cloud against the deep blue sky. Reed said he thought the animal was heading back, guided by instinct. He gave a sharp whistle, and although the horse did not come any closer, it followed at a distance all the way home.

41

Filthy, hungry, and silently thoughtful, Kate and Reed had been gone four and a half days by the time they rode into the corral area behind Benton House. Daniel had not spoken a word or made a sound. Nor had he cried. He had escaped to a place where hurt could not touch him anymore.

Scrappy hurried out of the kitchen door to take their horses. When he saw Daniel, the disconcerted expression on his face lightened, but not entirely. "You have any trouble?" he wanted to know.

Reed shook his head.

"Give you much of a fight, did he?" Scrappy studied Daniel carefully.

"None," Reed said.

"He don't look so good. Is he all right in the head?"

Reed quickly explained that Daniel had reached the camp and he and Kate had gotten to him shortly after an army raid on the small village and that his mother had been killed.

Scrappy shook his head, muttering something about Daniel being too young to have had such a passel of trouble in his life.

Kate couldn't have agreed more.

"Glad the boy's back," Scrappy grudgingly admitted. "Thought after you found him that life could get back to normal around here, but that ain't gonna happen any time soon."

"What do you mean?" Reed shifted Daniel on his shoulder.

"Preacher's here. Brought bad news about Captain Taylor."

"Oh, no," Kate groaned. "Not Jonah!"

Reed cursed and quickly shot Kate an apologetic shrug. "What happened? Is he alive?"

Scrappy bobbed his head. "He's alive. Took a bullet when the regiment went after a bunch of rustlers made up to look like Comanch'. Seems like ever'thin's going to hell around here this summer. Damned if it don't." Without further explanation, he led the horses off toward the barn.

Bone tired, sick with worry over how Charm must be taking the news, Kate trailed Reed across the veranda.

Inside the kitchen they found Charm crying at the table. Preston was there, too, sitting beside her, encouraging her in low, even tones. The minute they walked in, he stood and went directly to Kate. Reed pulled out a chair and sat Daniel down.

In her concern for Charm and Jonah, Kate had not thought of what Preston must think about her traveling alone with Reed. When the minister took his time noting her curious garb, she could only guess what he must be thinking. She tugged the ribbons on the poke bonnet, pulled it off, and set it aside. Before she could say anything, Reed asked Preston about Jonah. Kate hurried over to Charm and put her arm around her.

"He was tracking down some rustlers near Fort Griffin when he was wounded."

"How bad?"

"Enough that they brought him in to Lone Star yesterday. That's where he wanted to be. I knew the two of you were good friends and that you would want to know."

"Thanks." Reed's fingers pressed into the back of Daniel's chair, his knuckles white. "I appreciate it."

Kate hugged Charm tight. "Go to him," she urged softly. "We'll manage here."

"Do you think I should?" The girl wiped her tears with a checkered napkin.

"You have to. If you don't, you'll never forgive yourself."

Charmed threw her arms around Kate's neck, and Kate whispered, "If he proposes to you again, *promise* me you will say yes. If . . . if his life is in danger, it might keep him alive."

Charm's breath caught on a sob, then she whispered back, "I will."

Kate straightened and looked to Preston for help. "Will you please take Charm into Lone Star? She needs to be with Jonah. I think she can do more for him than any of us." She turned to Reed. "Besides, we can't leave Daniel right now."

After the slightest hesitation, Preston agreed.

Charm finally pulled herself together enough to stand, her eyes swollen from crying, her nose red. "I'll just go up and pack a few things, Reverend. I'll be right back," she promised.

As she hurried away, Reed took Daniel's hand. Kate was surprised to see the boy walking alone. She noticed, too, that he was barely limping and realized that he must have been fooling them for quite some time. Like a phantom, he followed Reed to the hall door.

"I'll get him to bed," Reed told her.

"I'll be right up." She could tell by the way Preston was lingering near the back door that he wanted to speak to her alone.

As soon as Reed was out of hearing, she walked over to the sink and pumped a glass of water. Taking a few sips eased her dry throat, but not her mounting agitation.

When Preston took her hand, her jitters multiplied.

"How are *you* holding up, Kate? You look exhausted."

"I am." There was no use dancing around the bald truth. "We were gone four days."

"Are you all right?" Preston studied her closely, searching for the truth in her eyes.

"Of course."

He seemed to be waiting for more, expecting her to say something else. "Have things changed at all between you and Reed?"

She wished she could have assured him that nothing happened, because nothing *had* happened other than a kiss, but on the ride back she had never stopped thinking about what Reed had done for Daniel, of his attention and concern. Nor could she dismiss her own reaction to him.

Nothing had changed and yet everything had changed.

As she stood there trapped in awkward silence, she tried to convince herself that Preston was by far the best choice. She tried to convince herself to go pack her things and leave with Charm, to move into town and take that job at the dry goods store. Then she would no longer have to see Reed day after day, no longer have to wonder what it would be like to be his wife, not just on paper, but for real. Forever.

She was so open, so vulnerable to temptation right now.

But she couldn't leave Daniel yet. Not when he needed her so. As did Reed, at least until he and Daniel were able to cope on their own.

"Everything is the same," she said, trying to assure herself as well as him. "I went along because I was afraid Daniel wouldn't come home with Reed."

As if he were aware of the debate going on inside her, he said, "This isn't the time or the place to press you. Just know that I still want you for my wife."

He was so genuine, so understanding and patient that she hated not being able to give him a definite answer.

Much to Kate's relief, Charm walked back into the room with a small bundle of her things. "I don't know when I'll be back," Charm said.

"Don't worry." Kate hugged her. "Take care of Jonah and remember what you promised. Keep your pretty chin up. Everything will be fine."

As Charm walked out, Kate thanked Preston again for taking her to town. "I know it can't be easy for you," she added. "People might object to you helping someone like Charm, but—"

"My job is to serve everyone in Lone Star. Saints and sinners alike. I'm happy to carry her back."

Saints and sinners. How much would he be willing to forgive in her own case? The fact that she wasn't a virgin? Her past? Her own lustful thoughts?

Preston was kind and gentle, handsome and sincere, but Reed had gotten under her skin.

"Kate?" Preston squeezed her hand.

Nudged out of her silent debate, Kate started. "I'm sorry." She looked into his eyes and saw such unbridled hope that it made her want to cry. "I'm not much of a rider. I'm afraid I'm on edge and worn to a frazzle."

He had been holding her hand throughout their conversation, but she had forgotten that entirely. She looked down at her hand in his, ashamed of her ragged, dirty nails.

She needed a bath in the worst way. She longed to be alone, to wash her hair, slip between clean sheets, and sleep on something besides the hard ground, but the idea of heating water and carrying it upstairs was beyond conception.

"I hope I see you again soon," he was saying. "Maybe you could have Scrappy bring you into town later this week. When things settle down."

She did not know how soon she could see him again, so she made no promises. He lingered, as if loath to leave. She felt the need to assure herself as well as him that she would be all right alone with Reed, so she put on a smile.

"Everything will be fine, Preston. We'll talk again soon. Please send my regards to Aunt Martha and take care of Charm. If anything happens to Jonah . . ." She could not bear to voice her fear.

"I'll get word to you as soon as I can. Tell Reed good-bye."

"I will."

He put his hand beneath her chin, tipped her face toward his. "May I kiss you?"

A test, she thought. *Nothing more.* She nodded.

His lips touched hers in a feather-light kiss. She fancied tasting respect, admiration, and boundless honor. Unfortunately, none of those sparked her passion the way Reed's kiss had done.

"Good-bye, Kate." He put on his hat and turned to go.

"Take care."

Watching him clear the veranda, she wished that she could be everything he wanted, wished that she welcomed his ardor, as would any woman in her right mind.

But as she watched him help Charm into the carriage, all she could think about was hurrying upstairs.

To Daniel. To Reed.

She heard Reed moving around in his own room, heard

water splash in the washbowl, so she walked down the hall to Daniel's door.

The boy was in bed, lying on his side, curled in on himself. His huge blue eyes were still open. She lowered herself to the mattress beside him, listened to the soft sound of his breathing, offered him nothing but silent companionship.

She reached up to stroke his hair, and he listlessly batted her hand away. It was the first real response he had made in two days.

Sensing movement behind her, she looked over her shoulder. Reed was framed in the doorway, watching them with worry etched around his eyes.

"My heart aches for him," she whispered. "I don't know what to do, what to say. Before he had hope. He had someone to return to. Now, he has nothing."

Reed walked over and stood with his thumbs hooked into his waistband, contemplating Daniel.

"He has us," he said.

Us.

A single father and a housekeeper.

He needs a real family. A permanent family.

The last thing this little boy needed was another temporary mother in his life.

As she sat there beside him, Kate realized that for Daniel's sake, she had to make a decision soon. She could not let him come to care for her, to think of her as a mother now that his Comanche mother was gone.

She stood up. "Would you like to tell him good night?"

Visibly uncomfortable, Reed shifted as he gazed down at the boy. Then he sat down where Kate had been perched beside Daniel's shoulder. Slowly, he reached into his shirt pocket, pulled out a choker beaded with multicolored glass of every hue. A dollar-size white shell, bright as a polished moon, dangled from it. Kate listened as Reed spoke softly to Daniel.

"I can't bring your mother back, but I saved this for you. You'll always have it to remember her by." Reed pressed the necklace into Daniel's hand. Slowly, his little fingers coiled around the choker and held it tight.

Kate could not bear to watch anymore, so she left them alone and walked out into the hall. Leaning against the wall, she let the tears come. Daniel would fall asleep tonight with his mother's choker clutched in his little hand, just as she had once clung to her mother's ragged handkerchief. The tattered piece of thin cotton was all she had left of Meg Whittington, a piece of her mother that she had never surrendered, even to this day.

Reed followed her and closed the door behind him, but tonight he did not lock Daniel in. "Are you all right?" he said softly.

She nodded, her throat working as she tried to swallow, searching for the right words. She, who knew the value of such a remembrance, had not thought to bring something back for Daniel, and yet Reed, a man she was convinced had a heart of stone, had managed to make the small gesture that would one day mean everything to his son.

She had seen a caring, loving, thoughtful side to him that threatened to make her even more vulnerable to him. As she watched him through her tears, he slipped his arm around her shoulders and started walking her down the hall.

"Why don't you go in and rest a few minutes? I'll get a bath ready for you."

Right now, nothing sounded more tempting than a bath, except remaining in the comfort and warmth of his embrace.

She sighed in resignation. "That sounds wonderful."

"Just promise to save me some room." Then he startled her by letting go a short laugh. "Don't look so shocked, Kate. I'm just teasing."

Smiling, she went into her room and sat down on the edge of the bed, afraid that if she closed her eyes even for a second, she would not stir until noon the next day.

42

Reed found her lightly dozing on top of her bed, still dressed in the ridiculous, oversize pants Charm had given her. She had unbuttoned her shoes, but hadn't taken them off.

He gently nudged her shoulder. She stirred.

"Sit up, Kate. You'll sleep better with the road dust off." He slipped his arm around her and helped her sit up. Then he knelt down, pulled off her shoes, and stripped away her stockings.

"No." Drowsy, she attempted to push him away. "I'm too sleepy."

"Let me, Kate." It was the least he could do.

Now that Daniel was safe, glorious relief had settled inside him, and everything Kate had done came into focus. She had dedicated herself to Daniel's care, enough to risk life and limb to go into Comanche territory. Any other woman would have walked out of their lives weeks ago.

But not Kate. Not his stubborn spinster.

Reed smiled down at the top of her head recalling how she had helped them all in one way or another, he, Charm, Daniel.

And she had asked nothing in return.

He picked her up and carried her down the hall, where

he lowered her to a stool in the middle of the floor. The water was still steaming, fogging the tiny room. From a table in the corner, a pair of candelabra cast the room in flickering shadows.

"Reed?" She was awake, barely, sleepily looking around.

He reached for the buttons on her purloined shirt. She made a halfhearted attempt to brush his hands aside. "Let me do this for you, Kate. Let me, please."

Somewhere between the second and third button, she stopped resisting. Somewhere between the third and fourth, he became fully aroused.

He leaned forward, pressed his lips to the tender white skin of her throat, and slowly opened the front of her shirt—*his* shirt—revealing a deep violet silk chemise. An insert of lace revealed bare breasts beneath it.

So daring. So unexpected. A spinster wearing a tantalizing, revealing, violet undergarment. Her breasts were full, her hard nipples enticing. Unable to resist, he slipped his palms beneath her breasts, rubbed his thumbs over the lace across her nipples. He expected her to pull away. Instead, Kate sighed and leaned into him. He closed his eyes.

She sat motionless while he cupped her breasts, stroking her. Collecting himself, he pulled out each and every pin until her long hair fell around her shoulders and down to her waist like dark, rich sable. It wasn't until he tried to slip his hand into her waistband to unfasten the ties that she stirred and pushed him away.

He yielded, letting her cling to her modesty. "I'll turn around while you undress and get into the tub."

"But . . ." She kept her eyes closed and her hands crossed over her breasts, unwilling to look at him even though she was still dressed.

"I'll stay and wash your hair for you. Scrub your back."

"Oh, my, no."

He leaned into her and whispered, "Oh, my, yes," against her lips. Then he got to his feet, crossed his arms over his chest and turned around.

Kate's limbs went liquid as she sat on the low stool, staring at Reed's back.

All this hot steam has gone to my head.

She felt downright dizzy and weak as a kitten. Her heart was pounding like the bass drum of the Lone Star Cowboy Band.

He had touched her breasts. Kissed her not once, but twice.

She hadn't protested, not any more than a whimper. But why would she? She was her mother's daughter.

Wasn't this what she had wanted ever since the first time? What she had longed for?

Her head told her to send him away. Her heart begged her not to. To deny him would mean denying herself.

Torn by the same conflicting emotions she felt the day she first read his father's advertisement—as if she were standing on a crossroads of a whole new life—she quickly reminded herself that she had turned down the wrong road once already. She glanced up at Reed; then pulled off the shirt and let it fall to the floor.

"Do you ever think about that night, Kate?"

His voice startled her so much that she nearly fell off the stool. "What night?"

"You know what night. The night I was feverish. The night you gave yourself to me."

She skimmed Charm's lucky chemise over her head and threw it atop the shirt. The windowless room was still warm, but she shivered anyway as she stood and quickly stripped off her pants before she lost her nerve. Careful not to slip on the damp floor, she quickly stepped into the tub and sank below the waterline. Thankful for the weak candlelight, she made a futile attempt to cover herself with her arms and hands.

Frustrated, she let go a long sigh. "I could lie to you, Reed. I could say that I have forgotten all about it, for believe me, I *have* tried to forget. But I've thought about that night every single day since it happened." Her voice faded to a whisper. "Every single one."

She sensed him there behind her before he asked her to lean forward, and then he wet her hair, expertly lathered, shampooed, and rinsed it. Then he dipped a piece of soap and a washrag into the water.

"I wish things could have been different," he said. "I'll be honest with you. What I remember of that night seems like a dream. It all comes back to me in fits and starts."

He slipped his hand behind her, lathered her shoulders, massaging them. He moved the soapy rag lower, to her waist, then ran it up and down her spine to its base.

She bit her lips, stifled a moan, trying to deny what his touch made her feel.

"I envy you," he went on. "I wish I could remember all of it."

His hands trailed through the slick soap on her back, slipped around to her breasts. He palmed them from behind, rubbed her nipples with his thumbs until she went as hot and liquid as the water around her. She closed her eyes, let her head drop against the edge of the tub.

Reed came around to the side of the tub, leaned over, and kissed her mouth. She kissed him back. Slowly, curiously, she traced his lips with her tongue, tasted and savored both Reed and the tenderness of the stolen moment.

When the kiss ended, he ran his tongue down her wet neck, brought it back to her ear, and made her shiver to her toes.

"I wish I could remember everything. I need to remember you, Kate," he said, his warm breath brushing her ear before he sucked on her earlobe. "What I recall is that it was never like that for me before. Never. Not knowing for certain has been driving me crazy. Don't you ever wonder, Kate? Don't you need to know if it was exactly the way you remember?"

He took her chin in his hand, made her look into his eyes. She felt herself falling into them. Why lie when she knew he could see the truth plain as day in her eyes?

The very last shred of her weak and worthless resistance fell away. "Yes. I need to know," she whispered.

He kissed her like a drowning man in need of air. The washcloth was lost somewhere in the tub, the soap forgotten, melting on the bottom.

This time he used his hands with no pretense of trying to bathe her. She let them wander over her seeking each and every hidden pleasure point, let him introduce her to places and feelings she never knew existed on her or in her.

She wanted more, begged for more than the gentle touch of his hand, and he obliged, stroking until she cried out with the shattering release. The sound of her voice echoed against the walls of the tiny room. Boneless and replete, Kate lazed against the back of the tub.

Reed moved away, sat on the stool, and pulled off his boots and socks. His hands were awkward. He fumbled with his shirt buttons, ended up tearing the last two out of the holes, wadding up his shirt, and tossing it aside. Once his pants and drawers were added to the heap, he grabbed a towel and spread it on the floor beside the tub.

Within a handful of heartbeats he was back at Kate's side. She stirred, gazed up at him, her thoughts unreadable.

"What I remember most from that night is that *you* pleasured *me*, Kate."

She pressed her fingertips to his lips. He sucked them into his mouth, lightly bit them, teased them with his tongue.

"I know what I did." She sighed and turned her face away.

"Don't be ashamed, Kate. Never be ashamed." He slipped his arms beneath her back and as he stood, drew her up. She came out of the tub slippery and wet, pressed fully against his length. There was no hiding his arousal. There was no hiding anything between them now.

He lifted her out of the tub, slid her down his body, skin against skin, took her with him until they were kneeling on the towel. He kissed her while they were pressed together from knees to lips. She clung to him as if she would never let go.

Easing her down to the towel, he released her long enough to spread her damp hair out around her head and then ran his hands over the thick rippling waves.

With hands and fingers he memorized every inch of her face, neck, shoulders, arms, as she watched. His hands mapped every curve and line, her breasts, her belly.

He touched her between her thighs, wanting only to give her pleasure. Her eyes closed, her lips parted.

"I need you, Kate," he whispered. "I need you."

He rose over her, parted her legs, found her warm and wet and willing. Kate wrapped her arms around him in silent invitation, an assurance that she understood what he wanted, that she wanted him, too.

He eased into her, felt her body open to accommodate him. He began to move slowly, reminding himself this was only her second time. But Kate began to thrust back, to lift her hips, inviting him to take all she had to give.

She was tight and hot as fire. She was innocent. She was wanton. Better than any memory.

She was Kate. Knowing that made having her infinitely more erotic.

His wants and needs were so deep, her sultry voice with its encouraging sighs and moans so unbridled and fervent, that it was over quickly, but he had the satisfaction of knowing he had brought her to fulfillment again before he surrendered.

They lay side by side on the damp, wadded towel. Droplets of water spattered across the varnished wood floor and shone like tiny stars in the candlelight.

Reed felt her shiver, traced her thigh. Goose bumps blossomed over her skin. He wrapped his arms around her and held her close.

"What do you say we find out if that water is still warm?" He whispered against her neck, amazed at the softness of her skin, the purity of it, golden ivory in the candlelight.

"We?" Her warm breath tickled his ear.

"With a bit of imagination that tub should hold two."

43

She overslept and woke up alone.

Kate rushed while getting dressed, pulling on her stockings and rifling through her drawers until she found a clean white chemise.

She closed her eyes, wondered about Charm's lucky one.

Dear Saint Perpetua, what happened to my clothes?

Were they still on the bathing room floor?

She slipped on her petticoat, tied the ties, and then donned her calico gown.

What now?

Where do we go from here?

More than once she paused to study herself in the oval mirror hanging over her chest of drawers, pressed her palms against her cheeks and wondered how on earth—since she was barely able to look herself in the eye—she could ever face Reed again.

She picked up her precious bottle of rose water, dabbed some on her throat and wrists. Before she left Maine she had splurged on a small amount, hoping to please her new husband. She wondered if Reed had ever really noticed the scent.

They had made love again in the tub and then in her bed and fell asleep in each other's arms.

He had whispered words of need, of want, but not of love.

Deftly, as she braided her hair, the recollection of his strong hands, of the care he took as he had washed her hair for her, nearly took her breath away.

What will I say to him?

How should I act?

As she tied a black ribbon around her braid, she suddenly remembered that Charm was in Lone Star. Dear Saint Perpetua, there was breakfast to be made!

She found her shoes under the bed, struggled to pull them on. The leather was cracked and dusty, the heels worn down on the outer edges. She struggled buttoning them up and then flew down the hall.

Daniel wasn't in his room. The bed was unmade, his dirty clothes lay in a heap on the floor, the dresser drawers were open.

Not again.

She rushed to the open window, drew aside the thin muslin curtain, and sagged with relief against the window frame when she saw Daniel currying Reed's horse in the corral.

Although she didn't see Reed anywhere, Scrappy stood close by, alternately repairing a section of fence and glancing at Daniel.

She went downstairs, expecting to find Reed. There was a pile of dirty dishes and a frying pan with a coat of egg stuck to the bottom, but no Reed. When she stepped out the back door and called to Scrappy, he motioned toward the front of the house.

Standing beneath the shade of the wide veranda, she debated whether to go find him or to put it off. She could take the coward's way out and go back to the kitchen, make breakfast, and wait for him to find her, or she could track him down.

Whatever she decided, sooner or later she was going to have to face him. Sooner or later they were going to have to talk about last night.

It was another hot, dry day. Not yet ten in the morning, and it already felt hot enough to bake bread outside. She walked around the veranda to the front. Sure enough, Reed was there, standing beside the hitching post, staring down the road.

Kate followed his gaze and recognized Gideon and Winifred Greene's buggy as it came up the drive.

Although she was loath to see them again, at least with the advent of the Greenes' arrival there would be no time to speak of last night. Smoothing down the front of her gown, Kate walked over to the steps. Reed heard her and turned around.

His jaw was set. There was tension in his stance, but at least when he looked up at her, he smiled.

"Good morning, Kate."

The sound of his voice held the power of a caress. Her knees went weak, but somehow she managed to walk down the steps and cross to where he was standing. Shielding her eyes with her hand, she concentrated on the buggy already halfway up the road.

"They must have started out before dawn." He was standing beside her.

"I was afraid we hadn't seen the last of them."

"The last thing I need is them bothering Daniel right now." He looked down at her again. "Let me handle this, Kate."

"Do you mean don't talk?"

He smiled again. "That's exactly what I mean."

Gideon turned the rig and set the brake. Reed and Kate crossed the yard to meet them as Gideon gave Winifred a hand climbing down. She was spry for her age, still wearing the same dour expression as when Kate first met her. It matched her somber clothes.

"We didn't realize you were here," Gideon told Reed without any word of greeting.

"I've taken over running the ranch." He paused and then casually slipped his arm around Kate's shoulders.

Surprised by such an outward display, Kate started to pull away until he squeezed her shoulder.

"You've already met my wife, Kate," he said.

As one, the Greenes looked her up and down from head to toe.

"We have, the day we . . ." Gideon began.

". . . came for Daniel and she turned us away," Winifred finished. "Real hard to believe you remarried, Reed."

"Why's that?"

Kate could tell he did not care for the Greenes any more than she did.

"After what happened to our poor Becky, it's a wonder you could find anyone who'd want you." Gideon rocked forward on his toes and then back on his heels.

"But then, she's not from around here, as I recall." Winifred was staring at Reed's hand on Kate's shoulder. "We came to see our grandson. We've got a right to see him."

"You certainly do," Reed acknowledged with a firm nod. "But not today. He's still getting settled in, and I don't want him upset."

Gideon's eyes hardened. "We went to town. Found out one of those whores is living here, too . . ."

". . . and we don't want the boy brought up around filth." Winifred primly folded her hands at her waist.

Reed kept a firm hold on Kate now. She was not about to let them malign Charm, but neither was Reed.

"Who I hire is none of your business," he said.

"Where *is* the boy?" Gideon craned his neck as if he could see around the width of the house.

"Working out back."

"When we saw him a few weeks ago he couldn't even speak English."

"He's still pretty quiet." Reed glanced down at Kate and quickly looked away.

She bit her lips and stared at the ground.

Gideon appeared to be gathering his courage. He tugged on the hem of his jacket, held his hand over his heart. "I won't beat around the bush, Reed. Winifred and I want that boy. You owe it to us to hand him over. He was Becky's boy after all, and since we don't have her anymore, we want to raise him. We figure it'll just be a matter of time before you take off again to rejoin the Rangers. You never wanted anything to do with this place."

Winifred picked up where he left off. "You got a new wife now. You and her will have a family of your own. Pretty soon, Daniel will wind up being the stepson around here. Why not give him to us . . ."

". . . so we can bring him up proper?" Gideon finished.

Kate realized she had been holding her breath until Reed let go of her shoulder and took a step toward them. "Daniel is *my* son. He belongs to *me*, and he's staying right here on Lone Star. I'd appreciate it if you left now, because like I said, I don't want him upset. He's just settling down." He paused, collected himself. "That's not to say you aren't welcome to visit some other time."

Kate was so very, very glad to hear him claim the boy that it was a moment or two before she realized he was already helping Winifred back into the high-sprung buggy.

Kate wished she were relieved to see them go, but now

that she was alone with Reed again, she had no idea what to say or do.

Reed took off his hat, wiped his forehead with his shirt-sleeve, and tried not to let the encounter with the Greenes haunt him. They were gone, hopefully for a long, long while. They had every right to visit Daniel, but after the way Becky turned out, there was no way he wanted the boy around them for any length of time.

They still blamed him for Becky's death and always would, but since in many ways he still blamed himself, he couldn't fault them for that.

Kate was still standing by the hitching post, watching the buggy rattle down the lane. He took a deep breath and wished what he was about to do would go as easy as his confrontation with the Greenes.

He walked back to where Kate was standing in her pretty flowered dress, looking radiant. He had never seen her more beautiful or more uncertain.

"Will you come up to the office with me, Kate?"

She paused, fingering the end of her braid. "What about Daniel?"

"Scrappy will keep an eye on him." Reed started toward the house. "Come with me, please." When he realized she had not budged, he added, "Just to talk."

"How is Daniel? I was surprised to see him outside."

"It's like he's moving around in his sleep. I dressed him, made him his breakfast. He picked at some eggs but only ate a few mouthfuls. He acts like sad walking."

"Can you blame him?"

He shook his head, holding the door for her. She passed through so close to him that he caught the scent of roses in her hair and shut his eyes. The scent intensified.

Once they were upstairs, Reed closed the office door. He had made the room his own, from the cluttered desk and the heavy leather chair to a map of Lone Star on the wall behind it. He walked over and opened a drawer, pulled out some folded papers, and then sat on the corner of the desk.

He held the papers out to her.

"What are these?" She took them and looked down.

"The legal documents that Jeb Cooley drew up for us."

He waited while she unfolded the pages and quickly scanned them. His signature was already at the bottom of each of them. He wished it weren't, but he had signed them in Jeb's office before he had come home.

He took a deep breath, looked out the window, across the lifts and folds of land, across endless miles of grass and blue sky. The land was everything his father had worked for. Lone Star was synonymous with the Benton name.

He watched her hand tighten on the corner of the pages. Saw the color drain from her face as she read them. He wished he didn't owe her total honesty.

"Let's stay married, Kate. Don't sign those papers."

He scratched his jaw, shifted his hip, and tried to think of the right words to say. He thought of the things he had read in her letters, of all the things she wanted out of life.

"I don't know that I'll ever be able to love you the way you want, the way you deserve to be loved. I don't know if I can ever love that way again. But we're good together. I'd be a fool to deny that, and so would you. Daniel needs a mother. Most of all, he needs a family to pull him out of this.

"If you tear those up, Kate, no one will ever know those proxy papers were forged. We can even get married before a judge if you want and file new ones. Reverend Marshall might even consent to marry us. I'm sure he wouldn't want you living in sin."

After last night he hoped that she would at least consider his proposal, but seeing her shock and the way her expression shuttered, he realized he had just made one of the most fatal errors of his life.

44

The papers in her hand shook when Kate began to tremble all over. The edges of the pages creased where her fingers dug into the them.

"Let's stay married."

Not for love. For Daniel.

"I don't know that I'll ever be able to love you in the way you want . . . the way you deserve."

Kate looked around the room, needing to sit before she fell down. Reed was beside her instantly, guiding her around the desk to his deep, leather-upholstered chair. She sank into it. The documents, suddenly too heavy to hold, dropped to her lap.

He wouldn't stop. He was pacing, waiting for her to answer, listing again his reasons for their remaining married. To him it was as simple as planning a cattle drive.

She had agreed to the proxy marriage after putting her trust into less than a dozen letters. She had believed in a paper dream.

That's all it was.

A paper dream.

The legal pages lay open in her lap—more paper. At some point Reed had signed them, wanting to be rid of her.

Now he was asking her to tear them up, to ignore his bold dark signature, ignore the fact that he could never cherish her as a husband should cherish a wife. As she would surely cherish him.

If she agreed to stay, she would have the house she always wanted, even marriage and a family—but the foundation of their union would be false. Nothing about it would be real, except for her own one-sided love for Reed, her unshakable love for Daniel, and whatever love the boy might come to have for her.

Would it be enough? Could it be enough?

If only there was a hint in Reed's eyes, even a distant glimmer of hope for the kind of love and regard that Preston felt for her. There was adoration in the preacher's eyes when he looked at her, an offering of the kind of love Reed did not consider himself capable of.

Oh, but what of last night in his arms?

Her body wanted him and no other. But could her spirit survive living with him as a lover, but never truly loved?

Across the room, Reed watched her intently. She gave him credit for not trying to seduce her into tearing up the documents, blessed him for not using the power of seduction to cajole her. Then again, perhaps he might not know how easily she would have acquiesced if he touched her, kissed her, begged her not to sign.

Somehow she found the strength to lift the papers again. She got to her feet. There was a pot of ink and a pen with a nib conveniently lying on the desk.

She reached out.

"Kate—"

Dipping the pen into the crystal pot, she fought looking at him. The tip of the nib disappeared into the dark India ink. She pulled it out, quickly signed her name, and then picked up a rocking blotter and rolled it over her signature. She dipped, signed, and blotted until all three copies were done.

When she stepped back and tried to hand him the papers, he would not take them, so she laid them out on the desk. She was forced to swallow twice before any words would come.

"I made a terrible mistake once, Reed. There is enough of a dreamer left in me to want to marry for love the next time. I want it all, not just the trappings. Not just a fine house and security, but the love that should dwell inside that home. I want a husband who can offer both commitment *and* love." She took a deep breath, forced herself to stay calm. "Do you really think that the lust we gave in to last night would be enough to hold us together forever?"

"That's already a hell of a lot more than some marriages are built on." He was angry now, doing nothing to hide it.

"But that's *not* enough for me. Not anymore. You know that I love Daniel." She willed herself not to cry, to stay strong. "Because I love him, I want what's best for him. He needs you to be a real father to him, and as long as I'm here, he will come to depend on me again."

And I on you.

Waiting and hoping for something you can't give.

"Maybe Daniel would even . . . maybe he would eventually come to love me. I can't let him begin to think of me as his mother. He is so very vulnerable now," she said.

"All the more reason you should consider my offer."

"All the more reason I have to leave."

"Leave?"

She looked out the window. It was still early. Not yet noon. She could be in town before the afternoon was through—if she packed and left right away.

"Yes. I'm leaving."

"When?"

"Today. As soon as I can."

Before I change my mind.

Before you do or say something that will make me stay.

"You're pretty calm about this, Kate. When *exactly* did you decide you were leaving? Last night after we made love the first time? Or after the last? Or was it when you called out my name when I came inside you? When *exactly* did you decide you didn't want to be here anymore?"

She thought of Sofia and of all the years she had given Reed Senior, years of loving him, caring for him enough to help him trick a naive young woman and shatter her dreams.

"Fight for what you want here, but not forever.

"Try, Señora, but do not waste your life waiting for Reed Benton to fall in love with you."

Under no circumstances, not even for Daniel, would she let herself become another Sofia.

"I agreed to stay on as a hired housekeeper, but what happened last night changed all of that completely." The ink on the pages was dry. She took a copy for herself, left one for Reed and one for the lawyer to file.

Would she ever see him again? She couldn't be sure, so she took a long last look into his eyes, at his mouth, his hands. Memories were all she would have to treasure. Memories and the photograph his father had sent her.

"Now, if you'll excuse me, I'm going to go ask Scrappy if he will take me into Lone Star. Then I'll pack . . . and tell Daniel good-bye."

Stunned, Reed watched her walk away. After last night, he had been sure she would agree to stay married, if not because of how good it had been between them, then surely for Daniel's sake.

But Kate wanted more. More than he could promise, and he wasn't about to lie to her, not when he knew that she deserved better. Hell, she deserved someone like the preacher.

So, he let her go. Through the window, he watched her walk out into the stable area and stop beside Daniel. She touched his hair, gently laid her hand on his shoulder and stood beside him for a while, offering silent companionship. Finally, she left him and walked over to Scrappy.

The old cowhand planted his hands on his hips and twice emphatically shook his head no. She kept talking until he rolled his eyes and finally nodded. Then Kate came back toward the house. Scrappy paused to watch her walk away, shook his head once more. Then the old wrangler picked up his hammer and moved on down the fence line.

It took her a surprisingly short time to pack. She found Charm's violet chemise and pants atop the mound of clothes in the tub room. She picked up Reed's shirt, held it close, and closed her eyes, inhaling his scent. Pulling herself together, she carefully folded his things and set them on the stool.

Towels lay around in dead wet heaps on the floor, so Kate picked them all up and hung them over the edge of the tub. If Reed did not find another housekeeper soon, there was no hope for the place.

Surprisingly calm, she finished packing up her life. Everything she owned still fit in one carpetbag. There was nothing new to take with her but the two dresses Charm had made, far too many memories, and a battered heart.

But she did have all the wisdom she had gained. She kept Reed Senior's letters to remind her that things are never as they seem. She packed the photograph of Reed. She would never, ever part with it. Then she slipped the brass photograph of Becky and Daniel in Reed's desk drawer.

Slowly she carried her bag downstairs. The house was as silent as Daniel.

She walked outside and found Scrappy waiting beside the buckboard. Handing him the carpetbag, she walked over to Daniel, now seated on the ground in the shadow of the horse barn. Unmindful of her calico dress, she sat beside him and took his little hand in hers.

"You'll never know how this hurts me to have to leave you, but I'm doing this for you and for Reed." She pressed his hand between her palms, promised to remember him always. "I'm going to miss you terribly, just the way you miss your mama, but I know that I'll see you again someday. When you're old enough, if you still remember the time we spent together and ask me why, I'll be able to explain."

She kissed the top of his head and prayed that his heart would soon heal. Then she cupped his chin, forcing him to look at her. "Good-bye, Daniel." She kissed his forehead and then let him go. He turned his face away.

Scrappy was waiting, so Kate climbed to her feet and brushed the dust off her skirt and then walked over to the buckboard. As if he had been waiting until the very last minute, the back door slammed and Reed came walking out to join them.

He went straight to Daniel, took the boy by the hand and pulled him gently to his feet; then he led him to the wagon. Kate was biting her lips so hard she was afraid they would bleed.

Reed stood behind Daniel with his hands on his shoulders as Scrappy helped her aboard. The old wrangler took his sweet time checking the lines before he finally climbed up on the seat. He let the brake go, stalled some more, and then turned to Kate. "You sure about this?"

"Yes. Please go."

Scrappy flicked the reins. As they slowly pulled out of the stable yard, she smiled down at Daniel and then looked at Reed.

"Good-bye, Kate," he said.

Afraid her trembling lips would give her away, she merely nodded in farewell.

Spewing dust in its wake, the buckboard bounced and rattled down the long, rutted road.

She didn't cry until the house was out of sight.

45

Kate found a room at the boarding house before she went to see Preston. He did not try to hide his joy, nor did he question her when she told him that she had moved to town. Instead, he immediately walked her down to Lone Star Mercantile to help her secure a position as a clerk.

After she had settled into her light and airy room, complete with a pretty indigo-and-yellow quilt on the bed, she ate dinner downstairs with four other boarders and then waited until just before sunset to walk to the end of town, knock at the back door of Dolly B. Goode's Social Club and Entertainment Emporium, and ask for Charm.

Dolly, a boisterous, robust woman in her fifties with jarring, carrot-colored hair and carmine lips, welcomed Kate with a startling bear hug, commended her for what she had done for Charm, and ushered her into the suite she had donated to Jonah and Charm until he recovered.

As soon as Dolly opened the door and Charm saw Kate, she left Jonah's bedside and raced across the room.

"Kate! What are you doing here?" Like Dolly, she hugged Kate hard and long before she stepped back. "Don't ever, ever come here again, do you hear me? Think what this might do to your reputation."

Kate had more to worry about than her reputation. Jonah, lying propped up against Dolly's satin pillowcases, surrounded by a barrage of fancy ruffled pillows, tried to smile. He was as gray as an overcast sky, but not feverish.

"How are you, Captain?" she asked.

"I'll live." Looking adoringly at Charm he added, "Now."

Charm adjusted his pillow and then offered Kate a chair. After they sat down, Charm took Jonah's hand.

"I want to thank you, Kate, for sending Charm to me," the captain said. "And we'd like you to be the first to know, outside of Dolly that is, that as soon as I'm up and around, Miss Riley is going to be my wife."

"We're getting married just outside of town at sundown," Charm added. "And I want you to stand up for me, Kate."

"We hope you'll consider it," Jonah added.

"I wouldn't miss it for the world."

Charm brushed his hair back off his forehead as the man's eyes drifted closed. "Thanks for coming to see him," she whispered. "Where's Reed?"

Kate noted Jonah's breath was coming deep and easy now, so she quietly confided in Charm. "I quit my job and signed the papers to undo the proxy marriage. I've moved to town and am staying at the boarding house."

"Oh, Kate." Charm's shoulders sagged. "What happened?"

Kate looked down at her hands. She had been unconsciously wadding her skirt. She smoothed out the wrinkles and tried to explain. "I didn't want Daniel to come to depend on me more than he does Reed. They need to learn to trust and love each other and I . . . I didn't want to be in the way—"

Charm reached over and laid her hand on Kate's arm. "What *really* happened?"

Before she knew it, Kate had told her everything that she wasn't ashamed to tell. Charm clucked and tsked and shook her head, and when Kate was through, she said how truly sorry she was that things had not worked out.

Kate collected herself. It was growing dark out, well past time to leave. Charm stood up to walk her to the door.

"Oh, Kate, I know Jonah plans to ask Reed to stand up for him. Can you still do the same for me if it means seeing Reed again?"

There could be worse fates, Kate was sure of it, but at the moment, none came to mind. But no matter what, she could never let Charm down.

"Of course I will," she assured her.

They reached the door to Dolly's suite. Charm insisted on walking her through the hall to the back door. Together they stepped out into the close August night. Piano music drifted out of the Social Club along with the sound of laughter, the murmur of hushed conversation, and an occasional squeal of delight.

Kate looked down the street toward the respectable end of town, where lights were shining inside the neat rows of houses. From here she could even see the two-story boarding house roof.

"I'll come visit you again tomorrow night and tell you all about my first day on the job at Lone Star Mercantile."

Charm shook her head vehemently. "No, you won't, Kate. As much as I would love to see you, I won't have you ruining your reputation. You have a chance to make something of yourself here. Besides, Reverend Marshall is smitten with you. You can't risk being seen coming in and out of this place."

"Don't be silly." Even though Kate knew it was true, loyalty compelled her to protest.

"Do you really want people talking about you now that you are starting over?"

"Your friendship means more to me than anything that people might say. Preston knows that." For the first time in her life, she had a friendship that meant much more to her than her name.

But Charm remained vehement. "I don't care. I mean it, Kate. Stay away from here until the wedding." A huge smiled bloomed across her pretty features, and she sagged. "After that, Jonah and I are going to move someplace where I can be respectable, too."

Kate had been gone a month before Reed stopped watching the road and came to the conclusion that she wasn't ever coming back.

Every now and again he expected to hear her voice, see her seated at the table in the kitchen or reading by an open window in the parlor. Once he thought he heard the heels of her sturdy brown shoes tapping sharply on the stairs.

Sleep tended to evade him these days, so he spent late evening hours in the office accompanied by Daniel. He had been with the boy day and night since he brought him home again. He bathed and dressed him, made him eat, carried on a running, one-way conversation just as Kate had done.

Slowly but surely, Daniel had come out of the spell of deep sorrow that ensnared him. In Kate's absence, the boy had begun following him around like a little lost lamb.

Daniel had taken to lugging around a box that contained his toys, a wagon and odd-shaped animals that Scrappy had made from wood scraps.

Tonight Reed was up late, hunched over his desk while Daniel played on the floor in the corner. He was busy lining up horses and cows, then shoving the wagon into them and knocking them over. Reed tried to concentrate despite the racket, reminding himself that it wasn't that long ago he worried Daniel was never going to come out of his silence.

Shaking his head at the pile of paper on the desk, Reed decided he was too tired to concentrate. It hadn't taken him long to realize that even though his father always made the effort of running the ranch seem minimal, Reed Senior had kept his hand in everything.

The four ranch foremen were veterans and competent, but someone had to coordinate the quarters of the ranch, and each one had its own particular problems. The sections that bordered the frontier had been hard hit by Comanche stealing stock. The eastern sectors had problems of their own with encroaching settlers making roads across the ranch. In the far southwest corner, drought threatened.

He stacked up bills and statements, ready to turn in for the night when Daniel threw his wagon into the wooden box with a clatter, stood up, and wandered over to the desk where he leaned against the arm of Reed's chair. He wore the beaded Comanche choker all the time, but the necklace was too big and was always coming loose. When Reed saw that it was about to fall off, he tightened the thongs at the nape of the boy's neck.

"There you go, son."

Daniel opened and closed all the desk drawers, a trick he had learned a few nights ago. Reed was reaching for the lamp when he realized Daniel had stopped dead still and was staring down into one of the open drawers. Inside, face up, lay the broken case with the photograph of Becky and Daniel.

Remembering the boy's first explosive reaction to it, Reed's first instinct was to quickly shut the drawer, but Daniel was studying it without any repercussion, so Reed slowly reached in and pulled out the broken silver case.

Daniel frowned, yet appeared to be waiting for Reed to say something.

Reed touched Becky's likeness. "That was your mama. Mama. Can you say it?"

Slowly Daniel reached out with his forefinger, extending his hand toward the picture. His finger hovered above the likeness before he touched the image of himself.

"That's *you* when you were almost three. That's Daniel."

The boy continued to point at his own likeness. Reed said again, *"Daniel."*

Certain the boy would soon tire of the game, Reed patted him on the head and started to put the photograph back in the drawer. Instead, Daniel pointed to his picture once more and then, in a barely audible voice, he said one word.

"Daniel."

Reed was too stunned to move. He looked around the room, but there was only emptiness to share the moment. With a lump in his throat the size of Texas, he wished like hell that Kate were there.

Finally, as calmly as he could, he said, "That's good, son. That's real good." He touched Daniel's chest and said again, "Daniel."

Daniel touched the image. "Daniel."

Then, much to Reed's amazement, the boy pointed to Becky and said, "Mama."

Daniel kept sliding his finger from Becky's image to his own, repeating the names over and over again.

To some, a nine-year-old repeating two simple words might not have seemed like much of an achievement. Reed knew that Kate would have rejoiced. To him, it was a start. A damn good start.

Fast Pony knew Tall Ranger, Reed, was proud of him when he spoke the white names—the way Many Horses had always been proud whenever he caught a rabbit or killed a badger. Even though Tall Ranger did not show it, Fast Pony could tell. The man was sitting very still, watching him closely, and when Fast Pony looked up, Tall Ranger was smiling.

At first he had been scared when he pulled the sliding wood box open and saw the ghostly faces staring up at him, but he refused to be afraid anymore, so he convinced himself they were flat and very, very small. They could do little harm.

Tall Ranger was warm and alive right there beside him, so there was no sense in fearing the ghosts on the paper. Tall Ranger would not let anyone hurt him. He was sure of that now.

At first, after his mother was killed, a strange, dense smoke had filled his head, and he wanted to die, too, like Painted White Feather. He had even decided to starve himself this time, but after a few days he was so hungry he ate.

As the mind-smoke began to clear, he remembered how Painted White Feather had told him that Tall Ranger might be his white father. Fast Pony watched and waited, and then he tried to learn some of the white ways.

He understood that the woman ghost on the paper was his white mother. *Mama.* But he had never seen her around here, just the image on paper. He decided she must be gone forever.

And what of Soft Grass Hands? For a time he wondered if she was his white mother, but she was gone now, too. Tall Ranger lived alone, with only him.

He often wondered when Soft Grass Hands was coming back. She had gone away once before, but had come before the sun had gone down on the day. And what of Yellow Hair? He missed her, too. There had been few sweets since she left them.

When his mind cleared he remembered the way Tall Ranger had buried Painted White Feather on the prairie and had given him the precious shell necklace she always wore. Every day now, he wore it. Every night he slept with it beneath his pillow. Before he fell asleep, he made a vow never, ever to forget his mother's last words to him.

"I want you to live, Fast Pony. I want you to grow up safe, away from death and sickness. With a full belly. You have always been the best son.

"Make me proud of your bravery."

He had begun to follow Tall Ranger and to learn his ways, to make Painted White Feather's spirit proud. He wanted to do what she asked of him before she died.

"You are a white man's son by blood."

Maybe Tall Ranger was his white father. Someday, when he learned the white tongue, he would ask.

One thing Fast Pony knew was that he would always be one of The People in his heart. For now, to please Painted White Feather, to honor her memory, he would be Daniel.

"Will that be all today, Mrs. Peabody?" Kate tucked a half dozen eggs in a small bucket of oatmeal to keep them from breaking. Annabelle Peabody's husband, Charlie, was one of the Lone Star ranch hands who also played trumpet in the town band.

Annabelle was much younger than Kate but already the mother of three boys under six. Each time she came into the store the poor woman looked more exhausted than the last.

She had opened her purse but was forced to corral the boys before she could count out her coins.

"That's enough for now, you hear me? Stop hitting Lawrence, Charlie Junior, or I'll tell your pa. An' I mean it this time." She looked back at Kate and sighed in frustration. "Lord, sometimes I don't know if it's worth it."

Kate's heart ached with envy as she watched the three towheads scrambling about below the countertops and playing hide and seek in the aisles. Melancholy, she shook her head and smiled. "Believe me, it is."

Annabelle paid Kate and gathered her purchases. Then she paused and reached over to give Kate's hand a sympathetic pat.

"Don't you never mind, Kate. You're pretty enough to find a man out here. Pretty soon you'll have a few youngsters of your own."

Embarrassed, Kate thanked Annabelle and then came out from behind the long wooden counter piled with goods to help her gather up the boys. Taking three-year-old Timmy's hand, she walked the Peabodys to the door.

The other boys raced ahead, careening down the sidewalk. Annabelle hollered for them not to step into the road, grabbed Timmy's hand from Kate, and hurried after them at a brisk trot with her poke hat dangling down her back and her arms full of supplies.

Kate watched Annabelle and the boys until they disappeared around the corner. After a heavy sigh, she was in the act of rubbing fingerprints off the front window with her sleeve when she heard a familiar voice behind her.

"Hello, Kate."

She turned around and saw Preston near the door and smiled. Her concerns when she first moved into town were that he might begin to pressure her into marriage and that he would want to spend all his free time with her— but neither proved true. He had been thoughtful enough to give her time alone to settle in and had kept his visits to a minimum.

If anything, he was determined to let her adjust to her new life.

"Come in and talk to me while I dust the shelves," she invited, happy to have him there. Aside from Annabelle Peabody and the boys it had been a slow morning. Empty hours seemed to drag of late.

"I don't want to get you in trouble with Harrison."

Kate laughed, knowing Preston was teasing. Harrison Barker, a recent transplant from Pennsylvania, owned the Lone Star Mercantile. Somewhere around forty, Harrison Barker was married and the father of one daughter. He was ambitious and highly motivated, busy putting together a proposition to expand the store, although for the life of her, Kate couldn't imagine why. The place was already stocked with more goods than the few inhabitants of Lone Star could purchase in five years.

"Harrison went to Dallas for a week to see some bankers about a loan. He left me to run the place."

Preston walked in after her and followed her to the counter in the rear of the store. Reed Senior had insisted that the folks who lived in Lone Star be able to buy almost anything, from ready-made pants and shirts to fabric, notions, dry food goods, even shoes and boots. There was a little of everything stuffed onto the shelves or piled in the back room.

Kate picked up a feather duster and walked over to a shelf of molasses and honey crocks. Preston began lifting the items while she dusted beneath them.

"I came to invite you to a salmagundi progressive, Kate. It's this coming Saturday night."

"What in heaven's name is a *salmagundi*?" She pictured a disgusting, fat-toed lizard lazing in a stream and wondered if it was some rare Texas specialty.

"Your nose looks incredibly tempting when you wrinkle it that way." Whenever he laughed, his entire face smiled.

Kate found herself blushing and quickly glanced toward the open door, suddenly very aware that they were alone.

Saint Perpetua, please don't let him kiss me.

He had never tried again, and she prayed he would not kiss her now. She was afraid—not of what she might feel—but of what she might not.

"What *is* a salmagundi?" She concentrated on her dusting, trying to divert his attention from her nose or any other body part he might admire.

"It's a progressive dinner that moves from house to house. There will be at least nine couples attending. I thought you might enjoy coming along with me."

Couples. They would attend as a couple.

It had been over a month since she left Lone Star. There was less than more of August left. Soon it would be fall and then winter. Christmastime.

It would be her first Christmas away from the orphanage. The girls and the school with all its yuletide activities, the special Masses, candles, and the scent of burning pine, and colorful decorations had all become synonymous with the holidays to her.

An endless stretch of aching loneliness yawned before her. "I'll go." She decided quickly, before she could talk herself out of it. "I'd love to go."

She wasn't actually in love with the notion, but nights in the boarding house were long, the hours overflowing with memories of Daniel and of Reed and the last tumultuous night she had shared with him.

"Well, then," Preston said, so delighted that he was absolutely beaming. "I'll walk down and pick you up at five on Saturday," he said.

.

"I'll be ready." She hoped she could muster half his enthusiasm by Saturday.

He lingered a bit longer, content to watch her dust. Kate wished a customer would walk in. Of all days for the place to be empty enough to fire a cannon through—

As if he sensed her discomfort, he pulled out a pocket watch and checked the time.

"Well, I should be going. I've a call to make before the noon meal," he said.

"And I have to finish dusting and then check Mr. Barker's endless stock inventory lists—but first I'll walk you out," she volunteered. "I've been meaning to sweep the sidewalk all morning." She grabbed a broom and started toward the front door.

Preston tipped his hat and bade her good-bye, off to visit a member of the congregation suffering from gout.

Kate soon finished sweeping the entire front of the store and then some and was on her way back inside when something crashed into her knees that nearly bowled her over.

46

A child's arms wrapped around Kate's thighs. At first she thought it was Timmy Peabody until she recognized the familiar striped fabric on his shirtsleeves.

"Daniel?"

She reached around, pulled him out from behind her, and immediately knelt down to his eye level. He was actually smiling. For the very first time, he wore a genuine, joyful smile. She couldn't help but notice that he looked more like Reed than ever. His hair was still uneven, but it had already grown to his collar. Without thinking, she brushed it back off his forehead.

"What are *you* doing here, young man?" She heard herself laughing for the first time in weeks. Unable to resist, she hugged him tight, then held him at arms' length so she could take a better look. He appeared to be doing fine. Healthier than ever and no longer trapped in mourning.

I made the right decision. Her heart swelled. They had done it without her. Reed and Daniel had survived on their own.

She reached out and touched the luminous shell hanging from the choker tied around his throat. If Daniel was here, Reed couldn't be far. She rocked back on her heels, scanned the street, and saw him headed across the thoroughfare, straight toward her. The sight of him took her breath away.

He was more handsome than she remembered as he moved with natural grace and ease, looking like a man comfortable in his own skin. Anyone who didn't know him would never guess the depth of pain he carried inside or what it had done to his heart.

He might be a rancher, but he still dressed like a Ranger in his tall boots and hat, with not one but two guns strapped to his waist.

His eyes never left hers, even when he paused to let a wagon loaded with hay rumble by. In his eyes she saw exactly what she had seen the night they made love—heat and fire and desperate need.

He wanted her still, but his mouth was firm with purpose. He was not smiling at her as Daniel was. Even if Reed was happy to see her again, he did not show it. Not like Preston, whose emotions were as clear as a teardrop.

Obviously, he was still upset that she had turned him down. He stepped up onto the walk and shoved his hat off his forehead. His gaze was intent, so much so that she feared he could see the hole where her heart used to be and knew how much she missed him.

"How are you, Kate?"

How am I?

I ache for you at night.

I long to hear your voice.

I wonder what you're doing all day long.

I wish you were here to talk to.

She left everything unsaid and smiled her most brilliant smile, determined not to let him see that she was standing amid the shattered pieces of her heart.

"I'm fine, thank you. I see you're both doing well." She smiled down at Daniel, who was hanging on to her hand, swinging her arm back and forth.

"He came out of it a whole new boy," Reed said.

"I'm so happy for you both." When she looked up again and caught Reed's gaze sweeping across her body, she almost dropped the broom.

"We came in to get some new shoes. He's growing like locoweed. We stopped in to see Jonah and Charm, and they told me you worked here." He easily explained away the chance meeting, indirectly letting her know they had not come just to see her.

"I believe we have everything you need in stock."

Happy to have a task, Kate held on to Daniel's hand and led them inside. The simple trusting act, the warm remembered touch of his little hand in hers threatened to undo all her determination not to let them see how much she missed them.

She helped Reed outfit Daniel with six new pairs of socks, two pairs of pants, three shirts, some suspenders, and new shoes. After he had the shoes laced up, Reed wanted Daniel to wear them home. Kate asked if she could pass the old ones down to Annabelle Peabody's boys, and Reed quickly consented.

Kate fumbled wrapping up all the new goods, caught her finger in the string, tore the paper. Through it all, Reed never took his eyes off her. By the time she finished she was perspiring and her hands were shaking.

Mr. Barker would want a full accounting of the inventory, so after handing Daniel half the pile, Kate quickly made note of everything Reed had purchased.

Then, as professionally as she could under the circumstances, Kate pressed her palms against the counter to keep them from trembling and evenly met Reed's stare. "Will that be all, or is there something else you need?"

"You don't really want me to answer that, do you, Kate?"

The sound of his voice poured over her like warm honey. Her imagination ran with the image, saw honey running down her spine, her thighs, her belly. She almost closed her eyes. Her knees went weak.

"No. No, I don't." She leaned against the counter for support.

"Then, I guess that's all. We'll be heading home now. Thanks for your help."

Reed started toward the door, walking off like any other customer. Daniel was trying to balance his pile of packages. Kate realized she would probably not see Reed again until Charm and Jonah's wedding—if he had agreed to be the captain's best man.

"How was your visit with Jonah?" she asked, stopping him in his tracks.

He turned, shifted the pile to his hip. "He told me he and Charm are getting married in a couple weeks, depending on whether or not he can walk without help. He asked me to stand up for him."

"Charm asked me, too."

"Will you?"

"Yes. Will you?"

"Of course I will."

"Well then. I suppose I'll see you at the wedding." She tried to sound lighthearted and gay but failed miserably.

Saint Perpetua, intercede for me. Help me live through this, and I will never ask another favor, I swear.

Unlike Preston, Reed was not of a mind to linger. Instead, he shifted impatiently. "Come on, Daniel." He walked back to where the boy was weaving between the flour bins and the pork barrels, trying to see over his load.

"Let me take those things or we'll never make it out of here." Reed relieved him of the pile and easily tucked it beneath his arm. When Daniel realized they were walking toward the door, he abruptly stopped and looked back at Kate expectantly.

"Come on, son," Reed called from the doorway.

Kate didn't think there were any whole pieces of her heart left to break, but yet another shattered when Reed called Daniel *son.*

Daniel ignored him and walked back to the counter. He grabbed the edge and stood on tiptoe to see over it. His bright blue eyes, the image of Reed's, shone up at her expectantly.

"Please, don't," Kate whispered. Then she cleared the ragged catch in her throat and said firmly, "You have to go home now, Daniel."

He did not budge. His forehead scrunched into a fierce, familiar frown.

"Daniel, we've got to go." Reed started back down the aisle.

Daniel frantically darted around the counter, grabbed her hand, and started tugging her toward the door. Kate didn't know what to do. She cast Reed a silent plea for help.

"Come on, Daniel." He put his hand on the boy's shoulder, lowered his voice. "Kate can't come with us." Then Reed straightened and locked eyes with her. "She wants to live here instead."

Daniel leaned back and put all his weight into tugging on Kate's arm. He pulled so hard his face turned pink. Finally out of frustration, he opened his mouth and yelled, "Come!"

Then he let go of her. Kate was so startled she nearly toppled over backward. She didn't know which moved her more, hearing Daniel speak, or having him so desperately want her to go back to the ranch.

Unable to look at Reed, she went down on one knee,

hugged the boy close, and kissed his smooth little cheek. Then she patted down his hair and slowly shook her head no.

"I love you, but I can't go with you, Daniel. You go on with your daddy now." She spoke softly, for his ears alone.

As she turned the child toward Reed and was about to give him a gentle nudge, Daniel slowly reached up and wiped a tear off her cheek.

As if that was a sign that her answer was final, he did not resist when Reed took him by the arm to lead him down the aisle and out of the store.

Kate watched them go. Not until they were out of sight of the huge storefront windows did she calmly walk down the very same aisle, close the door and lock it. She lifted the carefully lettered sign with the word CLOSED on one side and OPEN on the other, turned it CLOSED side out, and set it in the corner of the front window where folks knew to look for it.

That done, she started back down the aisle. By now she was crying so hard she ran straight into a heavy milk can, ricocheted off it and knocked over a tall, four-legged stool.

Without bothering to pick it up, listening to the hollow, lonesome click of her own heels against the floor, she ran all the way to the storeroom in back and threw herself down on a pile of burlap potato sacks.

Then she cried her heart out.

Reed kept his eyes on the road and the reins threaded through his fingers, wishing he and Daniel had ridden into town instead of taking the buckboard, but he was still a little leery of letting the boy ride alone.

Overvigilance wasn't a bad trait, Reed figured, not where Daniel was concerned. He had almost lost the boy twice and wasn't about to take the chance of losing him again.

They were nearly home. Daniel was sitting rock-still with his arms folded as the wagon bounced unmercifully over the hard, lumpy ground. Since they left town, Daniel had devoted serious time to pouting. He refused to look anywhere but straight ahead.

"You can sit there like a bump on a log if you want, but it won't change things one hell of a bit."

"Onehellovabit," Daniel said harshly.

Reed glanced over. Though he was shocked, he found himself biting back a smile. "You're as stubborn as the day is long, boy. Which is a Benton family trait that you will unfortunately have all your life. 'Course, you aren't near as stubborn as Kate. I never saw anyone so set on making herself unhappy. She could have stayed with us, you know, but she didn't want it that way. She had to have it all."

She wanted me to love her.

I didn't think I could.

Something unexpected slammed into him today when he caught sight of her sweeping the walk in front of the Mercantile.

Daniel had seen her, too, and took off like an antelope, darting across the street before he could grab him. He had stood and watched Kate's face light up when she realized Daniel was there and hugged the boy to her. Almost immediately after that, she had started looking around for him.

Seeing those huge dark eyes and the most tempting lips east or west of the Pecos had stirred him worse than ever, but after the first wave of hunger for her body had passed, he realized there was a lot more to what he was feeling than lust.

Just the fact that he had wanted her there with him the night Daniel first said his name, that he needed her to talk to, that he wanted to show her how well Daniel was getting along, had been a shock.

Over the past few weeks he had come to realize it was Kate he wanted to share the little triumphs and joys with, that he cared for *her*, Kate, more than just a little, more than he needed what her body could give. He missed her quiet, easy ways, missed the calm and order, the hope she had brought into his life.

He wanted Kate around for who she was, every bit as much as he wanted to make love to her again. That had been good. Hell, that had been *great*, but after seeing her today and more especially after having to leave her behind, he wanted her as far more than a lover.

He wanted to fill his empty house with life, and he wanted Kate to share it with him.

The wagon hit a bump because he hadn't been concentrating. He made a quick grab for Daniel's arm and hung on when the wagon jolted. Once they settled and were rolling along again, Daniel slid across the seat and put more space between them; then he continued his pout.

"You know what?" Reed acted as if Daniel might actually respond. "I hate to admit it, but I have the feeling something's been slipping up on my heart since the last time we saw Kate."

At the mention of her name, Daniel looked over at him inquisitively.

"Yeah, I know." Reed shrugged. "I swore I would never let it happen to me again. I swore that I wouldn't be crazy enough to let a woman own my heart again—and believe me, I tried not to. But somehow it happened when I wasn't looking.

"I don't particularly want to go crawling to her on bended knee, because I don't know if she would come back, even if I told her . . . you know . . . what she wanted to hear. By now the preacher's probably won her over, anyway."

Reed leaned over and ruffled Daniel's hair just to irritate him and thought he saw the boy fighting a smile. Then Reed adjusted the reins, squinted into the sunlight, and sighed.

"I doubt anything I say to her now would make any difference, but maybe if we both think on it for a while, we can come up with something convincing. What do you think?"

Daniel, of course, had nothing to say.

47

The progressive was enjoyable as Kate had hoped, a far cry from an evening spent alone reading at the boarding house. She donned her blue silk gown and Preston had arrived exactly at five o'clock, decked out in a new black suit and bowler hat. He proved to be so charming that everyone had naturally gravitated to him—and so, to her. All evening he was nothing but solicitous and kind, making certain she was never left out of conversations, always willing to explain whenever the talk drifted to Texas politics or other local issues.

Preston had taken her home before the party to please Aunt Martha, who wanted to see them dressed up. With her glowing cheeks and smiling gray eyes so like Preston's, his aunt reminded Kate of an elderly cherub. Martha hugged Kate and had even given her a small nosegay of blossoms fashioned from a climbing rose on a trellis beside the front porch.

Inside and out, the house was cozy and pleasant, filled with flowers and the lingering scent of lavender. Kate knew that it was charming because of his aunt Martha, but also because he cared enough to make his aunt happy.

Kate knew that Preston could offer her everything she

should ever need or want in a man and a husband. Not only was he well spoken and well educated, but he was a man of honor, strong moral fortitude, and convictions. She could not imagine that he would ever think of making love to her until after they were married.

Throughout the evening, as they laughed and talked with the other couples and progressed from house to house through the courses of the meal, Kate continually had to pinch herself. She found it hard to believe that her life had changed so very much in so short a time. There were long stretches that evening when she actually forgot about Applesby and her past.

But not once did she forget about Reed—or Daniel.

The salmagundi progressive was a complete success by the time the couples had dessert and coffee at the home of Jack and Bette Manning, two of Lone Star's first residents. Although their home was quite simple in comparison to Benton House, the couple seemed comfortable and happy there.

Partygoers sang while Bette pumped away, and her fingers flew over the keys of a lovely rosewood melodeon. Though Kate did not know the verses to many of the tunes, she was soon at ease and able to join in the chorus.

When Preston leaned back in his chair and declared himself too stuffed to walk and then immediately accepted another piece of apple pie from Bette Manning, everyone laughed. His gray eyes found Kate across the room, and she felt the warmth of his gaze as surely as she would a gentle, loving touch.

The salmagundi progressive came to a close as couples departed, calling out farewells and good-byes, disappearing down the lane to the various scattered houses. Preston tucked Kate's arm in the crook of his elbow and started walking down Front Street toward the boarding house. She held fast to Aunt Martha's nosegay.

The stars shone brightly despite the heat that enveloped them, the same stars she and Reed had slept under on the prairie. There was barely a sliver of a moon out tonight.

They had nearly reached the porch when Preston's steps slowed. "You seem sad tonight, Kate."

"Do I?" She truly was surprised to hear it. Whenever she fell into deep melancholy, she always tried hard not to let it show.

At the foot of the stairs, she noticed that Mrs. Brandon had left a lamp burning on the parlor table in the window and reminded herself to thank her landlady for her thoughtfulness.

She slipped her hand out of the crook of Preston's arm, but before she could thank him for the evening, he took her hand.

"Marry me, Kate," he said without preamble. "Let me give you a new life. I love you, you know."

I love you.

A lifetime. She had waited a lifetime to be loved, to be cherished by someone. To hear those very words spoken just for her and now they had been, easily and certainly. Words straight from his heart, spoken with sincerity and hope. Calm and unruffled as always, Preston was waiting for an answer.

She was ashamed of holding his love when somewhere out there was a woman who would give anything to have it.

He was a good man. A kindhearted man.

She owed him the truth. "You're too good for me," she said softly.

"Nonsense. Don't you think there are things that I've done in my life that I'm not proud of? During the war, long before I became a minister, I did things I'll never forgive myself for."

"That was war."

"There is nothing you could possibly say that would make me think less of you, Kate. Nothing."

"I've been with Reed. I'm not a virgin." She blurted it out, sparing him nothing.

Better to have it said plain as day, without mincing words or dallying around the truth. She was not about to muddy the waters by telling him all the sordid details of her childhood with Meg Whittington. It was enough for him to know she was ruined. That she had given herself to another man without the benefit of a legal, binding marriage. Worse yet, without shared love.

Another man would have walked away. Instead, Preston was silent, thoughtful. "I thought as much," he finally said. "I tried to ignore the way you looked at him whenever he was around. I know you wanted that marriage or you would not have come to Lone Star, but you can't blame yourself for doing everything you could to make it work."

"I wasn't trying to make it work. I was just weak."

"You are only human. None of us is without sin, believe me. I want you so badly right now, Kate, that I'm ashamed of the things I'm thinking. What's past is past, leave it there and marry me."

He was too good, too kind for her to let this go on. "I know what one-sided love is like, Preston, and I won't do that to you. Ever."

"That's the real reason you won't marry me, isn't it? You still love Reed Benton."

She was ashamed to admit aloud what her foolish heart had never denied. Dying of mortification, she fought to keep her head up, to look Preston in the eye and not at the ground. Ever since the day she had seen Reed in town, it had become harder and harder to put him out of her mind.

"I wish I could tell you different, but yes, I still love him. I wish I didn't, but I still do." She could barely whisper now. "I should leave Lone Star," she said, thinking aloud.

"How far would you have to go to outrun your feelings, Kate?"

"I don't know." She dipped her head so that he could not see her tears. "I don't know."

"I can tell you from experience that you can't run far enough. You'll just take it all with you." He dropped her hand, put his fingers beneath her chin, forced her head up. "Stay here. You don't love me now, I know that, but—"

"I treasure your friendship, Preston. But I can't be selfish. I want you to find the happiness you deserve, and if I stay—"

"Love doesn't just end when we want it to. It doesn't matter if you leave or not, I'm still going to love you. I told you before that I'm willing to wait, and that holds true now. I will be more than happy to be your friend until you can give me more."

"And if I can't?" She felt a tear slide down her cheek, cursing her own heart for condemning her to such aching loneliness.

He put his arm around her shoulder, drew her near, and she let him—needing the closeness, the comfort he so willingly offered. "If you can't," he said, "then I guess I'll just have to be content—but forever is a long, long time. Things could always change. We have a saying down South. 'The sun don't shine on the same dog's tail all the time.' " He shrugged. "Who knows? I just might get lucky here, Kate, as lucky as Reed. I promise, I won't put you in this position and propose to you again. Just know, if you change your mind, I'll still be waiting."

He let her go, but Kate was so moved she stayed beside him, then reached up and gently slipped her arm around his neck.

"Thank you, Preston, for understanding." She gave him a chaste kiss on the lips, wishing there were more she could give, wishing her heart was free. Somewhere not far away, a horse whinnied. The distant sound of piano music drifted out of Dolly's to taint the stillness.

He did not try to take more than she offered. Instead, ever the true gentleman, he stepped back and straightened his hat. "You best get on in now, or Mrs. Brandon will be out here chasing me off with a broom."

Knowing that she had hurt him did not make her feel any better, but his assurance that they would remain friends helped. "Good night then," she said as she headed for the stairs.

"Take care, Kate. I'll see you soon." He shoved his hand in his pocket and began whistling a lonesome tune as he headed down the street.

Reed walked into Dolly's crowded Social Club and Entertainment Emporium and let the door bang shut behind him. Everyone in the parlor looked up, from the scantily clad, satin-bedecked whores to local cowhands, a dry goods drummer, and a couple of gamblers just passing through. He sent one dark scowl ricocheting around the room and walked straight to the bar.

His sudden appearance sent Dolly herself hurrying to his side. "Well, hells bells and garters, Reed Benton, it's been more than a month of Sundays since you been in to see us. What brought you back to town? Jonah and Charm?"

He shook his head, and ordered a whiskey. "Stupidity," he mumbled.

"Did you just call me stupid, Reed-junah?"

"Naw. I was just telling you what brought me to town. Stupidity." He picked up the glass of whiskey, held it to the light in an admiring fashion, and then drank it down with one swallow.

"One more." He watched as the barkeep poured, and then he changed his mind. "Hell, might as well give me the whole bottle."

He started to toss out some coins, but Dolly stopped him. "If it wasn't for your daddy I wouldn't have this place, Reed, so put that money away."

A huge lamp adorned with antlers hung above the bar. The light set Dolly's garish orange hair aflame. She cocked one hand on an ample hip, tilted her head, and gave him a wry half-smile.

"You interested in spending a little time with one of the ladies? That's free to you, too." She thumbed over her shoulder at the women in various states of undress who were draped across parlor furniture like decorative pieces.

"Nope. The last thing I need to get tangled up with tonight is a woman. The whiskey's just fine, thanks."

"It looks like you got your work cut out for you with that bottle, so I'm just gonna let you get on with it." That said, she sashayed away and thankfully left him alone with his new purchase and his misery.

Within five minutes, he saw Jonah limping along the hall in back, leaning heavily on a cane, heading toward the parlor. Reed tipped his head and watched the captain rub his hip as he crossed the room.

"What are you doing here, Reed?" Jonah had lost weight, but aside from that, he looked content.

"Getting drunk."

"What's wrong?"

"Nothing."

Jonah scratched his ear. "The way I figure it is when a good man wants to look at the world through the neck of a bottle, then there's gotta be a powerful reason."

Reed offered Jonah a drink, but was turned down. He asked, "How many times does a man have to be hit over the head before he learns, you reckon, Jonah?"

"I don't know. It depends on how stubborn he is, I guess."

"Or how stupid."

"Is this about Kate?"

"Why do you ask?"

"Well, it's been my experience that when a man tries to drown himself in drink the reason's usually a woman, his conscience, or both every time. What happened?"

What happened was that he had let his guard down. He had dared to dream a little and let his heart soften to the consistency of pudding. Worse yet, he had been willing to smear it on his sleeve for Kate.

He had ridden into town prepared to tell her that he loved her and that he was ready to give her everything she wanted. All of it—love and marriage.

But when he was about to cross the street and tell her, he had seen her kissing the preacher outside the boarding house.

He'd wanted to show up earlier in the day, but then he had to ride halfway across the ranch and back to help settle a boundary dispute. Finally, unwilling to face another sleepless night thinking about her, he told Daniel and Scrappy good-bye, assured the wrangler that he would be back sooner than later, and headed to town.

The sight of Kate and Preston standing in the shadows of the porch had stopped him in his tracks. Unable to turn away, he had watched and cursed himself for waiting so long, cursed Kate for her fickle heart, even cursed the damn preacher for having enough sense to know when he was in love and to do something about it.

Thank God I never made Daniel a promise to bring her home.

He wasn't about to tell Jonah any of that, though. No use making even more of a fool out of himself.

"You better slow down or you're gonna be sorry," Jonah warned as Reed poured himself another round.

"I'm already sorry. I know you're trying to help, but how about leaving me alone tonight?"

He had expected an argument, but got none. "I'd be happy to. Just be certain you're able to stand up in time for the wedding next week." Jonah pushed away from the bar and walked off.

It was hard to see his friend in pain and dependent on a cane, but Jonah wasn't complaining. And why the hell should he? The woman he loved was waiting for him in the back room.

She wasn't down the road kissing some other man.

48

If God meant to punish Kate for her sins of the flesh, then standing up for Charm at the wedding was the perfect penance.

Not only did she have to be with both Preston and Reed at the same time, but Reed had brought Daniel with him. The boy would not budge from her side. He held her hand throughout the entire ceremony as she willed herself not to cry. Somehow, someway, she made it through.

Reed barely uttered two words to her. Nor had he looked her way once as the vows were exchanged. The ceremony crawled by for Kate until, with a dramatic flourish, Preston pronounced Charm and Jonah man and wife at almost the exact moment the sun touched the horizon. The sky erupted in vibrant hues, from orange to the palest pink, almost as if the entire universe were in accord with their union.

Dolly, decked out in a plum-colored confection adorned with yards and yards of ruffles and surrounded by her "ladies," sobbed into her handkerchief. Jonah turned nearly as red as the sky when he kissed his bride and everyone erupted into cheers.

Charm, resplendent in a gown that Jonah had sent from

Boston, looked like a china doll with fine blond curls cascading around her shoulders. Blushing like a virgin, she had eyes only for her husband.

For propriety's sake, Preston declined the invitation to attend the celebration at the Social Club. He wished the bride and groom well, bade everyone, including Kate, a polite good-bye, and started back to town.

Reed and Kate stood in clumsy silence as everyone else followed suit, then Reed looked down at Daniel, who was still holding Kate's hand.

"Would you mind taking him back to Dolly's in the buggy with you?" he asked.

"Of course not."

"I'm not sure I could get him to go with me yet."

Their exchange was very polite, very cool. Gone were other days and times. Even the hunger in his eyes had been extinguished, replaced by a guarded chill and unspoken irritation.

It's not your place to wonder why.

She turned and walked away with Daniel clinging to her hand.

Later, at the Social Club, Daniel was more intrigued with the wedding cake and bonbon dishes filled with assorted candies than with Kate. Dolly's ladies surrounded him, pinching his cheeks, cooing, and offering him sweets.

Uncomfortable among them, thinking of how much different and yet the same her mother's life had been, Kate had wandered away to stand alone at the end of the parlor when Charm caught her eye. The bride waved and slipped away from Jonah to come to her.

"How are you doing, Kate?"

"Why, I'm doing just fine," she lied. "Who wouldn't be on such a wonderful day? You make the perfect bride and groom, Charm. Anyone can see how much you two love each other."

Charm blushed prettily and followed Kate's gaze to where Reed and Jonah were leaning against Dolly's lavish mahogany bar, lost in deep conversation.

"What are you thinking, Kate?"

Kate toyed with the glass of champagne in her hand and shifted her gaze to Daniel, who was beaming up at four well-endowed women trying to tempt him with treats.

"That I did the right thing. Look how much Daniel has grown. He and Reed are getting along now. Reed seems to be doing a fine job with him."

"And what about you? Did you do the right thing for you?"

"Of course." Kate took a sip of champagne, another first, and Sofia's words came back to her.

"If you ever love a man the way I loved the señor, you will do anything for him."

"He was in here last week," Charm said.

"Who?" The champagne threatened to bubble back up Kate's throat.

"Reed." Charm was no longer smiling.

Kate's heart stumbled.

He came to the Social Club looking for what he needed.

What I can't give him anymore—not without losing my soul.

"What he does is none of my business," Kate said softly.

She couldn't keep from gazing around the room, wondering which of the women he had taken upstairs. Had it been the petite, soul-eyed girl with dusky skin and a wreath of coal-black hair? Or maybe he was partial to the voluptuous redhead covered with freckles.

Suddenly she wanted out. Out of this room. Out of Lone Star.

Preston had been very, very wrong to talk her out of leaving. She was going to run as fast and as far as she could go. She might not ever outrun the hurt, but given enough distance, at least she wouldn't have to be constantly tortured by seeing or hearing about Reed Benton.

"You don't have to worry about which girl he was with," Charm said, reading her mind. "He only came in to get roaring drunk."

Kate carefully set the champagne glass down, wishing sweet Charm would leave her alone, wondering when she could slip out without appearing rude.

"Jonah told me that it had something to do with you," Charm said.

"Me?"

"According to Jonah."

When Charm looked across the room at her new husband, he smiled, and her face lit up like sunshine. Reed had his back to both of them, but when he raised his head, his eyes met Kate's in the mirror behind the bar.

The hunger was back, so fleetingly that she was convinced she had imagined it.

"Go talk to him, Kate," Charm urged softly.

"That would be too forward." Of course, years of training had flown out the window before whenever her choices had concerned Reed. Why not now?

"You're standing in a whorehouse, Kate," Charm giggled. "Nothing's too forward here."

"I simply can't." Kate turned around. "It's over."

"Well, it looks like you won't have to go to him because he's headed this way." Charm's voice faded to a whisper. "I'm going to talk to Jonah."

"Don't go!" Kate made a grab for Charm but wasn't fast enough. Before she knew it, Reed was there, standing close beside her.

"Come with me." His voice was cold, as hard edged as she had ever heard it.

Saint Perpetua help me. Let it finally be over.

They walked through the parlor, through the overflowing noise, the heavy scent of cloying perfumes, the sound of frolicking piano music and enthusiastic off-key singing. Together, they stepped out into the night air.

Tonight there was a little more moon in a heavy canopy of stars. Kate took a deep breath, wondered what could be on his mind.

"Have you found a housekeeper?" She folded her arms tightly around her middle.

"Yeah. Believe it or not, one of the cowhands got his thumb torn off roping, but it turns out Ben likes to cook. He cleans like the devil. On top of that, he's fussy as an old hen, too. I never see him without a rag in his hand."

She half smiled, thinking of the piles of clothes and the dirty pans she had left behind.

"I came to see you last week," he said.

She should have known he wouldn't waste time with idle chat. Unskilled at coyness, she admitted, "Charm just told me you were in town."

"Did your preacher propose?"

"Yes. Yes he did, but that happened long before I left the ranch."

Reed shoved his thumbs in his waistband, paced a few feet away, turned, and headed back. "Did you say yes?"

"I don't see how that's any of your concern, Reed."

"Is that why you turned me down? Is that why you signed the papers? So you could marry him?"

"No, it's not. I turned Preston down, too."

"Why?"

"Because."

I don't love him.

I love you.

"You *sure* you aren't marrying him?"

"Yes. I'm sure. Why?"

"I saw you kiss him." He was simmering now, waiting for her to explain herself, as if she owed it to him. As if she owed him anything.

She pressed her hand to the base of her throat. "Have you been spying on me?"

"Last Saturday I came in to town to talk to you, but as I neared your place, I saw the two of you standing by the front porch. You kissed him."

"He's my friend."

He barked out a sharp laugh. "You kiss all your friends like that?"

"This is ridiculous. You have absolutely no right to question me." She turned and had not taken six steps before he grabbed her by the upper arm and spun her around.

"Don't touch me, Reed."

"I miss you, Kate."

I can't bear this.

"The house is too big for just Daniel and me. It's too quiet. All the life has gone out of the place. All I can think of are the empty rooms and the empty years ahead of me."

"What are you saying?" She trembled despite the heat.

"I love you, Kate."

"How do you know?" She was afraid to hope anymore.

He let go of her arm and shoved his fingers through his hair. "I ache for you at night. I long to hear your voice. I wonder what you are doing all day long and wish you were there to talk to. I keep wanting to tell you about all the little things Daniel has done. I've had to stop myself a hundred times a day from coming to see you. If all that doesn't mean that I'm in love, then I don't know what does."

Kate closed her eyes. Her lips were trembling so much, she was forced to press her fingers to her mouth.

"I want you to have what you want, Kate. I want to give you the whole damn dream. I love you."

Before she could say a word, before she even let herself believe, the back door slammed. Both of them started, looked over to see Daniel come barreling out of the Social Club. He ran straight into Kate and grabbed her around the knees so hard that he sent her reeling into Reed, whose arms gently closed around her before she could fall.

Kate was sandwiched between them, the boy and the man. Daniel started jumping up and down, tugging on Reed's pant leg.

Before Kate realized what was happening, Reed went down on one knee and took hold of her hand right there in the dirt behind Dolly's Social Club and Entertainment Emporium. Daniel grabbed hold of her other hand with both of his.

"Will you marry us?" Reed asked.

Kate glanced up at the heavens and the stars blurred. When she looked down at Reed and Daniel, tears spilled over her lashes. Identical pairs of Benton eyes stared up at her.

"I told him that he would have to do his part if we were going to get you back." Reed nodded to Daniel and said, "Now."

Daniel squared his shoulders and took a deep breath. "Come home now, Mama? Come home?"

"Will you marry us, Kate?" Reed asked again.

Then right there in the dirt behind Dolly's Social Club,

Kate sank to her knees, hooked an arm around each of them, and held them tight. She kissed Daniel on the cheek and then looked into Reed's eyes. Her every dream was waiting there.

With her future shining as bright as any star, she told them, "Yes, I'll marry you. I'll come home."

Epilogue

Kate listened to the hushed murmur of many voices in one place—a sound not unlike the prairie wind moving through tall summer grass—and gazed from her front-row seat at the standing-room-only crowd packed into the Dallas Opera House. Ladies and gentlemen in their Sunday best, some with older children in tow, filled every seat, crowded the aisles, and oozed through the doorways.

On her left, Reed shifted uncomfortably and tugged at his thin black tie. She laced her gloved hands together and placed them squarely on top of the two-page program in her lap, then leaned over and whispered to him.

"Darling, if you tug on that tie any harder, it's going to come undone."

His new black suit, complete with a matching wool vest sporting tiny, real gold buttons showed off his deeply tanned skin and sky blue eyes to perfection. There were touches of silver at his temples now, creases in the corners of his eyes and permanent smile lines around his full mouth, but to her the changes made him even more handsome.

She wasn't without more than a touch of gray hair of

her own. Thinking of her hair, she resisted the urge to reach up and see if any of the pins had escaped the elegant twist her daughter had created for her not an hour ago in their hotel room.

"Mama, please." The fifteen-year-old had started pestering Kate the moment she sat down at the dressing table in their suite of rooms. "You simply *must* let me do something a bit more modern with your hair. You have worn it in that topknot for years."

Now, as she looked down at Allison, her heart swelled with pride. As if she sensed her mother watching her, the girl turned and smiled up at her.

"Your hair looks lovely, Mama. I told you it would. Daddy likes it, too."

"I think he does," Kate said, keeping her voice low.

"He does what?" Reed wanted to know. He leaned over Kate, smiled at Allison. "What are you up to now, darlin'? Is it going to cost me anything?"

"Nothing, Daddy. I just told Mama that you liked the way I styled her hair."

"I like it any way she chooses to wear it, you know that." He pulled his watch out of his vest pocket, flipped the gold piece open, checked the time, and then snapped it shut. "How many more people are they going to crowd in here? It's five minutes past seven."

The room was stifling already. Hushed conversation had given way to a louder din as folks tried to hear each other over the low roar.

Allison looked around. "Do you think Daniel's nervous?"

Kate was the first to assure her. "Of course not. He's a gifted orator."

"And a fine teacher," Reed added proudly. "Did you know your mother taught elocution?" He reached for Kate's hand. She looked around the room and blushed but didn't let go.

"Of course. You've told me a hundred times already." Then Allison groaned, "Oh, no. Here comes that obnoxious reporter from the *Dallas Herald* again."

A spare young man in a full checkered suit, his oiled hair neatly parted in the center, was making his way between the occupants of the front-row seats and the stage, carefully easing past gents' crossed legs and ladies' skirt hems.

"Mr. Benton!" The reporter smiled and waved from down the row. There was a hush from those seated nearest them as the man propelled himself along, hastily apologizing as he pushed on through. Winded, he stopped before the Bentons and pulled a wrinkled wad of paper out of his sagging coat pocket.

"Thomas Barkley, reporter for the *Dallas Herald.*" He reintroduced himself as if they could forget anyone so obnoxiously tenacious. "I hope you folks don't mind a few more questions." Barkley licked the nub of a pencil and scribbled the date at the top of the page.

Allison groaned again and started fanning herself with her program. Kate patted the back of Reed's hand in a soothing fashion, praying he would be patient.

"The presentation is about to begin," Reed said coolly, keeping his voice even, setting Kate at ease.

"Is it true, sir, that you were a Texas Ranger during the seventies, at the height of the Indian wars?"

"Yes, it is."

The reporter wasn't dismayed by the curt brevity of Reed's answer. Kate wished the crimson curtain would rise. Around them, more and more folks were beginning to fall quiet and began to turn their way, hanging on every word of the exchange.

"Your son is beginning a world tour, speaking out for Indian rights, talking about what he calls atrocious conditions on the reservations, even appealing to folks to try and understand the Comanche and why they fought for so long. Did he ever ask you why you did what you did? How do you explain your part in killing off the people he is trying to help today?"

"My son knows what I did and why I did it. At the time, I fought for what I believed in, just as the Comanche fought for their way of life. Men start wars, Mr. Barkley, and at the time they make sense. I think that if you look back through history, you'll find that public opinion changes like the wind. I'm not the same man I was then. Times change, people change. We didn't honor our treaties with the Comanche any more than they did the ones they made with us."

"Are you saying all the killing and raiding that went on back then should be forgotten?"

"I'm saying we need to understand *why* it went on in the first place. Maybe we need to forgive, even if we can't forget. Listen to what Daniel has to say tonight. He's able to put it into words a lot better than I."

"Can I quote you on what you've said?" Barkley didn't look up as he scribbled frantically.

"Just as long as you get it right," Reed said.

The gaslights dimmed. The packed house fell silent. The only illumination came from the footlights on the stage. Barkley tipped his hat and hurried down the aisle, leaving an outburst of *oof*s and *ouch*es in his wake.

Kate looked over at her husband in the semidarkness. Their eyes met and held. He squeezed her hand and, as the curtain opened, Kate felt the same swell of pride she had already experienced the previous two nights when the curtain opened to reveal a podium at center stage. From the wings on the right, a tall, well-built young man came striding out to face the crowd.

He was secure in himself, at ease as he paused to smile and acknowledge the swell of applause.

Beside Kate, Allison scooted to the edge of her seat. "Don't I have the handsomest big brother in the world?" She turned around to whisper, "I think that new mustache he's grown makes him look even older than twenty-eight."

Kate couldn't do anything but nod, unable to squeeze a word past the lump in her throat. She watched him through a haze of tears, her son, comparing him to the child she had met that first day when he had kicked and spat and tried to lash out at her in such fear and desperation.

He had grown tall and firm, the image of Reed. Intelligent and inquisitive, Daniel had attended the university and become an accomplished teacher. Tonight was the last night he would appear in Dallas. Tomorrow they would see him off at the train, and he would start on a tour in hopes of teaching the world about a dying civilization, one he believed every bit as important as any of the others already lost to the tide of history, a people who once roamed the plains in countless numbers now reduced to less than fifteen hundred souls.

The applause continued, although he had yet to say a word. Many of those in the audience had been here on both previous evenings, and yet they had come to hear him again, to listen to his tale, to laugh, to cry, to wonder.

Finally Daniel raised both hands for silence, and the crowd quieted. Beside Kate, Reed sat as still as a statue, except that his hand was nearly squeezing the life out of hers while a smile as wide as the acres of Lone Star spread across his face.

She concentrated on Daniel again, amazed at his confidence. He scanned the crowd, looked down at where he knew his family was to be sitting and nodded to them.

Then he began. "I'd like to dedicate my speech tonight to

my family—my father, Reed Benton, my mother, Katherine Benton, and of course, my sister, Allison Benton. I'm here tonight to tell you a story, the story of the years I spent living among the Comanche and what I learned from them."

He paused dramatically, slowly stared into the footlights again. He had no notes, no written speech. Kate wiped away a tear that was heading for her chin, glanced down at her hand in Reed's, and then looked over at Allison, who was hanging on her brother's every word although she had heard the story many, many times before.

Daniel took a deep breath, drew back his shoulders. His strong, clear voice sounded throughout the hall.

"I remember living on the prairie, riding before I could walk. Back then, I was not Daniel Benton. I was Fast Pony, adopted son of Many Horses. . . ."